NEW SCIENCE FICTION
AND FANTASY

Eclipse
one

Other books edited by Jonathan Strahan:

The New Space Opera (with Gardner Dozois)
The Best Science Fiction and Fantasy of the Year: Volume One
Best Short Novels: 2007
Eidolon 1 (with Jeremy G. Byrne)
Fantasy: The Very Best of 2005
Science Fiction: The Very Best of 2005
Best Short Novels: 2006
Best Short Novels: 2005
Fantasy: Best of 2004 (with Karen Haber)
Science Fiction: Best of 2004 (with Karen Haber)
Best Short Novels: 2004
*The Locus Awards: Thirty Years of the Best in Fantasy and
    Science Fiction* (with Charles N. Brown)
Science Fiction: Best of 2003 (with Karen Haber)
*The Year's Best Australian Science Fiction and Fantasy
    Volume: 2* (with Jeremy G. Byrne)
*The Year's Best Australian Science Fiction and Fantasy
    Volume: 1* (with Jeremy G. Byrne)

NEW SCIENCE FICTION
AND FANTASY

Eclipse
one

EDITED BY
JONATHAN STRAHAN

NIGHT SHADE BOOKS
SAN FRANCISCO

First Edition

ISBN: 978-1-59780-117-1

Night Shade Books
Please visit us on the web at
http://www.nightshadebooks.com

For Justin Ackroyd, dear friend, fearless book supplier, and tireless supporter of my work.

Acknowledgements

This book grew out of a crazy conversation with Jason Williams. His faith and support made it possible. It then developed with contributions from my friend and anthology guru Jack Dann, and my science fiction mentor Charles N. Brown. It was made a reality by an incredibly talented group of authors who sent me some amazing stories. They dealt with crazy deadlines, insane turnarounds, and came through time and again. I couldn't be more grateful. Above all, though, I have to acknowledge my three angels, Marianne, Jessica and Sophie , who make every day an adventure and fill it with joy.

CONTENTS

INTRODUCTION

This is a good time for the short story in genre circles. Not maybe in business terms—we're yet to develop a twenty-first century business model that allows writers to make a living writing short fiction—but in artistic terms, it's extraordinary. Whether in anthologies like this one, or in magazines or on websites, short stories are being published in staggering numbers. Thousands each year, millions of words, and in amongst this torrent of content is some extraordinary work.

Over the past several years I've been reading through that torrent to compile my year's best annuals (most recently *The Best Science Fiction and Fantasy of the Year*), and as I've done so I've become more and more excited about the idea of publishing my own original anthology series, a series that would be a sort of counterweight to my year's best work. It took me a while, though, to figure out what that series would be like. A number of anthologies are being published at the moment that follow a theme, support a manifesto, or attempt to hark back to some grand moment in the history of science fiction and fantasy; anthologies that, no matter how good they may be, have some stated purpose beyond simply delivering a selection of great stories. That wasn't what I wanted to do.

When I began to sketch out what evolved into the book you're now holding, my intentions were clear. As I've written elsewhere, as an editor I have been greatly influenced by the work of the late, great Terry Carr who was, alongside Damon Knight, one of the best anthologists ever to work in science fiction. Through the 1970s and 1980s he edited two of the great SF anthology series: his *Best SF of the Year* and *Universe*. *Universe* was a truly exceptional anthology series which first appeared in 1971 and ran for seventeen volumes. It collected a broad variety of stories written by some of the best short story writers the field has seen, including Robert Silverberg, Harlan Ellison, R. A. Lafferty, and Gene Wolfe, including some of the best loved stories of the past thirty years. Each volume was short, tightly edited, and yet had a real variety to it. That was something I wanted to emulate: variety without sprawl, respected, well-known writers, and exciting newcomers, and both science fiction *and* fantasy.

That's why, in the beginning, I was going to call this series *Universe*. It seemed like a fitting tribute and an appropriate statement of intent. But then some time passed and I accepted that I'm not Terry Carr, that his tastes aren't necessarily mine, and that this isn't 1975, it's 2007. A different time calls for a slightly different approach and for a new name. So, last year my publisher and I put out a call to readers: give us a new name that would fit a series of anthologies that would contain great new science fiction and fantasy stories, something new, something resonant, something interesting. The suggestions poured in. Many were odd or dissonant in some way, some almost fit, but none were quite right. Some were too science fictional, some too fantastical, and some just didn't suggest much at all. And then, when I was ready to give up, *Interzone* editor Jetse de Vries suggested *Eclipse*. Some people who've heard it since think it suggests something exclusively science fictional, or that something must be being "eclipsed." I've been told it's negative, because it's either blocking something or being blocked *by* something. That wasn't what occurred to me, though, when I heard it.

An eclipse is a rare and unusual event. If you look at photos of the sun taken during a lunar eclipse you'll see a strange, dark, eldritch thing. The eclipsed sun becomes a weird, black, negative image of itself, and the landscapes it shines down upon are equally transformed. It seemed to me that wonderful things could happen under the strange skies of an eclipse. I was also struck by the fact that eclipses happen regularly. It seemed a perfect metaphor for a new science fiction/fantasy anthology series: a book published regularly that was filled with stories where strange and wonderful things happen, where reality was eclipsed for a little while with something magical and new. And as time passed and the stories for *Eclipse 1* began to arrive, it has seemed more and more appropriate.

So, with thanks to Jetse, welcome to the first volume of *Eclipse*. This is not a science fiction anthology. Nor is it a fantasy anthology. It's both and it's more. It's a space where you can encounter rocket ships and ray guns, zombies and zeppelins: pretty much anything you can imagine.

Most of all, it's somewhere you will find great stories. It does not have an agenda or a plan. There is no test of genre purity that it can pass or fail. There's only the test that every reader applies to any work that they encounter—is it good fiction or not?—and I hope we'll pass that one every time.

Every anthology is a community. Before you move on to the stories, I'd like to thank a few people. This book wouldn't exist without the extraordinary support of Jason Williams, Jeremy Lassen, and the entire Night Shade posse. I'd especially like to thank Marty Halpern for his heroic copyediting and Michael Fusco for his wonderful cover design. I'd also like to thank all of the contributors for their patience, support, and the wonderful stories that you're about to encounter. The path from proposal to publication was a particularly rocky one, and I could never have made it without them. I'd also like to thank my anthology guru and pal, Jack Dann, and my wife, Marianne, who have been there for every difficult moment I went through getting us here. And, last of all, I'd like to thank you for picking up this book and taking it home. I hope this is just the start of a beautiful friendship.

Jonathan Strahan
Perth, Western Australia
July 2007

UNIQUE CHICKEN GOES IN REVERSE

ANDY DUNCAN

Father Leggett stood on the sidewalk and looked up at the three narrow stories of gray brick that was 207 East Charlton Street. Compared to the other edifices on Lafayette Square—the Colonial Dames fountain, the Low house, the Turner mansion, the cathedral of course—this house was decidedly ordinary, a reminder that even Savannah had buildings that did only what they needed to do, and nothing more.

He looked again at the note the secretary at St. John the Baptist had left on his desk. Wreathed in cigarette smoke, Miss Ingrid fielded dozens of telephone calls in an eight-hour day, none of which were for her, and while she always managed to correctly record addresses and phone numbers on her nicotine-colored note paper, the rest of the message always emerged from her smudged No. 1 pencils as four or five words that seemed relevant at the time but had no apparent grammatical connection, so that reading a stack of Miss Ingrid's messages back to back gave one a deepening sense of mystery and alarm, like intercepted signal fragments from a trawler during a hurricane. This note read:

OCONNORS

MARY

PRIEST?

CHICKEN!

And then the address. Pressed for more information, Miss Ingrid had shrieked with laughter and said, "Lord, Father, that was two hours ago! Why don't you ask me an easy one sometime?" The phone rang, and she snatched it up with a wink. "It's a great day at St. John the

Baptist. Ingrid speaking."

Surely, Father Leggett thought as he trotted up the front steps, I wasn't expected to *bring* a chicken?

The bell was inaudible, but the door was opened immediately by an attractive but austere woman with dark eyebrows. Father Leggett was sure his sidewalk dithering had been patiently observed.

"Hello, Father. Please come in. Thank you for coming. I'm Regina O'Connor."

She ushered him into a surprisingly large, bright living room. Hauling himself up from the settee was a rumpled little man in shirtsleeves and high-waisted pants who moved slowly and painfully, as if he were much larger.

"Welcome, Father. Edward O'Connor, Dixie Realty and Construction."

"Mr. O'Connor. Mrs. O'Connor. I'm Father Leggett, assistant at St. John for—oh, my goodness, two months now. Still haven't met half my flock, at least. Bishop keeps me hopping. Pleased to meet you now, though." You're babbling, he told himself.

In the act of shaking hands, Mr. O'Connor lurched sideways with a wince, nearly falling. "Sorry, Father. Bit of arthritis in my knee."

"No need to apologize for the body's frailties, Mr. O'Connor. Why, we would all be apologizing all the time, like Alphonse and Gaston." He chuckled as the O'Connors, apparently not readers of the comics supplement, stared at him. "Ahem. I received a message at the church, something involving …" The O'Connors didn't step into the pause to help him. "Involving Mary?"

"We'd like for you to talk to her, Father," said Mrs. O'Connor. "She's in the back yard, playing. Please, follow me."

The back of the house was much shabbier than the front, and the yard was a bare dirt patch bounded on three sides by a high wooden fence of mismatched planks. More brick walls were visible through the gaps. In one corner of the yard was a large chicken coop enclosed by a smaller, more impromptu wire fence, the sort unrolled from a barrel-sized spool at the hardware store and affixed to posts with bent nails. Several dozen chickens roosted, strutted, pecked. Father Leggett's nose wrinkled automatically. He liked chickens when they were fried, baked or, with dumplings, boiled, but he always disliked chickens at their earlier, pre-kitchen stage, as creatures. He conceded them a role in God's creation purely for their utility to man. Father Leggett tended to respect things on the basis of their demonstrated intelligence, and on that universal ladder chickens tended to roost rather low. A farmer once told him that hundreds of chickens could drown during a single rainstorm because they kept gawking at the clouds with their beaks open until they filled with water like jugs. Or maybe that was geese. Father Leggett, who grew up in Baltimore, never liked geese, either.

Lying face up and spread-eagled in the dirt of the yard like a little crime victim was a grimy child in denim overalls, with bobbed hair and a pursed mouth too small even for her nutlike head, most of which was clenched in a frown that was thunderous even from twenty feet away. She gave no sign of acknowledgment as the three adults approached, Mr. O'Connor slightly dragging his right foot. Did this constitute *playing*, wondered Father Leggett, who had scarcely more experience with children than with poultry.

"Mary," said Mrs. O'Connor as her shadow fell across the girl. "This is Father Leggett, from St. John the Baptist. Father Leggett, this is Mary, our best and only. She's in first grade at St. Vincent's."

"Ah, one of Sister Consolata's charges. How old are you, Mary?"

Still lying in the dirt, Mary thrashed her arms and legs, as if making snow angels, but said nothing. Dust clouds rose.

Her father said, "Mary, don't be rude. Answer Father's question."

"I just did," said Mary, packing the utterance with at least six syllables. Her voice was surprisingly deep. She did her horizontal jumping jacks again, counting off this time. "One. Two. Three. Five."

"You skipped four," Father Leggett said.

"You would, too," Mary said. "Four was hell."

"Mary."

This one word from her mother, recited in a flat tone free of judgment, was enough to make the child scramble to her feet. "I'm sorry, Mother and Father and Father, and I beg the Lord's forgiveness." To Father Leggett's surprise, she even curtsied in no particular direction—whether to him or to the Lord, he couldn't tell.

"And well you might, young lady," Mr. O'Connor began, but Mrs. O'Connor, without even raising her voice, easily drowned him out by saying simultaneously:

"Mary, why don't you show Father Leggett your chicken?"

"Yes, Mother." She skipped over to the chicken yard, stood on tiptoe to unlatch the gate, and waded into the squawking riot of beaks and feathers. Father Leggett wondered how she could tell one chicken from all the rest. He caught himself holding his breath, his hands clenched into fists.

"Spirited child," he said.

"Yes," said Mrs. O'Connor. Her unexpected smile was dazzling.

Mary relatched the gate and trotted over with a truly extraordinary chicken beneath one arm. Its feathers stuck out in all directions, as if it had survived a hurricane. It struggled not at all, but seemed content with, or resigned to, Mary's attentions. The child's ruddy face showed renewed determination, and her mouth looked ever more like the dent a thumb leaves on a bad tomato.

"What an odd-looking specimen," said Father Leggett, silently meaning both of them.

"It's frizzled," Mary said. "That means its feathers grew in backward. It has a hard old time of it, this one."

She set the chicken down and held up a pudgy, soiled index finger. The chicken stared at the digit, rapt. The child took one step toward the bird, which took one corresponding step back. The child stepped forward again, and the bird retreated another step, still focused on her finger—its topmost joint slightly crooked, its nail gnawed to the quick. Third step, fourth step, fifth step. The chicken walked backward as if hypnotized, its steps both deliberate and without volition, like the plod of a marionette in unskilled hands.

"Remarkable. And what's your chicken's name, my child?"

She flung down a handful of seed and said, "Jesus Christ."

Father Leggett sucked in a breath. Behind him, Mrs. O'Connor coughed. Father Leggett tugged at his earlobe, an old habit. "What did you say, young lady?"

"Jesus Christ," she repeated, in the same dispassionate voice in which she had said, "Mary O'Connor." Then she rushed the chicken, which skittered around the yard as Mary chased it, chanting in a singsong, "Jesus Christ Jesus Christ Jesus Christ."

Father Leggett looked at her parents. Mr. O'Connor arched his eyebrows and shrugged. Mrs. O'Connor, arms folded, nodded her head once. She looked grimly satisfied. Father Leggett turned back to see chicken and child engaged in a staring contest. The chicken stood, a-quiver; Mary, in a squat, was still.

"Now, Mary," Father Leggett said. "Why would you go and give a frizzled chicken the name of our Lord and Savior?"

"It's the best name," replied Mary, not breaking eye contact with the chicken. "Sister Consolata says the name of Jesus is to be cherished above all others."

"Well, yes, but—"

The hypnotic bond between child and chicken seemed to break, and Mary began to skip around the yard, raising dust with each stomp of her surprisingly large feet. "And he's different from all the other chickens, and the other chickens peck him but he never pecks back, and he spends a lot of his time looking up in the air, praying, and in Matthew Jesus says he's a chicken, and if I get a stomachache or an earache or a sore throat, I come out here and play with him and it gets all better just like the lame man beside the well."

Father Leggett turned in mute appeal to the child's parents. Mr. O'Connor cleared his throat.

"We haven't been able to talk her out of it, Father."

"So we thought we'd call an expert," finished Mrs. O'Connor.

I wish you had, thought Father Leggett. At his feet, the frizzled chicken slurped up an earthworm and clucked with contentment.

The first thing Father Leggett did, once he was safely back at the office, was to reach down Matthew and hunt for the chicken. He found it in the middle of Christ's lecture to the Pharisees, Chapter 23, Verse 37: "O Jerusalem, Jerusalem, thou that killest the prophets, and stonest them which are sent unto thee, how often would I have gathered thy children together, even as a hen gathereth her chickens under her wings, and ye would not!"

Mrs. O'Connor answered the phone on the first ring. "Yes," she breathed, her voice barely audible.

"It's Father Leggett, Mrs. O'Connor. Might I speak to Mary, please?"

"She's napping."

"Oh, I see. Well, I wanted to tell her that I've been reading the Scripture she told me about, and I wanted to thank her. It's really very interesting, the verse she's latched on to. Christ our Lord did indeed liken himself to a hen, yes, but he didn't mean it literally. He was only making a comparison. You see," he said, warming to his subject, to fill the silence, "it's like a little parable, like the story of the man who owned the vineyard. He meant God was *like* the owner of the vineyard, not that God had an actual business interest in the wine industry."

Mrs. O'Connor's voice, when it finally came, was flat and bored.

"No disrespect meant, Father Leggett, but Edward and I did turn to the Scriptures well upstream of our turning to you, and by now everyone in this household is intimately acquainted with Matthew 23:37, its histories, contexts and commentaries. And yet our daughter seems to worship a frizzled chicken. Have you thought of anything that could explain it?"

"Well, Mrs. O'Connor—"

"Regina."

"Regina. Could it be that this chicken is just a sort of imaginary playmate for the girl? Well, not the chicken, that's real enough, but I mean the identity she has created for it. Many children have imaginary friends, especially children with no siblings, like Mary."

"Oh, I had one of those," she said. "A little boy named Bar-Lock, who lived in my father's Royal Bar-Lock typewriter."

"There, you see. You know just what I'm talking about."

"But I never thought Bar-Lock was my lord and savior!"

"No, but 'lord and savior' is a difficult idea even for an adult to grasp, isn't it? By projecting it onto a chicken, Mary makes the idea more manageable, something she can hold and understand. She seems happy, doesn't she? Content? No nightmares about her chicken being nailed to a cross? And as she matures, in her body and in her faith, she'll grow out if it, won't need it anymore."

"Well, perhaps," she said, sounding miffed. "Thank you for calling, Father. When Mary wakes up, I'll tell her you were thinking about her, and about her imaginary Jesus."

She broke the connection, leaving Father Leggett with his mouth open. The operator's voice squawked through the earpiece.

"Next connection, please. Hello? Hello?"

That night, Father Leggett dreamed about a frizzled chicken nailed to a cross. He woke with the screech in his ears.

The never-ending crush of church business enabled Father Leggett to keep putting off a return visit to the O'Connors, as the days passed into weeks and into months, but avoiding chickens, and talk of chickens, was not so easy. He began to wince whenever he heard of them coming home to roost, or being counted before they were hatched, of politicians providing them in every pot.

The dreams continued. One night the human Jesus stood on the mount and said, "Blessed are the feedmakers," then squatted and pecked the ground. The mob squatted and pecked the ground, too. Jesus and His followers flapped their elbows and clucked.

Worst of all was the gradual realization that for every clergyman in Georgia, chicken was an occupational hazard. Most families ate chicken only on Sundays, but any day Father Leggett came to visit was de facto

Sunday, so he got served chicken all the time—breasts, legs, livers and dumplings, fried, baked, boiled, in salads, soups, broths and stews, sautéed, fricasseed, marengoed, a la kinged, cacciatored, casseroled. Of all this chicken, Father Leggett ate ever smaller portions. He doubled up on mustard greens and applesauce. He lost weight.

"Doubtless you've heard the Baptist minister's blessing," the bishop told him one day:

"I've had chicken hot, and I've had chicken cold.

"I've had chicken young, and I've had chicken old.

"I've had chicken tender, and I've had chicken tough.

"And thank you, Lord, I've had chicken enough."

Since the bishop had broached the subject, in a way, Father Leggett took the opportunity to tell him about his visit with the O'Connor child, and the strange theological musings it had inspired in him. The bishop, a keen administrator, got right to the heart of the matter.

"What do you mean, frizzled?"

Father Leggett tried as best he could to explain the concept of frizzled to the bishop, finally raking both hands through his own hair until it stood on end.

"Ah, I see. Sounds like some kind of freak. Best to wring its neck while the child's napping. She might catch the mites."

"Oh, but sir, the girl views this chicken as a manifestation of our Lord."

"Our Lord was no freak," the bishop replied. "He was martyred for our sins, not pecked to death like a runty chicken."

"They seem to have a real bond," Father Leggett said. "Where you and I might see only a walking feather duster, this child sees the face of Jesus."

"People see the face of Jesus all over," the bishop said, "in clouds and stains on the ceiling and the headlamps of Fords. Herbert Hoover and Father Divine show up in the same places, if you look hard enough. It's human nature to see order where there is none."

"She trained it to walk backward on command. That's order from chaos, surely. Like the hand of God on the face of the waters."

"You admire this child," the bishop said.

I envy her, Father Leggett thought, but what he said was, "I do. And I fear for her faith, if something were to happen to this chicken. They don't live long, you know, even if they make it past Sunday dinner. They aren't parrots or turtles, and frizzles are especially susceptible to cold weather. I looked it up."

"Best thing for her," the bishop said. "Get her over this morbid fascination. You, too. Not healthy for a man of the cloth to be combing Scripture for chickens. Got to see the broader picture, you know. Otherwise, you're no better than the snake handlers, fixated on Mark 16: 17-18. 'And these signs shall follow them that believe; in my name shall they cast out devils; they shall speak with new tongues; they shall take up serpents; and if they drink any deadly thing, it shall not hurt them; they shall lay hands on the sick, and they shall recover.'"

"Perhaps this child has taken up a chicken," Father Leggett said, "as another believer would take up a snake."

"Not to worry, son," the bishop said. "Little Mary's belief will outlive this chicken, I reckon. Probably outlive you and me, too. Come in, Ingrid!"

A cloud of cigarette smoke entered the office, followed by Ingrid's head around the door. "Lunch is ready," she said.

"Oh, good. What's today's bill of fare?"

"Roast chicken."

"I'm not hungry," Father Leggett quickly said.

The bishop laughed. "To paraphrase: 'If they eat any deadly thing, it shall not hurt them.'"

"Mark 16:18 wasn't in the original gospel," Ingrid said. "The whole twelve-verse ending of the book was added later, by a scribe."

The bishop looked wounded. "An *inspired* scribe," he said.

"Wash your hands, both of you," Ingrid said, and vanished in a puff.

"She's been raiding the bookcase again," the bishop growled. "It'll only confuse her."

As he picked at his plate, Father Leggett kept trying to think of other things, but couldn't. "They shall lay hands on the sick, and they shall recover." Mary O'Connor had placed her hands upon a frizzled chicken and … hadn't healed it, exactly, for it was still a ridiculous, doomed creature, but had given it a sort of mission. A backward purpose, but a purpose nonetheless.

That day Father Leggett had a rare afternoon off, so he went to the movies. The cartoon was ending as he entered the auditorium, and he fumbled to a seat in the glare of the giant crowing rooster that announced the Pathe Sound News. Still out of sorts, he slumped in his seat and stared blankly at the day's doings, reduced to a shrilly narrated comic strip: a ship tossing in a gale, two football teams piling onto one another, Clarence Darrow defending a lynch mob in Hawaii, a glider soaring over the Alps—but the next title took his breath.

UNIQUE CHICKEN GOES IN REVERSE

"In Savannah, Georgia, little Mary O'Connor, age five, trains her pet chicken to walk backward!"

And there on screen, stripped of sound and color and all human shading, like Father Leggett's very thoughts made huge and public, were Mary and her frizzled chicken. As he gaped at the capering giants, he was astonished by the familiarity of the O'Connor back yard, how easily he could fill in the details past the square edges of the frame. One would think he had lived there, as a child. He thought he might weep. The audience had begun cheering so at "Savannah, Georgia," that much of the rest was inaudible, but Father Leggett was pretty sure that Jesus wasn't mentioned. The cameraman had captured only a few seconds of the chicken actually walking backward; the rest was clearly the film cranked in reverse, and the segment ended with more "backward" footage of waddling ducks, trotting horses, grazing cattle. The delighted audience howled and roared. Feeling sick, Father Leggett lurched to his feet, stumbled across his neighbors to the aisle, and fled the theater.

He went straight to the upright house on Lafayette Square, leaned on the bell until Mrs. O'Connor appeared, index finger to her lips.

"Shh! Please, Father, not so loud," she whispered, stepping onto the porch and closing the door behind. "Mr. O'Connor has to rest, afternoons."

"Beg pardon," he whispered. "I didn't realize, when I bought my ticket, that your Mary has become a film star now."

"Oh, yes," she said, with an unexpected laugh, perching herself on the banister. "She's the next Miriam Hopkins, I'm sure. It was the chicken they were here for. Edward called them. Such a bother. Do you know, they were here an hour trying to coax it to walk two steps? Stage fright, I suppose. I could have strangled the wretched thing."

"I've been remiss in not calling sooner. And how is Mary doing?"

"Oh, she's fine." Her voice was approaching its normal volume. "Do you know, from the day the cameramen visited, she seemed to lose interest in Jesus? Jesus the chicken, I mean. It's as if the camera made her feel foolish, somehow."

"May I see her?"

"She's out back, as usual." She glanced at the door, then whispered again. "Best to go around the house, I think."

She led the way down the steps and along a narrow side yard—a glorified alleyway, really, with brick walls at each elbow—to the back yard, where Mary lay in the dirt, having a fit.

"Child!" Father Leggett cried, and rushed to her.

She thrashed and kicked, her face purple, her frown savage. Father Leggett knelt beside her, seized and—with effort—held her flailing arms. Her hands were balled into fists. "Child, calm yourself. What's wrong?"

Suddenly still, she opened her eyes. "Hullo," she said. "I'm fighting."

"Fighting what?"

"My angel," she said.

He caught himself glancing around, as if Saint Michael might be behind him. "Oh, child."

"Sister Consolata says I have an invisible guardian angel that never leaves my side, not even when I'm sleeping, not even when I'm in the *potty*." This last word was whispered. "He's always watching me, and following me, and being a pain, and one day I'm going to turn around and catch him and *knock* his block off." She swung her fists again and pealed with laughter.

Mary's mother stood over them, her thin mouth set, her dark brows lowered, looking suddenly middle-aged and beautiful. Her default expression was severity, but on her, severity looked good. How difficult it must be, Father Leggett thought, to have an only child, a precocious child, any child.

"Mary, I've got cookies in the oven."

She sat up. "Oatmeal?"

"Oatmeal."

"With raisins and grease?"

"With raisins and grease." She leaned down, cupped her hands around her mouth, and whispered, "And we won't let that old angel have a one."

Mary giggled.

"You're welcome to join us, Father. Father?"

"Of course, thank you," said Father Leggett, with an abstracted air, not turning around, as he walked slowly toward the chicken yard. The frizzled one was easy to spot; it stood in its own space, seemingly avoided by the others. It walked a few steps toward the gate as the priest approached.

Father Leggett felt the gaze of mother and child upon him as he lifted the fishhook latch and creaked open the gate. The chickens nearest him fluttered, then stilled, but their flutter was contagious. It passed to the next circle of chickens, then the next, a bit more violent each time. The outermost circle of chickens returned it to the body of the flock, and by the time the ripple of unease had reached Father Leggett, he had begun to realize why so many otherwise brave people were (to use a word he had learned only in his recent weeks of study) alektorophobes. Only the frizzled Jesus seemed calm. Father Leggett stepped inside, his Oxfords crunching corn hulls and pebbles. He had the full attention of the chickens now. Without looking, he closed the gate behind. He walked forward, and the milling chickens made a little space for him, an ever-shifting, downy clearing in which he stood, arms at his sides, holding his breath. The frizzle stepped to the edge of this clearing, clucked at him. The hot air was rich with the smells of grain, bad eggs and droppings. A crumpled washtub held brackish water. Feathers floated across his smudged reflection. He closed his eyes, slowly lifted his arms. The chickens roiled. Wings beat at his shins. He reached as far aloft as he could and prayed a wordless prayer as the chicken yard erupted around him, a smothering cloud that buffeted his face and chest and legs. He was the center of a tornado of chickens, their cackles rising and falling like speech, a message that he almost felt he understood, and with closed eyes he wept in gratitude, until Jesus pecked him in the balls.

One afternoon years later, during her final semester at the women's college in Milledgeville, Mary O'Connor sat at her desk in the *Corinthian* office, leafing through the Atlanta paper, wondering whether the new copy of the McMurray Hatchery catalog ("All Flocks Blood Tested") would be waiting in the mailbox when she got home. Then an article deep inside the paper arrested her attention.

Datelined Colorado, it was about a headless chicken named Mike. Mike had survived a Sunday-morning beheading two months previous. Each evening Mike's owners plopped pellets of feed down his stumpy neck with an eyedropper and went to bed with few illusions, and each morning Mike once again gurgled up the dawn.

She read and reread the article with the deepest satisfaction. It reminded her of her childhood, and in particular of the day she first learned the nature of grace.

She clipped the article and folded it in half and in half and in half again until it was furled like Aunt Pittypat's fan and sheathed it in an envelope that she addressed to Father Leggett, care of the Cathedral of St. John the Baptist in Savannah. Teaching a *headless* chicken to walk backward: that would be *real* evangelism. On a fresh sheet of the stationery her grandmother had given her two Christmases ago, she crossed out the ornate engraved "M" at the top and wrote in an even more ornate "F," as if she were flunking herself with elegance. Beneath it she wrote:

> Dear Father Leggett,
> I saw this and thought of you.
> Happy Easter,
> Flannery (nee Mary) O'Connor

When Miss Ingrid's successor brought him the letter, Father Leggett was sitting in his office, eating a spinach salad and reading the *Vegetarian News*. He was considered a good priest though an eccentric one, and no longer was invited to so many parishioners' homes at mealtime. He glanced at the note, then at the clipping. The photo alone made him upset his glass of carrot juice. He threw clipping, note and envelope into the trash can, mopped up the spill with a napkin, fisted the damp cloth and took deep chest-expanding breaths until he felt calmer. He allowed himself a glance around the room, half-expecting the flutter of wings, the brush of the thing with feathers.

BAD LUCK, TROUBLE, DEATH, AND VAMPIRE SEX

GARTH NIX

I never thought Granny could die from the simple act of biting her own lip.

Not that it was quite as straightforward as that, of course. She would have been fine if that single drop of blood hadn't fallen in her brandy. Or to be fair, if I hadn't then jumped to attend her with a handkerchief and knocked the glass so that it flew across the room, brandy and blood entering the small open mouth of the bronze gargoyle on the corner of the mantelpiece.

All of which would have been no problem at all if it hadn't happened at the exact stroke of midnight, with the light of the moon falling just so through the dormer window.

I mean, how dumb is it to set up your immortality so that it can be rescinded as easily as that?

I looked down at the still corpse of the most powerful witch-queen in the nether-world, my own adopted grandmother, and was beset by a swirling mixture of powerful emotions, the uppermost one requiring me to vocalize it.

"Holy shit! What the fuck am I going to do now?"

The gargoyle licked its lips and answered me in a depressed monotone.

"You and me both. I'm gonna get my ass melted down for this. You, they'll probably string up by the—"

"Shut up!"

"With silver mandolin strings," concluded the gargoyle.

"They'll have to catch me first," I muttered. I bent down and took Granny's original 1911 model Colt .45 from her shoulder holster and thrust it through my belt. Then I started to go through the secret pockets of her bullet-proof cardigan. Not that I expected to get much. Granny's power had mostly been in her voice. She didn't go in much for charms and objets d'art. But there was always the chance I might find some money.

Outside, wolves began to howl and owls hoot in curious unison, soon joined by the clamor of the bells that hung at the top of the elevator shaft.

"They know," said the gargoyle. "They're coming. You're going to unscrew me or what? You don't want to leave no witness."

"I haven't got time to find a screwdriver," I muttered. There was nothing in Granny's pockets so I ducked into the fireplace and checked out the chimney. It wasn't wide enough for me to climb up unaltered, and there was a silver mesh grille across the top.

"There's a bunch of stuff in Dextrise and Malboc, volume four," said the gargoyle, indicating the bookshelf with its long, impressively scaly tongue. "Including a screwstone."

"Why would I want a screwstone *now*, for fuck's sake?" I hissed. There had to be another way out. The windows were barred with silvered iron rods. The fire door led not to a fire escape, but to a place no one would go without lengthy preparations, heavy-duty magical ordnance and a lot of backup. Well, no one except Granny.

"To undo me and the mesh on the chimney," said the gargoyle. "What did you think screwstones were for?"

I didn't waste time uttering a snappy retort, particularly since I'd have to think of one first. Where the hell was Dextrise and Malboc, volume four?

"They're all D&M on that shelf," said the gargoyle. "It's the one with the big gold '4' on the spine."

"I know," I snapped. The much heavier than expected volume slid out under my panicked fingers and fell open on the ground. A red leather bag with a gold drawstring lay inside the hollowed-out pages. I grabbed it and for a quarter of a second wondered if it would be wise to open the bag.

During this brief instant of caution, the elevator bell dinged, and the arrow above the door began to move from Z to A. The bells in the shaft ceased their jangle and the wolves and owls grew quiet. Little bastards probably didn't want to miss hearing my screams.

I opened the bag. Inside there was a rough grey stone the size of my fist, a mouldy bean that looked like it'd come off the rim of a bachelor's week-old lunch plate, and a copper coin green with verdigris. Or possibly a circular piece of verdigris that had got some copper on it.

I took out the stone and waved it in the direction of the gargoyle and the chimney, focusing what passed for my will on it to undo said items. Since I forgot to turn my head I was almost blinded by the rocketing screws that hurtled towards the stone, and one did scratch the middle knuckle of my left ring finger, which was probably a portent or an omen, or maybe both. What would I know, I failed Introductory Augury. Twice.

The gargoyle fell to the floor but managed to arrest itself with its tongue, ripping off most of the mantelpiece in the process. I hastily picked it up, shoved it in the red bag, put the bag in my mouth and transformed. I had a moment's unease as the .45 got stuck full-size in my groin for a second, before it transformed into a pistol-shaped patch of hair.

"That's your alter-form?" said a muffled voice from the bag, followed by a surprisingly girlish giggle.

"Shut the fuck up!" I snarled. Scotty dogs may not be very big and they may have curly hair but by god we can be vicious when we want to be. Just ask a rat.

On the other hand we can't climb as well as a cat, or I'd have been out of that chimney in half the time. Or fly like a bat, enabling an even speedier escape. Or do other cool and useful stuff that would be very helpful when trying to get the hell out of the lair of She Who Must Be Listened To Until She's Done.

I'd already been there for four hours when the brandy accident happened, and Grandma had hardly drawn breath the whole time. The key phrases in her diatribe were "Total disappointment," "I can't believe you tried to fuck a vampire" and "cancellation of contract forthwith".

That last bit wasn't going to look good when they wheeled in the guy with the Frankenstein-sewn back-to-front ears and he had a listen to Granny's last hours.

"They'll think I did it on purpose," I mumbled as I dropped the bag on the roof. Fortunately it only fell as far as the gutter. "Because she was going to cancel my deal."

"You mean you *didn't* do it on purpose?" asked the gargoyle. It had forced the top of the bag open with its tongue and I could see one baleful glowing eye peering at me. "It really was an accident?"

"Yeah," I said.

"Wow," said the gargoyle. "You been having a lot of accidents lately?"

"I don't think so—" I started to say, just as the tiles under my four little paws slipped and I flipped over and had to scrabble madly to avoid going over the side.

"You need to get checked out," said the gargoyle.

"I need to get the hell out of here first."

Getting out was going to be difficult. The rooftop was only a temporary haven and as I looked around it looked more and more temporary and less and less a haven. For a start, while the sky had been clear through the window, there were low, dark clouds clustering around the roof. I mean really dark clouds, the kind that usually flickered with internal lightning as they rumbled overhead and unleashed enough rain to make Noah piss himself. Which would only make matters worse when the lightning was unleashed. Conductivity-wise that is—

"You gonna sit there all night staring at the clouds or what?"

"Can't go down," I muttered. "Too far to jump to the Boaser building, and the Alleyn's roof is too sharp… what's with these clouds?"

The clouds were pushing in over the gutters, boxing me in to a space about ten feet wide. If they were clouds, which was becoming less likely with every passing second. They were clearly things that looked like clouds but were actually something else extremely horrible that I didn't know about and should never have had to even glimpse, let alone get up close and personal with.

"We'll have to translate," I said. "What are you over there?"

"You'll find out," said the gargoyle.

I did the dance as the clouds rushed in and just as their ghastly grey wispy tendrils were about to grab sensitive portions of my anatomy, I spoke the Word, and the gargoyle and I were suddenly somewhere else and I was no longer a Scotty dog and the gargoyle was no longer a small piece of gothic sculpture.

We were in a nondescript office corridor and she was a six-foot-six mahogany-skinned nightclub bouncer with a shaved head, wearing red wraparound sunglasses, a gold racing suit unbuttoned to the midriff and a mayoral-style chain of tiny ceramicised advertising patches from numerous oil and tyre companies that was doing very little to conceal her rather fascinating cleavage.

I, on the other hand, was back to my normal unprepossessing human self.

"Well, hello," I smirked, turning on the charm.

She smacked the sex charm out of my hand and slapped my cheek for good measure.

"What's got into you, moron? Your life's in danger. Besides, I'm simply not attracted to little men with weak sorcery."

"You didn't have to break my charm," I complained as I picked the pieces of the charm off the floor and clicked them together. Then just to be sure she wasn't toying with me, I tried my roguish smile and added, "Maybe you'd like to handle something—"

When I picked myself up off the floor she was grinding the remains of the charm into dust under her heel.

"Now I can believe you tried to hump a vampire," she said. "You must be desperate. Whatever gave you the idea that you would enjoy cold undead flesh anyway?"

"Books," I muttered. "Lot of 'em. Vampire hunters. Sexy undead. Thought some of it must be true. Leakage of reality from the nether-world…"

"You should know better than that."

"OK, the vampire sex wasn't so pleasant," I protested. "But I'm going to try a werewolf gal next, they're warm-blooded—"

This time I lay on the ground a bit longer before I got up, while the former gargoyle stood over me, frowning.

"That's to teach you to stop dreaming with your dick. Now get up. They'll be on our trail in a minute or two."

"What do I call you?" I asked gingerly. My lower lip was already starting to swell up from the latest punch. "I can't call you gargoyle."

"Call me Gurl."

"Girl? What kind of name is—"

"Gurl, with a 'u'. Can't you hear the difference? Uh oh—"

Both of us turned at the same time, just as the ceiling tiles exploded and something bright and shimmering blue dropped in, cold blasting ahead of it, sucking the breath out of my lungs. I had the .45 in my hand and I just managed to squeeze off two shots before my trigger finger froze, the gunshots booming in the enclosed space.

There was a horrible, high-pressure screech and then the thing collapsed in on itself and turned into a low wave of dirty iced water that rushed past me high enough to permanently stain the crotch of my pants. Gurl, of course, had managed to jump up and hang from a light fixture, escaping the air-conditioning elemental's final act of terror.

As warmth and feeling slowly returned to my hand, I eased my finger off the trigger, groaning slightly with the pain. Inside, I was giving thanks to Granny for packing a decent pistol with a full arcane load. A lot of folk who travel between the realms go for smaller caliber stuff, easy to conceal snub-nosed .38s, or 9mm autos with a big magazine, fourteen or fifteen rounds. But when it comes to stopping power, you can't beat a good old-fashioned Colt .45 with a 230gr Federal Hi-Shok round jacketed in silver. Well, of course, you can beat it with say a 10 gauge riot gun firing solid silver slugs or just the sheer firepower of a nice automatic weapon like a MAC-10 or an MP5K PDW or if the shit is really serious and you've got the room, some sort of light anti-armor weapon, like what they used to call a LAW, or SRAW, though nowadays if you can get your hands on an AT4—

"Wipe that drool off your face and let's move!" snapped Gurl. "That elemental was only the first across. Move it!"

"Uh," I grunted. What the hell was going on? I'd never had an internal monologue about the relative stopping power of various firearms before. And come to think of it, I never used to have a sex charm. Or wanted to fuck a vampire. I mean, I had a girlfriend… or I used to. Come to think about it, I wasn't even sure what had been going on in the last few weeks…

"I've been cursed," I croaked as Gurl dragged me down the corridor and down the internal fire escape.

"No shit!" snapped Gurl. "You only just realize that?"

"Yeah. It's just not me, this fascination with firearms and sex with the undead and—"

Gurl caught me as I tripped over the landing, arresting my movement an inch before I collided head first with the wall.

"Clumsiness," I finished weakly.

Gurl pushed the door open with her little finger and caught me again as I almost fell down the stairs.

"Concentrate!" she snapped. "It's a curse, remember? It can only get you when your mind wanders."

Like after four hours of Granny lecturing me. That was enough to make my mind wander about as far as any mind could go, thus letting the curse get a really good grip.

I concentrated. Steps, I told myself. Keep the feet on the steps. But who the hell would want to curse me? What had I been doing these last few weeks? Besides jumping vampire bones? What was happening with my current case? I could lose my investigator's licence—"

"I said concentrate!" said Gurl. She hauled me back and pushed me through the door to the lobby. "Do you recognize where we are?"

"The lobby of a building," I said weakly and then, "Ow! What did you do that for?"

Gurl ignored me. Lithe as a... a really lithe kind of animal that I couldn't quite think of... she ran to the revolving door and looked out. While she looked out, I looked around. It was a lobby, so I was right, there. But there was no one in it, despite the sunshine coming in through the front windows and the door. And the black-letter on white marble signboard had a lot of very strange entries. I mean the words weren't even English. Come to think about it, the letters weren't even English. Or Chinese. Or Cyrillic. This was a symbol puzzle, the kind that a top-flight private eye could solve in a few minutes, so I could do it in thirty seconds...

"Hold on," I said. "What's this private eye crap? I'm not an investigator in the alter-world! I'm a gardener. I own a company that does office plants! Green Thumb Inc., that's me! What the hell is going on?"

"Shut up!" said Gurl. "Listen."

I shut up and listened. It was quiet. Very quiet. Way too quiet for any kind of office block in the city. There should have been traffic noises. People shouting. Annoying beep-beep-beep sounds from pedestrian crossings and stupid escalating ringtones designed to deafen everyone except the owner of the phone.

"You idiot," said Gurl. "You've translated us to an ur-space."

"No I haven't," I protested. "Listen, I can hear *something*."

The something got louder and clearer. It was the distant baying of a very large number of hounds. Nasty, strangely metallic hounds. It sounded like a cross between a hundred hubcaps falling off the back of a truck on to a hard road and a similar number of dogs waiting in line to get neutered at the vet's.

"Uh, not anything normal though," I conceded. "Uh, sorry. I guess this *is* an ur-space. We must be close though, or you'd still be a gargoyle."

"Translate us!" demanded Gurl. The baying was getting louder, and it was coming from both outside the building and from the stairwell. It could only be a sorcerous hunting pack of firewrought hounds or maybe red iron firedogs or perhaps even brazen wolves, the kind of enemy where you wanted a nice secure pillbox with a narrow firing slit and a tripod-mounted M60 or better still a .50 cal, several boxes of silver-mercury explosive-tipped ammo, a few spare barrels—

"Concentrate! Translate us, wizard!"

"Oh yeah," I said. I'd forgotten I was a wizard too, a green wizard, not a somewhat sorcerous private eye with a proclivity for bizarre sex and firearms. "It's too soon to do the dance again. I'll have to do...

uh… something else."

"Be quick," said Gurl. She took a fire extinguisher and wedged it in the revolving door, then tore off the top of the reception desk and ripped it into three pieces. She chose one length as a club and put the other two through the handles of the stair door, barring it shut.

The desk was two-inch hardwood, so I was reminded once again to treat Gurl with respect. It wasn't so difficult, not since the sex charm had been destroyed. But my mind kept up its clumsy wandering, trying to go down paths liberally strewn with lady werewolves toting firearms. The curse was fighting my efforts to shake it off, and that meant that I had to get an unusually large and powerful handgun, perhaps a S&W Model 500 .50 revolver and hunt down the perpetrator—

I shook my head. The curse was too strong. If it had been a spell it would have been weakened in the translation from the nether-world and I could defeat the residual effects by mere force of will. That meant there was a curse locus on me somewhere, something powerful enough to stay with me through a shapechange and a translation.

I put my hand in my mouth and felt my teeth, quickly pulling each one to see if any were loose. One was. It came out with a stench of sulphurous gas that nearly choked me. Coughing and wheezing, I drop-kicked the tooth to the far side of the lobby.

Just then the first of the hounds arrived at the bottom of the stairs. The baying got a lot louder and now it was accompanied by terrible thuds and ominous cracking sounds as they threw themselves against the door.

I took stock very quickly. I had none of my usual apparatus. No trowel, no fertilizer, no seedlings, no selections of bark. Just a .45 pistol with perhaps five rounds in it which I was suddenly less interested in… and a red leather bag with a copper coin and a bean of unknown provenance. I could probably use the bean, but green magic is slow. I had to do something fast, but I didn't have anything…

Except that cursed tooth I'd just thrown away.

"Hold them off for a minute!" I shouted, as I dived across the floor and picked up the tooth again. I held it in my left hand as I took out the copper coin, holding that in my right fist as I mentally reached out to pull in whatever sorcerous power there was in this ur-space. Ivory, or ivory-equivalent, and copper were certainly not green magic, but people—particularly my enemies—often forgot that I wasn't just a green wizard.

I'd forgotten myself, but fear is a powerful mnemonic catalyst. I was also the owner of a not very successful office plant business that survived thanks to a grandmotherly subsidy in the alter-world. Not that this was relevant in the current circumstance. What was relevant was that in the nether-world I was a green wizard of the fourth circle (so only ninth-lowest of the low). But not only that, thanks to my grandmother's insistence on me signing up when I was twenty-one for three of the most miserable and toughest years of my life, I was also a duty-served Knight of the Bright Hill and so I could call upon aid from any of its outlying garrisons. Well, I could if I was prepared to pay for it in extra years of service.

Funnily enough, with imminent death by tooth and claw only the other side of a door and my only ally an admittedly extremely tough door-bitch, I was prepared to pay; and with ivory and copper, I could call in someone very heavy duty.

At least I hoped I could. I had no idea where we were, which garrison was closest, and even if anyone useful would be there. But at that point, even a knocked-kneed ancient arbalist would be better than nothing.

As my call went out, there was a particularly loud thud, a very sharp crack and the door burst open. A firedog pushed its flat, red-hot head through the smashed timbers and looked puzzled as Gurl smashed her club on its skull. The club burst into flames. The firedog growled, and swiped at Gurl with one very large, very hot paw. She leaped back, and it thrust itself almost through, its hindquarters stuck for the four or five seconds it would take for the door to finish burning down. At the same time, the revolving door shrieked and the top of the fire extinguisher blew off, a fountain of foam gushing towards the ceiling. Firedogs backed away from the foam, their burning rear-ends melting holes in the glass.

There was a lot of smoke, a lot of baying and quite a lot of screaming. Mostly that was Gurl's battlecry but I suspect some of it was more the pathetic scared kind coming out of my own throat.

There was also the shimmering sound of distant cymbals being struck with feathered hammers, and the floor shook as something very heavy arrived.

"Sir Gardner," said a voice behind me. "You beseech my aid?"

I didn't so much turn as revolve on the spot.

"Yes!" I said. There was so much smoke that it was hard to see our reinforcement. But as she took up so much of the lobby it was kind of hard to come to grips with the totality of her anyway. There was the sheen of bright scales, the glitter of a line of diamond teeth, the sudden sweep of a surprisingly prehensile tail about the size of a dozen firehoses braided together, a couple of talons the size of the firedogs... and then there weren't any firedogs. Just distant yelping that rapidly got more distant, and a nasty crunching sound, which would be the two or three of the pack that didn't turn tail fast enough.

I lay on the floor where the air was kind of OK and gasped. Gurl leopard-crawled across to me and propped nearby.

"It knows I'm with you, right?"

"She," I whispered. "Lady Alyss of the Corben Ravelin."

I raised my head a little and peered into the smoke.

"Gramercy, Lady Alyss," I said.

"A trifle," replied the dragon. "Have you the tokens?"

I threw the coin and the tooth up to where I thought her head was. Smoke swirled and parted, and I caught a glimpse of Alyss's serpentine head, dark as gunmetal, in stark contrast to her shining wings and body.

"Ach," grunted the dragon. There was a ghastly hawking sound and then the tooth shot past me like a stone from a slingshot and shattered on the floor. "A most disagreeable curse lay on that tooth, Sir Gardner."

"I regret that I was forced to rely upon such a token, and I apologise unreservedly for its use," I said. Possibly I had just got myself out of the skillet and onto the stove. Alyss was notoriously touchy about her honor, and I would have no chance fighting a duel with her. Even with all my stuff, and all my wits about me.

"Indeed," sniffed Alyss, her intake of breath clearing out most of the smoke. "I shall let the matter pass, as you were clearly in extremis, Sir Gardner. Till we meet again, at the Ebb Muster."

"Till we meet again, Lady Alyss," I said, standing up to bow. I'd just scored another obligation. Calling one of the Order's dragons was worth at least two years' service from the likes of me, and Lady Alyss had just made it official. Come the Ebb Muster, I had to report or be forsworn.

Of course, I'd be well dead by then, because Grandma's folk would catch up with me long before then. Or whoever put the curse on me in the first place.

Lady Alyss vanished, taking the remainder of the smoke with her, except for a little bit in my lungs that I had to cough out. Gurl clapped me on the back so hard I thought one of my natural teeth might fly out.

"The bastards got me at the dentist," I said, once I'd stopped cough-ing. "Or one of them was the dentist. I never should have let them give me the gas; they must have translated me while I was under, implanted the cursed tooth and then sent me back."

"Afraid of the pain, were you?" said Gurl. "Somehow I'm not sur-prised."

"Come on, it was a crown replacement," I said. "But I could have taken the pain, I just enjoy the gas… oh shit. *A crown replacement.* That is fiendishly clever. A cursed tooth for a crown replacement… Granny the witch-queen… they made me into an assassin that would kill with bad luck!"

"Got to give them points for that," said Gurl. "Has to be the new queen that set it up, I guess, and we get offed by the either the old queen's guards *or* the new queen's friends."

"I'm sure that's their plan," I said. My brain was finally getting itself into thinking order. "But if we can survive Granny's guards, we might have a chance."

"Why?"

"Because no one can guarantee who the new witch-queen will be. It's not something you can plan on, or subvert. I mean there's at least a hundred and one heirs of the blood, by birth or adoption. Each heir gets to hold the old witch-queen's knife, and put on the necklace and the stupid hat, and those three things *choose…* or not. The consequences of them not choosing are severe, so most potential heirs don't even try. Besides, who would actually want the job?"

"Whoever it is, we'd better find somewhere to hide out right *now*," said Gurl. "It'll be bats next. Or the Inner Coven. We'll have the best chance in the alter-world. Can you get us there yet?"

"Hang on a minute," I said. "I'm thinking."

"We have to—"

"Shhh!"

I was thinking. Very hard. The central part of it being my own question: *Who would want the job? Even Granny used to talk about giving it up.*

This was closely followed by another thought. What if someone just took Granny's place, without undergoing the test of the knife, the necklace and the hat? Sure, they'd lack the secret powers, but given enough front they could at least command the Inner and Outer Co-vens, the Familiar Circus and so on. If that's what they wanted to do, all that "say unto him go and he goeth" stuff.

"I think I've worked out what's going on," I said. "Part of it, anyway. We have to go back to the nether-world."

"Are you fucking crazy?" hissed Gurl. "Soon as we cross, they'll be on to us. And I'll be a gargoyle again, which let me tell you is not something—"

"I've got a plan," I said. I did too, or at least I had the seed of a plan. Hopefully it was going to grow into something. "Uh, why *are* you a gargoyle there by the way, and… uh… human here and in the alter-world? I mean, a gargoyle in the nether-world should just translate across as an ugly desk ornament or a novelty USB flash disk or something—"

"Thanks," snarled Gurl. "I'm not permanently a gargoyle in the nether-world. Your grandma turned me into one, because I wouldn't let her into a party."

"That's all? Seems a bit harsh, even for her."

"I did try to throw her down the steps," said Gurl.

"Well, you got off lightly," I said. "She must have liked you. But you won't be a gargoyle in the nether-world now. You translated out, which would break the initial working, and now Granny's dead the spell won't reattach."

"Oh yeah," said Gurl. Her face, which had been pretty much scowlified since we'd crossed over, suddenly brightened. "I forgot about that. It's hard to imagine her gone. I was kind of… kind of getting used to hanging out with her, if you know what I mean."

I did know what she meant and I realized in retrospect I should have wondered about it a lot more on my previous visits. Granny was the last person who'd let anything sentient hang out in her office. Which begged the question of why she'd stuck Gurl on the mantelpiece of that particular fireplace. It wasn't as if she'd been short of fireplaces. Or gutters, which is where you would expect her to put a once-human gargoyle as a punishment, out in the snow and rain for the owls to crap on.

It was another piece of the puzzle and though I now knew I wasn't and never had been a private detective, my brain had finally kicked into feverish activity and was sorting everything out.

Step one, of course, was to survive long enough to find out whether I was right or not.

"If we head a couple of blocks west in this ur-space, to the point that correlates with the Solomon Piazza in the nether-world, we can translate straight through. There'll be a crowd there for sure, waiting for news. We can give it to them."

"What?" snorted Gurl. "Like, 'Hi, Gardner here. I'm the guy who killed the queen, only it wasn't my fault'?"

"No," I said. My mind was really firing now. "What I'll do—"

"Explain as we run," said Gurl. Her head tilted to one side, and one of her pointy ears twitched. "Something else just came through up above."

I couldn't hear anything, but I didn't hang around to listen. We quickly climbed out through the broken revolving door and hot-footed it down the street—quite literally as there were hot... let's call them coals... all over the place from the frightened passage of the firedogs.

"Tell me," I panted. "How did you know the bag with the screwstone and stuff was in Dextrise and Malboc, volume four?"

"Granny talks... talked to herself a lot," said Gurl. "She was muttering to herself the other day about the screwstone, she kept on repeating it, 'The screwstone is in Dextrise and Malboc, volume four.'"

"Right at the next avenue," I interrupted. "The cunning old mad-am."

"What?" asked Gurl as we sprinted around the corner and both slowed at the same time. Third Avenue looked mostly like it would look in the alter-world, minus cars and people, except that about half a mile ahead it curved sharply upwards, as if someone had peeled the road back and let it curl. I allowed my gaze to follow the arching road up into a drearily blank sky of photographically neutral grey sky and wished I hadn't. That absence of color always makes me feel nauseous.'

"Shit!" exclaimed Gurl. "Not even a stable ur-space!"

She started running even faster, with me following as best I could. Unless this ur-space was completely whacked-out of alignment, the Solomon Piazza was contiguous with the weird little gothic shrine traffic island at the intersection a block ahead. All we had to do was get there before the whole avenue curled back on itself and disappeared into nothingsville.

Oh yeah, we also had to do it before the dozen witches on the heavy broom I could hear snorting overhead caught up with us. From the sound of it they'd stuffed at least a score of pegasi spirits into a serious lumberjack-territory pine pole to create a big, fast broom that could carry them and all their hardware.

Not that they'd need to actually catch up to us, though it is much harder to hit a running target from even a big broom than you'd think, either with a wand or a firearm.

This didn't stop them from trying. I wondered how they'd managed to get an antique punt gun aboard even a super-broom, as the hundreds of silvered pellets it fired bounced all over the road a few steps behind me and the bang echoed inside my ear-drums and a good proportion of the rest of my head.

"At least it'll take them five minutes to reload," I shouted. "Unless, they've got two, which is highly un—"

The boom of the second punt gun or rebored nineteenth century swivel gun or whatever the hell it was made us both leap rather than run the last five paces. As we landed, I immediately went into the dance, which strangely enough is much more difficult to do as a human than it is to do in dog-shape. Particularly the bit where you wag your tail widdershins in decreasing circles.

At the last moment, Gurl grabbed my hand and we translated, a microsecond ahead of some kind of hex that I saw as a horribly tusked boar of glowing red light racing towards us.

We landed in the middle of the piazza, which as I'd predicted, was full of nether-worlders of all shapes and sorceries. All of them craning their necks to look up at the perpetually dry fountain statue of Simon the Magus, upon whose broad shoulders the candidates for the succession would stand and try the knife, the necklace and the hat.

As I'd also expected, my no-good cousin J'nelle was rapidly taking the steps carved into Magus Simon's outstretched arm, jumping them three at a time. She had a broad-brimmed black hat on her head, a stone knife in her hand, and a necklace of gold and amber around her neck that went very nicely with her Dolce & Gabbana new season dress.

There was also a pack of ridiculously oversized timber wolves patrolling a nice clear circle around the statue, keeping everyone at a suitable distance, and overhead three score and seven traditional Athenian-style owls were doing the same service in the air. For all I knew, there were ninety-nine magical moles beneath the paving stones too, making sure all was hunky-dory underneath.

The wolves spotted us first. In the second before they started baying for blood, specifically mine, I ripped out the gold drawstring from the red velvet bag and flung it over Gurl's head. I managed that, but before I could get the bag on her head, she'd locked my arm behind my back and pushed me into a very uncomfortable position, one with which I had some familiarity from my student days when frequenting a particular pub.

Over on the statue, J'nelle pointed at me and hissed and the crowd went "oh!" as Grimmaur, the leader of the wolves (yeah, well his name was Cedric in the alter-world and he was a seeing-eye dog) growled out, "Get the assassin!"

Wolves leaped, wizards, witches and various beasties and denizens ran in all directions, owls hooted and began to dive, and the big broom with the punt guns translated through overhead and cleaned up the owls before scraping the side of the statue and crash-landing into the bowl of the fountain, where its dozen witches fell off. Through it all J'nelle was screaming something about claiming the throne.

"Put on the hat," I shouted to Gurl. "Put on the damn hat and take the .45! You're it, stupid! Granny wanted you to take over!"

The arm-lock tightened with a vengeance and for a second I thought I was done for. The wolves were mere yards away, J'nelle had drawn a wand from her sleeve. It was all over, I'd made a stupid gamble and I was going to pay for it with my life.

Then I was twisted around and thrown to the ground. Gurl leant over me. The velvet bag was on her head, only it didn't look like a bag anymore. It had grown a tall crown and a stiff brim and turned the color and texture of a very sleek black cat. The cord was around her neck, but it had also transformed into a narrow torc of reddish gold set with amber.

She slid the .45 out of my waistband, her finger around the trigger curling to match her smile. I heard the safety catch… catch on my belt and I shut my eyes. That pistol needed only the lightest trigger pull…

"Hold!" roared Gurl and I opened my eyes just in time to cop a face-full of wolf saliva as Grimmaur's jaws set open an inch away from my face with a very loud click. Gurl stood above me, looking taller and tougher than ever, with the hat and the necklace and a knife the color of gunmetal with a cross-hatched grip.

"Get to your kennels," said Gurl quietly. She looked up and added to the owls, "And you to your roost."

J'nelle squeaked something, possibly a protest, which was a mistake on both counts.

"Take her with you," added Gurl to the wolves and the owls. "Half each, mind."

I shut my eyes again, purely from exhaustion and a sudden failure of the massive amounts of adrenalin that must have been previously pumping through my system. I had no problem with watching cousin

J'nelle get dismembered. The crowd liked it too. I could hardly hear anything over the applause and the shouts of "Bravo!"

A sudden pressure on my chest made me open my eyes again. Gurl had set her boot on my sternum and was pressing quite hard.

"I don't need CPR," I croaked.

"Not yet," said Gurl. "You've got some questions to answer first. Like when did you figure it out, and what did you mean when you said 'cunning old madam'? And how come I'm eligible to be her heir?"

Gurl didn't need the wolves to keep a nice clear space about her, and everyone wisely had their backs to us, but I could see a lot of mostly pointy ears tilted in our direction. They all wanted to know the answers too.

"After the curse lifted, I could think a bit straighter," I said. "Eventually I realized that unlike me, Granny had passed portents and auguries with flying colors. I mean she *lectured* in prophecy and that thing they do with cold spaghetti to see potential futures… she must have always known when she was going to die, and of course she'd never just leave the choice of her successor to that stupid…"

I paused for a moment. Two slitted eyes had appeared in the crown of the hat, two baleful yellow eyes…

"She'd never leave it to chance, I mean," I babbled. "I figured it had to be you because she'd kept you in the office. So you could learn stuff from her, and overhear her talking to herself, and so you'd be there when the time came. Then you got adopted, in the classic way, by drinking her blood. One drop's enough to do the job."

"I don't really want to be queen. I just want to run my club, do some time on the door—"

The "really" was a giveaway. She was already into it. I could tell. Or I thought I could, which meant I probably couldn't. I opened my mouth anyway.

"The nether-city's just like a club really. Let some in, kick some out, take their money, entertain them, serve them expensive drinks . . "

"Technically you're still her assassin," said Gurl, getting back to the primary subject.

"Ah, can I get up now please?" I asked. "So I can grovel properly? And wipe some of this wolf snot off my face?"

Gurl lifted her boot. I staggered to my knees, palmed the old bean that I'd been lying on after it fell out of the hat, and wiped my face with my sleeve.

"I suppose it could be worse," she said thoughtfully. "It beats being a gargoyle. I have to thank you for that, anyway."

"You do?" I asked. I was more than a little bit nervous about what Gurl was going to do with me. The bit about "technically an assassin" hadn't helped.

"But I seem to remember that immediate execution is the normal punishment for regicide."

"I was set up!" I exclaimed. "J'nelle cursed me. I was only the assassination weapon, not the perpetrator."

I didn't mention the small fact that I now had a deep suspicion that Granny wasn't quite as dead as everyone thought—that J'nelle was almost certainly as much a patsy in the whole affair as I was—and that the whole thing wasn't so much a regicide as an abdication, with a little clearing up done for Granny's chosen heir.

"I guess you were just an unwitting pawn," said Gurl.

I bit back a retort. The old cursed me would have said something, but there is value in strategic silence. Not to mention bowing one's head lower and generally trying to be submissive. I even thought about whimpering but decided it wouldn't help.

"Don't plan on me supporting your stupid plant business in the alter-world though," said Gurl.

"Doesn't matter," I sighed. "I'll have to sell the company or shut it down anyway. Presuming you don't execute me, I'll be reporting to the Bright Hill soon enough and they only give us two weeks off a year."

"Yes, I suppose I owe you for the dragon's intervention too," said Gurl thoughtfully. "Under the circumstances, a pardon should be more than enough."

She touched my shoulder with the knife and I felt a chill strike through to the very marrow of my bones, and I have to tell you that is way colder than you ever want to get and it also greatly increases the chances of getting the flu somewhere down the track.

Gurl raised her voice and said, "You are pardoned, Wizard Gardner, and commended for all you have done for Us!"

There was a sprinkling of applause, and just about everyone turned around to watch me creakily rise to my feet, which just goes to show they were all listening like rabid keyhole eavesdroppers anyway.

I bowed and when Gurl offered her hand, air-kissed a point about six inches above the back of it. No point taking too many risks in one day.

"Come and see me when you're on furlough," said Gurl quietly, for my ears alone. "I am curious to see who you are actually, when not under a curse. And I still have a few questions—"

"As you command, ma'am," I said hastily, and backed away. When I'd done the obligatory thirteen steps, I bowed again, did my most courtly pirouette and resisted the temptation to run like the clappers for the nearest assisted exit to the alter-world.

I couldn't help but glance at the bean I had tightly clutched in my hand, noting the discolored patches that with every second were looking eerily like a familiar face. I wanted to plant it in a good self-watering pot and report early to the Hill before Granny grew herself a new body and once again engaged in the business of haranguing her descendents, particularly me.

I just knew the old bat wouldn't die as easily as that....

THE LAST AND ONLY
OR, MR. MOSCOWITZ
BECOMES FRENCH

PETER S. BEAGLE

Once upon a time, there lived in California a Frenchman named George Moscowitz. His name is of no importance—there are old families in France named Wilson and Holmes, and the first president of the Third Republic was named MacMahon—but what was interesting about Mr. Moscowitz was that he had not always been French. Nor was he entirely French at the time we meet him, but he was becoming perceptibly more so every day. His wife, whose name was Miriam, drew his silhouette on a child's blackboard and filled him in from the feet up with tricolor chalk, adding a little more color daily. She was at mid-thigh when we begin our story.

Most of the doctors who examined Mr. Moscowitz agreed that his affliction was due to some sort of bug that he must have picked up in France when he and Mrs. Moscowitz were honeymooning there, fifteen years before. In its dormant stage, the bug had manifested itself only as a kind of pleasant Francophilia: on their return from France Mr. Moscowitz had begun to buy Linguaphone CDs, and to get up at six in the morning to watch a cable television show on beginner's French. He took to collecting French books and magazines, French music and painting and sculpture, French recipes, French folklore, French attitudes, and, inevitably, French people. As a librarian in a large university, he came in contact with a good many French exchange students and visiting professors, and he went far out of his way to make friends with them—Mr. Moscowitz, shy as a badger. The students had a saying among themselves that if you wanted to be French in that town, you had to clear it with Monsieur Moscowitz, who issued licenses and *cartes de séjour*. The joke was not especially unkind, because Mr. Moscowitz often had them to dinner at his home, and in his quiet delight in the very sound of their voices they found themselves curiously less bored with themselves, and with one another. Their companions at dinner were quite likely to be the ignorant Marseillais tailor who got all of Mr. Moscowitz's custom, or the Canuck coach of the soccer team, but there was something so touching in Mr. Moscowitz's assumption that all French-speaking people must be naturally at home together that professors and proletariat generally managed to find each other charming and valuable. And Mr. Moscowitz himself, speaking rarely, but sometimes smiling uncontrollably, like an exhalation of joy—he was a snob in that he preferred the culture and manners of another country to his own, and certainly a fool in that he could find wisdom in every foolishness uttered in French—he was marvelously happy then, and it was impossible for those around him to escape his happiness. Now and then he would address a compliment or a witticism to his wife, who would smile and answer softly, "*Merci*," or "*La-la*," for she knew that at such moments he believed without thinking about it that she too spoke French.

Mrs. Moscowitz herself was, as must be obvious, a patient woman of a tolerant humor, who greatly enjoyed her husband's enjoyment of all things French, and who believed, firmly and serenely, that this curious obsession would fade with time, to be replaced by bridge or chess, or—though she prayed not—golf. "At least he's dressing much better these days," she told her sister Dina, who lived in Scottsdale, Arizona. "Thank God you don't have to wear plaid pants to be French."

Then, after fifteen years, whatever it was that he had contracted in France, if that was what he had done, came fully out of hiding; and here stood Mr. Moscowitz in one doctor's office after another, French from his soles to his ankles, to his shins, to his knees, and still heading north for a second spring. (Mrs. Moscowitz's little drawing is, of course, only a convenient metaphor—if anything, her husband was becoming French from his bones out.) He was treated with drugs as common as candy and as rare as turtle tears by doctors ranging from Johns Hopkins specialists to a New Guinea shaman; he was examined by herbalists and honey-doctors, and by committees of medical men so reputable as to make illness in their presence seem almost criminal; and he was dragged to a crossroads one howling midnight to meet with a half-naked, foamy-chinned old man who claimed to be the son of Merlin's affair with Nimue, and a colonel in the Marine Reserves besides. This fellow's diagnosis was supernatural possession; his prescribed remedy would cost Mr. Moscowitz a black pig (and the pig its liver), and was impractical, but the idea left Mr. Moscowitz thoughtful for a long time.

In bed that night, he said to his wife, "Perhaps it is possession. It's frightening, yes, but it's exciting too, if you want the truth. I feel something growing inside me, taking shape as it crowds me out, and the closer I get to disappearing, the clearer it becomes. And yet, it is me too, if you understand—I wish I could explain to you how it feels—it is like, 'ow you say...."

"Don't say that," Mrs. Moscowitz interrupted with tears in her voice. She had begun to whimper quietly when he spoke of disappearing. "Only TV Frenchmen talk like that."

"*Excuse-moi, ma vieille.* The more it crowds me, the more it makes me feel like *me*. I feel a whole country growing inside me, thousands of years, millions of people, stupid, crazy, shrewd people, and all of them me. I never felt like that before, I never felt that there was anything inside me, even myself. Now I'm pregnant with a whole country, and I'm growing fat with it, and one day—" He began to cry himself then, and the two of them huddled small in their bed, holding hands all night long. He dreamed in French that night, as he had been doing for weeks, but he woke up still speaking it, and he did not regain his English until he had had his first cup of coffee. It took him longer each morning thereafter.

A psychiatrist whom they visited when Mr. Moscowitz's silhouette was French to the waist commented that his theory of possession by himself was a way of sidling up to the truth that Mr. Moscowitz was actually willing his transformation. "The unconscious is ingenious at devising methods of withdrawal," he explained, pulling at his fingertips as though milking a cow, "and national character is certainly no barrier to a mind so determined to get out from under the weight of being an American. It's not as uncommon as you might think, these days."

"*Qu'est-ce qu'il dit?*" whispered Mr. Moscowitz to his wife.

"I have a patient," mused the psychiatrist, "who believes that he is gradually being metamorphosed into a roc, such a giant bird as carried off Sindbad the Sailor to lands unimaginable and riches beyond comprehension. He has asked me to come with him to the very same lands when his change is complete."

"*Qu'est-ce qu'il dit? Qu'est-ce que c'est, roc?*"

Mrs. Moscowitz shushed her husband nervously and said, "Yes, yes, but what about George? Do you think you can cure him?"

"I won't be around," said the psychiatrist. There came a stoop of great wings outside the window, and the Moscowitzes fled.

"Well, there it is," Mrs. Moscowitz said when they were home, "and I must confess I thought as much. You could stop this stupid change yourself if you really wanted to, but you don't want to stop it. You're withdrawing, just the way he said, you're escaping from the responsibility of being plain old George Moscowitz in the plain old United States. You're quitting, and I'm ashamed of you—you're copping out." She hadn't used the phrase since her own college days at Vassar, and it made her feel old and even less in control of this disturbing situation.

"Cop-out, cop-out," said Mr. Moscowitz thoughtfully. "What charm! I love it very much, the American slang. Cop-out, copping out. I cop out, *tu* cop out, they all cop out...."

Then Mrs. Moscowitz burst into tears, and picking up her colored chalks, she scribbled up and down and across the neat silhouette of her husband until the chalk screamed and broke, and the whole blackboard was plastered red, white, and blue; and as she did this, she cried, "I don't care, I don't care if you're escaping or not, or what you change into. I wouldn't care if you turned into a cockroach, if I could be a cockroach too." Her eyes were so blurred with tears that Mr. Moscowitz seemed to be sliding away from her like a cloud. He took her in his arms then, but all the comfort he offered her was in French, and she cried even harder.

It was the only time she ever allowed herself to break down. The next day she set about learning French. It was difficult for her, for she had no natural ear for language, but she enrolled in three schools at once—one for group study, one for private lessons, and the other online—and she worked very hard. She even dug out her husband's abandoned language CDs and listened to them constantly. And during her days and evenings, if she found herself near a mirror, she would peer at the plump, tired face she saw there and say carefully to it, "*Je suis la professeur. Vous êtes l'étudiante. Je suis française. Vous n'êtes pas française.*" These were the first four sentences that the recordings spoke to her every day. It had occurred to her—though she never voiced the idea—that she might be able to will the same change that had befallen her husband on herself. She told herself often, especially after triumphing over her reflection, that she felt more French daily; and when she finally gave up the pretense of being transformed, she said to herself, "It's my fault. I want to change for him, not for myself. It's not enough." She kept up with her French lessons, all the same.

Mr. Moscowitz, on his part, was finding it necessary to take English lessons. His work in the library was growing more harassing every day: he could no longer read the requests filed by the students—let alone the forms and instructions on his own computer screen—and he had to resort to desperate guessing games and mnemonic systems to find anything in the stacks or on the shelves. His condition was obvious to his friends on the library staff, and they covered up for him as best they could, doing most of his work while a graduate student from the French department sat with him in a carrel, teaching him English as elementary as though he had never spoken it. But he did not learn it quickly, and he never learned it well, and his friends could not keep him hidden all the time. Inevitably, the Chancellor of the university interested himself in the matter, and after a series of interviews with Mr. Moscowitz—conducted in French, for the Chancellor was a traveled man who had studied at the Sorbonne—announced regretfully that he saw no way but to let Mr. Moscowitz go. "You understand my position, Georges, my old one," he said, shrugging slightly and twitching his mouth. "It is a damage, of course, well understood, but there will be much severance pay and a pension of the fullest." The presence of a Frenchman always made the Chancellor a little giddy.

"You speak French like a Spanish cow," observed Mr. Moscowitz, who had been expecting this decision and was quite calm. He then pointed out to the Chancellor that he had tenure and to spare, and that he was not about to be gotten rid of so easily. Even in this imbecile country, a teacher had his rights, and it was on the Chancellor's shoulders to find a reason for discharging him. He requested the Chancellor to show him a single university code, past or present, that listed change of nationality as sufficient grounds for terminating a contract; and he added that he was older than the Chancellor and had given him no encouragement to call him *tu*.

"But you're not the same man we hired!" cried the Chancellor in English.

"No?" asked Mr. Moscowitz when the remark had been explained to him. "Then who am I, please?"

The university would have been glad to settle the case out of court, and Mrs. Moscowitz pleaded with her husband to accept their offered terms, which were liberal enough; but he refused, for no reason that she could see but delight at the confusion and embarrassment he was about to cause, and a positive hunger for the tumult of a court battle. The man she had married, she remembered, had always found it hard to show anger even to his worst enemy, for fear of hurting his feelings; but she stopped thinking about it at that point, not wanting to make the Chancellor's case for him. "You are quite right, George," she told him, and then, carefully, "*Tu as raison, mon chou.*" He told her—as nearly as she could understand—that if she ever learned to speak French properly she would sound like a Basque, so she might as well not try. He was very rude to the Marseillais tailor these days.

The ACLU appointed a lawyer for Mr. Moscowitz, and, for all purposes but the practical, he won his case as decisively as Darrow defending Darwin. The lawyer laid great and tearful stress on the calamity (hisses from the gallery, where a sizeable French contingent grew larger every day) that had befallen a simple, ordinary man, leaving him dumb and defenseless in the midst of academic piranhas who would strip him of position, tenure, reputation, even statehood, in one pitiless bite. (This last was in reference to a foolish statement by the university counsel that Mr. Moscowitz would have some difficulty passing a citizenship test now, let alone a librarian's examination.) But his main defense was the same as Mr. Moscowitz's before the Chancellor: there was no precedent for such a situation as his client's, nor was this case likely to set one. If the universities wanted to write it into their common code that any man proved to be changing his nationality should summarily be discharged, then the universities could do that, and very silly they would look, too. ("What would constitute proof?" he wondered aloud, and what degree of change would it be necessary to prove? "Fifty per cent? Thirty-three and one-third? Or just, as the French say, a *soupçon?*") But as matters stood, the university had no more right to fire Mr. Moscowitz for becoming a Frenchman than they would have if he became fat, or gray-haired, or two inches taller. The lawyer ended his plea by bowing deeply to his client and crying, "*Vive* Moscowitz!" And the whole courthouse rang and thundered then as Americans and French, judge and jury, counsels and bailiffs and the whole audience rose and roared, "*Vive* Moscowitz! *Vive* Moscowitz!" The Chancellor thought of the Sorbonne, and wept.

There were newspapermen in the courtroom, and by that last day there were television cameras. Mr. Moscowitz sat at home that night and leaned forward to stare at his face whenever it came on the screen. His wife, thinking he was criticizing his appearance, remarked, "You look nice. A little like Jean Gabin." Mr. Moscowitz grunted. "*Le camera t'aime,*" she said carefully. She answered the phone when it rang, which was often. Many of the callers had television shows of their own. The others wanted Mr. Moscowitz to write books.

Within a week of the trial, Mr. Moscowitz was a national celebrity, which meant that as many people knew his name as knew the name of the actor who played the dashing Gilles de Rais in a new television serial, and not quite as many as recognized the eleven-year-old Racine girl with a forty-inch bust, who sang Christian techno-rap. Mrs. Moscowitz saw him more often on television than she did at home—at seven on a Sunday morning he was invited to discuss post-existential film or France's relations with her former African colonies; at two o'clock he might be awarding a ticket to Paris to the winner of the daily *My Ex Will Hate This* contest; and at eleven PM, on one of the late-night shows, she could watch him speaking the lyrics to the internationally popular French song, *Je M'en Fous De Tout Ça*, while a covey of teenage dancers yipped and jiggled around him. Mrs. Moscowitz would sigh, switch off the set, and sit down at the computer to study her assigned installment of the adventures of the family Vincent, who spoke basic French to one another and were always having breakfast, visiting aunts, or making lists. "Regard Helene," said Mrs. Moscowitz bitterly. "She is in train of falling into the quicksand again. Yes, she falls. Naughty, naughty Helene. She talks too much."

There was a good deal of scientific and political interest taken in Mr. Moscowitz as well. He spent several weekends in Washington, being examined and interviewed, and he met the President, briefly. The President shook his hand, and gave him a souvenir fountain pen and a flag lapel, and said that he regarded Mr. Moscowitz's transformation as the ultimate expression of the American dream, for it surely proved to the world that any American could become whatever he wanted enough to be, even if what he wanted to be was a snail-eating French wimp.

The scientists, whose lingering fear had been that the metamorphosis of Mr. Moscowitz had been somehow accomplished by the Russians or the Iranians, as a practice run before they turned everybody into Russians or Iranians, found nothing in Mr. Moscowitz either to enlighten or alert them. He was a small, suspicious man who spoke often of his rights, and might, as far as they could tell, have been born French. They sent him home at last, to his business manager, to his television commitments, to his endorsements, to his ghostwritten autobiography, and to his wife; and they told the President, "Go figure. Maybe this is the way the world ends, we wouldn't know. And it might not hurt to avoid crêpes for a while."

Mr. Moscowitz's celebrity lasted for almost two months—quite a long time, considering that it was autumn and there were a lot of other public novas flaring and dying on prime time. His high-water mark was certainly reached on the weekend that the officials of at least one cable network were watching one another's eyes to see how they might react to the idea of a George Moscowitz Show. His fortunes began to ebb on Monday morning—public interest is a matter of momentum, and there just wasn't anything Mr. Moscowitz could do for an encore.

"If he were only a *nice* Frenchman, or a *sexy* Frenchmen!" the producers and the publishers and the ghostwriters and the A&R executives and the sponsors sighed separately and in conference. "Someone like Jean Reno or Charles Boyer, or Chevalier, or Jacques Pépin, or even Louis Jourdan—somebody charming, somebody with style, with manners, with maybe a little ho-*ho*, Mimi, you good-for-nothing little Mimi…" But what they had, as far as they could see, was one of those surly frogs in a cloth cap who rioted in front of the American Embassy and trashed the Paris McDonald's. Once, on a talk show, he said, taking great care with his English grammar, "The United States is like a very large dog which has not been—*qu'est-ce que c'est le mot?*—housebro*ken*. It is well enough in its place, but its place is not on the couch. Or in the Mideast, or in Africa, or in a restaurant kitchen." The television station began to get letters. They suggested that Mr. Moscowitz go back where he came from.

So Mr. Moscowitz was whisked out of the public consciousness as deftly as an unpleasant report on what else gives mice cancer or makes eating fish as hazardous as bullfighting. His television bookings were cancelled; he was replaced by reruns, motivational speakers, old John Payne musicals, or one of the less distressing rappers. The contracts for his books and columns and articles remained unsigned, or turned out to conceal escape clauses, elusive and elliptical, but enforceable. Within a week of his last public utterance—"American women smell bad, they smell of fear and vomit and *l'ennui*"—George Moscowitz was no longer a celebrity. He wasn't even a Special Guest.

Nor was he a librarian anymore, in spite of the court's decision. He could not be discharged, but he certainly couldn't be kept on in the library. The obvious solution would have been to find him a position in the French department, but he was no teacher, no translator, no scholar; he was unqualified to teach the language in a junior high school. The Chancellor graciously offered him a departmental scholarship to get a degree in French, but he turned it down as an insult.

"At least, a couple of education courses—" said the Chancellor. "Take them yourself," said Mr. Moscowitz, and he resigned.

"What will we do now, George?" asked his wife. "*Que ferons-nous?*" She was glad to have her husband back from the land of magic, even though he was as much a stranger to her now as he sometimes seemed to be to himself. ("What does a butterfly think of its chrysalis?" she wondered modestly, "Or of milkweed?") His fall from grace seemed to have made him kind again. They spent their days together now, walking, or reading Chateaubriand aloud; often silent, for it was hard for Mrs. Moscowitz to speak truly in French, and her husband could not mutter along in English for long without becoming angry. "Will we go to France?" she asked, knowing his answer.

"Yes," Mr. Moscowitz said. He showed her a letter. "The French government will pay our passage. We are going home." He said it many times, now with joy, now with a certain desperation. "We are going home."

The French of course insisted on making the news of Mr. Moscowitz's departure public in America, and the general American attitude was a curious mix of relief and chagrin. They were glad to have Mr. Moscowitz safely out of the way, but it was "doubtless unpleasant," as a French newspaper suggested, "to see a recognizable human shape insist on emerging from the great melting pot, instead of eagerly dissolving away." Various influences in the United States warned that Mr. Moscowitz was obviously a spy for some international conspiracy, but the President, who had vaguely liked him, said, "Well, good for him, great. Enjoy, baby." The government made up a special loose-leaf passport for Mr. Moscowitz, with room for other changes of nationality, just in case.

Mrs. Moscowitz, who made few demands on her husband, or anyone else, insisted on going to visit her sister Dina in Scottsdale before the move to France. She spent several days being taught to play video games by her nephew and enjoying countless tea parties with her two nieces, and sitting up late with Dina and her sympathetic husband, talking over all the ramifications of her coming exile. "Because that's the way I know I see it," she said, "in my heart. I try to feel excited—I really do try, for George's sake—but inside, inside…" She never wept or broke down at such points, but would pause for a few moments, while her sister fussed with the coffee cups and her brother-in-law looked away. "It's not that I'll miss that many people," she would go on, "or our life—well, George's life—around the university. Or the apartment, or all the things we can't take with us—that doesn't really matter, all that. Maybe if we had children, like you..." and she would fall silent again, but not for long, before she burst out, "But *me*, I'll miss *me!* I don't know who I'll be, living in France, but it'll be someone else, it won't ever be *me* again. And I did...I *did* like me the way I was, and so did George, no matter what he says now." But in time, as they knew she would, she would recover her familiar reliable calmness and decide, "Oh, it will be all right, I'm sure. I'm just being an old stick-in-the-mud. It *will* be an adventure, after all."

The French government sent a specially chartered jet to summon the Moscowitzes; it was very grand treatment, Mrs. Moscowitz thought, but she had hoped they would sail. "On a boat, we would be nowhere for a few days," she said to herself, "and I do need to be nowhere first, just a little while." She took her books and CDs about the Vincent family along with her, and she drew a long breath and held onto Mr. Moscowitz's sleeve when the plane doors opened onto the black and glowing airfield, and they were invited to step down among the roaring people who had been waiting for two days to welcome them. "Here we go," she said softly. "*Allons-y*. We are home."

France greeted them with great pride and great delight, in which there was mixed not the smallest drop of humor. To the overwhelming majority of the French press, to the poets and politicians, and certainly to the mass of the people—who read the papers and the poems, and waited at the airport—it seemed both utterly logical and magnificently just that a man's soul should discover itself to be French. Was it not possible that all the souls in the world might be French, born in exile but beginning to find their way home from the cold countries, one by one? Think of all the tourists, the wonderful middle-aged tourists—where will we put them all? Anywhere, anywhere, it won't matter, for all the world will be France, as it should have been long ago, when our souls began to speak different languages. *Vive* Moscowitz then, *vive* Moscowitz! And see if you can get him to do a spread in Paris-Match, or on your television program, or book him for a few weeks at the Olympia. Got to make your money before Judgment Day.

But the government had not invited Mr. Moscowitz to France to abandon him to free enterprise—he was much too important for that. His television appearances were made on government time; his public speeches were staged and sponsored by the government; and he would never have been allowed, even had he wished, to endorse a soft drink that claimed that it made the imbiber twenty-two per cent more French. He was not for rent. He traveled—or, rather, he was traveled—through the country, from Provence to Brittany, gently guarded, fenced round in a civilized manner; and throngs of people came out to see him. Then he was returned to Paris.

The government officials in charge of Mr. Moscowitz found a beautiful apartment in safe, quiet Passy for him and his wife, and let them understand that the rent would be paid for the rest of their lives. There was a maid and a cook, both paid for, and there was a garden that seemed as big as the Bois de Boulogne to the Moscowitzes, and there was a government chauffeur to take them wherever they wanted to go, whenever. And finally—for the government understood that many men will die without work—there was a job ready for Mr. Moscowitz when he chose to take it up, as the librarian of the Benjamin Franklin library, behind the Odeon. He had hoped for the Bibliothèque nationale, but he was satisfied with the lesser post. "We are home," he said to his wife. "Having one job or another—one thing or another—only makes a difference to those who are not truly at home. *Tu m'comprends?*

"*Oui,*" said Mrs. Moscowitz. They were forever asking each other that, *Do you understand me?* and they both always said *yes.* He spoke often of home and of belonging, she noticed; perhaps he meant to reassure her. For herself, she had come to realize that all the lists and journeys of the family Vincent would never make her a moment more French than she was, which was not at all, regardless. Indeed, the more she studied the language—the government had provided a series of tutors for her—the less she seemed to understand it, and she lived in anxiety that she and Mr. Moscowitz would lose this hold of one another, like children separated in a parade. Yet she was not as unhappy as she had feared, for her old capacity for making the best of things surfaced once again, and actually did make her new life as kind and rewarding as it could possibly have been, not only for her, but for those with whom she came in any sort of contact. She would have been very surprised to learn this last.

But Mr. Moscowitz himself was not happy for long in France. It was certainly no one's fault but his own. The government took the wisest care of him it knew—though it exhibited him, still it always remembered that he was a human being, which is hard for a government—and the people of France sent him silly, lovely gifts and letters of welcome from all across the country. In their neighborhood, the Moscowitzes were the reigning couple without really knowing it. Students gathered under their windows on the spring nights to sing to them, and the students' fathers, the butchers and grocers and druggists and booksellers of Passy, would never let Mrs. Moscowitz pay for anything when she went shopping. They made friends, good, intelligent, government-approved friends—and yet Mr. Moscowitz brooded more and more visibly, until his wife finally asked him, "What is it, George? What's the matter?"

"They are not French," he said. "All these people. They don't know what it *is* to be French."

"Because they live like Americans?" she asked gently. "George—" she had learned to pronounce it *Jhorj*, in the soft French manner—"everyone does that, or everyone will. To be anything but American is very hard these days. I think they do very well."

"They are not French," Mr. Moscowitz repeated. "I am French, but they are not French. I wonder if they ever were." She looked at him in some alarm. It was her first intimation that the process was not complete.

His dissatisfaction with the people who thought they were French grew more apparent every day. Friends, neighbors, fellow employees, and a wide spectrum of official persons passed in turn before his eyes; and he studied each one and plainly discarded them. Once he had been the kind of man who said nothing, rather than lie; but now he said everything he thought, which is not necessarily more honest. He stalked through the streets of Paris, muttering, "You are not French, none of you are—you are imposters! What have you done with my own people, where have they gone?" It was impossible for such a search to go unnoticed for long. Children as well as grown men began to run up to him on the street, begging, "*Monsieur Moscowitz, regardez-moi, je suis vraiment français!*" He would look at them once, speak or say nothing, and stride on. The rejected quite often wept as they looked after him.

There were some Frenchman, of both high and low estate, who became furious with Mr. Moscowitz—who was *he*, a first generation American, French only by extremely dubious mutation, to claim that they, whose ancestors had either laid the foundations of European culture, or died, ignorant, in its defense, were not French? But in the main, a deep sadness shadowed the country. An inquisitor had come among them, an apostle, and they had been found wanting. France mourned herself, and began wondering if she had ever existed at all; for Mr. Moscowitz hunted hungrily through all recorded French history, searching for his lost kindred, and cried at last that from the days of the first paintings in the Dordogne caves, there was no evidence that a single true Frenchman had ever fought a battle, or written a poem, or built a city, or comprehended a law of the universe. "Dear France," he said with a kind of cold sorrow, "for all the Frenchmen who have ever turned your soil, you might have remained virgin and empty all these centuries. As far back in time as I can see, there has never been one, until now."

The President of France, a great man, his own monument in his own time, a man who had never wavered in the certainty that he himself was France, wrote Mr. Moscowitz a letter in which he stated: "We have always been French. We have been Gauls and Goths, Celts and Franks, but we have always been French. We, and no one else, have made France live. What else should we be but French?"

Mr. Moscowitz wrote him a letter in answer, saying, "You have inhabited France, you have occupied it, you have held it in trust if you like, and you have served it varyingly well—but that has not made you French, nor will it, any more than generations of monkeys breeding in a lion's empty cage will become lions. As for what else you may truly be, that you will have to find out for yourselves, as I had to find out."

The President, who was a religious man, thought of Belshazzar's Feast. He called on Mr. Moscowitz at his home in Passy, to the awe of Mrs. Moscowitz, who knew that ambassadors had lived out their terms in Paris without ever meeting the President face to face. The President said, "M. Moscowitz, you are denying us the right to believe in ourselves as a continuity, as part of the process of history. No nation can exist without that belief."

"*Monsieur le Président, je suis désolée,*" answered Mr. Moscowitz. He had grown blue-gray and thin, bones hinting more and more under the once-genial flesh.

"We have done you honor," mused the President, "though I admit before you say it that we believed we were honoring ourselves. But you turn us into ghosts, *Monsieur* Moscowitz, homeless figments, and our grip on the earth is too precarious at the best of times for me to allow you to do this. You must be silent, or I will make you so. I do not want to, but I will."

Mr. Moscowitz smiled, almost wistfully, and the President grew afraid. He had a sudden vision of Mr. Moscowitz banishing him and every other soul in France with a single word, a single gesture; and in that moment's vision it seemed to him that they all went away like clouds, leaving Mr. Moscowitz to dance by himself in cobwebbed Paris on Bastille Day. The President shivered and cried out, "What is it that you want of us? What should we be? What is it, to be French, what does the stupid word mean?"

Mr. Moscowitz answered him. "I do not know, any more than you do. But I do not need to ask." His eyes were full of tears and his nose was running, "The French are inside me," he said, "singing and stamping to be let out, all of them, the wonderful children that I will never see. I am like Moses, who led his people to the Promised Land, but never set his own foot down there. All fathers are a little like Moses."

The next day, Mr. Moscowitz put on his good clothes and asked his wife to pack him a lunch. "With an apple, please," he said, "and the good Camembert, and a whole onion. Two apples." His new hat, cocked at a youthful angle, scraped coldly beside her eye when he kissed her. She did not hold him a moment longer than she ever had when he kissed her goodbye. Then Mr. Moscowitz walked away from her, and into legend.

No one ever saw him again. There were stories about him, as there still are; rumors out of Concarneau, and Sète, and Lille, from misty cities and yellow villages. Most of the tales concerned strange, magic infants, as marvelous in the families that bore them as merchildren in herring nets. The President sent out his messengers, but quite often there were no such children at all, and when there were they were the usual cases of cross-eyes and extra fingers, webbed feet and cauls. The President was relieved, and said so frankly to Mrs. Moscowitz. "With all respectful sympathy, Madame," he told her, "the happiest place for your husband now is a fairy story. It is warm inside a myth, and safe, quite safe, and the company is of the best. I envy him, for I will never know such companions. I will get politicians and generals."

"And I will get his pension and his belongings," Mrs. Moscowitz said to herself. "And I will know solitude."

The President went on: "He was mad, of course, your husband, but what a mission he set himself! It was worthy of one of Charlemagne's paladins, or of your—" he fumbled through his limited stock of non-partisan American heroes—"your Johnny Appleseed. Yes."

The President died in the country, an old man, and Mrs. Moscowitz in time died alone in Passy. She never returned to America, even to visit, partly out of loyalty to Mr. Moscowitz's dream, and partly because if there is one thing besides cheese that the French do better than any other people, it is the careful and assiduous tending of a great man's widow. She wanted for nothing to the end of her days, except her husband—and, in a very real sense, France was all she had left of him.

That was a long time ago, but the legends go on quietly, not only of the seafoam children who will create France, but of Mr. Moscowitz as well. In Paris and the provinces, anyone who listens long enough can hear stories of the American who became French. He wanders through the warm nights and the cold, under stars and streetlamps, walking with the bright purpose of a child who has slipped out of his parents' sight and is now free to do as he pleases. In the country, they say that he is on his way to see how his children are growing up, and perhaps there are mothers who lull their own children with that story, or warn them with it when they behave badly. But Parisians like to dress things up, and as they tell it, Mr. Moscowitz is never alone. Cyrano is with him, and St. Joan, Roland, D'Artagnan, and Villon—and there are others. The light of them brightens the road for Mr. Moscowitz to see his way.

But even in Paris there are people, especially women, who say that Mr. Moscowitz's only companion on his journey is Mrs. Moscowitz herself, holding his arm or running to catch up. And she deserves to be there, they will tell you, for she would have been glad of any child at all; and if he was the one who dreamed and loved France so much, still and all, she suffered.

THE LOST BOY: A REPORTER AT LARGE

MAUREEN F. MCHUGH

On June 13, 2014, Simon Weiss came into the mechanic's shop where he worked in Brookneal, Virginia. He was a quiet kid in Carharts overalls. He had started working at Brookneal Goodyear two years before at 16. He was enrolled at the vocational school and living with a foster family. His auto mechanics teacher had found him the job after school. In the aftermath of the Baltimore attack, Brookneal had taken in more than its share of Baltimore homeless. Jim Dwyer, who owns Brookneal Goodyear, said that some of those people were problems. "A lot of those people were not used to working for a living," Dwyer says. "They expected to go on in Brookneal pretty much the way they had in Baltimore. I guess a lot of them had drug problems and such." But not Simon. He never missed work. He was always on time. Dwyer thought that work was the place Simon felt most comfortable. On Saturdays while he was still in high school, Simon arrived early in his lovingly maintained '08 Honda Civic. He made coffee and read the funnies while waiting for everyone else to arrive. He looked up to Dwyer and had asked Dwyer advice about a girl. The girl hadn't lasted. His foster parents were, in Dwyer's words, "decent people" but they had two other foster kids, one of whom had leukemia from the effects of the dirty bomb.

On this hot summer Friday morning, two weeks after Simon's graduation from high school, a couple came in at about 9:30 and asked to see Simon. There was something about them that made Dwyer watch closely when Simon came in from the back where he was doing an oil change. "When he came through that door," Dwyer said, "his expression never changed. He thought it was something about a car, someone complaining or asking a question or something, you could tell. He had a kind of polite expression on his face. But there wasn't a flash of recognition or anything. There was nothing."

When the woman saw him she started sobbing. She called him William. He looked at Dwyer and then at her and said okay. She was his mother and she had been looking for him for five years.

"Why didn't you try to find us?" she asked.

"I don't remember," Simon said. And then he walked back into the garage, to the Lexus he was doing the oil change on. Dwyer followed him back. Simon did not respond when Dwyer spoke to him. He stood there for a moment and then he started to cry. "I'm crazy," he told Dwyer.

When I met Simon, I asked him what he wanted me to call him. He shrugged and said most people called him Simon.

"Is that your name, now?" I asked.

"I guess," he said.

He was tired of talking about himself, he said. Tired of talking about his family and Baltimore. He was a quiet, passive kid, dressed in an oversized shirt. He answered my questions but didn't volunteer anything. We were meeting in a park, sitting at a picnic table. His car, a gold Civic, was parked not far away. It was impeccably maintained and had a handsome set of after market wheels and some "mods." I admired it and said that I had a Civic in the '90s.

Simon murmured something polite.

I said it was the first car I ever bought with my own money. I lived in New York, I explained, and didn't own a car until I was thirty. But I had moved and I loved that car.

He looked at me, nodding. I said I liked his wheels, which was true. They were in keeping with the car, not too flashy, I said.

In minutes I had learned the history of the car. Hands waving, he talked about how he saved for the wheels. We talked about the joys of spending a couple of hours really cleaning a car and the relative merits of different ways to clean interiors. I had assumed that the diffident young man was Simon. That this was the affect of someone with a problem. Instead, what I had found was a shy but normal boy who was not comfortable talking to a journalist. I am accustomed to people being wary of being interviewed, but I had forgotten that with Simon.

I had done research on memory loss like Simon's. It's called Dissociative Fugue. Like most psychological diagnoses, it probably says as much about our culture as it does about Simon. I had expected someone in a mental fog and had projected that onto him.

Amnesia is a relatively common phenomenon, but mostly it's transient. Anyone who has ever been in a car wreck and can't remember the moment of the accident has experienced amnesia. But contrary to its popularity in movies and television, it is rare for a person to forget who they are.

Dissociate fugue is a condition where a person leaves home for hours, sometimes months. They have no memory of who they are and sometimes adopt another identity.

Two months after the Reverend Ansel Bourne disappeared from his home in Providence in January of 1887, his nephew got a telegram telling him that a man in Norristown, Pennsylvania, was acting strangely and claiming to be Ansel Bourne. Six weeks before, a man calling himself A. Brown had opened a fruit and candy store. He was normal, rather quiet. He cooked his meals in the back of his shop. One day Ansel Bourne "woke up" and found himself in a strange town. He had no memory of A. Brown and no idea where he was.

William James hypnotized Ansel Bourne and was able to call forth "A. Brown." A. Brown had never heard of Ansel Bourne. He complained that he felt "hedged in at both ends" because he could remember nothing before opening his shop and nothing from the time Ansel Bourne had woken up. Why had he come to Norristown? He said "there was trouble back there" and "he wanted rest."

Ansel Bourne's case perfectly fit the psychoanalytic category of hysteria, a diagnosis that was prevalent at the turn of the twentieth century but which has largely disappeared. He was a very intellectual man with high standards for behavior, who had dissociated himself from a life that exhausted him and picked up a different life. Bourne, it was said, had a strong aversion to trade. The personality of Brown was a shrunken version of Bourne.

Today we can surmise that starting a store from scratch, traveling to Philadelphia to establish suppliers, joining a new community and learning a new town may not be "simpler" than the intellectual life of a well-off, comfortable reverend. Like my assumptions about Simon, William James' analysis of Ansel Bourne includes unexamined assumptions about class and personality.

Simon took me for a ride in his Civic (which was far better maintained than mine ever was). He was a good driver. He was interested in autocross and was saving money to take a class. I'm no judge of drivers, but I would say he had a natural feel for driving. While we were driving around the park, I asked him if he felt as if William was a different person.

"No," he said. "I'm William, too."

"Does it make you feel odd to be called William?" I asked.

He nodded, concentrating as he took a turn. "If people are calling me William, then Brookneal feels, you know, kind of not real. But if people are calling me Simon, then I can not worry about that."

"Do you ever think about Pikesville?" I asked.

"I don't like to," he said. And then the conversation turned back to cars.

Dissociate fugue is most common after some sort of trauma. It is most likely to occur after combat or natural disaster. It is assumed that the events in Baltimore triggered William/Simon's fugue. It is just not known exactly what happened to him. Or why, unlike most people, after a few hours or a few days, or at most, a few weeks, he didn't tell someone his real name or seek his family out.

Luz Anitas Weil, William's mother, was at work when two dirty bombs exploded in Baltimore. A divorced mother of three, she lived in Pikesville, a suburb north and west of Baltimore. The Weils were not the typical Pikesville family. Hispanics make up about 1% of the student population. They're outnumbered by whites, blacks and Asians. Luz had hung on in Pikesville after her divorce because she thought that her kids would get a better education there. More important, she thought they would grow up thinking middle class. Luz grew up in Belton, Texas. Her father runs a landscaping company. She met Nick Weil when he was stationed at Fort Hood. They were engaged in six weeks, married in nine months. Luz says, "We partied pretty hard. I was a wild child. We drank too much. We had big fights. I gave as good as I got." After two and a half more years, Nick Weil was discharged and they returned to Maryland. Soon after, Luz got pregnant and had William. She shrugs. "After William was born, I stopped partying. I stopped drinking. Nick didn't. That's when I realized his hitting me, that wasn't us fighting, that was abuse." They tried going to counseling. A second boy, Robert, was born two years after William. After that, they were separated for two years, got back together instead of divorcing, and seven years after William, Inez was born. But by then Luz says she knew it was over and they were divorced soon after.

She got a job working in the kitchen at the Woodholme Country Club. Fancy dinners for fancy people. It was the first place in Maryland where she was around people speaking Spanish. Like a lot of restaurants and kitchens, most of the help was from Central America. But they were men and they didn't have much patience with a Texas born Latina. "Everyday I had to prove myself again," Luz said. Which she did, moving up until she was catering. "You know, $30,000 weddings, where everything has to be just right." She liked the work, except for the hours, which, she felt, kept her away from her kids too much. When someone came into the kitchen that Friday afternoon and said, "There's been a bomb," she says she didn't understand. "I thought they meant that there has been a bomb at Woodholme. The first thing I thought was that I didn't hear anything, you know? I thought it couldn't be that big a deal." Normally, William, then 13, would have been home with his brother and sister, Robert, 11, and Inez, 6. William was the oldest and had just that year turned old enough to baby-sit. Child care was expensive and having a child old enough to watch the other two was making a huge difference. But William was at the Maryland Science Museum in the Imax Theatre with his seventh grade class. They were watching *Andean Condors, Lords of the High Reaches,* when the first bomb exploded across the harbor in Patterson Park. The wind from the northwest pushed the plume south and east across Dundalk, away from Harborplace and the museums.

William's classmates say he was there at the Imax, but no one knows what happened next. William says he doesn't remember. For the famous fifty-one minutes when no one knew the bomb was a dirty bomb and that radioactive materials were being dispersed in the plume, William's class continued to enjoy the museum. Several boys got in trouble for getting each other wet with an exhibit and then a drinking fountain. The first indication that there was any trouble was when the museum announced that they would be closing. It was 2:35. Cell phones started ringing from parents checking on their children. At 2:42, the second bomb exploded near the Baltimore/Washington International Airport. By the time the buses were rolling for Pikesville, roads were already congested.

William wasn't on his bus.

No one knows what happened or how he got separated. Teachers did counts and called attendance but it was pretty chaotic. Kids were on cell phones and not paying attention. Children were crying. Teachers were trying to check on their own families. The cell phone system was completely overloaded and people couldn't get anything beyond the "circuits are busy" message. Luz was trying to call William and getting no answer.

Luz was at the school with Robert and Inez in the car when the buses got to Pikesville Middle School. The car was packed with clothes, photo albums, and the cat, Splinter. Luz says she waited with growing dread as the busses emptied and left, one by one. When William didn't get off with his classmates, she told herself he was on another bus. But eventually, all the busses were emptied. She went and found the assistant principal and told him that William hadn't gotten off. The assistant principal assumed that she had just missed him in the crowd and they searched inside the school.

But he had children and he was desperate to get home and maybe get them out of the city. Luz tried to drive downtown and was turned back by police. "I told them that I had to find my boy," she says, and the tears well up. "They told me that I couldn't go any farther, that the city was contaminated. They said people were helping anyone left behind." She tried to insist, but a policeman finally said to her that she had more than one child to think about and did she want to expose the other two.

She turned the car around and drove north, joining the slow crawl of vehicles out of Baltimore. Her plan was to find a safe place for the other two kids and then turn back. She ran out of gas in Dillsburg, Pennsylvania. A passing motorist stopped, called police for advice, and she and the two children were taken to a school gymnasium that had been turned into a shelter. There, a volunteer (a member of the VFW) passed a Geiger counter over her and the two children, gave them sheets and blankets and directed them towards cots. It was two more days before she could find someone to give her a ride to a gas station and then back to her car. She drove back to Baltimore but was again turned away, this time with instructions to contact the Red Cross. She did contact the Red Cross, but they had no mention of William. For the next week she made the hour and a half trip to Baltimore every day, only to be turned away.

Finally, there was simply no more money for gas.

There is something compelling about the idea of someone who has lost their memory. It taps into an almost universal desire to wipe the slate clean, to start over. In fiction and in film, it is often a chance for a person to redeem themselves.

THE LOST BOY: A REPORTER AT LARGE • 57

Doug Bruce walked into a Coney Island police station on July 3, 2003, and said that he didn't know who he was or where he lived. He had woken up on the subway without wallet or identification. He could speak, he had skills—since he knew how to swim before he lost his memory, he still knew how. But he could not remember ever having seen the ocean. He couldn't remember family or friends. Police found a phone number in a knapsack that Bruce was wearing and a friend came and picked him up. He was a stockbroker with a loft, cockatoos and a dog. He became a *cause celebre*, in no small part because he was so charmed by the world. Everything was new. It was his first rain, his first snow, his first exposure to the Rolling Stones, his first shop window. Friends said that before he lost his memory, he was somewhat arrogant, and that afterwards he was much more…delightful.

He has never had MRIs, which would go a long way toward verifying whether or not he has amnesia (recall of memories cause certain kinds of visible brain activity), and there is considerable doubt as to whether or not he is lying. Complete retrograde amnesia, the kind of amnesia Doug Bruce claims to have, is extraordinarily rare. It rarely persists for more than a few months at most. In 2005 Bruce was the subject of a documentary called *Unknown White Male*. After it was released he stopped giving interviews.

A boy with no identification but who said his name was Simon Weiss was found on the streets of downtown Baltimore five days after the bombs exploded. He was hungry and mildly dehydrated, but he had obviously eaten and drank in the five days. He was brought to a Red Cross relief center where his name was entered in a data bank for missing persons. When he was asked where his family was, he said he didn't know. He was asked his mother's name and said he didn't know. Area hospitals were still overwhelmed with people who had been, or thought they had been exposed to radioactive waste from the bombs. His file was marked for follow-up with a psychologist and he was transported to the refugee center outside Richmond, Virginia.

A number of refugees were moved to the Virginia National Guard station at Fort Pickett and put in barracks-style housing. The boy who called himself Simon was there for five months.

"Yeah, I remember it," he said. "It wasn't so bad. Boring. I watched a lot of television. I had never seen *Lost* so I watched the whole thing from beginning to end in reruns. They were showing two episodes a day from 9:00 to 11:00. I remember that. And then one night I saw *The Simpsons* where they did the last episode about *Lost* where they all get rescued and they mixed *Gilligan's Island* in with it and Homer Simpson was the old guy, the Skipper." His face crinkled with laughter. He was animated. He was present in the memory. Asked about what he remembered from before Fort Pickett, he described the Red Cross worker who asked him questions, a somewhat scary lady with gray hair, he said. Asked for before that and his face changed, went oddly slack.

"Do you remember going to school in Pikesville?"

"Yeah," he said. Pressed for what he remembers, he said, "The monkey bars." He shrugged. Looked away.

Eventually, when no one came forward to claim him, Simon Weiss was placed in the foster care system and ended up with a family in Brookneal. (The family did not want to be identified in this article.)

Jim Dwyer, the mechanic that the boy eventually came to work for, believes that there is a reason that he doesn't remember. "I don't know exactly what happened," Dwyer says, "but something obviously wasn't right with the family." He won't be pinned down, but the implication is he suspects abuse or at least neglect. He believes that the boy separated mentally and emotionally.

Luz, Robert (now 16) and Inez (now 11) deny that there was abuse. "We were never abused," Robert says. "I don't know who said that, but it's not true."

Robert is a soft-spoken boy who remembers William as "a great kid. A great older brother." He remembers that William was the one that their mother left in charge sometimes, but until that last year, he says, they always had a babysitter. Inez has memories but they are more vague. What she remembers better is the home after Baltimore. "We were always hearing about William," she says. "About where he might be. Mom was always calling someone because of something on the internet or on television."

No one but Luz and the children believed that William was alive. There are about a hundred people who have never been accounted for and it was assumed that William had been killed, either during the bombing, or had died in the day after. Luz moved them back to Pikesville as soon as they were able in case William was looking for them. In the year before the Woodholme Country Club took her back, she worked a series of jobs. The kids remember going to a school that was mostly empty, so few people came back. There is no doubt that William's disappearance affected the family both financially and emotionally. Robert had nightmares, and Inez wet the bed. Both were afraid that things were contaminated. Inez got food poisoning from a hot dog and refused to eat for days. Even now she is in therapy once a week because she is afraid to eat.

Luz was haunted by the fear that William had been exposed to radiation and was sick. The amount of radiation in the bombs was small, and it dispersed in plumes that trailed south and east, no where near Pikesville. She obsessively tracked down as much information as she could about the dispersion of the contaminants. She knew that William's school trip should not have exposed him (and it didn't) but she wondered if he had left the museum for some reason. She couldn't understand, if he wasn't sick, why he hadn't shown up on a list of displaced persons, somewhere.

But she couldn't give up. Finally, a relief worker found a list of children who had been placed in foster homes and gave Luz the number of the social worker who had Simon's case. The social worker wasn't sure that Simon and William were the same person, but she gave Luz the phone number of the foster parents. That was on Friday. I asked Luz if she called right away.

"I couldn't," she admits. "I started thinking, why didn't he call us? What's wrong? I thought that it couldn't be him. I thought a thousand things. I thought he was angry because I hadn't come and gotten him." The next morning she put the kids in the car and they drove to Brookneal where she rang the doorbell of the foster parents. They sent her to Simon's job.

"I did it all wrong," she says. "I should have called him. I didn't know about the memory thing. I thought maybe something had happened to him, that he had been hurt or abused or…I didn't know."

But she had to make the trip. Had to see him. She didn't know what she would do if it was William and he didn't want to see them. "When we were in Pennsylvania and I kept driving back, trying to get into Baltimore to look for him, every time I got to a barricade and they turned me around, I felt as if William thought I was abandoning him. I wasn't going to abandon him. I promised him every night, lying in bed, I would not give up. I would find him." She looks fierce. "And I did."

Finally in therapy, Simon/William was unable to talk much about either his life in Brookneal or his life in Pikesville. In the presence of his family, he became almost mute. It was too much. Something triggered the creation of Simon, but Stein Testchloff, an authority on Dissociative Disorder at Cornell University Medical, says it didn't have to be either abuse or some terrible event in Baltimore—or at least, nothing more terrible than getting separated from his class. It appears that some people are predisposed to dissociation. "When someone goes missing for weeks," he explains, "it usually turns out that they have experienced fugue states before, usually for only a couple of hours." Luz says that as far as she knows, William never forgot who he was and left home, but as Testchloff points out, William was young, and may not have had a fugue experience before. But if he did have a predilection for fugue, then the fear and chaos of his experience in Baltimore could certainly have brought it on.

Usually the treatment for someone with dissociative fugue is to bring them out of the fugue state, but William Weil/Simon Weiss doesn't appear to be in a fugue. Testchloff says that can be deceiving. "We think of this as a dramatic thing, a kind of on/off switch. He was William, now he is Simon. But the brain can be much more fuzzy. After five years of living as Simon Weiss, I think it is going to be very difficult for him to bring those two histories together."

Testchloff feels that what has happened to William is close to Dissociative Identity Disorder (DID), which used to be called Multiple Personality. He is reluctant to make that statement because there is so much misinformation about DID. "Everybody thinks Sybil," he says. But there is a lot of doubt about Sybil, and again, everyone assumes it is like the movies. That the separate personalities don't leak over into each other. When in many cases, some personalities know all about other personalities, and there can be a kind of fluidity where personalities merge and break apart. Again, popular literature and movies have given an impression that is perhaps less complicated than reality. Testchloff has not seen William, and has only reviewed his chart (with the permission of William, his therapist, and his family). He says it seems that Simon now has memories of growing up in Pikesville, but there is some sense in which he has assigned all that to William and holds it at arm's length.

When asked what he wants, Simon says he wants to keep working for Jim Dwyer. Does he want to continue to see his family?

He does, although he expresses no enthusiasm.

What does he think of his family?

He looks shy. "They're nice," he says, almost too soft to hear. "I like them okay." Then after a moment: "I always wished I would have a family."

(Shortly after this piece was written, Simon disappeared for seventy-two hours. He called Jim Dwyer from Norfolk, Virginia, saying he didn't know how he got there. Dwyer drove to Norfolk and picked him up. Luz and Robert and Inez are still living in Pikesville, but they see William almost every weekend. He has plans to spend Thanksgiving with them.)

THE DROWNED LIFE

JEFFREY FORD

One

It came trickling in over the transom at first, but Hatch's bailing technique had grown rusty. The skies were dark with daily news of a pointless war and genocide in Africa, poverty, AIDS, desperate millions in migration. The hot air of the commander in chief met the stone-cold bullshit of Congress and spawned water spouts, towering gyres of deadly ineptitude. A steady rain of increasing gas prices, grocery prices, medical costs, drove down hard like a fall of needles. At times the mist was so thick it baffled the mind. Somewhere in a back room, Liberty, Goddess of the Sea, was tied up and blind-folded—wires leading out from under her toga and hooked to a car battery. You could smell her burning, an acid stink that rode the fierce winds, turning the surface of the water brown.

Closer by, three sharks circled in the swells, their fins visible above chocolate waves. Each one of those slippery machines of Eden stood for a catastrophe in the secret symbolic nature of this story. One was *Financial Ruin*, I can tell you that—a stainless steel beauty whose sharp maw made Hatch's knees literally tremble like in a cartoon. In between the bouts of bailing, he walked a tightrope. At one end of his balancing pole was the weight of the bills, a mortgage like a Hydra, whose head grew back each month, for a house too tall and too shallow, taxes out the ass, failing appliances, car payments. At the other end was his job at an HMO, denying payment to people with legitimate claims. Each conversation with each claimant was harrowing for him, but he was in no position to quit. What else would he do? Each poor sop denied howled with indignation and unallied pain at the injustice of it all. Hatch's practiced façade, his dry "Sorry," hid indigestion, headaches, sweat, and his constant, subconscious reiteration of Darwin's law of survival as if it were some golden rule.

Beyond that, the dog had a chronic ear infection, his younger son, Ned, had recently been picked up by the police for smoking pot, and the older one, Will, who had a severe case of athlete's foot, rear ended a car on route 70. "Just a tap. Not a scratch," he'd claimed, and then the woman called with her dizzying estimate. Hatch's wife, Rose, who worked twelve hours a day, treating the people at a hospital whose claims he would eventually turn down, demanded a vacation, with tears in her eyes. "Just a week, somewhere warm," she said. He shook his head and laughed as if she were kidding. It was rough seas between his ears and rougher still in his heart. Each time he laughed, it was in lieu of puking.

Storm Warning was a phrase that made surprise visits to his consciousness while he sat in front of a blank computer screen at work, or hid in the garage at home late at night smoking one of the Captain Blacks he'd supposedly quit, or stared listlessly at *Celebrity Fit Club* on the television. It became increasingly difficult for him to remember births, first steps, intimate hours with Rose, family jokes, vacations in packed cars, holidays with extended family. One day Hatch did less bailing. "Fuck that bailing," he thought. The next day he did even less.

As if he'd just awakened to it, he was suddenly standing in water up to his shins and the rain was beating down on a strong southwester. The boat was bobbing like the bottom lip of a crone on Thorozine as he struggled to keep his footing. In his hands was a small plastic garbage can, the same one he'd used to bail his clam boat when at eighteen he worked the Great South Bay. The problem was Hatch wasn't eighteen anymore, and though now he was spurred to bail again with everything he had, he didn't have much. His heart hadn't worked so hard since his twenty-fifth anniversary when Rose made him climb a mountain in Montana. Even though the view at the top was gorgeous—a basin lake and a breeze out of heaven—his t-shirt jumped with each beat. The boat was going down. He chucked the garbage can out into the sea and *Financial Ruin* and its partners tore into it. Reaching for his shirt pocket, he took out his smokes and lit one.

The cold brown water was just creeping up around Hatch's balls as he took his first puff. He noticed the dark silhouette of Captree Bridge in the distance. "Back on the bay," he said, amazed to be sinking into the waters of his youth, and then, like a struck wooden match, the entire story of his life flared and died behind his eyes.

Going under was easy. No struggle, but a change in temperature. Just beneath the dark surface, the water got wonderfully clear. All the stale air came out of him at once—a satisfying burp followed by a large translucent globe that stretched his jaw with its birth. He reached for its spinning brightness but sank too fast to grab it. His feet were still lightly touching the deck as the boat fell slowly beneath him. He looked up and saw the sharks still chewing plastic. "This is it," thought Hatch, "not with a bang but a bubble." He herded all of his regrets into the basement of his brain, an indoor oak forest with intermittent dim light bulbs and dirt floor. The trees were columns that held the ceiling and amid and among them skittered pale, disfigured doppelgängers of his friends and family. As he stood at the top of the steps and shut the door on them, he felt a subtle tearing in his solar plexus. The boat touched down on the sandy bottom and his sneakers came to rest on the deck. Without thinking, he gave a little jump and sailed in a lazy arc ten feet away, landing, with a puff of sand, next to a toppled marble column.

His every step was a graceful bound, and he floated. Once on the slow descent of his arc, he put his arms out at his sides and lifted his feet behind him so as to fly. Hatch found that if he flapped his arms, he could glide along a couple of feet above the bottom, and he did, passing over coral pipes and red seaweed rippling like human hair in a breeze. There were creatures scuttling over rocks and through the sand—long antennae and armored plating, tiny eyes on sharp stalks, and claws continuously practicing on nothing. As his shoes touched the sand again, a school of striped fish swept past his right shoulder, their blue glowing like neon, and he followed their flight.

He came upon the rest of the sunken temple, its columns pitted and cracked, broken like the tusks of dead elephants. Green vines netted the destruction—two wide marble steps there, here a piece of roof, a tilted mosaic floor depicting the Goddess of the Sea suffering a rash of missing tiles, a headless marble statue of a man holding his penis.

Two

Hatch floated down the long empty avenues of Drowned Town, a shabby, but quiet city in a lime green sea. Every so often, he'd pass one of the citizens, bloated and blue, in various stages of decomposition, and say, "Hi." Two gentlemen in suits swept by but didn't return his greeting. A drowned mother and child, bugling eyes dissolving in trails of tiny bubbles, dressed in little more than rags, didn't acknowledge him. One old woman stopped, though, and said, "Hello."

"I'm new here," he told her.

"The less you think about it the better," she said, and drifted on her way.

Hatch tried to remember where he was going. He was sure there was a reason that he was in town, but it eluded him. "I'll call, Rose," he thought. "She always knows what I'm supposed to be doing." He started looking up and down the streets for a pay phone. After three blocks without luck, he saw a man heading toward him. The fellow wore a business suit and an overcoat torn to shreds, a black hat with a bullet hole in it, a closed umbrella hooked on a skeletal wrist. Hatch waited for the man to draw near, but as the fellow stepped into the street to cross to the next block, a swift gleaming vision flew from behind a building and with a sudden clang of steel teeth meeting took him in its jaws. *Financial Ruin* was hungry and loose in Drowned Town. Hatch cowered backward, breast stroking to a nearby dumpster to hide, but the shark was already gone with its catch.

On the next block up, he found a bar that was open. He didn't see a name on it, but there were people inside, the door was ajar, and there was the muffled sound of music. The place was cramped and narrowed the further back you went, ending in a corner. Wood paneling, mirror behind the bottles, spinning seats, low lighting, and three dead beats—two on one side of the bar and one on the other.

"Got a pay phone?" asked Hatch.

All three men looked at him. The two customers smiled at each other. The bartender with a red bow tie, wiped his rotted nose on a handkerchief, and then slowly lifted an arm to point. "Go down to the grocery store. They got a pay phone at the Deli counter."

Hatch had missed it when the old lady spoke to him, but he realized now that he heard the bartender's voice in his head, not with his ears. The old man moved his mouth, but all that came out were vague farts of words flattened by water pressure. He sat down on one of the bar stools.

"Give me something dry," he said to the bartender. He knew he had to compose himself, get his thoughts together.

The bartender shook his head, scratched a spot of coral growth on his scalp, and opened his mouth to let a minnow out. "I could make you a Jenny Diver...pink or blue?"

"No, Sal, make him one of those things with the dirt bomb in it... they're the driest," said the closer customer. The short man turned his flat face and stretched a grin like a soggy old doll with swirling hair. Behind the clear lenses of his eyes, shadows moved, something swimming through his head.

"You mean a Dry Reach. That's one dusty drink," said the other customer, a very pale, skeletal old man in a brimmed hat and dark glasses. "Remember the day I got stupid on those? Your asshole'll make hell seem like a backyard barbecue if you drink too many of them, my friend."

"I'll try one," said Hatch.

"Your wish is my command," said the bartender, but he moved none too swiftly. Still, Hatch was content to sit and think for a minute. He thought that maybe the drink would help him remember. For all of its smallness, the place had a nice relaxing current flowing through it. He folded his arms on the bar and rested his head down for a moment. It finally came to him that the music he'd heard since entering was Frank Sinatra. "'The Way You Look Tonight,'" he whispered, naming the current song. He pictured Rose, naked, in bed back in their first apartment, and with that realization, the music went off.

Hatch looked up and saw that the bartender had turned on the television. The two customers, heads tilted back, stared into the glow. On the screen there was a news show without sound but the caption announced *News From The War*. A small seahorse swam behind the glass of the screen but in front of the black and white imagery. The story was about a ward in a makeshift field hospital where army doctors treated the wounded children of the area. Cute little faces stared up from pillows, tiny arms with casts listlessly waved, but as the report obviously went on, the wounds got more serious. There were children with missing limbs, and then open wounds, great gashes in the head, the chest, and missing eyes, and then a gaping hole with intestines spilling out, the little legs trembling and the chest heaving wildly.

"There's only one term for this war," said the old man with the sunglasses. "Clusterfuck. Cluster as in cluster and fuck as in fuck. No more need be said."

The short man turned to Hatch and, still grinning, said, "There was a woman in here yesterday, saying that we're all responsible."

"We are," said the bartender. "Drink up." He set Hatch's drink on the bar. "One Dry Reach," he said. It came in a big martini glass—clear liquid with a brown lump at the bottom.

Hatch reached for his wallet, but the bartender waved for him not to bother. "You must be new," he said.

Hatch nodded.

"Nobody messes with money down here. This is Drowned Town... think about it. Drink up, and I'll make you three more."

"Could you put Sinatra back on," Hatch asked sheepishly. "This news is bumming me out."

"As you wish," said the bartender. He pressed a red button under the bar. Instantly, the television went off, and the two men turned back to their drinks. Sinatra sang, "Let's take it nice and easy," and Hatch thought, "Free booze." He sipped his drink and could definitely distinguish its tang from the briny seawater. Whether he liked the taste or not, he'd decide later, but for now he drank it as quickly as he could.

The customer further from Hatch stepped around his friend and approached. "You're in for a real treat, man," he said. "You see that little island in the stream there." He pointed at the brown lump in the glass.

Hatch nodded.

"A bit of terra firma, a little taste of the world you left behind upstairs. Remember throwing dirt bombs when you were a kid? Like the powdery lumps in homemade brownies? Oh, and the way they'd explode against the heads of your victims. Well you've got a dollop of high-grade dirt there. You bite into it, and you'll taste your life left behind—bright sun and blue skies."

"Calm down," said the short man to his fellow customer. "Give him some room."

Hatch finished the drink and let the lump roll out of the bottom of the glass into his mouth. He bit it with his molars but found it had nothing to do with dirt. It was mushy and tasted terrible, more like a sodden meatball of decay than a memory of the sun. He spit the mess out and it darkened the water in front of his face. He waved his hand to disperse the brown cloud. A violet fish with a lazy tail swam down from the ceiling to snatch what was left of the disintegrating nugget.

The two customers and the bartender laughed, and Hatch heard it like a party in his brain. "You got the tootsie roll," said the short fellow, and tried to slap the bar, but his arm moved too slowly through the water.

"Don't take it personally," said the old man. "It's a Drowned Town tradition." His right ear came off just then and floated away, his glasses slipping down on that side.

Hatch felt a sudden burst of anger. He'd never liked playing the fool.

"Sorry, fella," said the bartender, "but it's a ritual. On your first Dry Reach, you get the tootsie roll."

"What's the tootsie roll?" asked Hatch, still trying to get the taste out of his mouth.

"Well, for starters, it ain't a tootsie roll," said the man with the outlandish grin.

Three

Hatch marveled at the myriad shapes and colors of seaweed in the grocery's produce section. The lovely wavering of their leaves, strands, tentacles, in the flow soothed him. Although he stood on the sandy bottom, hanging from the ceiling were rows of fluorescent lights, every third or fourth one working. The place was a vast concrete bunker, set up in long aisles of shelves like at the Super Shopper he'd trudged through innumerable times back in his dry life.

"No money needed," he thought. "And free booze, but then why the coverage of the war? For that matter why the tootsie roll? *Financial Ruin* has free reign in Drowned Town. Nobody seems particularly happy. It doesn't add up." Hatch left the produce section, passed a display of starfish, some as big as his head, and drifted off, in search of the Deli counter.

The place was enormous, row upon row of shelved dead fish, their snouts sticking into the aisle, silver and pink and brown. Here and there a gill still quivered, a fin twitched. "A lot of fish," thought Hatch. Along the way, he saw a special glass case that held frozen food that had sunk from the world above. The hot dog tempted him, even though a good quarter had gone green. There was a piece of a cupcake with melted sprinkles, three French fries, a black Twizzler, and a red and white Chinese take-out bag with two gnarled rib ends sticking out. He hadn't had any lunch, and his stomach growled in the presence of the delicacies, but he was thinking of Rose and wanted to talk to her.

Hatch found a familiar face at the lobster tank. He could hardly believe it, Bob Gordon from up the block. Bob looked none the worse for wear for being sunk, save for his yellow complexion. He smoked a damp cigarette and stared into the tank as if staring through it.

"Bob," said Hatch.

Bob turned and adjusted his glasses. "Hatch, what's up?"

"I didn't know you went under."

"Sure, like a fuckin' stone."

"When?" asked Hatch.

"Three, four weeks ago. Peggy'd been porking some guy from over in Larchdale. You know, I got depressed, laid off the bailing, lost the house, and then eventually I just threw in the pail."

"How do you like it here?"

"Really good," said Bob, and his words rang loud in Hatch's brain, but then he quickly leaned close and these words came in a whisper, "It sucks."

"What do you mean?" asked Hatch, keeping his voice low.

Bob's smile deflated. "Everything's fine," he said, casting a glance to the lobster tank. He nodded to Hatch. "Gotta go, bud."

He watched Bob bound away against a mild current. By the time Hatch reached the Deli counter, it was closed. In fact, with the exception of Bob, he'd seen no one in the entire store. An old black phone with a rotary dial sat atop the counter with a sign next to it that read: Free Pay Phone. NOT TO BE USED IN PRIVACY!

Hatch looked over his shoulder. There was no one around. Stepping forward he reached for the receiver, and just as his hand closed on it, the thing rang. He felt the vibration before he heard the sound. He let it go and stepped back. It continued to ring, and he was torn between answering it and fleeing. Finally, he picked it up and said, "Hello."

At first he thought the line was dead, but then a familiar voice sounded. "Hatch," it said, and he knew it was Ned, his younger son. Both of his boys had called him Hatch since they were toddlers. "You gotta come pick me up."

"Where are you?" asked Hatch.

"I'm at a house party behind the 7-11. It's starting to get crazy."

"What do you mean it's starting to get crazy?"

"You coming?"

"I'll be there," said Hatch, and then the line went dead.

He stood at the door to the basement of his brain and turned the knob, but before he could open it, he saw way over on the other side of the store, one of the silver sharks, cruising above the aisles up near the ceiling. Dropping the phone, he scurried behind the Deli counter, and then through an opening that led down a hall to a door.

Four

Hatch was out of breath from walking, searching for someone who might be able to help him. For ten city blocks he thought about Ned needing a ride. He pictured the boy, hair tied back, baggy shorts, and shoes like slippers, running from the police. "Good grief," said Hatch, and pushed forward. He'd made a promise to Ned years earlier that he would always come and get him if he needed a ride, no matter what. How could he tell him now, "Sorry kid, I'm sunk." Hatch thought of all the things that could happen in the time it would take him to return to land and pick Ned up at the party. Scores of tragic scenarios exploded behind his eyes. "I might as well be bailing," he said to the empty street.

He heard the crowd before he saw it, faint squeaks and blips in his ears and eventually they became distant voices and music. Rounding a corner, he came in sight of a huge vacant lot between two six-story brownstones. As he approached, he could make out there was some kind of attraction at the back of the lot, and twenty or so Drowned Towners floated in a crowd around it. Organ music blared from a speaker on a tall wooden pole. Hatch crossed the street and joined the audience.

Up against the back wall of the lot, there was an enormous golden octopus. Its flesh glistened and its tentacles curled, unfurled, created fleeting symbols dispersed by schools of tiny angel fish constantly circling it like a halo. The creature's sucker disks were flat black as was its beak, its eyes red, and there was a heavy, rusted metal collar squeezing the base of its lumpen head as if it had shoulders and a neck. Standing next to it was a young woman, obviously part fish. She had gills and her eyes were pure black like a shark's. Her teeth were sharp. There were scales surrounding her face and her hair was some kind of fine green seaweed. She wore a clamshell brassiere and a black thong. At the backs of her heels were fanlike fins. "My name is Clementine," she said, "and this is Madame Mutandis. She is a remarkable specimen of the Midas Octopus, so named for the beautiful golden aura of her skin. You see the collar on the Madame and you miss the chain. Notice, it is attached to my left ankle. Contrary to what you all might believe, it is I who belong to her and not she to me."

Hatch looked up and down the crowd he was part of—an equal mixture of men and women, some more bleached than blue, some less intact. The man next to him held his mouth open, and an eel's head peered out as if having come from the bowels to check the young fish-woman's performance.

"With cephalopod brilliance, non-vertebrate intuition, Madame Mutandis will answer one question for each of you. No question is out of bounds. She thinks like the very sea itself. Who'll be first?"

The man next to Hatch stepped immediately forward before anyone else. "And what is your question?" asked the fish-woman. The man put his hands into his coat pockets and then raised his head. His message was horribly muddled, but by his third repetition Hatch as well as the octopus got it—"How does one remove an eel?" Madame Mutandis shook her head sac as if in disdain while two of her tentacles unfurled in the man's direction. One swiftly wrapped around his throat, lurching him forward, and the other dove into his mouth. A second later, the Madame released his throat and drew from between his lips a three-foot eel, wriggling wildly in her suctioned grasp. The long arm swept the eel to her beak, and she pierced it at a spot just behind the head, rendering it lifeless. With a free tentacle, she waved forward the next questioner, while brushing gently away the man now sighing with relief.

Hatch came to and was about to step forward, but a woman from behind him wearing a kerchief and carrying a beige pocketbook passed by, already asking, "Where are the good sales?" He wasn't able to see her face, but the woman with the question, from her posture and clothing, seemed middle-aged, somewhat younger than himself.

Clementine repeated the woman's question for the octopus. "Where are the good sales?" she said.

"Shoes," said the woman with the kerchief. "I'm looking for shoes."

Madame Mutandis wrapped a tentacle around the woman's left arm and turned her to face the crowd. Hatch reared back at the sudden sight of a face rotted almost perfectly down the middle, skull showing through on one side. Another of the octopus's tentacles slid up the woman's skirt between her legs. With the dexterity of a hand, it drew down the questioner's underwear, leaving them gathered around her ankles. Then, wriggling like the eel it removed from the first man's mouth, that tentacle slithered along her right thigh only to disappear again beneath the skirt.

Hatch was repulsed, fascinated, aroused, as the woman trembled and the tentacle wiggled out of sight. She turned her skeletal profile to the crowd, and that bone grin widened with pleasure, grimaced in pain, gaped with passion. Little spasms of sound escaped her open mouth. The crowd methodically applauded until finally the object of the Madame's attentions screamed and fell to the sand, the long tentacle retracting. The fish-woman moved to the end of her chain and helped the questioner up. "Is that what you were looking for?" she asked. The woman with the beige pocketbook nodded and adjusted her kerchief before floating to the back of the crowd.

"Ladies and gentleman?" said the fish-woman.

Hatch noticed that no one was too ready to step forth after the creature's last answer, including himself. His mind was racing, trying to connect a search for a shoe sale with the resultant... What? Rape? Or was what he witnessed consensual? He was still befuddled by the spectacle. The gruesome state of the woman's face wrapped in ecstasy hung like a chandelier of ice on the main floor of his brain. At that moment, he realized he had to escape from Drowned Town. Shifting his glance right and left, he noticed his fellow drownees were still as stone.

The fish-woman's chain must have stretched, because she floated over and put her hand on his back. Gently, she led him forward. "She can tell you anything," came Clementine's voice, a whisper that made him think of Rose and Ned and Will, even the stupid dog with bad ears. He hadn't felt his feet move, but he was there, standing before the shining perpetual motion of the Madame's eight arms. Her black parrot-beak opened, and he thought he heard her laughing.

"You're question?" asked Clementine, still close by his side.

"My kid's stuck at a party that's getting crazy," blurted Hatch. "How do I get back to dry land?"

He heard murmuring from the crowd behind him. One voice said, "No." Another two said, "Asshole." At first he thought they were predicting the next answer from Madame Mutandis, but then he realized they were referring to him. It dawned that wanting to leave Drowned Town was unpopular.

"Watch the ink," said Clementine.

Hatch looked down and saw a dark plume exuding from beneath the octopus. It rose in a mushroom cloud, and then turned into a long black string at the top. The end of that string whipped leisurely through the air, drawing more of itself from the cloud until the cloud had vanished and what remained was the phrase *322 Bleeter Street* in perfect, looping script. The address floated there for a moment, Hatch repeating it, before the angel fish veered out of orbit around the fleshy golden sac and dashed through it, dispersing the ink.

The fish-woman led Hatch away and called, "Next." He headed for the street, repeating the address under his breath. At the back of the crowd, which had grown, a woman turned to him as he passed and said, "Leaving town?"

"My kid..." Hatch began, but she snickered at him. From somewhere down the back row, he heard "Jerk," and "Pussy." When he reached the street, he realized that the words of the drowned had crowded the street number out of his thoughts. He remembered Bleeter Street and said it six times, but the number... Leaping forward, he assumed the flying position, and flapping his arms, cruised down the street, checking the street signs at the corners and keeping an eye out for sharks. He remembered the number had a 3, and then for blocks he thought of nothing but that last woman's contempt.

Five

Eventually, he grew too tired to fly and resumed walking, sometimes catching the current and drifting in the flow. He'd seen so many street signs—presidents' names, different kinds of fish, famous actors and sunken ships, types of clouds, waves, flowers, slugs. None of them was Bleeter. So many storefronts and apartment steps passed by and not a soul in sight. At one point, tiny starfish fell like rain all over town, littering the streets and filling the awnings.

Hatch had just stepped out of a weakening current and was moving under his own volition when he noticed a phone booth wedged into an alley between two stores. Pushing off, he swam to it and squeezed himself into the glass enclosure. As the door closed, a light went on above him. He lifted the receiver, placing it next to his ear. There was a dial tone. He dialed and it rang. Something shifted in his chest and his pulse quickened. Suffering the length of each long ring, he waited for someone to pick up.

"Hello?" he heard; a voice at a great distance.

"Rose, it's me," he screamed against the water.

"Hatch," she said. "I can hardly hear you. Where are you?"

"I'm stuck in Drowned Town," he yelled.

"What do you mean? Where is it?"

Hatch had a hard time saying it. "I went under, Rose. I'm sunk."

There was nothing on the line. He feared he'd lost the connection, but he stayed with it.

"Jesus, Hatch... What the hell are you doing?"

"I gave up on the bailing," he said.

She groaned. "You shit. How am I supposed to do this alone?"

"I'm sorry, Rose," he said. "I don't know what happened. I love you."

He could hear her exhale. "OK," she said. "Give me an address. I have to have something to put into MapQuest."

"Do you know where I am?" he asked.

"No, I don't fucking know where you are. That's why I need the address."

It came to him all at once. "322 Bleeter Street, Drowned Town," he said. "I'll meet you there."

"It's going to take a while," she said.

"Rose?"

"What?"

"I love you," he said. He listened to the silence on the receiver until he noticed in the reflection of his face in the phone booth glass a blue spot on his nose and one on his forehead. "Shit," he said, and hung up. "I can take care of that with some ointment when I get back," he thought. He scratched at the spot on his forehead and blue skin sloughed off. He put his face closer to the glass, and then there came a pounding on the door behind him.

Turning, he almost screamed at the sight of the half-gone face of that woman who'd been goosed by the octopus for her shoe sale query. He opened the door and slid past her. Her Jolly Roger profile was none too jolly, he noticed. As he spoke the words, he surprised himself with doing so—"Do you know where Bleeter Street is?" She jostled him aside in her rush to get to the phone. Before closing the door, she called over her shoulder, "You're on it."

"Things are looking up," thought Hatch as he retreated. Standing in the middle of the street, he looked up one side and down the other. Only one building, a darkened storefront with a plate glass window behind which was displayed a single pair of sunglasses on a pedestal, had a street number—621. It came to him that he would have to travel in one direction, try to find another address, and see which way the numbers ran. Then, if he found they were increasing, he'd have to turn around and head in the other direction, but at least he would know. Thrilled at the sense of purpose, he swept a clump of drifting seaweed out of his way, and moved forward. He could be certain Rose would come for him. After thirty years of marriage they'd grown close in subterranean ways.

Darkness was beginning to fall on Drowned Town. Angle-jawed fish with needle teeth, a perpetual scowl, and sad eyes came from the alleyways and through the open windows of the apartments. Each had a small phosphorescent jewel dangling from a downward curving stalk that issued from the head. They drifted the shadowy street like fireflies, and although Hatch had still to see another address, he stopped in his tracks to mark their beautiful effect. It was precisely then that he saw *Financial Ruin* appear from over the rooftops down the street. Before he could even think to flee, he saw the shark swoop down in his direction.

Hatch turned, kicked his feet up, and started flapping. As he approached the first corner, and was about to turn, he almost collided with someone just stepping out onto Bleeter Street. To his utter confusion, it was a deep-sea diver, a man inside a heavy rubber suit with a glass bubble of a helmet and a giant nautilus shell strapped to his back feeding air through two arching tubes into his suit. The sudden appearance of the diver wasn't what made him stop, though. It was the huge chrome gun in his hands with a barbed spearhead as wide as a fence post jutting from the barrel. The diver waved Hatch behind him as the shark came into view. Then it was a dagger-toothed lunge, a widening cavern with the speed of a speeding car. The diver pulled the trigger. There was a zip of tiny bubbles, and *Financial Ruin* curled up, thrashing madly with the spear piercing its upper pallet and poking out the back of its head. Billows of blood began to spread. The man in the suit dropped the gun and approached Hatch.

"Hurry," he said, "before the other sharks smell the blood."

Six

Hatch and his savior sat in a carpeted parlor on cushioned chairs facing each other across a low coffee table with a tea service on it. The remarkable fact was that they were both dry, breathing air instead of brine, and speaking at a normal tone. When they'd entered the foyer of the stranger's building, he hit a button on the wall. A sheet of steel slid down to cover the door, and within seconds the seawater began to exit the compartment through a drain in the floor. Hatch had had to drown into the air and that was much more uncomfortable than simply going under, but after some extended wheezing, choking, and spitting up, he drew in a huge breath with ease. The diver had unscrewed the glass globe that covered his head and held it beneath one arm. "Isaac Munro," he'd said, and nodded.

Dressed in a maroon smoking jacket and green pajamas, moccasins on his feet, the silver-haired man with drooping mustache sipped his tea and now held forth on his situation. Hatch, in dry clothes the older man had given him, was willing to listen, almost certain Munro knew the way back to dry land.

"I'm in Drowned Town, but not of it. Do you understand?" he said.

Hatch nodded, and noticed what a relief it was to have the pressure of the sea off him.

Isaac Munro lowered his gaze and said, as if making a confession, "My wife Rotzy went under some years ago. There was nothing I could do to prevent it. She came down here, and on the day she left me, I determined I would find the means to follow her and rescue her from Drowned Town. My imagination, fired by the desire to simply hold her again, gave birth to all these many inventions that allow me to keep from getting my feet wet, so to speak." He chuckled, and then made a face as if he were admonishing himself.

Hatch smiled. "How long have you been looking for her?"

"Years," said Munro, placing his teacup on the table.

"I'm trying to get back. My wife Rose is coming for me in the car."

"Yes, your old neighbor Bob Gordon told me you might be looking for an out," said the older man. "I was on the prowl for you when we encountered that cutpurse Leviathan."

"You know Bob?"

"He does some legwork for me from time to time."

"I saw him at the grocery today."

"He has a bizarre fascination with that lobster tank. In any event, your wife won't make it through, I'm sorry to say. Not with a car."

"How can I get out?" asked Hatch. "I can't offer you a lot of money, but something else perhaps?"

"Perish the thought," said Munro. "I have an escape hatch back to the surface in case of emergencies. You're welcome to use it if you'll just observe some cautionary measures."

"Absolutely," said Hatch, and moved to the edge of his chair.

"I take it you'd like to leave immediately?"

Both men stood and Hatch followed through a hallway lined with framed photographs, which opened into a larger space; an old ballroom with peeling flowered wallpaper. Across the vast wooden floor, scratched and littered with, of all things, old leaves and pages of a newspaper, they came to a door. When Munro turned around, Hatch noticed that the older man had taken one of the photos off the wall in the hallway.

"Here she is," said Isaac. "This is Rotzy."

Hatch leaned down for a better look at the portrait. He gave only the slightest grunt of surprise and hoped his host hadn't noticed, but Rotzy was the woman at the phone booth, the half-faced horror mishandled by Madame Mutandis.

"You haven't seen her, have you?" asked Munro.

Hatch knew he should have tried to help the old man, but he thought only of escape and didn't want to complicate things. He felt that the door in front of him was to be the portal back. "No," he said.

Munro nodded and then reached into the side pocket of his jacket and retrieved an old-fashioned key. He held it in the air but did not place it in Hatch's outstretched palm. "Listen carefully," he said. "You will pass through a series of rooms. Upon entering each room, you must lock the door behind you with this key before opening the next door to exit into the following room. Once you've started you can't turn back. The key only works to open doors forward and lock doors backward. A door can not be opened without a door being locked. Do you understand?"

"Yes."

Munro placed the key in Hatch's hand. "Then be on your way and Godspeed. Kiss the sky for me when you arrive."

"I will."

Isaac opened the door and Hatch stepped through. The door closed and he locked it behind him. He crossed the room in a hurry, unlocked the next door and then passing through, locked it behind him. This process went on for twenty minutes before Hatch noticed that it took less and less steps to traverse each room to the next door. One of the rooms had a window, and he paused to look out on some watery side street falling into night. The loneliness of the scene spurred him forward. In the following room he had to duck down so as not to skin his head against the ceiling. He locked its door and moved forward into a room where he had to duck even lower.

Eventually, he was forced to crawl from room to room, and there wasn't much room for turning around to lock the door behind him. As each door swept open before him, he thought he might see the sky or feel a breeze in his face. There was always another door but there was also hope. That is until he entered a compartment so small, he couldn't turn around to use the key but had to do it with his hands behind his back. His chin against his chest. "This has got to be the last one," he thought, unsure if he could squeeze his shoulders through the next opening. Before he could insert the key into the lock on the tiny door before him, a steel plate fell and blocked access to it. He heard a swoosh and a bang behind him and knew another metal plate had covered the door going back. He was trapped.

"How are you doing, Mr. Hatch?" he heard Munro's voice say. By dipping one shoulder he was able to turn his head and see a speaker built into the wall.

"How do I get through these last rooms?" Hatch yelled. "They're too small and metal guards have fallen in front of the doors."

"That's the point," called Munro, "you don't. You, my friend, are trapped, and will remain trapped forever in that tight uncomfortable place."

"What are you talking about? Why?" Hatch was frantic. He tried to lunge his body against the walls but there was nowhere for it to go.

"My wife, Rotzy. You know how she went under? What sunk her? She was ill, Mr. Hatch. She was seriously ill but her health insurance denied her coverage. You, Mr. Hatch, personally said *No*."

This time what flared before Hatch's inner eye was not his life, but all the many pleading, frustrating, angry voices that had traveled in one of his ears and out the other in his service to the HMO. "I'm not responsible," was all he could think to say in his defense.

"My wife used to tell me, 'Isaac, we're all responsible.' Now you can wait, as she waited for relief, for what was rightly due her. You'll wait forever, Hatch."

There was a period where he struggled. He couldn't tell how long it lasted, but nothing came of it, so he closed his eyes, made his breathing more steady and shallow, and went into his brain, across the first floor to the basement door. He opened it and could smell the scent of the dark wood wafting up the steps. Locking the door behind him, he descended into the dark.

Seven

The woods were frightening, but he'd take anything over the claustrophobia of Munro's trap. Each dim light bulb he came to was a godsend, and he put his hands up to it for the little warmth it offered against the wind. He noticed that the creatures prowled around the bulbs like waterholes. They darted behind the trees, spying on him, pale specters whose faces were like masks made of bone. One he was sure was his cousin Martin, a malevolent boy who'd cut the head off a kitten. He'd not seen him in over thirty years. He also spotted his mother-in-law, who was his mother-in-law with no hair and short tusks. She grunted orders to him from the shadows. He kept moving and tried to ignore them.

When Hatch couldn't walk any further, he came to a clearing in the forest. There, in the middle of nowhere, in the basement of his brain, sat twenty yards of street with a brownstone situated behind a wide sidewalk. There were steps leading up to twin doors and an electric light glowed next to the entrance. As he drew near, he could make out the address in brass numerals on the base of the banister that led up the right side of the front steps.

He stumbled over to the bottom step and dropped down onto it. Hatch leaned forward, his elbows on his knees and his hands covering his face. "That's not me," he said, "it's not me," and he tried to weep till his eyes closed out of exhaustion. What seemed a second later, he heard a car horn and looked up.

"There's no crying in baseball, asshole," said Rose. She was leaning her head out the driver's side window of their SUV. There was a light on in the car and he could see both their sons were in the back seat, laughing and pointing at Hatch.

"How'd you find me?" he asked.

"The internet," said Rose. "Will showed me MapQuest has this new feature where you don't need the address anymore, just a person's name, and it gives you directions to wherever they are in the continental United States."

"Oh, my god," he said, and walked toward Rose to give her a hug.

"Not now Barnacle Bill, there's some pale creeps coming this way. We just passed them and one lunged for the car. Get in, Mr. Drowned Town."

Hatch got in and saw his sons. He wanted to hug them but they motioned for him to hurry and shut the door. As soon as he did, Rose pulled away from the curb.

"So, Hatch, you went under?" asked his older son, Will.

Hatch wished he could explain but couldn't find the words.

"What a pile," said Ned.

"Yeah," said Will.

"Don't do it again, Hatch," said Rose. "Next time we're not coming for you."

"I'm sorry," he said. "I love you all."

Rose wasn't one to admonish more than once. She turned on the radio and changed the subject. "We had the directions, but they were a bitch to follow. At one point I had to cut across two lanes of traffic in the middle of the Holland Tunnel and take a left down a side tunnel that for more than a mile was the pitchest pitch-black."

"Listen to this, Hatch," said Ned, and leaned into the front seat to turn up the radio.

"Oh, they've been playing this all day," said Rose. "This young woman soldier was captured by insurgents and they made a video of them cutting her head off."

"On the radio, you only get the screams, though," said Will. "Check it out."

The sound, at first, was like from a musical instrument, and then it became human—steady, piercing shrieks in desperate bursts that ended in the gurgle of someone going under.

Rose changed the channel and the screams came from the new station. She hit the button again, and the same screaming. Hatch turned to look at his family. Their eyes were slightly droopy and they were very pale. Their shoulders were somehow out of whack and their grins were vacant. Rose had a big bump on her forehead and a rash across her neck, but at least they were together.

"Watch for the sign for the Holland Tunnel," she said amid the dying soldier's screams as they drove on into the dark. Hatch kept careful watch, knowing they'd never find it.

TOOTHER

TERRY DOWLING

As Dan Truswell gave his signature three-three knock on the door in the modest hospital tower of Everton Psychiatric Facility that Friday morning, he couldn't help but glance through the second-floor window at the new sign down in the turning circle. *Everton Psychiatric Facility*, it said. He'd never get used to it. That was the more politically correct name for Blackwater Psychiatric Hospital, just as words like *client* and *guest* had completely replaced *patient* and *inmate*.

"Peter, it's Dan."

Dan didn't enter Peter Rait's room, of course. That wasn't their arrangement. He just waited, looking at his reflection in the small mirror Peter kept hanging outside his door, surprised not so much by the slate-grey eyes and flyaway hair but by how white that hair had become. He was fifty-nine, for heaven's sake! It was something else he'd never get used to.

Finally the door opened and Peter stood there in his pyjamas.

"Careful, Doctor Dan. That's a dangerous one."

"They all are, Peter. Carla said you've been yelling. Another nightmare?"

Peter looked tired, troubled. His black hair was tousled from sleep. "They don't usually come this often now. Harry's going to phone."

"Harry Badman?" Dear industrious Harry was two years out of his life, distanced by the usual string of promotions, secondments and strategic sidelining that marked the lives of so many career detectives in the New South Wales Police Force. "All right, Peter, so how does this dream relate?"

"Ask Harry about the teeth, Doctor Dan."

Dan's thoughts went at once to the recent desecration at Sydney's Rookwood Cemetery. "Is this about—?"

"Ask him."

"What do you have, Peter?"

"I can't say till he confirms it. Ask him. He'll know."

Dan made himself hold back the rush of questions. "It's been a while."

Peter did finally manage a smile, something of one. "It has, Doctor Dan."

Dan smiled too. "Phil knows?"

"Some of it. I'll give him an update at breakfast. But it's important. Very important."

"Tell me the rest, Peter."

"I really can't."

"There are voices?"

"God, yes. But strange." Neither of them smiled at the bathos. What internal voices weren't? "They're coming over time."

Dan frowned. This was something new. "Across years?"

"The first is from the sixties."

"More, Peter."

"Let Harry start it."

You've started it! Dan almost said, but knew to hold back, just as Peter had known how much to use as a tease.

"Listen, Peter—"

"Talk later. I'll leave you two alone."

And he closed the door. Dan, of course, looked straight into Peter's mirror again, had the good grace to laugh, then headed downstairs.

Forty-nine minutes later, as Dan sat in his office reviewing the patient database, Harry Badman phoned from Sydney. There was the inevitable small-talk, the polite and awkward minimum that let them stitch up the years as best they could. Dan Truswell and Harry Badman liked one another a great deal, but their friendship had never been easy far from where their respective careers met: for Harry, pursuing the more dangerous exponents of extraordinary human behaviour; for Dan, fathoming the often extraordinary reasons for it.

Finally Harry's tone changed. "I need to see you, Dan."

"It's about what happened at Rookwood last Saturday night, isn't it?"

"What have you heard?"

"What was in the news. A grave was desecrated. A recent burial." Dan said nothing about teeth. This had been one of Peter Rait's dreams after all, and it had been a while since the intense, still-young man had been "active" like this. More importantly it was Dan's way of testing Peter's special talent after all this time.

"Samantha Reid. Aged forty-one. Buried on Friday, dug up on Sunday sometime between two and four in the morning. Cold rainy night. No one saw anything. The body was hauled from the coffin and left lying beside the grave."

"So, not just a grave 'tampered with,' like the papers said. Your people are good, Harry. Why the call?"

"Things were removed from the scene. I'd like your take on it."

"Stop being coy. What was 'removed'?"

"The teeth, Dan. All the teeth."

Dan had an odd rush of emotion: revulsion, fascination, the familiar numb amazement he always felt whenever one of Peter's predictions played out like this. And there was the usual excess of rationalism as if to compensate. "What do the deceased's dental records show? Were there gold fillings?"

"Dan, *all* the teeth. And it's not the first desecration. Just the first to make the news."

Dan knew he'd been slow this time, but allowed that he was out of practice too. "There were others?"

"From secluded and disused parts of the cemetery. Much older graves."

"But recent desecrations?"

"Hard to tell conclusively. Not all were reported back then. It didn't look good for the cemetery authorities. The graves were tidied up; nothing was said. We would have assumed these earlier violations were unrelated except…" He actually paused. Had the subject been less serious, it would have been comical.

"Come on, Harry. Someone's collecting teeth. What else do you have?"

"That Rattigan murder in Darlinghurst a month back. The pensioner, remember?"

"Go on."

"She wasn't strangled like the media said."

"No?"

"She was bitten to death."

Dan was surprised to find that his mouth had fallen open in astonishment. "Bitten?"

"At least two hundred times. Increasing severity."

"These could be different crimes, Harry. What makes you think they're related?"

"Teeth fragments were found in some of the wounds. Very old teeth."

But not in very old mouths, Dan realized. "Dentures made from these older desecrations?"

"Exactly."

"Surely there was saliva DNA from whoever wore them."

"No," Harry said.

Dan grasped the implications. "So, not necessarily biting as such. Someone made dentures from these older corpse teeth and— what?—killed the Rattigan woman using some sort of hand-held prosthesis?"

"Spring-loaded and vicious. All we can think of. And that's *several* sets of dentures, Dan. We've traced teeth fragments back to the occupants of three older desecrations: graves from 1894, 1906 and 1911. All female. No fragments from newer teeth—"

"Too new to shatter."

"Exactly. But there could be other teeth used, from other desecrations we don't know of. There are some very old graves there; we wouldn't necessarily be able to tell. So all we have is a major fetish angle. Something ritualistic."

"My phone number hasn't changed, Harry." The accusation hung there. *You didn't call sooner!*

"You've got your life, Dan. Annie. Phil." The barest hesitation. "Peter. I didn't want to intrude."

Dan stared at the midmorning light through his office windows and nodded to himself. "You've profiled it as what?"

"I'd rather not say. That's what this is about. Getting another take."

"Official?"

"Can be. You want the file? I'll email a PDF right now. Drive up tomorrow first thing."

"See you at the Imperial Hotel at eleven."

"See you then."

Seventeen hours later they were sitting with light beers in a quiet corner of the Imperial on Bennet Street trying to make the small-talk thing work face to face. They did well enough for six minutes before Harry put them both out of their misery.

"You got the file okay. Anything?"

Dan set down his glass. "A question first. You kept something back on the phone yesterday. You said the Rattigan woman was bitten to death."

"That's what happened," Harry said. He looked tanned, less florid than Dan remembered; in his casual clothes he could have been another tourist visiting the local wineries.

"Her teeth were taken as well, weren't they?"

Harry barely hesitated. "How'd you know?"

Dan lifted a manila folder from the seat beside him. "The results of Net searches. Know what a toother is, Harry?"

"Tell me."

"It was a vocation, to call it that, associated with body-snatching back in the eighteenth, nineteenth centuries. Back when resurrection-ists—lovely name—dug up bodies to sell to medical academies for their anatomy classes. There were people who did the same to get the teeth. Sold them to dentists to make false teeth."

"Dug up corpses?"

"Sometimes. Or did deals with resurrection men already in the trade. Mostly they'd roam battlefields and take teeth from dead soldiers."

"You're kidding."

"Not when you think about it. It was much better than getting teeth from the gibbet or the grave. Ivory and whalebone were either too expensive or decayed. No enamel coating. Teeth made from porcelain sounded wrong or were too brittle. Corpse teeth were better, soldiers' teeth usually best of all, injuries permitting. Sets of authentic Waterloo Teeth fetch quite a bit these days."

"What, dentures made from soldiers who died at Waterloo?"

Dan nodded. "Fifty thousand in a single day. Mostly young men. Supply caught up with demand with battles like that. But that's the thing. There weren't many battles on that scale. Demand outstripped supply."

"You already knew this stuff?"

"Some of it. You know what I'm like. And that's quite a file you sent. I stayed up late."

Harry had his notebook on the table in front of him. He opened it and began making notes. "Go on."

"Back then there just weren't enough corpses of executed criminals or unknown homeless to satisfy the demand. Not enough from the right age or gender, even when you had poorer people selling their own teeth. Some resurrectionists began killing people."

"And these toothers did too."

"There's little conclusive evidence that I'm aware of. But that's the point, Harry. You do a job like this, you try to make sure there isn't."

"But body-snatchers can't be doing this."

"It presents that way is all I'm saying—a similar MO. If the cemetery desecrations and the Rattigan death *are* related, as the fragments suggest, we need to allow a context for it."

Harry wrote something and looked up. "So this joker could be proceeding like a modern-day toother."

Dan shrugged. "Just putting it forward, Harry. He took the Rattigan woman's teeth. Used others to kill her. So, a psychopath possibly. A sociopath definitely, probably highly organized. A latter-day resurrectionist? Not in the sense we know it. But we only have the teeth being taken and the single recent murder. I assume there are no similar cases in the CID database?"

Harry shook his head. "The usual run of biting during domestics and sexual assault. Random mostly. Nothing like this."

"Then he may be escalating; either a loner doing his own thing or someone acquainted with the old resurrectionist methodology."

Harry started writing again. "Do you have more on that?"

"Going back a hundred, two hundred years, he'd see a likely subject, get them alone and have an accomplice grab them while he slapped a pitch-plaster over their mouth and nose—"

Harry looked up. "A what?"

"A sticky mass of plaster mixed with pitch. Mostly used during sexual assault, but what some resurrectionists used too. Silenced your victim and incapacitated them. Suffocated them if that was the intention. All over in minutes."

Harry was suitably horrified. "They just held them till they expired?"

"Or did a traditional 'burking'—covered the mouth and nose with their hand till the victim asphyxiated."

"This actually happened?"

"It did. The biting takes it in a completely different direction, of course. Was the Rattigan woman drugged or bound?"

"Not that we can tell."

"That tends to suggest an accomplice. Someone to help restrain her.

Do Sheehan's people have anything?"

"Just the fetish, ritual angle, Dan. A loner after trophies. It's early days. But you're taking it further, saying there could be an accomplice, someone getting the teeth for someone else—who then makes dentures and uses them to kill."

Dan glanced around to make sure that they weren't being overheard. They still had the bar virtually to themselves. "Just another possibility, Harry. Much less likely. And no conventional client. There's no economic reason for it now. It presents like that is what I'm saying."

"Okay, so either a loner or a gopher for someone who originally wanted the teeth for fetishistic reasons but is escalating. He now kills people and does the extractions himself. Focusing on females?"

"Seems that way. But until we know more I'm still tempted to say a loner with a special mission."

Harry drained his glass and set it down on the table. "So why do a *new* grave? Why show his hand like this? Was he interrupted before he could finish? Did he *want* people to know?"

"He's fixated. He may have seen the Reid woman alive and wanted that particular set of teeth. Like in the Poe story."

Harry frowned. "What Poe story?"

"'Berenice.' A brother obsessed with his sister's teeth extracts them while she's in a cataleptic coma."

"Where do you get this stuff, Dan?"

"They're called books, Harry. But this guy is doing it for himself. And I definitely believe it's a he. He could be using the more traditional techniques."

"Drugs would be easier."

"They would. But he wants them fully conscious. So we're back to the ritual aspect you mentioned."

"That emblematic thing," Harry said.

"The what?"

"Two—three years back. That conversation we had at Rollo's. You said that people try to be more. Have emblematic lives."

Dan never ceased to be amazed by what Harry remembered from their conversations. "Emblematic? I said that?"

"Four beers. You said that. Make themselves meaningful to themselves, you said. Do symbolic things."

"Okay, well this is his thing, Harry. We can't be sure if he's following aspects of the old toother/resurrectionist MO but Sheehan's right. Given the special dentures he's made for himself, doing this has some powerful fetishistic or symbolic meaning for him. And he may have done this a lot: gone somewhere, seen a lovely set of teeth on someone, arranged to get them alone, then suffocated or bitten them and taken their teeth."

"That's horrible. You actually think he may have already done that and hidden the bodies?"

"Because of the desecrations, the older teeth being used, that's how I'm seeing it, and it may get worse." Dan thought of Peter Rait's voices. *They're coming over time.*

"How could it—ah! He may start removing the teeth while the victims are alive. And conscious?"

Dan deliberately left a silence, waiting for Harry to say it.

It took a five-count. "You think it's already got to that! But the coroner's report for the Rattigan woman showed the extractions were post-mortem."

"Harry, I think that may have been her one bit of good fortune. She died just as he was starting."

Harry shook his head. "Then we can definitely expect more."

"I'd say so. And it depends."

"On what, Dan? On what?"

"On whether it's local. Someone developing his ritual. Or if it's something international that's been relocated here."

"International?"

"Ask Sheehan to check with Interpol or whoever you guys work with now. Find case similarities. Forced dental extractions. Post- and *ante*-mortem."

"Can you come down to Sydney?"

"Phone me Monday and I'll let you know. I need to speak with someone first. You could stay around. Visit some wineries, come over for dinner tonight. Annie would love to see you."

They both knew it wouldn't go that way. Not this time. Not yet. "Sorry, Dan. I need to get going with this. Take a rain-check?"

"Roger that," Dan said.

At 2 pm that afternoon, Dan met with Peter Rait and Phillip Crow at a picnic table sheltered by the largest Moreton Bay Fig in the hospital grounds. Peter, thin, black-haired, pale-skinned, on any ordinary day looked a decade younger than his forty-two years, but his recent nightmares had given him an intense, peaked quality that Dan found unsettling. He sat with a manila folder in front of him.

To his left on the same bench was Phil, four years older, fair-headed, stocky, with the sort of weathered but pleasant face that Carla liked to call "old-school Australian." He looked up and smiled as Dan arrived. "Just like old times, Doctor Dan."

"It is, Phil," Dan said as he sat across from them. He had to work not to smile. Peter and Phil were his "psychosleuths," their talent pretty well dormant these last three years. Officially, both men had been rehabilitated back into society; both had elected to stay, their choice, taking accommodation and rations in return for doing odd jobs. And called it Blackwater Psychiatric Hospital, of course.

Given Peter's present state, Dan couldn't enjoy the reunion as much as he would have liked. He went straight to the heart of it.

"Peter, tell me about the voices."

Peter took two typed pages from the folder in front of him. "Here are the transcripts," he said, sounding every bit as tired as he looked.

Dan was surprised by the odd choice of words. "Transcripts? How did you manage that?"

"They keep playing over. Two different conversations now. Two different victims."

"But how—?"

"I just can, Doctor Dan, okay? It's pretty distressing. You can't know how awful it is."

Dan saw that Peter wasn't just tired; he was exhausted. "You can't stop it?"

"Giving you these might do it. Getting them out."

"Nothing else?"

"Not yet. Please, just read them."

Dan looked at the first page.

TRANSCRIPT 1

[miscellaneous sounds]

[male voice / mature, controlled]

"As they say, there is the good news and the bad news."

[terrified female voice, quite young]

"What do you mean?"

"You have a choice here. The good news is that you'll wake up. All your teeth will be gone, but we'll have a relatively easy time with the extractions and you *will* wake up. You'll be alive. The alternative—you make my job difficult and you won't wake up. That's the deal."

"Why are you doing this?"

"What's it to be?"

"Why?"

"It's necessary. What's it to be?"

"There has to be a reason!"

"I'll count to three."

"Just tell me why! Please!"

"One."

"For God's sake! Why are you doing this? Why?"

"Two. Choose or I will."

"You can't expect me—"

"Three. Too late."

"No! No! I want to wake up! Please! I want to wake up!"

"All right. Just this once."

"One question."

"Go ahead."

"You could drug me and do it. Do whatever you want. Why do I even have to choose?"

"Now that's the thing. And, really, you already know why. I need you conscious for it. I may drug you at the end. Oh, dear, look. You're pissing yourself."

[sobbing]

"Why? Why? Why?"

"You're not listening. It's my thing. I need to see your eyes while I'm doing it."

"Another question."

"There always is. What is it?"

"What will you do with—with *them?* Afterwards?"

"Make a nice set of dentures. Maybe I could sell them back to you. That would be a rather nice irony, wouldn't it? Irony is quite our thing."

"What about me? Afterwards?"

"You'll wake up. Hate us forever. Go on with the rest of your life."

"But I'll wake up? I *will* wake up?"

"Make it easy for us now and, yes. You have my word."

"You're saying 'us' and 'our'."

"Oh dear. So I am."

"What's that over there?"

"I think that's enough questions."

"What *is* that?"

[sundry sounds]

[victim screaming]
[audio ends]

Dan looked up. "Peter—"

"The next one, Doctor Dan. Read the next one, please. Same male voice. Different female victim."

Dan turned to it at once.

TRANSCRIPT 2

[miscellaneous sounds]

"You're crazy!"

"I hope not, for your sake. Major dental work needs a degree of control."

"But why? Why me?"

"The usual reason. Chance. Purest hazard. You were on hand."

"Then pick someone else!"

"From someone else's viewpoint I did. But enough talk. We have a lot to do."

"Listen. Listen to me. My name is Pamela Deering. I'm a mother. I have two little girls. Emma and Grace. Aged 7 and 5. My husband's name—"

[muffled sounds]

"Ssh now, Pamela. No more bonding. We have a lot to do."

"What? What do we have to do?"

"Let's just say that your girls and hubby will have to call you Gummy instead of Mummy." [pause] "That's our little joke, Pamela."

[sobbing]

"Please. Please don't do this."

"We have to, Mu—er—Gummy. It's our thing. It won't take long."

"You're saying 'we,' 'us.' You're not alone. There's someone else."

"Tsk. How rude of me. You want to meet my associate. Over here. Try to turn your head a little more."

[sundry sounds]

"But that's not—"

[victim screaming]

[audio ends]

Dan lowered the pages. "There are two of them. He's not a loner."

"Seems that way," Peter said.

"Do you get accents at all?"

"Educated male. Educated enough. Enunciates carefully so it's hard to know. The first woman sounds English. The Deering woman sounds Australian."

"But not recent. Over time, you said."

Peter nodded. "Sixties, seventies." He gestured to include Phil, as if he were equally part of this, both of them hearing the voices. "You have to protect us, Doctor Dan."

"I always do. That comes first."

"How will you?"

"Our old method. You aren't mentioned. Any locations you give, I'll have Harry say a phonecall came in, anonymous. Someone overheard a disturbance, cries, screaming. Wouldn't give their name."

"They'll buy it?"

"Why not? It happens more and more these days. Remember, we *all* need to stay out of this."

Phil leant forward. "What happens now?"

"We have a name," Dan said. "Pamela Deering. Harry can check that out. Meanwhile, Peter—"

"I'll keep dreaming."

"You don't have to. We can give you a sedative."

"No," Peter said. "I'm doing it for them."

Dan saw the haunted look in the tired dark eyes. "We need this, Peter."

"I know."

Thirty-two cases were listed in the international database, Harry told Dan on the phone that Monday morning, different countries, different cities, different decades, though it was the sort of statistic that convinced them both that many others existed.

"They say two thousand people a year in New Guinea are killed by coconuts falling on their heads," Harry said. "How do you get a statistic like that? It can only ever be the ones you *hear* about. It's like that here. These are just the ones that came to the attention of different national authorities and have anything approximating a similar MO."

"What about the time-frame, Harry?"

"Dan, we've got cases going back to the thirties and forties, even earlier. Prague. Krakow. Trieste. Bangkok, for heaven's sake! They can't be the same person. It can't be a generational thing. It doesn't work like that."

"I'd normally agree," Dan said. "But you say the MOs are similar for these thirty-two?"

"Victims bitten to death, post- or ante-mortem; the various odon-tologists' findings give both. Their own teeth removed before, during or after; again there's a range. Older fragments in the wounds in some instances, say, nineteen, twenty per cent."

"Harry—"

"You're not going to say a secret society. An international brother-hood of toothers."

Dan gave a grim smile. "No, but look how it presents. It's as if a very old, well-travelled sociopath has been able to find agents across a lifetime and still has at least one accomplice now, doing his dirty work. The Reid disinterment was done manually, not using a back-hoe. That took a lot of effort."

"You believe this? Sheehan may not buy it."

"At this point I'm just trying to understand it, Harry. Rookwood and Darlinghurst suggest he may be local, at least for now."

"Can you come down to Sydney?"

"On Thursday. I'll be bringing Peter Rait."

Harry knew enough about Peter's gifts not to question it. "He has something?"

"For your eyes only."

"What, Dan?"

"Check if you have a missing person, a possible victim named Pam-ela Deering." He spelled out the name. "It could be from the sixties or seventies."

"How on earth did—?"

"Harry, you know how this has to be done. Yes or no?"

"Yes. Yes. Pamela Deering. Bring Peter with you. You got somewhere to stay?"

"I've arranged for unofficial digs at the old Gladesville Hospital on Victoria Road. There's a coffee shop on the grounds called Cornucopia. Meet us there around midday Thursday, okay?"

"Cornucopia. Got it."

"And bring a map of Rookwood Cemetery, will you? The adjacent streets."

"You think he lives in the area?"

"Peter needs it."

"Done."

At a convenience store roadstop in Branxton on their drive down that Thursday morning, Peter presented Dan with a third transcript.

"You need to factor this in," was all Peter said as he handed it over. He looked more drawn than ever, as if he had barely slept the night before.

"Last night?"

"Last two nights."

"You kept it to yourself."

Peter ran a hand through his dark hair. "Look, I have to be sure, okay? I have to know that it's not—just coming from me. That I can trust it."

"And you do?"

"I'm satisfied now, Doctor Dan. I couldn't make this up."

Dan leant against the car door and read the carefully typed words.

TRANSCRIPT 3

[miscellaneous sounds]

"You're the one who took the Kellar woman. Those poor women in Zurich. You're going to take out all my teeth!"

[sounds]

"Take them out? Oh no. Not this time. Toother was very specific."

[sounds, like things being shaken in a metal box]

"Toother?"

"Yes. Your name please?"

"What difference does it make?"

"But isn't that what the experts advise? Always try to use names? Don't let them dehumanise you. My name is Paul."

"Your real name? Not Toother?"

"It'll do for today."

"Then I'll be Janice. For today. Who is Toother?"

"Why, your host, Janice-for-today. The one who taught me all I know. Mostly he takes, but sometimes he gives."

"Gives?"

"Sometimes. I have my little hammer and my little punch, see? And you have such a full, generous mouth. Today we are going to put teeth back in. Lots and lots, see?"

[more rattling sounds]

"Big teeth. Men's teeth. We're going to call you Smiler."

[more rattling sounds]

[victim sobbing]

[victim screaming]

Dan left Peter to drowse for much of the journey south, but as they were on the bridge crossing the Hawkesbury River, he glanced aside and saw the dark eyes watching him.

"You okay?" he asked.

"Sorry for losing it back there," Peter said, as if resuming a conversation from moments before. "Things are escalating for me too. With this latest—exchange—I get something about his trophies."

Dan wished he weren't driving right then. He pulled into the low-speed lane. "You see them?"

"Just lots of—grimaces. You know, teeth without lips. It's the most terrifying thing. Bared teeth. No skin covering. Like eyes without lids. Horrible."

"Are they on shelves, in drawers, boxes, what?"

"Displayed. Arranged somehow, secretly. Nothing like smiles or grins. I just see them as bared teeth, Doctor Dan. In a private space. Sorry. It isn't much."

"Try, Peter. Whatever you get. These voices—"

"It's more than just voices. It's reciprocal now."

"Reciprocal? What does that mean?"

"It isn't just going one way. He knows I've been listening. Accessing his files. He was very angry at first, but now he's enjoying it. He's fighting back."

"How, Peter? How does he fight back?"

"Sending things, thoughts, images. They're not mine. It's more than delusions, Doctor Dan, I'm sure of it. More than my usual hypersensitivity. I just had to be sure."

"Understood. Go on."

"It's Rookwood. All those graves. I keep seeing the bodies, vulnerable, helpless, keep seeing the teeth. They're mostly all teeth, lots of dentures too. But there's such anguish. Such rage."

"Female burials?"

"Female *and* male. They're all murmuring, chattering. Some desperately wanting to be picked, calling 'Pick me! Pick me!' Others hiding. Desperately hiding. As if alive. They're not, but it's like they are for him."

"Is there a voice talking to you now?"

"*Like* a voice, Doctor Dan. *Not* a voice, but like one. I have certainties, just know things. He wants it like that."

"He's found someone he can share with. He hears the bodies calling to him you say?"

"How he sees them. Calling, begging. 'Pick me! Pick me!' Or hiding, resisting. Furious. Either way he sees it as liberation, sees them as all waiting to be chosen. The living victims too."

"He's *saving* them?"

"Liberating them is his word, yes. Living or dead, it doesn't matter. It just means a different method of retrieval."

"Retrieval!" Dan gave a laugh, completely without humour. "But he's in the area?"

Peter shrugged. "It's a huge cemetery, Doctor Dan. It's not called the Sleeping City for nothing. He's committed so many desecrations there. You can't begin to know. Secretly. Passionately. This is his place for now."

"Peter, I trust you completely. Just let me know what you get. Anything."

It was strange to walk the grounds of the decommissioned, largely deserted mental hospital at Gladesville later that morning. The former wards and out-buildings had been turned into offices for various governmental health services, so by day it was like a stately, manicured, museum estate. There were still vehicles in the carparks, people walking the paths, roadways and lawns, giving the place a semblance of its former life.

Dan walked those daylight roads now, glad that he wasn't doing it at night. After dark the offices and carparks were deserted, but had a strange new half-life, quarter-life, life-in-death. Instead of being left to stand as part of a vast col of blackness overlooking the Parramatta River, the old sandstone buildings and empty roads were lit, as if beckoning, urging, waiting for those willing to surrender bits of their sanity to make the place live again.

When Dan reached Cornucopia, he found Harry waiting at a table outside the café door.

"I've driven past this place a thousand times," Harry said, "and never knew how big it was. Where's Peter?"

"He sends his apologies. Said he wants to keep his mind off this for now."

"Doesn't want me asking questions," Harry said. "I can understand that."

"Harry—"

"Dan, I know how it can be for him. How it *was*. Just say hi for me."

They went in and placed their orders, then sat watching the clear autumn sky above the sandstone walls. Harry took out his notebook.

"The Deering woman went missing from a holiday house at Cottesloe Beach in 1967."

"That's Western Australia, isn't it?"

"Right. There was blood, definite signs of a struggle, but no body. And before you ask, there were no teeth fragments."

"You've been thorough."

"Now that there's international scrutiny, we have different resources available."

"What did you tell Sheehan?"

"That it came up in a missing persons keyword sweep. In the last three decades alone there are thirty-six names of missing persons nationally where blood mixed with saliva was found at locations where each of them was last seen."

"Oral blood?"

"Right. So tell me what Peter has found."

Dan passed him the transcript folder. "Harry, you might want to finish eating first."

Dan found it hard to sleep that night. They were in separate rooms in an otherwise empty, former staff residence at the southern end of the hospital grounds, a converted single-storey brick house. It was a cool, late autumn night, pleasant for sleeping, but with all that had happened, Dan felt restless, too keenly aware of the empty roads outside and the lit, abandoned buildings, so normal, yet—the only word for it—so abnormal, waiting in the night.

The lights are on but nobody's home.

The old euphemism for madness kept coming back to him. No doubt there were security personnel doing the rounds, one, possibly more, but, just the same, there was the distinct sense that Peter and he were the only living souls in the place.

Dan kept thinking of what Peter had told him that morning, of the bodies as repositories for teeth, grimaces, smiles, lying there waiting, hiding, some calling, chattering in darkness, wanting any kind of life, others dreading such attention.

It was absurd, foolish, but Rookwood Necropolis was barely ten kilometres away, 285 hectares of one of the largest dedicated cemeteries in the world, site of nearly a million interments.

In his half-drowsing state, Dan kept thinking, too, of the old 1963 movie, *Jason and the Argonauts,* of King Aeëtes collecting and sowing the teeth from the skull of the slain Hydra, raising up an army of skeletons to combat Jason and his crew. Dan imagined human teeth being first plucked and then sown in Rookwood's older, less tended fields. If the Hydra's teeth raised up *human* skeletons, what sort of creature would human teeth raise up?

He must have fallen asleep at last, for the next thing he knew Peter was rousing him.

"Doctor Dan?" Peter said, switching on Dan's bedside light.

"Peter? What is it?"

Peter was fully dressed, his hair and eyes wild. "He's got someone! Right now. He has someone!"

Dan grabbed his watch, saw that it was 12:16 am. "He told you this?"

"No. But I saw anyway. He's furious that I saw."

Dan climbed out of bed, began dressing. "The reciprocal thing?"

"It backfired, yes. Showed me more than he wanted. He's so angry, but he's enjoying it too! He's still enjoying it."

"The drama. The added excitement."

"Yes. We have to hurry!"

Dan reached for his mobile. "Where, Peter? I need to call Harry."

"Good. Yes. An old factory site in Somersby Road. A few streets back from the cemetery. But I need to be there. I have to be closer, Doctor Dan. Her life depends on it."

"Those women in the transcripts…?"

"Never woke up. None of them."

"Understood."

Harry answered his mobile before Dan's call went to voicemail. He sounded leaden from sleep until Dan explained what they had. "You'll be there before I will, Dan, but I'll have two units there. Four officers. Best I can do for now. Where are you?"

"Still at the hospital. Heading out to the car. We'll need an ambulance too, Harry. The Somersby Road corner closest to the cemetery. Tell them to wait for us. No sirens."

"Right. You're sure about this, Dan?"

"Peter is."

"I'm on my way!"

"Harry, Peter stays out of it. How do we cover ourselves?"

"Anonymous tip. A neighbour heard screaming. I'll have a word with whoever turns up. Go!"

Two patrol cars and an ambulance were waiting at the corner of Somersby Road, lights off, ready. There was no sign of Harry's car yet.

"You Dr Truswell?" an officer asked, appearing at Dan's driver-side window when he pulled up.

"Yes. Look—"

"Harry explained. I'm Senior Constable Banners. Warwick Banners. Just tell us where to go."

"It's there!" Peter said, pointing. "That building there!"

"Right. Follow us in but stay well back, hear?"

"We hear you," Dan said, and turned to Peter. "You have to stay in the car, okay?"

"I know," Peter said. "And keep the doors locked."

Dan joined the police officers and paramedics waiting at the kerb. It took them seconds to reach the building two doors down, a large brick factory-front with closed and locked roller-doors and smaller street door. The premises looked so quiet and innocent in the night, and not for the first time Dan wondered if Peter could be mistaken.

There was a single crash as the street door was forced. In moments they were in off the street, standing in utter quiet, in darkness lit by the beams of five torches.

Again it was all so ordinary, so commonplace. But Dan knew only too well how such places could be terrifying in their simplicity. He had seen the Piggyback Killer's rooms in Newtown, such a mundane blend of walls, hallways and furniture until you opened that one door, found the two coffins. He had seen Corinne Kester's balcony view and the shed with its treacherous windows, had seen Peter Rait's own room come alive in a wholly unexpected way right there at Blackwater. Such simple, terrifying places.

This, too, was such an ordinary, extraordinary space. Who knew what it had been originally: a warehouse, a meat packing plant, some other kind of factory, but taking up the entire ground floor, large and low-ceilinged, with painted out windows and a large, windowless inner section that took up most of the back half of the premises. Given the absence of screams being reported in the neighbourhood, it was very likely double brick or sound-proofed in some other way.

Dan followed the police and paramedics as they pushed through the double doors into that inner precinct. At first, it seemed totally dark. Then Dan saw that intervening pillars concealed an area off to the left lit by a dim yellow bulb. The police deployed immediately, guns ready, and crossed to it. There was no one there, just signs of where the occupant had been: a table and chair, a cupboard, a modest camp-bed with tangled bed-clothes, a hot-plate and bar fridge to one side where it all stretched off into darkness again.

Deliberate darkness. Darkness as controlled theatrical flourish, prelude to shocking revelations, precisely calculated anguish and despair.

The police led the way around more pillars. The stark white light of their torches soon found the old dentistry chair near the back wall, securely bolted to the floor, revealed the victim strapped down, alive but barely conscious, gurgling through a ruined mouth filled with her own blood.

The paramedics rushed to her aid, began working by torchlight as best they could.

Dan made himself look away, forced himself to look at what else there was in the shifting torchlight that *wasn't* this poor woman, gurgling, groaning and sobbing. He noted the straps for securing the chair's occupant, the elaborate padded clamp for holding the head, the metal tables and dental tools, other tools that had no place in dental work, the stains on the floor, dark and rusty-looking. The air smelled of disinfectant, urine and blood and something else, something sour.

An officer finally located a light switch. A single spot came on overhead, illuminating the chair and the woman, showing her ruined face and more: an array of mirrors on adjustable stands, video and audio equipment, shelves with old-style video and audio tapes, newer-style DVDs.

Souvenirs. An archive.

Dan scanned the row of audio tapes; the first were dated from the sixties.

Peter Rait's voices.

But all so mundane in a worrying sense. Though terrible to say, these were the workaday trappings of sociopaths and psychopaths the world over, how they, too, made mundane lives for themselves out of their horrific acts.

But there was a large, heavy door beyond the woman in the chair, like a rusted walk-in freezer door with a sturdy latch. Dan focused his attention on it as soon as the torch beams revealed the pitted metal surface. An exit? A hideaway? Another inner sanctum in this hellish place?

An officer approached the door, weapon ready, and pulled it back.

It was a storeroom, a small square room empty but for a large chalk-white post nearly two metres tall. The post was as round as three dinner plates, set in concrete or free-standing, it was hard to tell, but standing like a bollard, one of those removable traffic posts used to stop illegal parking, though larger, much larger, and set all over with encrustations.

Not just any encrustations, Dan knew. Sets of teeth in false mouths, fitted at different heights, randomly but carefully, lovingly, set into the white plaster, fibre-glass, concrete, whatever it was. Dentures made from real teeth, corpse teeth, teeth taken post- and ante-mortem, some of them, all of them spring-loaded and deadly!

A trophy post.

This was where Toother kept his terrible collection, displayed it for his pleasure—and, yes, for the calculated and utter terror of others.

A door slammed somewhere in the building.

The police reacted at once. The officer holding the storeroom door let it go. It was on a counterweight and closed with a resounding boom. Another shouted orders. One hurried back to secure the main entrance. The rest rushed to search the outer premises, to find other exits and locate their quarry. Footsteps echoed in the empty space.

It all happened so quickly. Dan stood listening, hoping, trusting that Peter was still out in the car, safe.

Movement close by caught his attention, brought him back. The paramedics had the woman on their gurney at last. The awful gurgling had stopped and they were now wheeling her away.

For a terrible moment, Dan was left alone with the chair under its single spot, with the tables and instruments, the archive shelves and heavy metal door, now mercifully closed.

Then there were cries off in the darkness, sounds of running, more shouting. Two gunshots echoed in the night.

Then, in seconds, minutes, however long it was, Harry was there, two officers with him.

"We got him, Dan."

"Harry. What? What's that?"

"We got him. Toother. He's dead."

"Dead?" Peter was there too, appearing out of the darkness. "You did? You really got him?"

"We did, Peter," Harry said. "He was running out when we arrived. Officer Burns and me. He was armed and wouldn't stop. Colin here had to shoot."

Dan placed a hand on Peter's arm. "No more voices?"

"No," Peter said. "No voices at all now."

"We got him, Peter," Harry said.

But Peter frowned, gave an odd, puzzled look as if hearing something, then crossed to the heavy door and pulled it back. "Harry, I don't think we did. Not this time. Not yet."

The storeroom was empty, of course.

UP THE FIRE ROAD

EILEEN GUNN

-Andrea-

The main thing to understand about Christy O'Hare is he hates being bored. Complicated is interesting, simple is dull, so he likes to make things complicated.

Used to be the complications were more under his control. Like one time he went down to Broadway for coffee, but the coffee place was closed. So he hitched a ride downtown, but the driver was headed for Olympia on I-5, so Christy figured he'll go along for the ride and get his coffee at that place in Oly that has the great huevos. He ended up thumbing to San Francisco and coming back a week later with a tattoo and a hundred bucks he didn't have when he left home. I think he was more interested in doing something that would make a good story than he was in getting a cup of coffee. But I did wonder where the hell he was.

He's not a bad guy. I don't agree with what my mother said about him being a selfish son-of-a-bitch. But Christy is the star of his own movie, and it's an action flick. If life is dull, just hook up with him for a while. And if life seems slow and meaningless, go somewhere where you depend on him to get you back.

Like the ski trip. It's not that he *wanted* us to get lost on Mt. Baker, where we could have died of exposure, but ordinary cross-country skiing, on groomed trails, with parking lots and everything, is just so crowded and boring. Starting out way too late makes things more interesting. Drinking a pint of Hennessy and smoking a couple joints makes things *much* more interesting and gives the Universe a head start.

That's how we found ourselves, last year, four miles up a fire road as the sun was setting. Early March: warm days, cold nights. Slushy snow, pitted with snowshoe tracks, turning to ice as the temperature dropped. Did we bring climbing skins for our skis? Of course not. Did we bring a headlamp, or even a flashlight? Nope.

"We've got an hour of visibility," I said. "Let's get back."

"It's all downhill. Won't take long. There's a trail that cuts off to the hot-spring loop about half a mile ahead. We can go back that way, and stop by the hot spring." He extended the flask to me. "Here, babe, take a drink of this."

I pushed it away. "It'll be dark by then," I said. "How will we find our way out?"

"The hot spring is just off the main road, the paved one that we drove up. We can walk back down the road to our truck in the dark. No problem."

As it turned out, the hot spring was a lot farther away than that, but it was a natural enough mistake, because we didn't have a map. We didn't have much food, either, just a couple of power bars, and we didn't have a tent or even a tarp, and we didn't have dry clothes. Oh, yeah—we had the cellphone, but its battery needed a charge.

By the time we found the hot spring, it was dark. There was a moon, but it was just a crescent, and it wasn't going to last more than an hour or two before dipping below the trees. I was starting to shiver.

"We got plenty of time," Christy said. "Let's warm up in the hot spring, then we can take our time getting back to the road, 'cause you'll be warmer."

Well, it made a certain amount of sense. Of course, we didn't have any towels or anything, but our clothes were wool, so they'd keep us pretty warm, even though they were wet with sweat from climbing up the fire road. All I had to do was get my body temperature up a bit, and I'd be fine for a couple of hours.

It was slippery and cold getting down to the hot spring. It wasn't anything fancy, like Scenic or Bagby. No decking, no little hand-hewn log seats, just a couple of dug-out pools near a stream, with flat stones at one side, so you don't have to walk in the mud.

We took off our skis, took off our clothes, put our boots back on without tying the laces, and moving gingerly and quickly, in the cold air and the snow, climbed down to the spring, shed our boots, and started to get into the water.

Hotter than a Japanese bath. We dumped some snow in, tested again. Still hot, but tolerable. Soon we were settled in and accustomed to the heat. It sure felt good—I was so tired—but adrenalin kept me alert. We still had a ways to go to get back to the truck.

That's when I saw the old guy, watching us from behind a tree, the moonlight making his outline clear. Creepy, I thought.

I whispered to Christy, "There's somebody watching us. Don't look like you're looking. Over to my left, past the big fir."

Christy liked that, I could tell: it suddenly made things even more interesting. He liked danger. He liked the idea of someone watching us get naked. He sidled around for a better look, and tried not to look like he was looking.

Then he froze. "It's not a guy," he said. "It's a bear."

"What do we do?"

"Stay here and hope it goes away."

"Do bears like hot springs?" I asked.

"Fuck if I know. I don't think so."

I kept my eye on the figure in the forest. It still looked a lot more like a guy than a bear to me. It came closer. It obviously could see us. It waved a mittened hand, and resolved into a guy with a big beard and a fur hat. "How you folks doing tonight," it said.

"Whattaya know," said Christy, "a talking bear."

-Christy-

I met Andrea at Burning Man. She was welding together a giant sheet-metal goddess robot with glowing snakes for hair. She was wearing a skirt made of old silk ties, and nothing else. No shoes, no shirt. Great service, though.

I lost my heart to her. I would do whatever she wanted. It's been that way ever since. She wanted a baby, and now she's got one. Doesn't need me anymore. Neither of the women do—her or Mickey. The babies need me, though. I'll stand by my kids, if their mothers will let me.

I'm not going to say that Andrea lies, but what happened on Mt. Baker wasn't my fault. I didn't even want to go skiing that day. It was dark and rainy in the morning, and it was a long drive to Mt. Baker. That's why we got there so late: she kept changing her mind about going. And if I hadn't been stoned, I wouldn't have misjudged the distance to the hot spring.

She's always saying that it's my fault when I screw up. Sure, I screw up, but why assign blame like that? Everybody screws up—even Andrea screws up sometimes. That's why I like skiing cross-country: because, when you screw up, you can recover. Usually, anyway.

You can make more mistakes, going cross-country, like finding yourself in the middle of fucking nowhere without a sandwich. But sometimes you get a chance to see stuff that most people, in their safe little lives, never even dream of.

Like the sasquatch. Where would you ever see a sasquatch, if you didn't go cross-country skiing? Or a talking bear, either. Whatever.

I figured it would calm Andrea down if she thought it was a talking bear, because that's an idea she's familiar with: *ursus fabulans*, the talking bear. We all know the talking bear. Even the Romans knew the talking bear. *Introit tabernum ursus et cervisiam imperavit,* as the book says. A bear goes into a bar and orders a beer.

But I knew it was a sasquatch—I'm not an idiot, Mt. Baker is crawling with them—and I wanted, naturally enough, to find out more. Besides, we were sitting there in the hot spring, facing a long, cold, dark walk back down the side of the mountain to the truck. The sasquatch asked us, real friendly, how we were doing. I saw no problem with partaking of his hospitality, you know? Maybe the sasquatch had a nice little cabin somewhere, or a warm cave with a fire already going. Maybe the sasquatch had a treasure and would bestow it upon us if he took a shine to us.

So I said, well, man, my sister's not feeling so good, and we sure could use a place to sleep tonight. You know any place around here, any place warm? Andrea looked at me hard when I called her my sister, but she didn't say anything. She's cool, Andrea. We didn't want to tell the sasquatch our whole story. Everybody needs to keep some truths to themselves. It's the only way.

And the sasquatch invited us back to his place. Polite as can be. Seemed like a good man, this sasquatch.

We leaped out of the hot spring, and got dressed real fast. It was colder now. We were all warmed up, so the hot spring was not a dumb idea, no matter what Andrea thought.

Skiing behind the sasquatch, she gave me a *what-the-fuck?* look. It was so dark, I couldn't see her face, but Andrea can do the *what-the-fuck?* look with her entire body.

I gave her a shrug that said *later*. Of course, Andrea was gonna have to rethink what I told her, and she was gonna have to ask why, and she was gonna have to just fuck with me on it, but she knew enough not to do any of those things while we were following a sasquatch through a frigid forest in the middle of the night.

We skied in the dark for maybe a half hour or so: it was slow going. The sasquatch, I noticed, had furry webbed feet that worked like snowshoes. Obviously, sasquatches evolved in the snow, like yeti. That's part of my theory. I'm just learning about this stuff. I found a couple of websites that have been helpful.

So, we were climbing on some kind of a narrow path. Climbing is relatively easy on my mountaineering skis, even without skins, but going down you don't have the control you'd have with steel edges. It was steep and it's icy. I was hoping we could get out of there in the morning without having to side-step all the way down. When we came to the sasquatch's cave, it didn't look like anything was there at all—just a wall of granite with a row of Doug firs in front of it. But somehow there was a gap in the rock, and the sasquatch gestured us in.

Inside, of course, it was bare ground, so we took off the skis and carried them in. No sense leaving them out there, risking that it would snow during the night and cover them up. I've done it, can you tell? Even if you know exactly where you put your skis, it's scary, out in the middle of nowhere, you don't see 'em.

The squatch struck a spark and lit a funny little oil lamp, and me and Andrea looked around inside the cave.

Back from the mouth of the cave, the ground sloped down and the roof was higher than I could see, in the dark. It seemed big inside, even though we couldn't see. I wonder if humans have some kind of sonar, like bats or dolphins.

We followed the wall, and, not far from the entrance, we came to a house made of logs and rocks. We went by several sets of doors and windows, like some old tourist motel, right in the cave.

We went in one of the doors and entered a big room. The floor was covered with the skins of deer and mountain sheep. No bearskins, I noticed. There was a strong musky smell, like raccoon or bear. Sasquatch, I bet.

There was another lamp, and there were big piles of balsam boughs, which I knew were comfortable to sleep on, and they smelled good. The sasquatch had a pretty nice place. Cold, though.

The sasquatch soon had a little fire going in a firepot, and there must have been a way for the smoke to get out, because the room didn't fill with smoke. There was a pot of water on the fire, and, criminy, the squatch even had a bunch of those heavy, handmade pottery mugs, like the kind you find cheap at the Goodwill. What, did he carry those things all the way into the woods? Sasquatches shop at thrift stores?

Soon we were drinking fir-tip tea, which was good, if somewhat redundant in the mountains.

After a couple cups of tea, Andrea went outside to take a leak, and I got the sasquatch alone. I dug in my pack and pulled out the Hennessy, of which there was still a little left, and offered the sasquatch some. He took a pull, I took a pull, and pretty soon I was breaking out the grass. While I was rolling a couple fat joints, I told the sasquatch that I thought my sister had the hots for him.

He took this a good bit cooler than I might have expected. I mean, Andrea is a good-looking woman. I wondered what sasquatch chicks looked like, that he was so unimpressed. Or maybe there was just no accounting for taste.

I told the sasquatch that when Andrea came back inside, I could set it up for him with her. I told him this all had to be above board. But I could tell, I said, that he was a stable fellow—solid, responsible—and my sister was ready to settle down and have kids. This last part was true, actually: Andrea and I had had The Conversation, though we didn't come to any conclusion, or at least not one that made her shut up about it.

The sasquatch just nodded at what I said, and I took this as agreement. We smoked a joint on it.

-Andrea-

When I came back into the room, the old guy was warming up some kind of a soup he's got in a pot near the fire.

"You folks are probably pretty hungry, eh?"

He and Christy had been smoking that homegrown Christy carried with him. Pretty punk stuff.

"Yeah," I said. "We didn't bring much to eat."

"Well, honey, let me tell you." He patted my shoulder, left his hand there just a little too long, y'know? "You and your brother shouldn't go off skiing like this without bringing some emergency rations. You're lucky you ran into me. I'll take care of you."

Yeah, I thought, I'm sure.

But he was nice enough, and the soup was okay, though lord knows what was in it. Roots and stuff. No meat. There was something potato-like, but it wasn't a potato. I didn't ask, because I didn't want to make the old guy feel bad. I've eaten a lot of weird stuff—a little more wouldn't hurt me.

He had these handmade wooden bowls to eat out of. I'd seen bowls like that before. Very rustic, kind of Zen, you know? I took some meditation classes in Berkeley, and the monks, they had bowls kind of like that.

The cave was warming up a bit from the fire, but I wouldn't have called it warm. The old guy noticed I was shivering, and put an arm around me. Christy moved away. Bastard.

"What's your name?" I asked. He said something, but I didn't catch it. It came out kind of funny, like he was clearing his throat at the same time.

"What?" I said.

"Call me Mickey," he said.

"Like the mouse?" I asked.

"Like the mouse," he said.

After supper, I left Christy and the old man talking, and lay down on a pile of balsam branches. I was tired, and it was soft and kind of cozy.

In the middle of the night, I heard a noise in my sleep, and I opened my eyes. Was it a noise I dreamed, or a noise in the real world? It took me a while to wake up. The oil lamps were out, but the fire was still burning, and by its dim light, I could see the old man moving across the room. He was wearing some kind of a tall hat. Other people came up behind him. It was very dark and shadowy, and completely silent. I wondered a bit if I was dreaming, but it didn't seem to be a dream.

Where was Christy? He wasn't next to me. One of those people looked like him.

I got up from the pile of branches and slipped my boots back on. I stood there in the dark, very quietly, thinking they couldn't see me.

The old man came closer to me, and the group moved with him. Yes, that was Christy there.

The people moved so strangely, like they weren't used to walking upright, and the cave was so dim, lit with a faint orange glow that seemed to come from within the people themselves, that I thought again that it was a dream. They were carrying ropes of twisty brown vines with yellow and orange berries on them, like swags of tinsel from a Christmas tree, and they encircled me, looping strands of vines over my head. It wasn't scary, though, it was like an interesting slow-motion dream. I felt that I could duck out of the vines and run away if I wanted, or wake up from it, but I didn't want to. The berries seemed to give off a dim light, and I was able to see better, like my eyes were getting used to the dark.

The people were all dressed in rags that looked like dead oak leaves. Their garments fluttered, although there was no movement of the air. I tried to talk to them, but they couldn't seem to understand what I was saying. I'm not sure there was any sound coming out of my mouth. The visitors looped the vines around me and Christy and the old man and pulled them tight, bringing us closer and closer, until we were bound together as if we were sticks in a ball of twine.

Then, suddenly, as if a bubble had popped, the room was dark again. The visitors disappeared, and then the orange berries went out quietly, one by one, and the vines bound us less and less until they were gone. We sank onto the balsam boughs, Christy on one side of me, and Mickey on the other.

Christy fell asleep right away. I was feeling dizzy, but I wasn't falling asleep. It was like being stoned, maybe because I'd been asleep already. Mickey was staring at me intently. He didn't seem so much like an old man, just like another human being who was concerned about me.

"I'm okay," I said. "I'm just a bit out of breath."

He ran this hand down the center of my back to just below my waist, and pulled me towards him. He kissed me very lightly on the lips, and I could feel my whole body respond to those two points of contact, his hand and his lips. Now he didn't seem like an old man at all.

-Christy-

I can tell you that nobody was more surprised than I was to find out that the squatch was a girl. How could I have thought the squatch was a bear or an old guy? It must have been some trick of the light. But she had looked like a guy—how was I to know?

And of course, when I found myself in bed with this beautiful girl, what could I do? I was putty in her hands, just like with Andrea. Obviously she had targeted me right from the beginning, there at the pool. She didn't say anything about that, but she didn't have to. I could tell.

So Mickey was there, she was willing, and I was certainly able. That was just how it goes sometimes: the right moment, the right two people. Andrea was asleep next to us, but I knew that this was okay, that she wouldn't wake up. I mean, she was out cold.

All I can say is we had a blast. Mickey was hot, she was juicy, she was gorgeous, and boy did she give good head.

Afterward, when all the other people appeared, it was strange but familiar to get up and join them. Mickey gave me a tall hat. It was a sort of a wedding, I think, but I was not a one-hundred-percent co-operative bridegroom. I just walked around in a fog, and then Andrea woke up and she walked around, too, with me and with Mickey, and I thought that made everything okay. The three of us being together like that, I mean. Andrea must have known, when she woke up and saw us. But I thought, what would Andrea do, now that Mickey and I had this thing going?

The other people, they had ropes of bittersweet, which I thought was odd. I'd never seen real bittersweet in the Northwest. They have something else here that they call bittersweet, the stuff with the little purple flowers and the red fruit, but I call it nightshade. Where I grew up, the bittersweet has orange berries with little yellow shells that cover them. Beautiful, but it strangles everything that comes near it. My mom used to have me busting my butt out there in the back field, cutting bittersweet away from the trees, because it would just take over, climb all the trees and overwhelm them. It was real pretty in the wintertime, though, with the yellow and orange berries sticking up in the snow. So I loved seeing those people with the bittersweet vines, even though I knew that if it took hold, they'd never get rid of it.

Andrea was dancing faster and faster, sort of pulling us along in this frenzy. The visitors roped her in with the bittersweet, her and me and Mickey, all together, until we fell on the bed of balsam branches, all hot and sweaty, and I had a brief thought that maybe we could get a threesome going, and I was getting a hard-on, and then I was coming and falling into a deep sleep at the same time. You know, a lot of that night is just a blur to me. That was some weed, I'll tell you. I don't remember any more.

The next morning, the three of us were like old married people, chewing on roots around the fire, eating some kind of a porridge of seeds. Andrea and Mickey, they seemed pretty friendly, in spite of what went on last night. So things were okay in that area. I didn't notice the musky smell anymore. Probably that was what I smelled like myself at this point.

There was a thing about caves that I actually hadn't thought through: they're dark. If you stay in your cave, the sun might as well never have come up. I needed to get out of the dark, get outside, take a dump, and prepare for a long ski out, maybe through the woods, the way we'd come up. I hoped there was a forest road nearby, but my guess was the sasquatch was a deep-woods guy, as far from civilization as he could get.

And we needed to get going pretty soon too.

So I put on my parka, and went out to the mouth of the cave, and you know what? It was raining, raining hard. Water was flowing in the snow, down the slots of our tracks, down the slope of the mountain, down through the trees, down to the hot spring, down to the road, which was, by my guess, a couple thousand feet below us. Staying over had not been a very good idea, if getting home soon was our goal.

But I'll tell you what I do when something doesn't work out: I go with the flow. I let life keep happening. I keep an eye out for opportunity.

And, to my mind, the opportunity at this point was to find out about the treasure. Easiest thing would be to get the info directly from Mickey, not poke around in acres of rock. Might involve smoking a few more joints, a bit more bonding. I could handle that. Andrea would find something to keep her busy.

-Andrea-

Mickey wasn't bad in bed. He was younger than I had thought, and he gave good head. He was a lot gentler than Christy, too. Christy likes it kind of rough and fast. Not that there was anything wrong with that, but Mickey was a gentleman, and quite attractive in a way. Kind of hairy, though. Some guys are just, like, bears if they don't wax it all off, but I'd never slept with a guy who was as hairy as Mickey.

So he was talking afterward, real quiet, the way some guys do, just trying to find out a little about you, and maybe trying to impress you a bit with who they are. He mentioned this workshop that he had. To hear him tell it, he could make anything he wanted, which I guess explains about the bowls and the cups. Well, what he said was "it" could make anything he needed, but he was a little vague about what "it" was. Didn't trust me, I guess. But he said he'd bring me something nice, something that was useful. I wondered what he meant, because if he could have anything he needed, why would he be living in a cave?

Maybe "it" was the secret treasure that Christy told me about. I asked if it could make money. But Mickey said he didn't need money. I guess that made sense to me: having what you need is not the same thing as having money. Because the only thing that you *need* about money is the ability to turn it into something else.

So the next day, Mickey gave me a silk undershirt. It was warm and light, and I could wear it without Christy wondering what it was and where it came from. It was kind of a weird color, not olive-green, not an earth-tone, but something that could be described as either of those things. Mickey said it was a wedding present, that we were now, the three of us, bound to one another.

I noticed that Christy has a new wool hat, because he'd lost his old one when we skied up to the cave. I wondered if Mickey had given it to him, also as a wedding present. I bet that was true. I wondered what else it could make.

In the days after our first night together, I didn't see any of the other people who were there that night. It was like there wasn't anybody in the cave but the three of us. I figured there were other caves with the other people in them, or maybe they lived further back in our cave. I asked Mickey where his neighbors went, they seemed so nice. He said something about they were "respecting our privacy." Okay, okay. If he didn't want to give me a straight answer, he didn't have to.

So I thought I'd take a look further back in the cave, and just see if there was any sign of people living back there, plus maybe that was where the warehouse was. Maybe they were all together in a workshop there, making pottery and knitting hats and tie-dying shirts, like some ancient hippie cult. I mean, anything seemed possible.

I got one of the oil lamps, which are pretty bright, and I walked back in the cave, which got narrower as I went back. It wasn't scary, as it would have been when we first came to the cave. It was a bit damp, sure, but it wasn't dripping, and there didn't seem to be any animals or big spiders moving around. When I got way to the back, the cave was much more like a tunnel than the big room it seemed like out near the front.

On one of the walls, I noticed some painting, right on the rock. A large group of dancing figures, one with a tall hat, just like the one Mickey had worn at our wedding. They were carrying garlands of red-orange berries with yellow casings. Bittersweet.

The figures had recognizable faces. There was Mickey, there was Christy, there was me. And there was my mother. Had my mother been there at the wedding? I didn't remember her being there, for sure, and it seemed so unlikely that she would have just appeared there in the woods and gone away without taking me back with her.

Had Mickey come back here and painted this scene? I was touched, really. It was sweet, in a mystical sort of way. I stood there looking at the drawings for a little while, and my oil lamp started guttering. The figures had looked so lifelike, and now they started to move. My mother turned to look at me, and she seemed to be speaking. What was she saying? The oil lamp guttered more, and went out.

I stood there in the dark, not knowing which way to move, and for the first time I was afraid. I heard my mother's voice. "Calm down,

Andrea," she said. "You never get anywhere by panicking." I waited for a minute, and took a few deep breaths. The darkness did not seem so deep. Was my mother there with me or not?

As I stood debating the question, it became clear that there was a dull light coming from a part of the darkness, and I thought that maybe that was the direction from which I'd come. "Go ahead," said my mother's voice. "Trust yourself." Well, that certainly sounded like my mother. All that new-age crap. I walked towards the dim light, and as I walked the light got stronger. Soon I was back at the front of the cave again.

Christy and Mickey weren't anywhere to be seen. I looked out the front of the cave, and it was fucking pouring down rain. Where had they gone? Mickey's little house was empty. I yelled out a bit, calling Christy's name. Everything seemed so much like a dream. Was I on some kind of strange drug? Was I in the woods at all? Was I at my mom's house, and having some kind of a psychotic episode? I thought I was past that kind of thing, really.

The fire was still going, and I lit a couple of the oil lamps from it. Just about the time I was starting to get worried, Christy and Mickey came out of the back of the cave. Christy had an oil lamp. I wondered where they had been, since I hadn't seen any light back there at all. They looked funny, but I couldn't put my finger on why. Christy had his hand on Mickey's shoulder, but he moved it when he saw me.

"Andrea! There you are!" he said, as though he's been looking for me. I know that lying tone.

"Where'd you go? I was worried," I said.

"Everything's fine. Just go with the flow, babe. Just go with the flow." That's good advice if you've got a flow to go with. Christy did, Christy always did, but he wasn't going to tell me about it.

Mickey had started poking at the fire, stirring it up, and was putting the big pot on the hook over it, and tossing stuff in the pot. I thought maybe I could help with that, and pretty soon we were working together on chopping up stuff and it was starting to smell pretty good. Christy didn't make himself useful, but then he never does, you know?

I asked Mickey about the paintings I'd seen in the back of the cave. He said maybe we should go back there while the stew was cooking, and he squeezed my shoulder. Christy was nodding off anyway, so we slipped away easily, grabbing a lamp on the way out.

Walking towards the back of the cave, I noticed more pictures and some strange writing, like lines and circles. I asked Mickey what it meant.

"Instructions and rules, mostly. Stuff you need to know to raise your kids right."

"Do you have kids?"

"Mmmmph." It was a yes, I thought.

"Where are they? Are they grown up?"

He made some more noises. "Old enough. Scattered."

Poor guy, I thought. Getting old up here in the mountains, and his kids off somewhere, probably don't visit. I wonder if they even know he's living in a cave now.

"That was nice, last night," I said. "I was wondering about the pictures in the cave, of us dancing." Mickey didn't say anything, He just kept leading me deeper into the cave. "Haven't we already gone past the painting I was talking about?"

"It's a circular path," said Mickey. "We'll come by it again." We walked, and it did seem as though we were going uphill and around a curve.

This isn't what I thought it was like, but I have to agree that it did look as though the picture was coming up again.

"There!" I said. "There's the picture." We stopped, because I made us stop. Mickey would have continued on by.

"See that?" He nodded. "That's us there, isn't it?" He nodded again. "And there, towards the back, that's my mother." He nodded again.

"Okay," I said. "How did my mother get there?"

"Your mother is a very strong soul," said Mickey. "Whatever has been done to her, she has fought back, and has entered the realm from which there is movement back and forth."

"I don't understand," I said. "Do you know my mother?"

Mickey kissed me. "And you are also a very strong soul. I am sure I am seeing your mother in you."

"Was she here? Do you know my mother? What is she doing in the cave?"

"We need to keep walking, just past here," said Mickey. He moved a curtain aside, as we passed, and there was a small room cut into the rock. We stopped and went inside, and he was so nice and gentle, and he has a deliciously masculine scent.

-Christy-

So we figured to stay for a few days. Seemed like the easiest thing to do. A lot pleasanter than walking down the mountain in the mud.

Mickey was totally great, and Andrea seemed to be okay with what was going down, whatever she thought. She never said a word to me about it.

Mickey and I had a lot of chances to get together, and we took advantage of them. She was a total delight. Not to say that Andrea wasn't neat, but it's the unexpected treat that is sweetest, isn't it? Even Andrea would understand that.

Andrea and Mickey seem to be becoming friends too, which is more than I could have hoped for. They went off for long walks into the cave together, and they always came back hand-in-hand and smiling. I wondered sometimes if they were talking about me, but Andrea had no idea, and Mickey seemed to live on another planet when it came to fucking.

The few days became a week, and the rain continued. It was a lot of work, just to get water and roots and dry wood for fuel. I always liked to camp out, but then I had those packets of freeze-dried shit. The week became several, and then a month. But I will never complain about rainy weather again. It was the happiest time of my life, at least to date: two women, both of them great in bed, and each of them devoted to me.

Though, clearly, Mickey was a lot more devoted than Andrea. This is completely understandable, and I don't fault Andrea for it in the least. She was much more the modern woman, with her complaints, and, let's face it, her neurotic shit. There are consequences for that, is all. I totally support her in her struggle for getting a handle on what goes on between men and women, I just think she's taking her own sweet time at it.

I asked Mickey a few times about the people who were there that first night. Who were they? Where are they? How come they don't come around at all, and she said they were giving us the time we needed to create our family, our oneness. And this made sense, though I did feel I was getting the shut-up explanation. I mean, it's no skin off my ass if her friends don't want to come around and see us. Really. What do I care?

But they never did come around during the daytime. Or even at night, except that once. And we were there for, well, it was nearly six weeks, I think. We stayed—and I would have stayed longer, let me be clear about it—until Andrea started throwing up and said she thought she was pregnant.

I tried to convince her that this was no problem. Lots of women give birth at home, away from hospitals, but she wasn't hearing any of this.

She said she had to go home, she had to get hold of her mother, and she had to have some answers. Naturally, I thought the answers thing meant she'd finally decided that it wasn't okay about me and Mickey, but that wasn't what Andrea meant at all.

Turns out she'd been stewing on this wonky idea that her mother was some kind of alien or something, and that she was in like psychic communication with her. Fuck. Andrea's mother is the least-psychic middle-aged woman I have ever met. She's all business, she's an accountant or something, and she always treats me as though I had a communicable disease, which I'm quite sure I don't have, and if I did, she'd be the last person I'd give it to.

When Andrea told me she was pregnant and wanted to go home, I confess I had to think about it for a little. Not that I wouldn't have taken her home, but I needed to think about what I would say to Mickey, and whether I would want to come back to the cave after taking Andrea home. On the other hand, Andrea and her child were my responsibility too, and it's funny how, well, connected I felt to her, knowing it was my kid she was pregnant with.

When I talked to Mickey, it turned out she was very cool with it and didn't seem surprised or hurt. Kind of the ideal woman.

And then she told me that she might be pregnant too. As you might imagine, this was both a pleasure and a shock. Two babies? I was always aware that unprotected sex could create a baby: I was completely with that program. But I confess I hadn't considered the idea that unprotected sex could create two babies in a month.

Okay, okay, it was dumb of me. I hadn't thought it through, okay? But I can tell you I was pretty proud of myself. Or at least that was my first reaction. And then I thought, well, I am going to have to get a job.

But the women, Andrea and Mickey, were so much more practical. With them, it was always, what am I going to do now? Andrea was for going home to her mother, and Mickey was for staying there in the cave and giving birth all alone by herself.

This was a little too close to the mama-bear-baby-bear thing for me, but Mickey seemed so at home with the idea, it seemed to make sense to me as a solution. Only it wasn't one, was it?

So when Andrea told me that she wanted to go back to the city, I figured I'd take her there and then come back to be with Mickey. After all, Andrea has her mother, right? And Mickey hasn't got anybody, since her friends—her supposed friends, the useless twats—never come around.

I tell this to Mickey, figuring it'll make her feel better. Instead, she goes all weird on me. Like, we've never fought. We've never even disagreed. But all of a sudden, she's like, "How could you?" As if I'm some monster because I want to stay with her.

"Andrea will need you," she says. "How could you leave her at a time like this?"

"Her mother will take care of her," I say, wondering what the big deal is. "Her mother will, in fact, take much better care of her than I could."

"That old bat?" says Mickey. "She can scarcely feed herself. She can barely walk and chew gum at the same time. Look what happened to Andrea, under her care."

"What? What happened to Andrea?"

"She was running wild, and Lord knows what all. She got involved with *you*."

My feelings were hurt, but I wasn't inclined to let her know that. "So did you."

"That's different. I can take care of myself. I know what I want and how to get it. But Andrea just sleepwalks though life, accepting whatever is handed to her, not taking charge. Somebody needs to take charge."

"Excuse me for not grasping your point here, but what's your point? If I'm such a dolt, how come you want me to take care of Andrea and the baby?"

"That's a very good question, Christy. But I'm not going to answer it just now. You just get her out of here and get her back to Seattle safely. Can you do that?"

Yeah, I could do that, and I did. But the price of that is I was shut out of Mickey's life. She made it clear she wanted me out, and I didn't need to come back.

-Andrea-

As we left, I was not sure whether I was going home or leaving it, going out into a strange and dangerous world. I wasn't anxious to go back to the city with Christy. Would he and I stay together? I didn't want to be with him, but I had to worry about having a baby by myself and taking care of it.

I understood Christy better than I ever had before, but I didn't like what I understood. Never had, I guess, but when it was just me, it didn't seem so important, as long as life was interesting. Maybe I hate being bored almost as much as Christy.

We slogged down the side of the mountain, carrying our skis. It was a pleasant-enough spring day, a little overcast. The snow was long gone, and the trees were starting to bud green. There was skunk cabbage poking up in the wet places, and some little white flowers here and there. What were they? I couldn't remember. As we walked, everything that had happened in the past six weeks seemed like an extended dream.

It was a hassle getting down to the car, because the fire road in some places was pretty soggy. When we got down to the main road and looked for our car, of course it was gone. "Forest Service towed it, babe," said Christy. Well, duh. We started walking, and after a few miles we got a lift from a guy in a pickup truck.

"Mud skiing?" the guy says when he stops, nodding at our skis. A humorist.

Christy says, "We been up the mountain for a while."

"Whoa," said the guy. "Are you those two skiers vanished a month ago? You're alive?"

"Six weeks ago," said Christy, "but who's counting? I think we're alive."

"Rescue copters were over here for three days, combing the area. How do feel? Need water? Something to eat? You want me to drive you to a hospital?"

"I just want to get my car back, man. I need to get my girlfriend here to her mom's house. She's pregnant. My girlfriend, I mean."

"I think I better take you to the sheriff's office. They'll know what to do. Where you been, anyway?"

"Ripvanwinkleville," said Christy.

Great. The sheriff's office. I hope Christy's not packing out any of that homegrown.

-Christy-

When we got back, I figured I had to do something fast to support me and Andrea and the baby. I mean, Andrea wasn't going to be able to bring in much from waitressing after a few months.

I figured there should be a book in there somewhere, if I could just find somebody to write it. Any real writer would jump at the chance. So I got hold of this guy I knew at *The Stranger*. We'd talked about doing this Hunter Thompson thing once, over a pitcher or two of margaritas, but nothing ever came of it. He wasn't against the idea, but he said it would be easier to sell the book if it was a news story first. He said if the story had legs, it would walk, and then he'd write the book. First he had to finish a book on hiking in Peru, anyway. But he thought his friend Darla could help with the news story.

Darla was kind of a mistake—all she knew was the confession market. So the story broke in *News of the World*, and everybody thought it was a big joke. I guess I can't blame them. That headline wouldn't have been my first choice: *He fathered a bigfoot baby… and became a deadbeat dad.*

I got phone calls and email from all my old buddies, who basically figured I'd pulled off a scam of some kind. I mean, it's nice to be congratulated, but if it's your life and not a scam, it's a little embarrassing.

It wasn't my idea to contact Maury. That was Darla, came up with that. I had had my sights on Oprah, actually. A lovely woman, a bit matronly, but clearly someone who could converse on a higher plane, who would not judge me because I had left my little one behind with a loving parent. I could hear her: she would extend her generous hand to me, and she would say, "You sharing your story here with us today has brought us all a bit closer to an understanding of our relationship to the wilderness." That's how I wanted to tell my story.

But Darla couldn't get the Oprah people to even return her calls, so she went on this website and sent my story to *The Maury Show*. So we don't hear from them, and we don't hear from them, and we don't hear from them. They are really into deadbeat dads there, which isn't my story, in my opinion. But like Darla said, we didn't have time to wait for them to do a show on bigfoot babies. I had to fit into the story they were doing.

So, anyway, I went to the show, and they had a woman up there and three deadbeat dads. Maury talked for a while, and the woman cried, and then the deadbeat dads talked. And then I interrupted, and I took the dads to task for not taking better care of their kids. I really pitched into them. I was like, I'd give anything to get back to my kid and take care of him or her. And this was true, or it seems true when I think about it. Anyway, I did my stuff, and pretty soon I was sitting up there with the deadbeat dads, and we were all crying and Maury was comforting us.

The part I didn't understand was that not only did Mickey not want to spend any time with me, but neither did Andrea. She was into the whole idea of having a baby, but not into the idea of me anymore.

So then, Maury kind of jumped all over me, y'know? He asked how come if I was such a good dad I wasn't supporting my kid either?

Even the deadbeat dads joined in. I think this is the result of all those therapy programs at prisons. We've raised a whole generation of ex-cons who are in touch with their sensitive sides.

It was rough—Oprah, like I said, would have been a much better choice—but I stood up for myself, and Maury even said I was making a good case for parental responsibility in the abstract, if not in actuality. Eventually, we all hugged, and I got out of there alive.

The Maury people liked how I handled it, and they did a follow-up show a few weeks later, where they had me working with this psychic who said she could lead me to the cave again, but she couldn't. We got a couple of TV shows out of it, including one where people who've been cheated by psychics confront the cheats. And then I met this guy that wanted to do a film script. When he finished it, he said, he was hoping they could get Ben Stiller or Luke Wilson to play me. I always liked Owen Wilson better than Luke, but apparently he wasn't available or something.

-Andrea-

Well, it's like I thought. Christy always lands on his feet.

We had a hard time getting along after we got back to Seattle. Before, we had mostly the same opinions about things, but now, it seemed like whatever he wanted to do was totally screwed. I don't know why, but I just didn't want to go along with his schemes. Me being pregnant made a difference, for sure. Christy was completely sure it's his baby, but how could he be so sure of that? I didn't rub his nose in it, but I think he knew there was something going on between me and Mickey. He would believe what he wanted to believe, just like he would tell the stories that get him the biggest reaction from other people, when you got right down to it, whether he believed them or not.

He wasn't a bad dad, though. He's very into the baby, and he doesn't seem to care whose it is. When I was pregnant, he was always bugging me to eat right, and exercise, and all this stuff. And once little Baker arrived, Christy was all over me with baby-care advice from the shopping channel.

But, give me a break, I knew how to take care of a baby. I used to be a babysitter. It's no big deal. Just keep them breathing and don't drop them.

And of course my mother was delighted. She certainly didn't think it was Christy's baby. When Baker was born, she took one look at him, and she said, "We've got to talk." And of course, when we sat down to talk, which was, with one thing and another, a month later, she wormed the whole story out of me, just as you have.

"I knew it," she said. "I knew it. I had a dream."

The thing that I wondered about was the story that Christy told—about him and the bigfoot baby. I mean, I'm the one that should have been on Oprah or something, technically. Mickey threw us out of the cave, after all—so didn't that make *him* the deadbeat dad? I mean, really, if Mickey is Baker's dad?

It's kind of soon to tell, but there's something about Baker that is *so* not like Christy.

So I watched *The Maury Show*. It's not something I'd ordinarily do, but I had to watch it, when he said he'd be on it.

It was a show on deadbeat dads, and while "deadbeat" probably does describe Christy pretty well, I didn't figure that he was completely aware of that. So I thought there would be some acknowledgement by Christy of just where he went wrong, you know?

So I tuned in, and it wasn't like Christy was actually on the show: Christy was in the audience. Why did I believe him? I thought. Had again.

And then, when he spoke up from the audience, and accused those young guest guys, I thought, what?! He wasn't telling this straight. What was going on? And then I realized that he was talking about Mickey.

He even mentioned his name: he even called him Mickey. But he was talking about him like he was a girl. This I didn't understand. Christy embroiders, you know, but he doesn't usually tell bald-faced lies. It's too easy to get caught, for one thing, telling bald-faced lies. Christy is smarter than that.

And he was crying like she broke his heart and stole his baby. Mickey? Hey! It's my heart that was broken. I'm the one who got seduced and abandoned. Mickey's the deadbeat dad, not you, I thought. And I've got the baby.

So after the show, I went to the Maury people. I told them Christy was taking advantage of them. They weren't interested in that story. And why should they be? They had a good story already in Christy. But I said, you're on a roll here. If they kept it going, and maybe they could bring Mickey in, too.

They liked that idea. "Do you know where she is?" the guy asked.

"He's a he!" I said. "Mickey is a he. I ought to know. He got me pregnant. I don't know why Christy is pretending he's a girl. This is my story, and he swiped it!"

I would have thought they'd be surprised by this, but it turned out they're used to this kind of a story. If it's a love triangle, they can keep bringing people back until the cows come home. If it's got a bi angle, they love that too.

So I met with them again, with a story doctor. Very professional, very slick. They do this hundreds of times a season. Kind of creepy, actually.

I had little Baker with me, 'cause I was nursing him, and they glommed onto him. "So this is Bigfoot's baby?" they asked. For Pete's sake, he's just a baby, I said. Leave him out of this.

So the deal was, they were not going to tell Christy that I was going to be on the show, or Mickey, if they could find him. They kept calling Mickey "she."

-Christy-

What did I look like? I wondered. Wardrobe had tried to spiff me up a bit, with a haircut and some clothes that weren't too bad. They even shaved me, sort of, with a razor that left me with a nice even stubble.

I wasn't expecting Andrea. They had made her up to look very wholesome and earth-mother-y, with a peasant skirt and embroidered blouse, like some sort of old-country woman headed for the market. Her hair was wound into a braid, and the braid was curled into a large round bun at the back. I felt like I'd been set up. Where was the hot babe with the welding gun who had won my heart at Burning Man? This was a mom!

They brought us out like the contestants in some old game show, sitting on chairs in front of the audience.

Then Maury came out and he introduced us, and he started asking us questions about where we live and how we met. Pretty soon we started talking, and I didn't think it would amount to all that, or that we could talk about it in public.

Then they started showing the videos of the kid. I mean, babies are babies, and we're hardwired to find them cute. But gee whiz, the audience went a little wild at the baby video. I admit, Baker is a cute kid. I looked a lot like that when I was a toddler. I can show you the photos.

And then they said they had photos of the other baby, but they ran videos of some bear cub instead. The audience was confused, but game. It was a tease, I thought. They don't have any photos, because they've never been able to find Mickey, because I've never been able to find Mickey. Cute little cub, though.

And then they brought out Andrea's mother.

-Andrea-

So my mother was on the show, which I wouldn't have agreed to if anybody had asked me. And she and Maury, I swear, they tag-teamed me, and pretty soon I was telling the unexpurgated version.

I said, which I had never said out loud to anyone, even Christy, that I didn't think the baby is Christy's. My mom said, basically, that she certainly hoped not, and that Christy was an aimless good-for-nothing.

Christy acted like he was outraged, and he threw himself off the chair and onto the floor and kicked his heels a lot and yelled. Since he knows perfectly well how my mother feels about him, I felt this was a little stagy, but I think it's something that men have to do on *The Maury Show*.

I said that I was just a bit annoyed that my own mother would rather see me with a fatherless kid from some hookup with a grizzly halfway up a volcano, than for me to have a baby with Christy.

But my mom just looked at me and said, "That's the way it is."

Maury was still in control, though, whatever my mother thought, and he started talking to my mom about her entirely misspent youth. And she told this perfect stranger—she doesn't even watch his show—stuff she had never told me in my entire life. My mother told Maury that she used to hike on Mt. Baker, and that she, in fact, had had her own fling with the sasquatches, way back before I was born.

She made it sound like a picnic of some kind. No long weeks in a cave. It was summer, and the weather was warm and sunny. It was like some fantasy romance. The love sasquatches. I don't know why I got so angry about that.

But I was pretty incensed by it all. My mom had always been so tight with the details about my dad that I assumed he was some kind of criminal. And now I find out he's a sasquatch, and on network television. If I were a typical Maury guest, I'd be jumping up and down and crying.

But I know that doesn't work with my mom. So I just ask her: Was Mickey my father?

She said, "Honey, I don't know. It was a long time ago. Life was different then, before I took the accounting course. I didn't always keep track of stuff."

There was a lot of yelling from the audience, some of them laughing and some scolding her.

And then they brought out Mickey.

-Christy-

I don't know how they do this stuff. I certainly didn't have anything to do with it. They didn't ask me for any advice or help. But somehow they found Mickey, or maybe Mickey just decided to allow herself to be found.

Either way, she walked out onto the stage at *The Maury Show* and paused. She looked great. Elegant, all spiffed up in some kind of classy New York clothes. She looked like Candice Bergen, maybe, or that woman who lives in Connecticut and does the magazine—Martha Stewart. Older, you know, and maybe a little authoritative, but still pretty great-looking. I guess I hadn't thought about it, but maybe Mickey does that craft stuff too, like Martha—that's how she gets all those hats and bowls and coffee cups and stuff.

They told me later that, to the studio audience, Mickey looked like a sasquatch. Some people screamed, other people laughed. But I wasn't paying a lot of attention to the audience reaction at the time.

Of course, I wanted to run to Mickey, but Maury gestured to me and Andrea to stay in our seats. He went over to her, rather cautiously, I thought, and guided her to a seat next to Andrea's mother, who looked at Mickey speculatively.

Andrea looked at Mickey too. Tears welled up in her eyes, and she said to me and the studio audience, "He's lost weight."

I swear, I thought at the time, "She's not even seeing the same person I'm seeing." I said, "Looks to me like she gained about ten pounds, but I figure, she had a baby, she's going to gain a little weight."

Andrea looked at me intently for the first time, like she was actually listening to me. "What are you talking about?"

I said, "Well, you gained weight."

Andrea gave me the evil eye. I said, "I'm talking about Mickey, that's who. She had the baby, and she's still carrying a few extra pounds. But it's nothing to me. She looks great. You look great. Jeez."

Then Andrea said to me, right on camera in front of the TV audience, "Mickey is a man, you idiot."

I was surprised, but I was not going to put up with being treated that way. Idiot. Huh. I said, "I understand how you could have thought that, but the fact is that she's a girl. I found out for myself in the traditional manner."

Of course by now, there were more people in the audience screaming and laughing. I've done some street theater, and this happens—people act out, and certainly on *The Maury Show* the audience is encouraged to act out. I've found that the best way to deal with it is to ignore it.

And then Maury turned to me and Andrea, and he looked sort of sad. "Christy and Andrea," he said. "Is this your friend Mickey?" We each nodded. "And you each say you've slept with Mickey?" We each nodded. Andrea's mother just shrugged, and then she nodded too.

"Well, you've shown us here today that not everyone is seduced by Hollywood's ideal of beauty..." I was about to object to that statement, when I saw Mickey sort of focus on Maury. He did kind of a double-take, then said, "...though of course you... you would carry it to a... new standard." He shook his head a little, like there was something wrong with his eyes.

Then Maury pulled himself together and held up a manila envelope. "I've got the tests right here," he said. *The Maury Show* is very supportive with the paternity test thing, and I was looking forward to the results. Maury tore the envelope open and pulled out the lab report.

At that point, Mickey stood up and said, "I don't think we need to hear this." She gestured with one hand, and an opening appeared in the floor of the stage right in front of us. It looked like it led into a cave, and it sure was dark down there.

Then people started coming out of it, people with tall hats and clothing that looked like it was made from dead oak leaves. They were carrying bittersweet vines and two babies, neither of whom looked to me like a bear cub, though I've been told that, to the audience, they both looked like bear cubs.

The people in hats danced with Mickey and Maury and Andrea's mother, and they handed the babies about while they danced. Maury danced, but Andrea and I did not dance. We watched, slightly paralyzed, while Mickey and Andrea's mother entangled themselves in the bittersweet, and then entangled Maury. Then they all danced down into the trapdoor with the babies, even Maury.

But Maury looked a little worried, just a tiny bit. As he descended down into the floor, he looked right at the cameraman and said, "Keep it rolling, Anthony." He disappeared into the cave, wrapped in bittersweet. Maury was a pro, I thought, and I respected that.

Andrea and I were left sitting on the sound stage, looking at the audience. I'm sure you've seen the clip on YouTube.

IN THE FOREST OF THE QUEEN

GWYNETH JONES

Aymon Bock was not taken with the Montsec American Monument. It seemed inflated: a Doughboys' monster donut, dominating a landscape that *really* didn't need any more reminders of war and death. Surely the hectares of white crosses, another thick-sown field of them every time you turned a bend, were sufficient? The only way to escape the thing was to drive up there, which Aymon and his wife Viola duly did. They left the car, climbed a momentous flight of steps and walked around the circuit of massive fluted columns. Built in 1930, damaged in WWII, restored in 1948.

"Designed by Egerton Swartwout," remarked Viola. "Sounds like a German name, and it looks like Nazi architecture, isn't that ironic."

"The Doughboys didn't fight Nazis. They were here in 1918, they fought one of the last great battles of the Great War, down there below—"

Viola sighed and nodded. She knew all about the Doughboys of the American Expeditionary Force, their gallant part in licking Kaiser Bill; the various rationales suggested for that nickname (the dumpling shape of an Infantryman's buttons, the dust of battle, a derogatory reference to apprentice bakers' boys...) The Doughboys were the reason, or one of the reasons, for this pilgrimage to North Eastern France.

The only other visitor was a stooped young man in mismatched tweed jacket and tan chinos, laden with camera equipment, who did not have kin remembered here, he was just interested in the AEF. So Aymon was in his element: pointing out his great-grandfather's name, explaining the strategic importance of the Meuse-Argonne offensive, General John J Pershing's objectives, the difficulties that beset the

American boys, in their biggest operation on French soil—and Viola was released to gaze in peace at the landscape of what had been the "St Mihiel salient." The wooded ridges, the lush green, lake-dotted plain, the tide of forest lapping at its shore.

Aymon remembered that his penchant for talking to strangers tended to get him into trouble with Viola, and he wanted her on his side, today of all days. He bid the young man from Kentucky a courteous goodbye, before he'd even scratched the surface of his knowledge, and came to join her.

"It looks so peaceful now."

"Did you know," said Viola, "this is *still* one of the most sparsely populated areas in Europe? Right here, practically next door to Paris, and all those big, packed, developed cities? It's a boneyard, a grave-yard, a derelict munitions dump. I warned you. Didn't I warn you? The eastern flank of *La Belle France* is just battlefield after battlefield. Who'd want to come here, work here? How do you plan to attract the good people?"

"Money," muttered Aymon. "Space, freedom, natural beauty. You're so wrong: this location is perfect. We'll be fighting them off with sticks—"

Aymon Bock was an extremely wealthy man. He'd been loaded before he was thirty, avoided getting his fingers burned in a long career of daring start-ups; and finally, in what he still felt was youthful middle age, he wanted to give something back. He looked on the grinning slackers who were this generation's overnight billionaires, not with envy but with trepidation; and felt his long-ago hippie roots stirring. He meant to do something *good*, and since this region of France was (according to family legend) his ancestral home, he had chosen the forests of Argonne for the site of his Foundation. Having a French son-in-law also helped; though Jean-Raoul had been almost as hard to convince as Viola herself.

"There's another Great War going on, Vi. The world's in crisis, don't you understand that? The Bock Foundation is going to be a beacon in the storm: here, where my people came from. I'm the one to do it, I know I am. I have the experience, the talent for spotting ventures that will *fly*, and for hiring the guys, the scientists, the technologists, who are really going places. I'm tired of all the defeatism, the denial and plain lies. It's time to get organised, pull together, and see this Global Warming, Climate Change bogey for what it is: a dazzling *opportunity*. A new industrial revolution."

"You're such a romantic. If you want to be a war hero like your great-granddaddy was, why don't you set up a Sustainable Technology Centre in the Sudan? Or closer to home, in Down South, Black Hispanic USA, the newest Desperate Developing Nation on the block?"

"I give a heap of money away to good causes, Vi. You know I do. But it's pouring water in a leaky bucket: and you know that too. A man like me, with my expertise, is better employed turning out new buckets."

"Those Developing Nations," remarked Viola, heading for the steps, "can be such a hassle to deal with. Where there's human suffering there's dirty politics. Business dies, and God forbid Aymon Bock should get his fingers burned at last."

"I'm doing this for you, too. It's going to reboot your career. You're going to design for me."

"Now you're talking crazy. Designers have to be cool, and middle-aged women are not cool. Only youth is cool, in a woman."

"That's ridiculous! That's antediluvian thinking, this is the Age of the Grey Tigress. What about Vivienne Westwood?"

"She's in fashion and she's pushing seventy. Thanks a lot."

"Hell, did I say the Bock Foundation? I misspoke myself. It's going to be the Viola Canning Bock Foundation."

Viola laughed, touched in spite of herself. Say what you like about Aymon Bock, he could do irony: he could laugh at himself. She took an antique Hermès scarf from her $6,000 shoulder bag, and tied it over her hair, Grace Kelly style. He liked to drive the gun-metal Aston Martin he'd chosen for this trip with the top down, and the wind in his golf-tan wrinkles.

Of course he did.

She was a disappointment to her husband because she'd taken a career break, long ago, and never got around to mending it. She couldn't convince him that it would be madness for her to return to the fray: a wealthy woman, playing with her husband's newest toy. She'd be a laughing stock. But Ay's own "career" was in the same state. The money produced itself now, without Aymon's assistance: churning out mounds and mounds of cash, like that infernal salt mill in the fairytale. The moneymaker and his wife were over. They were on the downslope, and this eco-technology fantasy just proved it.

"We're barely middle-aged," cried Aymon, as they drove away. "We have half our lives ahead!" And went off into one of his one-man brainstorms: Microgeneration. Virtual Tourism. The billions to be made in the development of *efficient* recycling. Get the basic patents, the ones that are going to change the entire world… We are both drowning, thought Viola, fully aware that her age was no excuse for anomie. We are both lost, we've always been lost. It's just that Ay doesn't know it. And deep inside her, like a tiny stone fetus curled around her heart, she felt what she might have been: shining, shining.

Discontent was all she had left, her only proof that life could have been better, could have been *wonderful*—

Down on the plain, when they finally reached the boundary of Aymon's new real estate, there was certainly a sense of crossing some kind of crucial border. The wide fields of ethanol-fated corn (where Aymon muttered about the dumb European energy policy, not yet woken up to the exploded concept of biofuels) gave way to water meadow; and then suddenly they faced a wall of trees. There was no signage. The road surface, equally suddenly, deteriorated to dirt, with a few scabby patches of asphalt.

"Are you sure this is the right place?"

Aymon had been enlarging on the fortunate partnership of Jean-Raoul and Madeleine. Their daughter the biochemist, brilliant and flighty, who'd taken up computer science as a sideline, currently spent her time modelling neurotransmitters, out in the wild blue yonder. Jean-Raoul Martigny, however, was a scientist with a sound business mind, always took Aymon's advice, understood that *sustainable* dies if it means *non-profit-making*.

He paused in this pleasurable rant—leaving Maddy with her head in the clouds, Raoul with his feet on the ground— and punched up the help menus on the dashboard map.

"Heck. Something's wrong with this—"

The Aston Martin was a beautiful car, and as guilt-free as a classic performance roadster can well be, but its subsystems had proved un-reliable. Or else there was something in the air, interfering with the signal… Aymon could feel the prickling heaviness, an electric storm on the way.

There was an old man watching them from the edge of the trees.

A welcome sight, in the ringing, silent *emptiness* of this countryside, where you could hardly believe that crowded old Western Europe was all around. Aymon had pulled up, meaning to try some diagnostics. He leaned out, and made his inquiry. The old fellow set down his axe—he really was carrying a long-handled, ancient-looking axe— and came ambling over, cautious of his joints as the Tin Woodsman.

"Hi," said Aymon, ever trustful of the universal power of the English language. "Would you mind telling us where we are, sir?"

The old fellow stared at the foreign car as if he'd never seen anything like it, and said something that Aymon didn't catch at all, except that the word *forêt* was in there. Viola explained the problem, in her passable French. The Tin Woodsman scratched his seamed and bristly chin, peered into the car and looked long at their GPS screen, shaking his head and murmuring, a voluble excursion, presumably in the local dialect: from which Viola could only snag "unbelievable!" She tried again, and managed to learn that he'd never heard of the projected Bock Foundation, and didn't recognise the number of the minor Departmental Road they were looking for—

"But there *are* roads through the forest?" she persisted, still in French.

The old man looked completely blank, a senior moment, then he spoke again, in a careful, strangely accented English. "There are plenty of paths." He smiled. "Perhaps too many. You can go in, easily. But you may not come out." He nodded, pleased with his joke, and went back to his axe.

"Let's go," snapped Viola. "We were heading in the right direction five minutes ago. And we have the paper maps. "

"What a damned language," remarked Aymon, consolingly, as they passed into the embrace of the trees, and the world behind disappeared. "Don't feel bad. It's okay in print, but I can never understand a word when they start talking. Beyond restaurant dialogue, anyhow."

"I understand French. I can't do quaint dialects."

"Yeah, well. They always remember a little English in the end."

The forest had a placid, timeless air of expectation: as if it had been waiting for them, and welcomed them with quiet satisfaction. The trees were poplar and ash, oak, beech and hazel, and other nameless European species. None of any great size. The understory was a mass of climbers, vines and briars and ferns: but there was nothing sinister, no dripping, ghostly lichens. Still no signage, and the GPS screen was a fuzz of grey. Aymon grinned at his wife, and took a turn at random down another of the dirt-paved tracks. He drove slowly, appreciating the experience. Strangely, although the driving surface was horrible, the broad verges were evenly shorn to the height of a healthy suburban lawn. Maybe the Tin Woodsman came down here regularly, on a horse-drawn mower—

"Are you trying to get us lost? I should be throwing out a trail of breadcrumbs," Viola commented, uneasily.

"I want to get a feel for the place. Never been here in the flesh before. We'll meet a landmark of some kind soon. If we don't, there's a compass on the dash. You're sure we have the right *numéro* in that map folder of yours?"

Viola was not sure. She kept paper maps out of nostalgia for the old days, when she'd been the map-navigating queen of their travels; but she'd come to rely on that fickle modern technology… She decided, in the interests of marital harmony, that she wouldn't check the folder yet.

Aymon had been noticing long, regular shapes among the trees by the roadside: mostly wrapped in some kind of tarp. Then he saw the numbered tags, like mailboxes without the mailbox, and it dawned on him that he was seeing cords of firewood. The forest belonged to the commune; to the local people. It was not farmed for timber, it was portioned out, household by household, for winter fuel: which was sound energy policy for a change. This was one of the rights he'd agreed to respect, for an interim period, while he investigated the issue. But now the woodpiles, the dismembered flesh of the wood laid out like that, right under the noses of the living trees, were somehow very disturbing. He found himself wondering how the forest felt about the arrangement. Death by inches, endlessly repeated. Reminded him of the story of the hillbilly with the three-legged pig.

"*A hog as good as that, you don't eat him all at once…*"

Viola felt nothing, except a practical concern about the coming storm—something in the air, not exactly oppressive, but electric. She looked up. The sun was invisible, the flowing band of sky was cloudless, a billowing deep blue canopy, a bride's train, a robe… At last they reached a crossing place where several tracks met, around an open green crown. Aymon pulled up, carefully parallel to the mown grass, as if he feared a sudden rush of traffic. The sun was still invisible, the electric sky without a cloud, the forest vistas unbroken. A jaybird flashed across the clearing and called loudly, one indignant note. They smiled at each other.

"The old guy said we were '*À L'Orée de la Forêt de la Reine*'," said Viola. "On the threshold of the Forest of the Queen. So we're in the right woods, unless there are multiple Queens' Forests around here. Which queen was it, Ay? When did she reign? What was her name?"

"I don't remember. Could be Marie-Antoinette for all I know. The history's on file, it's in the documents, we can find out. Let's take a walk."

"Not out of sight of the car."

"Okay, okay… Hey, I have my pocket knife, I'll cut flashes on the trees. It's just a small, suburban, European forest, honey. It won't bite."

"Oh no? I bet there are mosquitoes."

"So bring your repellent."

Aymon didn't suffer from mosquito bites. Viola hated them, and hated the smell of any effective repellent, but she shared his mood. There was something about this place that made you want to let go and *drift…* They took one of the tracks, deeper into the world of green. There were mosquitoes. She stopped to anoint her bare legs and stooped lower, curious about the texture of the turf. It didn't seem to have been mown recently, every shining blade was pristine, curved like a baby's fingernail—

"What's the matter?"

She was startled at the edge on his voice. Was the forest, like Viola, a disappointment? Or was he spooked? She felt a little spooked herself: the enticing lethargy had a thread of tension in it, a tug of adrenalin. An insect, a butterfly with pretty marbled wings, looked up at her from the grassblades under her nose, and seemed to *wink* one of its faceted eyes.

What the hell—?

"A butterfly. A really tiny one, very pretty. It's gone now."

"I wonder who does the mowing," muttered Aymon. "And *why*. What for? I don't see this as a picnic spot—"

But the reproach of the living harvest, those piles of dead limbs, had aroused his defiance, so he proposed they leave the path. Viola followed him without a murmur, though she was hardly dressed for it. She prided herself on her docility: it was one way of dealing with constant low-level despair. Aymon could complain of her negativity, her lack of enthusiasm, her sarcasm. He could never call her high maintenance.

She picked her way, getting scratched, hoping this would soon be over. Aymon kept stopping and peering at bark, examining leaves. She knew he was looking for an unusual bug to match the "pretty butterfly" he'd missed. It was one of his strengths, maybe all wealthy men were the same. He was *always* playing to win, every second, on every scale. It could be exhausting. But it was Viola who first noticed that the leaf mould underfoot was alive with hopping, creeping dark-skinned little frogs.

"My God," said Aymon.

"So *many* of them—" whispered Viola, horrified, afraid to take another step, repulsed at the thought of carnage on her shoe soles.

"My God," breathed Aymon again. "Now I call that a *good* omen. So much for the worldwide catastrophic decline of amphibians."

He managed to catch one of the critters without crushing it, and held it up to his eye, threadlike limbs dangling. It had a pointed snout, and two green stripes down its crooked back that glittered when they caught the light and disappeared in shadow. Its irises were striated gold around the slippery, bulging pupils. The frog grinned tooth-lessly, and Aymon laughed. His unease vanished. He felt innocent and adventurous, like a little boy—

"These little guys are having a ball."

"My watch has stopped," announced Viola, rummaging in her over-sized, arm-and-a-leg purse. "Damn, and my cell seems to have run out of charge, however that happened. What time is it?"

"About midafternoon. It doesn't matter, does it?"

She looked up. He'd dropped the frog and his hands were dug so deeply into his pants pockets that both his wrists were hidden. She guessed at once that *his* watch had stopped too, and a chill ran down her spine.

"Where's your cell, Ay?"

"Calm down, honey, what's the panic? It's in the car."

They could not see the car. Every direction looked the same.

Something has happened, thought Viola. I *felt* it, when we drove in here. Wild thoughts went through her mind. Hostage-takers with some kind of ray, killing their digital communications. Electromagnetic Pulse, the Third World War, UFOs, a natural disaster—

"We left the fucking car wide open," she said. "These trees all look identical, and there's just about to be a cloudburst."

"We can retrace our steps. You stay where you are, marking our last known position, I'll cast around for our footprints."

He cast about, examining the leaf mould and the creepers. Viola doubted if even Aymon could suddenly acquire finely honed tracker skills, from nowhere. She stayed put because she hated the idea of taking another step into chaos, and stared all around her: intently, slowly—

"Aymon! There's light over there! Sunlight, it must be the clearing where we left the car!"

"No, it's not, honey. It can't be. You're pointing downhill, we were *coming* downhill. We left the car on kind of a hilltop, don't you remember?"

"I can see buildings."

She was right. Aymon could see the leaf-broken outlines too: hard to say what *kind* of buildings, they could be in ruin… Defiantly, silently daring her to laugh, he took out his pocket knife and sliced a rectangle of white bark from the pink flesh of a birch tree beside him. "I'm going to go on doing that. So we can get back to *here*, whatever else."

"Go ahead. Be a vandal."

The sunlight lay over the valley of a clear brown stream that ran between beds of flowering rushes. Fine trees, untrammelled by close neighbours, grew on the natural turf on either side. There was a footpath, well-maintained if not well-trodden, and the buildings they'd seen were close. They saw white weatherboard and cranky little gabled roofs, a crooked white wooden bridge, the glimmer and the laughter of a modest weir—

"It's an old mill," said Aymon.

"So now you know where we are?"

He shrugged. "If you'd taken an interest, you'd know there are several of them on the property, all disused."

"Oh my God, look at that!" cried Viola.

But what she'd taken for an exquisite glass statue, a naked, transparent young woman crouching in the stream, was gone at a second glance. All she could see was a mass of iridescent, blue-green damselflies, *demoiselles*, darting over the surface. The cloud of wings suggesting, maybe, the turn of a girl's smooth shoulder, the waves of her hair—

"How perfectly lovely," she finished, uncertainly.

"Told you." Aymon beamed, striding along. I will make her happy, he thought. I will do one great deed before I die, and she'll be proud. "I told you. This place is a dream. It's going to be great, inspirational, relaxed: our people will love to work here."

He was somewhat piqued to discover that the "disused mill" seemed to be in use, as a shabby old-fashioned forest information point. They wandered the covered porches, looking at quaint, half-effaced pictureboards. Forest animals, birds, flowers—

"Did you know about this place, Ay?"

"I don't exactly remember."

He was looking for a map of the forest (a tourist guide place like this has to have a map, even if it's out of date). He couldn't find one, but he discovered that if he looked at the picture boards *directly*, with attention, they *changed*. The animals, birds and plants came alive, he couldn't put it any more clearly. As if something extra was passing from the vaguely suggested images directly through his eyes to his brain. They were more than alive, they were conscious, these images *were the creatures themselves*, looking back at him, wise and wicked, fun to know, but by no means entirely friendly—

He was fascinated, and passed from one array to another for several minutes (for time without measure) before he noticed how *weird* this was, and began to get scared. What the hell have I eaten, drunk, *smoked* today: without knowing it? Was there something in the slimy skin of those tiny frogs? Some hallucinogen that passed through my skin?

A door opened, and a young woman came out, smiling. She wore a full-sleeved, black, belted smock and cap, with a white bib and collar at the throat—like an old-fashioned nun; except that her slim brown legs and feet were bare. She greeted them in pretty French, which for once they found easy to understand, announced herself as the *gardienne* of this Centre, and ushered them inside. The room she showed them was a store, selling natural forest products: toiletries, herbal infusions, food and candy: not the usual tourist lines, but genuinely unusual, quirky products; Viola was charmed. Aymon followed her around, grinning loosely: feeling young again.

"Do you take cash or cards?" asked Viola, hoping she had enough euros. There was no sign of a PayPoint or a till, nothing to suggest the twenty-first century at all.

The little *gardienne* dipped her head. "We accept all the usual kinds of currency, or credit. Would Madame and Monsieur like to take something to drink? We have tables on the terrace."

She brought them eglantine tea in the souvenir forest china, which was pattered blue-green, iridescent as a damselfly's wings. They were the only customers on the rustic terrace above the weir. It was the kind of place, thought Viola, where you *want* to be the only customers, you want to have discovered a hidden treasure. But it was a little disquieting.

"I wonder what happens in the other buildings."

"I wonder where they've hidden the damn car park," growled Aymon, trying to frown, to mask his drug experience. "It's got to be around here somewhere. Hidden up in the canopy, maybe, with the big butterflies—"

Viola's attention had been caught by a frog on a lily pad, on the water right below the rail beside their table. He was bright green all over, and much larger than the minute creatures teeming on the forest floor, maybe the size of the palm of her hand. Or larger than that: it was hard to be sure of the scale of him, there was a trick of perspective—

The frog looked up, bright-eyed, beamed at her and began to sing.

"Dedans ma chaumière
Pour y vivre heureux
Combien faut-il être?
Il faut être deux…"

Or rather, he began to *croak:* but it wasn't a bad voice, not at all.

In my li-tel co-ttage,
what do I need there?
for to be so happy,
what I need is you!

The words, that turned to English in her head with no effort at all, seemed so charming. And his bright eyes, his lipless, toothless grin, were so lively, so funny; and, if this wasn't too ridiculous, decidedly *sexual*—

"Oui, ma chaumière,
Je la préfère!
Avec toi, oui avec moi
Avec toi, oui avec moi!
Au palais d'un roi…!"

"I think I'll take a little walk," said Viola, abruptly: very startled by the feelings she was getting about that frog—

She thought she was abrupt, but thankfully Aymon didn't seem to care. He seemed content with his own thoughts, his own daydreams, whatever was happening to *him*… She knew she should find the ladies' room, splash her face, recover her poise. Instead, on a whim, she walked by the stream. The tender grass that had never been mown was starred with secret flowers. She knelt and dug into it with her fingers. Even the dirt itself was jewelled complexity, shimmering and edgy with endless life. The deeper you looked the more you saw. Everywhere, *everywhere,* *everywhere* tiny knowing eyes looked back at you…

Something gleaming on the ground attracted her attention. She followed the gleam and found a golden corpse, lying as if annealed into the earth, the limbs and trunk sealed together and shining, shining, the face half-hidden by polished waves of hair. Now she had found a dead body, no wonder the forest had felt spooky. She bent for a closer look, knowing she must touch nothing, because this was a murder mystery and she would destroy the evidence. But the golden corpse sat up, the glimmering girl fled, leaving only a forest boulder; and Viola had never seen her face. Even stone is alive, stone is the mineral matrix of all life. It was the queen, she thought.

"That was the queen—" croaked the frog.

He must have followed her from the terrace. Did he really have a tiny yellow Disneyfied *crown* perched on his head? Could that *happen*? He winked at her and began to dance, hopping from one webbed, splay-toed foot to the other, singing the chorus of his French folksong, English in Viola's head:

Oh yes, my little home!
I would prefer it,
For you and me,
for you and me
To the palace of a king!

This time she went with the feeling. She jumped into his arms, the frog grabbed her and held her tight. He became man-sized, and outrageously, unamphibianly male. They were swimming in the millpool now, and a wanton, winged companion, great-eyed, androgynous and slender, hovered over them, making its wishes plain. Viola and the frog kissed and parted, Viola passed happily to the other partner. They went zooming away, over the shining surface of the water, their wings shivering in delight, hooked up *en soixante-neuf*, never had an orgasm like it, excitement, innocence and delight such as she hadn't known since, since, since forever—

Life is wonderful.

"You have very old-fashioned minds," confided the *gardienne*, as she handed over several exquisitely wrapped packages, in a delightful raw raffia bag. "May I ask where are you from?"

"From the USA," confessed Viola, knowing this was not always a good answer in Europe. She had raided the store. The taste of eglantine tea was still on her lips. She hoped she'd remembered to buy a box of those relaxing *tisanes*: she was a little hazy about the last few minutes—

"Ah!" said the *gardienne*, dipping her round black head, as if this explained everything (although, Viola thought, in fact the little nun was completely mystified, something lost in translation again). "Many thanks for your visit. Please come again."

They followed the flashes Aymon had cut in tree bark, back to the "last known position," without any trouble. Maybe their eyes were better accustomed to the veil of green now; or maybe there'd been a touch of needless panic earlier. They spotted the gun-metal Aston Martin immediately, parked in that clearing, no more than a couple of hundred yards away.

"You see," said Aymon. "We were never lost."

Viola stood on one foot and then the other, to shake scraps of leaf mould and bark out of her sandals. "We'd better hurry. There's going to be a thunderstorm, I can feel it."

Aymon took his best guesses at the route out, using the compass on the dash (there was still nothing but grey fuzz on their GPS). Eventually they saw an ochre-washed cottage standing by the track, though as yet no tyre marks, no vehicles, no signage, no human activity—

Aymon pulled up and jumped out, eagerly. "Civilisation! C'mon, you're the linguist, you do the talking—"

But the forest grew right up to the stained, derelict walls, swamping what had been a little railed yard. "I don't think so, Ay."

The cottage had been walled up. The bricked door and boarded windows stared at the intruders, somehow stirring inexpressible emotions... "There's a plaque on the wall," said Aymon.

Viola kept her distance, nervous as a wild animal. "It's an old forester's house," he reported. "It's been fitted out as a bat refuge, a kind of memorial thing, wait there's more, think I can find out where we are—"

Aymon knew that there was a village called Boucq around here. He'd never nailed the genealogy (people who check out their family legends often find things they wish they didn't know); but he believed the Bocks could have come from there, long ago. And here was the name itself, on this bat refuge plaque, but strangely, it came in the English spelling...

"Let's get back on the road. I don't need to know about bats."

"Did you find out where we are?"

"No. We'll find out by driving, we have to hit a real road soon."

She sighed, concluding that his ability to read French had betrayed him: better not press the point. They returned to the car. Aymon punched the button, at last (always reluctant to give up the freedom of the open-top). The roof performed its slick, robotic manoeuvre, and they looked at each other, sealed and safe. Soon after that, the GPS screen came back to life.

"*Now* do we know where we are?"

"Never in doubt," said Aymon.

He drove on. Almost immediately they reached a junction, and they were back in the world of traffic, of powerlines, of isolated farms and miles of corn; and the sky finally opened. But Viola felt—maybe it was the sudden attack of the rain—as if the country had changed, as if she had to start "being in France" all over again, in a much less confident key. She remembered her purchases, and couldn't think what she'd done with them. Nothing in her purse. Where was that pretty raffia bag? Her arms ached with emptiness.

"What's the matter?"

"Nothing…really."

He kept his eyes on the streaming grey road. "Honey? Did you notice anything *strange* about that place we found?"

She'd have denied everything, doubting her sanity and/or the eglantine tea, but the tremor in his voice convinced her to speak. "I'm not sure. Tricks of the light, maybe. Or things I can't explain."

"Did you see the girl in black, the *gardienne,* turn into a water bird?"

"I didn't see that. Did you see the transparent girl in the stream?"

"No. But I saw those tall pink flowers, the rushes, come alive, and turn into, er, people. What happened to *you*? After you followed that dragonfly?"

"Damselfly." Viola shook her head, realising with a shock that she wanted to tell him *all* about it, but not right now, not in a moving car. "I don't want to say, not yet. Aymon, what happened to us, where have we been?"

"You mean what did we take?" he countered, with a tight grin.

The windscreen wipers fought with pounding grey battalions.

"I don't believe that. Oh, I know we took the eglantine tea, but we were in another world before that. You know it. You and that tiny frog, the way you were, you were *communing* with each other. Aymon, we should compare notes. We should do it right now, before we lose our nerve, before we stop believing."

The rain was so heavy he could see nothing but the starred red tail-lights of the truck ahead of him. The two-lane road was narrow, traffic heavy, no chance to overtake. Aymon's heart was racing, better maintain the speed of the traffic but it felt too fast, almost uncontrollable—

Viola pressed her hand to her mouth. "In another world, my God. I've heard of a story like this, Ay, it's famous… Two English women were visiting Versailles, in the nineteen twenties, no, earlier. They had a strange experience and published it, they called it *An Adventure*. They believed they'd been through a timeslip, back to 10 August 1792. They'd visited the Petit Trianon in the days of Marie-Antoinette, and seen the queen herself—"

"It wasn't Marie-Antoinette." Aymon gripped the wheel fiercely. "The queen of that forest was *not* Marie-Antoinette."

"That's not what I'm saying. The account the authors of *An Adventure* published didn't check out. It's famous as a hoax. But I think they'd added stuff, because something incredible *had* happened to them, and they wanted people to believe. That's why we have to get this straight, you and I, *now*. Pull over, next chance you get—"

"Did you see the animal images on those boards come alive? As if they were getting directly into your brain, and *looking back at you?*"

"No, but I… something like that. Did you see the singing frog?"

"I've got a better idea. I'm going to find somewhere to pull over, a quiet spot, maybe a *bar tabac*. We're going to call Piper, right now, tell her the whole thing, have *her* record it."

Bette Piper was Aymon's long-time personal assistant, a very smart woman whom they both trusted implicitly.

"Yeah, yeah! Great idea, let's do it!"

Viola felt twenty, thirty years younger. She felt as if something inside had shattered and been remade. She had a mission, a cause, *this would be big*, she had her own instincts, she could almost taste it. The natural world is *alive*, sexual, conscious, full of living spirits, I'll write a book, a bestseller—

"The nearest I can come," she exclaimed, imagining the tv audience, trying out her lines on him, "to putting a name on what happened to us, is to say that we visited Fairyland. That's not *adequate*, but it's the word people have used, traditionally, for the dimension we entered: where, where every flower is conscious, and nature spirits inhabit insects, animals—"

"*Fairyland???*" Aymon exploded, hands still locked on the wheel, eyes fixed on those blurred taillights. "What the *fuck?* You are *shitting* me, honey. That was a *timeslip*. That was my future we visited. That was the future. Shit, those noticeboards: I can almost figure it. Information coded in light, direct to the cortex, and hijacking the processes of consciousness, that's what causes that weird 'everything is looking at me' effect—"

"SHUT UP!" shouted Viola. "Shut up, shut up. You and your *codes!*"

He held the wheel, but inside he was shaking, reliving the moment when—spelling out that memorial plaque— he'd had the strangest conviction that if he read another word he'd discover the date of his own death. He knew he was right, oh God, he knew. But it was a crass error to shoot her down, far more important to get her to talk, get *her* experience on record: before vital clues to those unborn developments were lost—

"Okay, okay. I'm sorry, honey, calm down, didn't mean to offend."

"Maybe we're both right," whispered Viola, marvelling. "Maybe the future *is* a fairyland, and that's what we have glimpsed—"

A tiny voice in his ear brought Aymon up short. He gripped the wheel harder, his eyes bulging. He could see a little figure squirming up out of the walnut fascia, a tiny face, incredibly malevolent, made of *polished wood grain*, a flayed body—

"Think of the consequences!" it squeaked, waving its knobbly little arms. "Where is your evidence? What did you bring back? Nothing! No one will believe you. You'll be treated as cranks! You will be ridiculed!"

Hordes more of them, a different variety, came pouring out of the strengthened glass, and flew around their heads, jabbering urgently, flickering in and out of focus, liquid and abrasive.

"They will say you have ingested illegal substances, your trusted assistant will report you to the authorities, you will be ruined!"

Multicoloured creatures whose bodies were ever-shifting crowns and chains came out of the door panels and the floor, and cried out, passionately:

"We are not life, we were once life, deep in the ancient fern-forest time: we are naked chemicals, stripped and crucified now. Beware, beware, Viola! Our cousins in your brain have told us this: your happiness will vanish, if you betray your lovers."

"Don't betray us! Don't betray us! We never betrayed you! Cowards! Cowards!"

The Egyptian cotton fairies danced on Aymon's shoulder, pleading to be heard, telling him how they had been tortured into thread—

"And think, if you are believed," shouted the Parisian artisan leather spirits, crawling out of the sleek hide of Viola's purse. "If your visit can be detected as changes in your brain chemistry? What then? By interfering, by trying to make it happen, you may destroy the very salvation that you have glimpsed, that you so desire, and it may never come to be—!"

Viola had succumbed to hysterics, she was trying to open the passenger door, sobbing and batting at the glass-sprites.

Never come to be, never come to be, hissed the voices in Aymon's ear, not a single voice but a varied choir: in fact the voices of the different materials confined in his pacemaker. He struggled to go on driving, though his heart was jumping like a jack-hammer, convinced, like his wife, that there was hope in flight… But the rain kept raining madly, the taillights were too close, and a party of young male deer, inspired by who knows what *diablerie*, decided to bolt across the road ahead of that truck, bounding from the forest margin.

"Ay!" yelled Viola, terrified out of her panic attack—

Aymon failed to apply the brakes, probably because he had already succumbed to a fatal heart attack. Viola, who had unclipped her seat belt whilst trying to escape, went through the windscreen, despite its toughness. She was technically alive when the Emergency Services arrived, but she never recovered consciousness, and died on the way to the hospital.

The Woodsman put away his axe. Many members of the commune preferred to cut and stack their fuel in winter, when the trees were sleeping, but he saw no harm in being open about these things. He stood beside his toolshed (which he had cultured himself, from living timber, a proud feat), scratching his chin and pondering. Those tourists now, where exactly had they got to?

There were Centres all over the world, where anyone who wished could experience, in forest, in meadows, desert, savannah or ocean, full communion with the woken world—or as much of that reality as they could stand. But foreign visitors who came to this oldest meeting place, the original Martigny Centre of the Forest of the Queen, often had very mistaken ideas. There was no raw primeval innocence in this forest, for the forest was not *old* at all. It had died and been reborn as often as France herself, and the consciousness of nature was imbued with the character of the human culture. This meant that strangers could get into trouble. The *woken* world here (a misnomer, for it was the human mind that had been *woken*, by the miracles of science) could be mischievous, bawdy, a little dangerous to the unwary.

Tourists who arrived in the flesh irritated the Woodsman: Why could they not be content with the virtual access, which was excellent? But he thought fondly of the American couple, for the sake of that remarkable grey steed of theirs; for the sake of a past which he remembered with the nostalgia of a survivor. Nowadays, the living world could *compel* human beings to deal with its peoples fairly and decently. Trade agreements had been made, laws had been drawn up, which humanity must respect. My God, yes, the human race had learned a hard lesson, when the change first came… But even now, in the peace after the ages-long conflict, there was bitterness, and one had to take care. It must be a challenge to keep a machine from the o.d days, happy!

And perilous.

His own car had been drowsing in a hazel thicket. He led it out and checked its skirts for burrs and prickles (its wheels were rarely deployed, they weren't very practical for this terrain)—as he studied the satellite views of the forest and its environs, which he habitually kept open at the back of his eyes when he was guarding these gates. The grey steed was nowhere to be seen. No mark of their passage anywhere. Perhaps they had given up trying to find the Centre, and left the area while his attention was elsewhere.

"After all," he murmured, as he gave the little white car a gentle touch on the wheel, to guide it across the water meadows—where it tended to shy at the rise of a heron, or the curiosity of the cattle. "It was a *very* old map."

QUARTERMASTER RETURNS

YSABEAU S. WILCE

"…That he escaped that blow entirely is due to the consummate good luck which enabled him to steer clear of that military maelstrom…he never had to be post quartermaster."

Trials of a Staff Officer
Captain Charles King, 3ʳᵈ U.S. Cavalry

I. Wet

When Pow walks into the hog ranch, everyone turns to stare at him. At the whist table, the muleskinner gurgles and lets fall his cards. The cardsharp's teeth clatter against the rim of his glass. The cowboy squeaks. At the bar, the barkeep, who had been fishing flies out of the pickle jar, drops her pickle fork. On the bar, the cat, a fantastic mouser named Queenie, narrows her moon-silver eyes into little slits. At the pianny, Lotta, who'd been banging out *Drink Puppy Drink* on the peeling ivory keys, crashes one last chord and no more.

Even the ice elemental, in the cage suspended over the whist table, ceases his languid fanning. He's seen a lot of boring human behavior since the barkeep bought him from a junk store in Walnuts to keep the hog ranch cool; finally a human has done something interesting. Only Fort Gehenna's scout doesn't react. He wipes his nose on a greasy buckskin sleeve, slams another shot of mescal, and takes the opportunity to peek at his opponents' cards.

The barroom is dead silent but for a distant slap and a squeal—Buck and the peg-boy in the back room *exercising*—and the creak of the canvas walls shifting in the ever-present Arivaipa wind.

Pow wobbles over to the bar—just a couple of boards laid across two empty whiskey barrels—leans on it—the boards creaking ominously at his weight—and croaks: "Mescal." His throat feels as though he's swallowed sixty pounds of sand. The barkeep stares at him, her mouth hanging slightly ajar. Against her garish blue lip rouge her teeth look as yellow as corn.

Pow licks his lips with a cat-coarse tongue and whispers: "Come on, Petty, give me a mescal. I'm powerfully dry."

"You're dripping wet," The barkeep answers. Pow looks down, and yes indeed he is dripping, brown water seeping from his dirty uniform, turning the ground he stands upon to mud.

"Sorry," he says. "Is it raining outside?" He looks back towards the door, which is a blazing rectangle of sunlight, bright enough to blind—it's not raining outside. Arivaipa is a goddess-forsaken wilderness of a desert, where it only rains occasionally, and then usually in the dead of night. And anyway, if it were raining outside, it would be raining inside too, for the hog ranch's roof is made of brush and it is not water tight. The last good downpour was two weeks ago, and it had almost swamped the hog-ranch out.

"Lotta—get the lieutenant a towel," the barkeep says, but Lotta does not spring to the order. She shrinks back behind the wall of the pianny and wishes she were invisible.

"Lotta!" The barkeep repeats, "Get Lieutenant Rucker a towel or I'll kick ya in yer hinder."

While Lotta reluctantly follows the barkeep's order, Pow wipes his face on the mustachio towel nailed to the bar; the towel, none to white to begin with, comes away black with dirt. The barkeep hands him a sloshily poured glass; he drinks it in one draught, and bangs his glass down for more. The mescal is bitter and burning but it washes away the taste of mud in his mouth. He feels very clammy, and from the itch, there is sand in his drawers. The barkeep pours him another.

"Thanks, darling," Pow says, and bolts his second drink. The whist game has not resumed; the players are still staring at him, and he returns their glance, saying, "Ain't you people never seen a man drink before?"

No one responds to this quip, and then the canvas curtains over the doorway to the back room part. Out staggers Buck, laughing, struggling to get her sack coat back on. She's got her right arm in the left sleeve and that's not going to work no matter how much she pulls. The peg-boy follows her, grinning, and snapping his galluses up over red-checkered shoulders. An air of satisfaction hovers over them both.

Buck outranks him, so Pow wafts a salute at her, and she waves at him drunkenly, collapsing in a chair at the other rickety table. The peg-boy sticks a cigarillo in her mouth, another in his, and lights them both.

"Where the hell you been, Pow?" Buck says. The barkeep has already anticipated her desire, and plunks a bottle of whiskey before her. Pow licks the dirt from his lips and realizes that he has no idea.

II. Desiccated

Arivaipa Territory, where the sun is so hot that it will, after dissolving your flesh into grease, melt your bones as well. A territory of bronco natives and bunco artists, wild religiosos and wild horses, poison toads and rattling snakes. A hard dry place, an endless expanse of Nowhere. Why the Warlord wants to keep a thread of authority in such a god-dess-forsaken place is a mystery, but the Army doesn't question orders, just follows them. Thus Fort Gehenna, and a scattering of other army posts, sown like seeds across the prickly rocky dusty landscape of the remote territory.

The hog ranch sits on Fort Gehenna's reservation line, just beyond the reach of military authority, and technically off-limits to army personnel. There are no hogs at this ranch, just cheap bugjuice, cheap food and cheap love, but these three attractions make the hog ranch a pretty attractive place to Gehenna's lonely bored hungry soldiers. So a well-worn track starts at the hog ranch's front door and wends its way through the desert scrub, up and down arroyos, by saguaro and paloverde, across the sandy expanse of the Sandy River to terminate behind Officers' Row.

Down this track, known as The Oh Be Joyful Road, Pow zigzags. His feet kick up dust, and the sun hits his shoulders, his bare head, with hammer-like intensity. The heat has sucked the wet right out of his uniform, which now feels gritty and coarse against his skin. His sinuses tingle and burn. He feels in his sack coat pocket for his bandana, but the pockets are full of sand. So he blows his nose into his sleeve, but only a thin gust of dust comes out.

His boots are full of sand too; near the cactus priest's wikiyup he sits on a rock and pours them out. Were his toes always that black? They look like little shriveled coffee beans. His brain feels thick, as though his skull is full of mud. Pow marches on, his eyes slits of grittiness, his eyelids scrape at his eyeballs like broken glass. He can hardly see where he is going, but the urge to go is strong, and he can't help but follow it.

Pow reaches the Single Officers' Quarters, and staggers up the steps into the blessed shade of the porch—a few degrees cooler and the air slightly moist from the water olla hanging from the porch eaves. He pulls down the olla, hearing his muscles crackle like dried cornstalks.

The olla is fat and round, beaded with moisture, but almost empty. He licks the droplets off the clay, oh delicious wetness, and then throws the pot on the ground, where it shatters.

As a first lieutenant, Pow's only entitled to one room, and this room is now empty of his gear, its only furniture a steamer trunk and an iron cot. Pow collapses on the iron cot, unable to take another step. His thirst is sharp and pointed, it's overwhelming and all encompassing, it leaves little room inside him for anything else. All around him he can sense moisture, but he himself is parched.

He shakes his head, feeling the tendons in his neck wheeze and burn. There's a rattling sound inside of his skull—his brain perhaps, now shrunken to a desiccated nubbin. That would account for the thickness of his thoughts. Something falls into his lap; at first he thinks it's a piece of jerky, then he realizes it's his ear. He tries to stick his ear back onto his head, but it won't stay, so he puts it in his pocket for safe keeping.

A shadow slinks in the corner of the room; two silver eyes glitter. Freddie, Pow's pet Gila monster, which he raised from an egg, is peeking out of its den, a hole in the adobe wall. The lizard waddles across the floor and nips at the toe of Pow's boot, its usual method for requesting a treat. Lacking anything else, Pow gives the Gila monster his ear—his hearing seems fine without it—and Freddie nibbles daintily. Pow reaches for the lizard; Freddie spits a shiny squirt of silvery poison at him. Pow licks the slippery venom off his fingers—it's lovely wet.

The lizard is fat with moisture; underneath that scaly skin, it's heavy with wetness, its meat saturated with blood, bile, venom, juice. Pow makes a dry clucking noise with his splintery tongue, and reaches for Freddie again. As if sensing his intent, the Gila monster scuttles away, but desperation makes Pow quick. He snatches.

III. Dry

Pow's retreat from the hog ranch to his quarters did not go without notice; indeed, when he had staggered onto Fort Gehenna's parade ground, a long file had straggled behind him. In addition to the habitués of the hog ranch, who gave him a respectable head start before following, the brigade included the herd guard, a couple of privates who were loitering in the shade of the sinks watching an ant fight, the tame broncos (as the soldiers call Arivaipa's natives) who live behind the remuda corral, and the dog pack, tempted out of the arroyo by Pow's smell, which, now that his clothes have dried, is quite strong: a meaty kind of decay.

This crowd now stands outside the SOQ, and it has attracted the attention of Lieutenant Brakespeare, Gehenna's adjutant and current acting quartermaster, and Sergeant Candy, Gehenna's ranking noncom. When they arrive to investigate, a multitude of voices in several languages all begin to babble at once. Lieutenant Brakespeare ignores the shouting and enters the SOQ only to find Pow's room empty. The contents of his trunk are strewn about the room and every item packed therein that once contained anything moist—boot polish tin, a bottle of Madama Twanky's *Sel-Ray-Psalt Medicine*, fly ointment—lies wrecked upon the floor.

The destruction continues across the hallway and into Lieutenant Brakespeare's quarters—the lieutenant swears horribly when she sees the mess—and on into the kitchen beyond. There Berman, the lieutenant's striker, stands surveying a battlefield of crumpled tin cans, smashed sauerkraut crocks, broken wine bottles, and the splintered remains of a water barrel.

"He went that way," Berman says, *that way* being into the back yard. There Lieutenant Brakespeare and Sergeant Candy find Pow face down in a laundry tub, sucking up soapy water, while the laundress stands over him, whacking at his shoulders with her washboard. They heave Pow out of the almost empty tub. He burps a giant soap bubble, which pops into an appalling stench of sweet-sour decay, and shakes the soldiers off. He feels deliciously waterlogged, heavy and solid. He feels much much better.

The crowd has rushed around the back, and now a rotund figure— Captain de Poligniac, Gehenna's commanding officer—pushes through, almost invisible underneath a huge black umbrella, an item that officers in uniform are strictly forbidden to carry. When he reaches the SOQ back porch, and lets drop the shade, Polecat (as the good captain is called even to his face) reveals that he's not in uniform anyway, just a pair of dirty red drawers and a white guayabera. He'd been in his quarters, riding out the furnace of the afternoon on an herbal haze, and he is annoyed at being disturbed.

"What's all that infernal racket, Lieutenant Brakespeare?" Polecat complains. He catches sight of Pow, and his voice trails off. His lips pucker in puzzlement, and he stares at the rapidly dehydrating lieutenant.

"Pow!" Polecat says. "I thought you were dead!"

IV. Arid

Of course, First Lieutenant Powhatan Rucker is dead. Not just dead, but drowned. How can you drown in a desert? In an Arivaipa thunderstorm, all too quickly. One minute the sky is as blank as a sheet of paper; the next minute it roils with quicksilver clouds, from which lunge enormous purple-silver prongs of lightning. And then rain bullets down, water floods into the arroyos and anything not on the high ground is swept away. Ten minutes later the desert is dry as a bone again, and the sky empty.

He died a hero's death, Lieutenant Rucker did, trying to save, not another comrade, but rather the hog ranch's entire supply of beer. The story is short and tragic: the freight train dropped fifteen cases of beer at the hog ranch, before proceeding on to Rancho Kuchamonga; an inexperienced drover off-loaded the beer in the arroyo below the hog ranch; when the storm came up, Pow organized his fellow whist players into a bottle brigade, and supervised the shifting of fourteen cases to higher ground; the water was already foaming when Pow went back for the last case—refusing to allow the others to join him in harm's way; Pow heroically managed to shove that case up the bank, just as a wall of water twenty feet high came roaring down the ravine.

After Pow's battered and soggy body was found tangled in an uprooted paloverde tree, he was borne off to Gehenna's sandy cemetery, where he was given a full military funeral, and toasted by the entire garrison with bottles from the fateful case that killed him. But now that sandy cemetery has spit Pow back up, a circumstance that no one in Gehenna can ever remember occurring before.

"If Pow is dead, how can he be alive?" Polecat says, in bewilderment. They've retired to his office, for privacy, although the crowd still loiters outside, hoping that voices will be raised enough to facilitate eavesdropping. Considering that the walls of the office are mud-covered brush, and the ceiling more brush, under which hangs a piece of canvas which keeps centipedes from falling on your head, the voices do not have to be very loud. Polecat plops behind his desk, trying to look official, while the Lieutenants Brakespeare and Rucker stand before him, in semi-respectful stances. Lieutenant Fyrdraaca, retrieved from the privy, isn't quite as drunk as she was before, but she's not sober enough to stand at attention, so she has sprawled upon Polecat's well-used daybed.

Polecat puts his spectacles on to examine Pow more closely; the lieutenant is still crusted with a fine silt, but the few bits of skin visible look downright shriveled. He is twenty-two years old, but now he looks a hundred.

"I think *alive* is stretching it a bit, Polecat," Buck says. "I mean, Pow is animated, but he looks a bit rough to actually be alive. I would say he's definitely dead."

"Then what am I doing here?" Pow asks, bewildered.

"I called you back." Lieutenant Brakespeare says. She sounds rather smug.

"You brought him back from the dead?" Polecat moans. "Why in Califa's name did you do that, Azota?"

"His quartermaster accounts were a mess—and short, too." Lieutenant Brakespeare purses her mouth into a small knot. "I'm not going to be responsible for his shortages, or pay for his mistakes."

At the time of his death, Pow had been Gehenna's quartermaster, and thus responsible for all of Gehenna's rations, uniforms, equipment, ordnance and equipage, for the previous three months. During that time he'd not done a lick of paperwork, preferring instead to while away the days playing mumblety-peg with the QM clerks. To say that Pow's QM accounts were a mess, was being charitable. Actually, they were a catastrophe.

When Lieutenant Brakespeare (only shortly graduated from Benica Barracks Military Academy but already well on her way to being a properly stuck-up yaller dog, as staff officers are called) assumed the QM duties upon Pow's death, it had taken her fourteen days of nonstop paper pushing to complete the QM returns properly, and even then she couldn't account for all the shortages in the QM inventories. Since officers in the Army of Califa are personally responsible for items on their inventory returns, someone is to going to have to pay for these shortages. Lieutenant Brakespeare has no intention of being that someone.

Polecat complains: "But you shouldn't summon someone back from the dead just to make up a shortage."

"I didn't," Lieutenant Brakespeare says primly. "Officers are forbidden by *The Articles of War* to attempt or achieve any magickal acts. Article 3, Section I, Subsection 2."

Buck, from the settee, observes: "Maybe forbidden themselves, but there's nothing in *The Articles of War* about paying someone else to attempt or achieve magickal acts for you, eh? Who'd you get to do it?"

"The curandero," Lieutenant Brakespeare admits. The curandero is an elderly bronco who, having decided he was too old and wise to fight, made peace with the Califians and moved into a wikiyup near the river, from which he dispenses charms, foul smelling ointments, and philosophical advice, in return for rations. "Anyway, Lieutenant

Rucker can go back where he came from as soon as he either produces the inkwell, or pays for it. I don't care which."

"Inkwell?" says Polecat.

"Ayah, so. Pow signed a receipt for fifteen glass inkwells, shipped from Fort Ludwig to here—" Lieutenant Brakespeare fishes a sheet of paper out of her sack coat and consults it. "On Martes 12. One arrived broken and was dropped from the inventory. One was issued to Corporal Candy on Martes 15; one was issued to the AG, and one to the CO. Leaving eleven on the return. But there were only ten in the QM store. Where's the missing inkwell?" She looks accusingly at Pow.

"I don't know." Pow says. He has no idea where the missing inkwell is, but there's a burning feeling in his throat, a scratchy roar that is extremely distracting. The dry Arivaipa air has sucked his moisture away and his thirst has returned, with a vengeance. Something wiggles on his neck; despite the canvas a centipede has fallen from the brush. Pow pops the flailing bug into his mouth and it squishes wetly between his teeth. The others don't notice.

"How much is the inkwell valued at?" Polecat asks.

Lieutenant Brakespeare consults the receipt again. "Fifteen lisbys."

"Fifteen lisbys!" Polecat reaches for the cigarillo box on his blotter, which does not contain cigarillos. "Fifteen lisbys! That's pocket change!"

"You always gotta do things the hard way, Tiny Doom," Buck chortles, and Lieutenant Brakespeare gives her a poisonous look.

"Have you got fifteen lisbys, Pow?" Polecat asks.

Pow feels in his pockets, but if he ever had fifteen lisbys, the Arivaipa desert has them now. He tries to answer; his jaw creaks like dry wood, and no words come out, only a puff of dust.

"I'll take that as a no. Here, I'll give you fifteen lisbys, Pow, and you can pay Lieutenant Brakespeare, and that will be that," Polecat says, his head now wreathed in soothing herbal smoke. He fishes around in his top desk drawer. "Buck, do you have two lisbys?"

There's an ink bottle sitting on Polecat's desk, half-full of ink. Pow can smell the dark delicious wetness—

"I don't want your money, Captain," Lieutenant Brakespeare complains. "It's Lieutenant Rucker's responsibility and he should either find that inkwell or pay up—"

Pow's entire focus is now pointed at that ink bottle and the promise of liquidity within. His thirst burns; his blood has long evaporated, and his veins feel like rawhide thongs, taut and stretched. He reaches a clawlike hand towards the bottle. The ink tastes thick and dark, but most deliciously, it tastes wet.

The others have stopped their squabbling, and are staring at him. Pow licks his now black lips and sets the empty bottle back on Polecat's desk.

"Anyway, it's not just the inkwell." Lieutenant Brakespeare says triumphantly. "There's also a small matter of the paymaster funds, which are also missing, and which Pow, as QM, is responsible for."

Polecat blanches. "How much?"

"Five thousand divas."

"Paper or gold?" Polecat asks faintly.

"Gold."

V. Parched

Suddenly Lieutenant Brakespeare's actions no longer seem quite so drastic. Fifteen lisbys is nothing; even a private can probably scrounge up fifteen lisbys, the price of a beer. But five thousand divas in gold—Fort Gehenna's entire payroll for the entire year! If the troopers find out their pay is gone, they'll riot, they'll mutiny, they'll desert. They'll raise a howl that will be heard in the War Department back in Califa, a howl that, since Pow is dead, will thunder down upon the shoulders of his superiors: Polecat and Lieutenant Brakespeare. They'll be court-martialed for sure, and lucky to escape cashiering. And they'll still have to pay back the cash. Five thousand divas in gold is a pretty good reason for raising the dead.

Polecat and Lieutenant Brakespeare pounce on Pow, but their berating questions get nowhere. He can hardly hear them; they are distant mirages in his parchedness. The ink has only whetted his thirst—not quenched it—and now his only interest is in moisture. He can smell the wetness; not in the air, which is as dry as dust, but in the living bodies around him—wet blood, wet bile, wet sweat, wet saliva. They are soggy with wetness, fair dripping, and he can feel himself shriveling for the lack of it.

Pow stares at Polecat, upon whose white brow stand little drops of sweat, whose rosy cheeks are flushed and bedewed. Polecat's lips are moving, opening to display the moist cavern of his mouth—the desire to lunge towards that wetness—tear Polecat's tongue out by the roots, suck out all its moisture—is rising like a dust devil inside of Pow, twisting and turning and—

"Hey," says Buck. She's now standing next to him, a bottle in her hand. "Have a drink, Pow. You look like you could use it."

His hands are too gnarled now to grasp the bottle; creakily he leans back, and Buck pours the coarse whiskey into his mouth; as it flows down his throat he feels his flesh expanding, reconstituting itself, plumping out. Delicious delicious wetness.

Lieutenant Brakespeare turns on Buck: "You could be helping. You signed the receipt for the paymaster. This will hit you, too."

Buck protests: "I am helping. While the two of you shriek like owls, I've been thinking. You know, the night Pow died, I was at the hog ranch, too."

"Where else?" says Lieutenant Brakespeare bitterly. She's never set foot in the place.

"*Cállate*, Azota, I wasn't feeling so well so I left early—*cállate*, Azota!—and thus missed Pow's heroism, but I do recall now that when I left, Pow was playing cards with the scout, Lotta, Pecos and some other guy. Pow was losing, and losing in gold, too."

"Who was winning?" Lieutenant Brakespeare asks.

"The scout," says Buck triumphantly.

So Polecat puts his sack coat on and orders Lieutenant Brakespeare to arrest Pow, which she does. Then, they all march, under colors, down to the hog ranch to demand the return of the payroll. They find the scout eating pickles and playing mumblty-peg with the ice elemental. He freely admits that he won the divas off Lieutenant Rucker, but he refuses to return them. A bet lost is a bet won by someone else, fair and square.

While Polecat dithers, and Buck and Pow have themselves another drink (or two), Lieutenant Brakespeare puts the screws on the scout. She starts out politely persuasive, then turns to choleric threats, but neither attitude makes the slightest dent. The scout is part-bronco, part-coyote, rumor has it, and a shavetail lieutenant don't scare him at all. Lieutenant Brakespeare sends a detail to search the scout's miserable shebang. No gold. Another detail holds the scout down and searches his greasy buckskin-clad person. No gold. She's urging Polecat to allow her to tie the scout to a wagon wheel and set his hair on fire—*I'll wager he'll cough up the gold then!*—when Buck offers a lazy solution.

"A wager." Buck says. "Let's make a wager."

Arivaipa Territory is arid and dull; the soldiers must make their own fun and what's more fun than a wager? At Gehenna, they'll bet on anything. *I'll stand you four divas, five lisbys, six glories that you can't*: leap a prickly pear cactus; eat six jars of jalapeño pickles; stand on your head for six hours; ride that strawberry roan; stay in bed two weeks; walk from the hog ranch to the flagpole blindfolded. The inhabitants of Gehenna have bet on ant wars; mule races; tennis matches; foot races; marksmanship; whose bed sheets are whiter; whose corporal is fatter; and whether or not lightning is attracted to a picket pin dangling from the flagpole. (Yes.)

The scout's eyes, deep in red-painted sockets, gleam. "A wager?"

"Ayah," Buck answers. "A bet. You won the divas off Pow, now give him a chance to turn about fair play. A contest of skill."

"What skill?"

"Who can hold their breath longest?" Buck suggests.

The scout shakes his head. "He's dead. He don't breathe. A foot race?"

Even in life, Pow was pokey; in death, he's moving at a snail's pace. Buck quickly counters: "Who can stay on Evil Murdoch the longest?" Evil Murdoch being the most notoriously un-rideable bite-y mule ever seen in Arivaipa.

The scout shakes his head. "Evil Murdoch kicks me in the head, I'm dead. The lieutenant, he's already dead, why should he care? Not good odds."

Lieutenant Brakespeare suggests: "How about a penmanship contest?" This suggestion is so boring that she is ignored.

"A drinking contest, then," says Buck, grinning. She knows that the scout takes particular pride in his ability to consume large quantities of bugjuice, with no outward effect. Only last year he drank the barkeep under the table, and she's a professional.

"Done!" says the scout quickly, "I got five thousand divas in gold. What is he going to put up?" This question is a legitimate stumper. The cumulative value of everything at Fort Gehenna, from Polecat's silver cigarette case to the hay in the hay yard, probably isn't worth five thousand divas in gold. What can Pow wager that even remotely begins to match the value of the gold?

"How about his soul?" the scout says.

"Done!" says Buck.

VI. Drink

By now, night is falling. To the northeast, in a cliché suitable for a yellowback thriller, a storm is forming up over Mount Abraxas, garish purple and pink lightning splitting the iron-blue twilight sky. A dust devil spirals across the parade ground; the howling dog pack chases after it. Fort Gehenna is now mostly deserted; every soldier not currently on duty is at the hog ranch, along with every one else for miles. A drinking contest between the scout and a dead man is probably the most exciting thing ever to happen at Fort Gehenna. The hog ranch is standing room only; slits soon appear in the canvas walls, each rent accommodating an avid pair of eyes. No one wants to miss the show.

The officers have had a whispered conversation regarding Pow's stake, which Pow has objected to. With his body liable to crumble to dust any minute, Pow's soul is all he's got left—he doesn't want to chance losing it. And besides, he doesn't care about the five thousand divas, why should he? He's dead. They can't court-martial him or cashier him. No, Polecat agrees, they can't. But they can confine him to the guardhouse, which is a dry place, where the water dipper is offered only twice a day. Here, they are offering Pow an opportunity to drink all he can, *set me up another round, keep 'em coming.* Suffer thirst or quench it. When it's put like that, Pow agrees that getting the money back is his responsibility after all.

As for the value of Pow's soul, how can it match the value of five thousand divas? Strictly speaking, it does not. Pow, in life, was an affable fellow, always good for a laugh and a loan, but he wasn't a famous magician, or a holy man, or anyone else who might have accumulated great animus, a weighty powerful soul. No matter to the scout. He has a little collection of souls; he keeps them in a leather pouch he wears on a cord around his neck. He's got the soul of a baby who died at birth; a dog that could read; a woman who lived to be one hundred and four; a coyote with two heads; a man who was hung for horse-stealing; and a woman who changed into a flamingo during the dark moon. The soul of a man who drowned in the desert would be a nice addition to this collection.

The rumble of thunder is growling nearer, like the distant approach of cannon fire, when Pow and the scout sit down across from each other at the whist table. The peanut gallery—no peanuts, no gallery—crowds around.

The rules, as Buck explains them loudly, are simple: whoever quits drinking first loses.

They start with the rest of the beer that Pow rescued from the flood—the last case, the one that Pow died for. After the funeral, the barkeep had put this case away for a special occasion and Pow's return is certainly a special occasion. It's very poor beer (the good stuff has no hope of surviving the long journey via steamer and mule train to

Arivaipa) but the people who drink at the hog ranch aren't picky. As long as the beer is cheap and wet, they are satisfied.

Pow, of course, only cares that the booze is wet. He and the scout chug down the beers as quickly as Lotta places them on the table. Six bottles each. With each swig, Pow feels his flesh expanding, fattening. The alcohol doesn't affect him at all, only the moisture. His muscles and sinews flex, his jaw relaxes. His brain swells back to its normal size, and he is beginning to think clearly again. The scout starts out strong, matching Pow sip for sip, but Gehenna's officers are not yet worried. The beer is weak stuff; even Lieutenant Brakespeare can drink several bottles of the stuff to no ill effect.

The scout finishes sucking the last few drops of beer out of the last bottle and tosses it over his shoulder. A yelp indicates that his aimless aim still found a mark.

"I gotta piss," he announces.

Pow needs no piss break; so he waits at the table, while the scout saunters out back to the saguaro that became the default urinal after the big storm washed the privy away. He returns a few minutes later and the contest resumes.

Now the beer is gone, and at Buck's bidding, the barkeep brings out the hog ranch's supply of mescal: six large ollas. This mescal is rough and strong; Buck doubts if the scout will make it through the second olla. She winks at Pow. Now that he is better hydrated, his eyes don't feel quite so much like glass marbles, so he winks back.

"Ut!" Pow says, raising his glass. The mescal looks exactly like urine, and it tastes, Pow realizes, almost exactly like soap. By the end of the first olla, a thin glaze is starting to creep across the scout's face. He puts his glass down and burrows into his buckskin jacket. The room stiffens and other hands stray towards hips, shirt fronts, waists, and boot-tops—any place a weapon could be stashed.

But when the scout's hand reappears, it's with a leather cigarillo case. He aims the cigarillo for his mouth, and makes the target on the second try. The scout accepts the trigger that the drover, leaning in, offers.

"Cigarillo?" The scout asks Pow.

Pow shakes his head. He's ready for another drink. And anyway, even when alive he never smoked. The scout gets the cigarillo lit on the third try; his hands are definitely shaking now. He probably won't even make it through the next glass. Gehenna's officers exchange triumphant glances.

But the scout makes it through the next glass, and the next one too.

They are into their fourth glass when the scout finishes his cigarillo and casually flicks the butt away. But his aim is impaired, and the flick sends the butt flying, not towards the floor, but directly at Pow. It lands in his hair, which, now well saturated with flammable liquid, immediately ignites into a halo of fire.

The crowd recedes in a squawk of horror. The barkeep has had patrons burst into flames before, and experience has taught her to keep a blanket handy. While Buck and Polecat slap Pow with their hats, she elbows through the crowd and tosses the blanket over Pow, pushes him on the floor, and sits on him.

When they unwrap the blanket, they find Pow a bit charred around the temples, but otherwise no worse for wear. They haul him to his feet and sit him back down at the table. The fire has quenched his deliciously moist feeling, and he's ready for another drink.

"No more smoking," Buck warns the scout. She doesn't believe for a minute that the scout's flick was unintentional, but since she can't prove this belief, she's going to watch him like a hawk. Pow's thirst is the insatiable thirst of a desiccated dead man. The scout is neither dead nor desiccated and he should have long succumbed. Buck is getting suspicious. The scout grins at her, pointy blue-stained teeth gleaming, and raises his glass.

But by the time they've killed the mescal, the scout is looking a bit done. His eyes are tarnished silver coins, and, in between chugs, he's clawed his hair into jagged clumps. The canvas walls are now sucking in and out, as though the hog ranch itself is trying to gasp for breath, stifled by the interior tension and the stench of hair pomade, tallow, dog and bugjuice. A guttural rumble overhead reminds them the storm is coming in.

But the scout doesn't drop. They finish the mescal, and pause so that the barkeep can send Lotta out to the back to dig up the whiskey that's been mellowing in a grave near the corral. The scout staggers off to relieve himself of some of his liquid burden and Gehenna's officers worriedly confer.

"He's cheating. He's got to be," Buck says. "No one can drink that much and live. Even Pow's starting to look waterlogged."

Pow *is* looking rough. As he has absorbed the liquid, he's puffed up, ballooning like a sponge. Where he had been stringy and dry, he's now round and plump, but it's a strained kind of plumpness. His skin, burned black with decay, looks shiny and stretched, like the skin of a balloon. The bony claws of his fingers have swollen into fat sausages.

In short, Pow looks about to burst. The scout has an outlet for his excess liquid. Pow is drinking faster than he can absorb. Something is gonna give.

"I know he's cheating," Buck repeats.

"How can he be cheating?" Polecat whispers. "What are we going to do?"

Pow is no longer paying attention to the whispered accusations flying between the officers. Something cold and hard has just bopped him on the beezer: an ice cube. He looks up to see the ice elemental, suspended in its silver cage above the table, waving a small blue hand at him. Pow sloshily waves back.

The elemental grabs at its scrawny neck and pulls, making an agonized face. Then it points to the scout's empty seat. Pow is mystified. The elemental grabs at its neck again—no, it's not grabbing at its neck, it's pretending to pull on a pretend something that is not actually hanging around its neck. The elemental points at the scout's empty seat again, and then mimes chugging a bottle. Pow glances around. The scout has not returned; the spectators have thinned out, some ducking outside for the same reason the scout did, others for a smoke. Buck has also disappeared, but Lieutenant Brakespeare and Polecat are still whispering worriedly. No, Polecat is whispering worriedly. Lieutenant Brakespeare is also staring at the ice elemental, who seeing her gaze, opens his little blue beak. A few teeny tiny sparkles fly out: Gramatica, the language of magick.

Pow may be dead, and also alive, and therefore somewhat magickal, but he still can't understand Gramatica. But Lieutenant Brakespeare, who is not magickal in the slightest, cannot be magickal at all per *The Articles of War*, upon pain of death (except at remove, of course)—a tiny little flicker of comprehension flits across her face, a flicker that almost instantly is reabsorbed back into her normal mulish scowl. The elemental tugs on the imaginary thing again. Pow and Lieutenant Brakespeare make eye contact, and the lieutenant raises her eyebrow oh-so-very-slightly. Pow is still clueless but Lieutenant Brakespeare seems to have understood.

A bright blue light briefly electrifies the hog ranch interior, its whiplike *crack* provoking shrieks. The roar of thunder drowns out the shrieks. The storm is almost upon them.

The scout returns and takes his place across the table. Buck returns and she and Polecat resume their positions of support behind Pow. But Lieutenant Brakespeare has realigned herself until she stands directly behind the scout. Buck gives her a glare, which is ignored. The barkeep pours from a dirt-encrusted bottle.

"Ut!" The scout says, raising his glass.

"Ut!" says Pow. The brief hiatus has left him thirsty. He raises the glass and drinks; the liquid flows like oil down his throat.

The scout sputters and puts his glass down. "This is not whiskey!"

The barkeep holds the bottle up so that the label reading *Madama Twanky's Amber Apple Schnapps* is visible. "The whiskey bottles broke," she explains. "This is all I could salvage. Don't you like apple schnapps?"

The scout sniffs the glass again, suspiciously. "It don't smell like apples."

"If you ain't thirsty anymore, we can stop right now," Buck says "Call an end, and Pow the winner. Get home before the flood."

Pow swallows; death has ruined his palate pretty good, but even in death he knows the aftertaste of apple schnapps, his mamma's favorite *digestif*. He also now knows the aftertaste of gun oil. And he knows the difference between the two.

"Finish now and we can be out of here before the storm blows us away," Buck suggests. Her smile is very smug.

In response, the scout raises his glass and bolts its contents. Then he chokes. Coughs and wheezes. His eyes roll upward, and the snake tattoo on his forehead ripples. Tears spring to his eyes, snot dribbles from his nose. He swallows hard, and slumps forward.

The hog ranch is silent. The wind has stopped, but the roof brush rustles, and a few drops of rain slip through, an advance guard. Another bolt of electric blue scorches the night. This time the crack sets ears a-ringing, and the accompanying thunder has almost no delay. Lieutenant Brakespeare leans over and jiggles the scout's shoulders, but he doesn't respond.

"I hereby declare—" Buck starts to say, and then the scout lifts his head. His eyes glitter green and gold, and he says: "Set us up again."

The barkeep pours them each another round of gun oil and this time the scout doesn't hesitate. Smiling, he drains the glass and slams it so hard upon the tabletop that it shatters. He grins, a rill of amber fluid dribbling down his chin.

"Set me—" The scout's voice turns thick and then trails away. His head flings back and his eyeballs roll up and then roll down. A bubble of foam appears on his lips and as he gurgles this bubble forms a beard, dripping down his chin to cover his chest. The scout begins to vibrate, his arms and legs twitching like he's been hit by lightning. The foam turns reddish brown, as the scout paws at his neck, moaning creakily.

"Looking for this?" Lieutenant Brakespeare dangles a small buckskin bag for all to see. In her other hand, the knife she used to snip the buckskin cord while pretending to be solicitous gleams sharply. She smiles, and that smile, in combination with her jagged scars, one on each cheek, is extremely malevolent.

The scout croaks as she opens the bag, waving his hands weakly. Six wisps of light—the souls the scout has collected—fly up and out, floating through the brush roof to disappear into lightning-spattered darkness. Lieutenant Brakespeare shakes the bag over the table, and something small and glittery falls out: a scorpion.

"What is that?" Buck asks. The scorpion curls its tail up, stinger gleaming. Arivaipa scorpions are dull brown and white, bland. The carapace of this scorpion is milky green, like translucent jade, and its stinger is a small barb of bright fuchsia.

"Ha!" says Lieutenant Brakespeare. "That scorpion is a Potable Sigil. It makes any liquid drinkable. Pretty useful in the desert, no?"

"I told you he was cheating!" Buck crows.

"You cheated too," the scout says thickly. "That weren't no apple likker."

"Evening the odds," Buck retorts. "And anyway, your cheat cancelled out mine—so that makes your cheat bigger!"

The scout is gagging and retching; Candy thrusts a spittoon towards him just in time. The scout vomits up a copious amount of bad booze and gun oil and then keels over backwards. Lieutenant Brakespeare winches his head up via a fistful of greasy hair and says: "Where's the gold?"

The scout burbles and Lieutenant Brakespeare nods, satisfied. Candy and the drover carry him off, to recover (if he can) in the guardhouse. Lieutenant Brakespeare and Polecat follow, to plan the excavation of the payroll gold as soon as the storm blows through. Outside, the rain is starting to come down, which means inside it is starting to come down, as well. The spectacle over, the spectators scatter for cover from the storm.

"Can I have another drink?" Pow asks, but no one refills his glass—they've all disappeared. He's killed the bottle of gun oil (Buck had switched the liquids when everyone thought she was pissing), but, of course, he's still thirsty, and so he's rather sorry the contest is over.

The scorpion-sigil skitters, tail waving frantically, trying to find shelter from the raindrops. Pow's interior is starting to feel rather odd. There's a ticklish feeling in his tummy, a funny rustling that makes him want to giggle. Pow unbuttons his sack coat, and something hard butts his hand. He looks down, and sees a scaly nose poking out from a tear in his shirt.

Freddie. The Gila monster erupts from Pow's chest, and darts forward to snap up the insect sigil, then scuttles back to safety. A gust of wind has almost taken down one of the canvas walls; another gust blows off half the roof and Pow's hat. A falling viga narrowly misses Pow's head; it lands instead on the table, smashing it. Then something large drops into Pow's lap: the ice elemental's cage. Inside, the elemental has a death-grip on the bars, tiny sanguine-colored sparks flashing from its mouth. Pow doesn't need to speak Gramatica to understand the elemental's shrieks for help. As the rest of the roof blows away, Pow fumbles at the cage's door. The door springs open and the elemental springs out, disappearing into the howling electrified night.

Pow lets drop the cage, and raising his face, opens his mouth to the wet wet rain.

ELECTRIC RAINS

KATHLEEN ANN GOONAN

Ella sat by Nana's body for two days before she pushed it out the window.

She had spent the first half-day realizing what death was, the next half-day grieving, the following morning waking and feeling reverent if somewhat nauseated, and trying to decide what to do.

It was three in the morning when she finally did it, and it was almost the season of electric rains.

There had been one already, fitful and slight, harbinger of spring and the season of avoidance. Once the weather warmed in Washington, D.C., thunderstorms boiled up almost every evening, preceded by the leaves in the park across the street turning up silver undersides. Ella was twelve, and had grown up knowing that she could not let the rains, or the rare snows, touch her.

But Ella had to take Nana home. Besides, she was beginning to smell bad. Night was a good time, the time least likely to rain.

In the end it was easy. There was no heat in the old lady's three-room apartment with the toweringly high ceilings and the hole in the plaster that looked like South America, so she'd not gotten very warm. The old lady had an electrical setup but used it only for cooking and powering a space heater in the most bitterly cold weather, hooking up big sparking clamps which scared Ella. There were people who kept the grid alive, down by Anacostia. Engineers, and those whom they taught, people who had escaped the first electric rains, like Ella and Nana.

By now, the body was very stiff. Ella was not surprised to find that the tiny old lady was not terribly heavy. She wrapped the body in the sheet upon which she had died, which made her easy to pull over the shiny wood floor, through the sitting room with its yellowed lace doilies and once-valuable international knickknacks—the ancient Chinese vase, the intricately carved Vietnamese table, the rug from nineteenth century Bagdad—and managed to lift her to chairs and then push her onto an oval table of shiny hardwood, a table she herself had polished only days before, one of the unending chores the old lady had her do so they could "live with dignity in this shit-eating world."

She shoved the table on its clawed wheels to the window. Grunting, she pushed up the reluctant sash. Paint chips flurried in the moonlit air, and the gust of wind took Ella by surprise: it was warm.

That was not good.

She leaned out the window; sniffed the air. It smelled too warm, like sudden spring. Perhaps it was. And the stars were obscured by cloud.

No matter. She had to do this, and soon.

She looked up and down the length of the street, waited until a lone car stopped at the light and then moved past, low, prowling beams of light ahead. She leaned out further, saw a few ragged shapes curled on the sidewalk. She swallowed. The rain people, those who didn't go down into the Metro but let the rain wash them countless times, could sometimes be normal, harmless. But sometimes…

She looked back at Nana's face, her delicately curved nose, her imp-like face overwhelmed by wrinkles, her high lacy collar always kept clean and white.

A middle-aged man used to visit, and talked to Nana blusteringly, with wide frantic gestures. He always frowned at the sight of Ella and she knew that the man did not like her being there and couldn't do a damned thing about it. She didn't like him much either. "Little bitch," he called her, the time he had squeezed her back in among Nana's spicy-musty clothes, but she had kicked him hard and he hadn't tried it again.

She sat down in one of the high-backed chairs and watched Nana for a moment.

Then, through the doubled wavy glass of the high windows, she saw a light streak through the heavens. A monitor plane, checking for contagion. Very rare. Nana laughed derisively whenever they saw one. "It won't be safe in our lifetimes, missy. At least," her voice gentled, "not in mine."

Ella knew, though, that the light was the spirit of Nana and that it was all right, that she did not have to tell anyone, that she could stay here as long as she wanted to. That was Nana's plan. Nana had talked about papers she had signed, and showed her the key to the safety deposit box at the bank. That nasty old man would do something about it, she was sure. He blabbered about the apartment being a "gold mine," and called Nana stupid all the time, even though he was her nephew.

But because of the newspaper room, she knew that both of them might well be insane. In the back of the townhouse was a huge room filled with stacks of old *Washington Posts,* yellowed, crumbling, musty-smelling. Nana had her cut out the crossword puzzles from each day, right by the funnies, and put them into a box from which she drew; she did one a day.

The newspapers were sorted roughly into years, but the year that Ella was most interested in was the year, the very day, that terrorists had run an Amtrak Silver Eagle from New York into Union Station in downtown Washington at full speed, crashing right into the lobby of the station.

They had hoped that in the resulting confusion they would be able to get into the Capitol Building, a block away, and set off their dirty bomb.

Their particular dirty bomb was not full of radioactive material. It was, instead, full of what became taken up by the atmosphere, rather than filling up the Capitol Building. That material was what had turned into electric rains.

The *Post* headline for that day said TERRORISTS DECIMATE DIRTY BOMB.

The terrorists had, apparently, been Ella's parents. She deduced this by reading several month's worth of *Washington Posts,* and hid them from Nana. That was not difficult in a room full of newspapers.

There was probably no bank anymore with the important papers in it; or, if there was, there was no one to pay attention to them, anyway.

Ella knew that Nana had lived here all her life and had seen her beloved city change and change and change and all the relatives and friends who really cared for her die until she was all alone, except for Ella, in the place she owned; the rest of the building she had divided into apartments when younger and rented them. Now, she kept the squatters out with fierce bars, preferring them to be empty rather than full of the "rain riffraff" which now inhabited Washington.

Ella climbed onto the table, knelt, and pushed the woman's shoulders. She leaned forward and grunted. It was harder than she thought it would be. Finally Nana's legs and her hips were outside and Ella, with a shriek, let go.

The window had a deep sill which overlooked 14th Street in Washington D.C., between R and S Streets. It was a place, Ella had been made to understand from listening to endless stories of hell and glory from Nana, burnished to mahogany smoothness by many tellings, which had felt the ebb and flow of time. When Nana's grandfather had bought the building, the street was genteel, alive with a shop for each need, even if that need was for fresh flowers, a need which Nana and now Ella felt keenly as stomach-hunger: brilliant purple zinnias mixed with broad creamy spider chrysanthemums, studded with red baby rosebuds, ah! Set on the grand dining room table, they made one feel royal.

But Nana, Ella often observed, had no problem feeling royal. She told Ella tales of the city lights being akin to blood for her, tales of being young and speeding about the city in a fine gray car, and then jolting on the farting busses when they still ran. Now, there were no busses, and the Metro entrances glowed. People had taken refuge underground when the electric rains had begun, but of course it had been too late: the rains, with their voices, had gotten them, had spread its contagion among them.

Now, if they went anywhere, they had to walk, even after Nana was attacked and raped. After that she walked her same route, head held high, Ella in tow and terrified, a heavy gun in her pocket that she practiced with once a week in the back alley on bottles and cans, laughing every time she blew one to bits. Once she dropped a young woman gangster just like that, when the gangster walked toward them holding a knife, and then she became known and feared, even by the people who danced up and down the street singing, "What a glorious feeling, I'm happy again!" The electric-rain people sometimes had ragged parades which marched beneath their window. They blew horns, and usually wore hats to hide their terrible deformities.

A warm breeze stirred the curtains. Ella was filled with terrified reverence as she gazed down on Nana, who had landed spread-eagle, face-up. The sheet had caught on a ledge and fluttered just below Ella, so Nana gazed at the stars.

Nana loved the stars, and had taught Ella their names; she had a formidable telescope she kept inside a little concrete room on the roof. On clear nights, cold or hot, they would go up, unlock the giant padlock, roll out the telescope onto the bumpy roof, and gaze all night, drunk on pulsing lights arranged with the precision of numbers. "If you got close they'd change position so you wouldn't recognize them but of course you can't get that close," Nana told Ella. One night, as a great treat, she'd shot out the six remaining park lights so that the sky would be darker. "Ha!" she laughed. "Think the cops will show up? Not a chance."

Ella knew there was not a chance—she knew what cops were, but had never seen one. She only knew that now that park would be dark at night forever.

"I used to go to lectures with my dad every Friday night at the Naval Observatory," she told Ella in her deep, rough voice, sticking her gun back in her pocket. "Now that's *dark*. Gentle man, so kind, too good for this world. Nothing like me."

But Ella saw gentleness everywhere in her, in the way she took care of Ella, how she took care to keep her in fine silk pajamas, how she made sure the linens were always clean, lowering the laundry down to Ella waiting nervously on the street with a red wagon that said Radio Flyer on the side, then trundling down to the Deep-Clean Laundro-Mat. "Shitty machines," she always said, "and they cheat us on the drying time but what can you do?"—a litany Ella had grown quite used to. Once she asked if they could not just dry the clothes on a clothesline and had received a lecture about the possibility of electric rain polluting the clothes. The Deep-Clean was operated by an old man who wore very clean clothes, a fine and eccentric mix of clothes—thin wool suits in winter with vests and colorful silk ties and combat boots; beautiful, starched cotton dresses with aprons in the summer that he claimed he'd stolen from the Smithsonian Historic Collection. He ran his machines with a generator and spent most of his time gathering fuel.

Well, now Nana had returned to the streets.

Ella was very unhappy as she gazed down at her. She should have wrapped her more tightly, she thought now; she should have hidden her from the world; she should have cushioned the fall.

Suddenly frantic, she ran for the linen closet. Every sheet was ironed and folded; Nana knew how to take up the time of day, that was certain. Ella pulled a chain and the closet lit up and she felt the neat but sparse row with her finger and lit on the smoothest, oldest one, white cotton limp with age and use, smooth as glass, and yanked it out.

She paused to look around the apartment. She felt in her pocket for the key. She went to Nana's bedroom; got her purse which she had never before violated, a shapeless black leather affair, and pulled out the wallet, stuck it next to the key in her pocket. The gun was already there. She stepped out into the hall holding the sheet, locked the door, and ran down five flights of stairs.

At the foot of the stairs she pulled out the key chain and felt for the key to the closet beneath the stairs. Unlocking the storage closet, she pulled out the laundry wagon.

Once outside, she felt exposed. She'd never been outside, alone, that she could remember. She took a deep breath and looked down at Nana.

She expected blood but there was none. Maybe death had dried it; maybe it was frozen in Nana's veins now that there was no heart to move it. She heard glass break a block away, and distant gunfire. She felt in her pocket Nana's heavy gun, filled with bullets; she had checked as Nana had taught her.

She hastily spread the sheet on the sidewalk next to Nana. Taking a deep breath, she knelt and shoved her hands beneath Nana's shoulder and bony hip and pushed. Nana rolled on to the sheet, twice, there, now she was well on and Ella took the edge of the sheet, pulled it over her face, and felt better. Pushing with all her might, she rolled the woman up in the sheet like an egg roll, tucking the ends in.

Now for the hard part. Nana was not tall; in fact, she was no taller than Ella and often complained of having shrunk.

Ella tipped the wagon on its side and pulled it next to Nana. Now what? She set the wagon back up. She could do it. She had lifted her onto the chairs, the table, hadn't she? But she was a lot more tired now.

She heard shuffling footsteps behind her and whirled.

A shape of rags was making its way toward her.

The shape had a greasy silk scarf folded like a triangle and tied beneath the chin; probably a woman. She looked at Ella, the wagon, and the sheeted shape. Squatting, she shoved her arms beneath the body and lifted it into the wagon. Ella noticed that she had very large feet in dark untied boots. She stammered, "Thank you."

The… person said, "'S'allright," and shuffled along.

Nana's torso and thighs took up the wagon; her legs stuck out stiffly behind and her head was just a bump. Ella picked up the handle and paused.

She looked out across the park, her only playyard for so long, and then only rarely. She remembered little before Nana: a beautiful face framed by smooth, sweet-smelling, pitch-black hair which swung forward and tickled Ella's face; an older brother. Ella would always remember him, his baggy sweater hanging from wide shoulders; she never told these things to Nana, nor did she tell her about the special school she attended, and though she knew that her whole family had died, she no longer believed the story Nana told her, that they had been shot all of them by a thin white man for no reason at all as they left a restaurant in Georgetown while Nana watched from inside, then rushed out and grabbed her, then jumped into a taxi, when Ella was about four or five. She had no memory of such a thing, and she remembered things before.

She knew who she was. She had been there. At the train crash. And now, she had seen the newspaper article.

TERRORIST'S CHILD SAVED BY DECORATED ADMIRAL

She took another deep breath of sharp air. The park benches across the street were filled with dark lumpy shapes. She and Nana planted tulips there every fall, which they got from the cold basement of a deserted nursery, and nothing delighted them so much as to see them come up every spring; they did not even mind when people picked them, for flowers are meant to be picked, Nana said. But for a precious two weeks they flamed gold and red and when the twisty old trees were darkened with rain the flowers took on deeper color and then everything was so absolutely beautiful.

But now the blooms had come and gone. A match flared tiny across the street then went out. Fourteenth Street stretched before her. She had a very long walk ahead of her. She picked up the wagon handle, glad that the street was level here.

Her memory of the route was of changing constellations of lights, for once a month they had walked this route, at night, Nana swinging her gun in her hand openly. "Exercise," she would exclaim with satisfaction at regular intervals. "Exercise! This is my city too, dammit!"

Now, Ella was terrified. Here she was, all alone, pulling a dead old woman in a wagon through no-man's land. She leaned forward and yanked hard.

She was wearing her glasses. She felt like taking them off, but did not. When she walked with Nana, she had often removed them, until their absence was noticed and Nana demanded that she put them back on. She had noticed Ella stumbling several years earlier and checked her eyes. It was then that Ella found out that there were such people as ophthalmologists, and that Nana was one—or had been one. After the months of the first electric rains, when her parents, fifth-generation Americans from Kansas City, had been on trial for treason, everyone who could, fled the city, or were drawn into the Metro station, where, rumor had it (and they so claimed), her parents had placed some of the first uploading devices. Even the *Washington Post* faltered, but then cloaked their intrepid reporters in rain gear—ineffective, they soon learned—and soldiered on.

Nana's office was two blocks away from the apartment, dark and full of mysterious shapes until Nana flicked on the lights. "Ah," she said. "Electricity. And my equipment is still here. Amazing. Sit up there in that chair, missy. Here's a pillow." And she looked into Ella's eyes and clicked this and that until the world was sharp enough to draw tears; sharp enough to force Ella to leave fuzziness behind, enough to make her behold, remember, yearn, and regret.

Nana let Ella pick out several frames and made lenses for them all. "Who knows if this will even be here, next month," she said, sighing. "I loved my work. Not many can say that, missy."

Ella had been amazed to see, once the glasses had been slid onto her face and they stepped out into the night, that the moon was a single sharp sliver, and not white mounds resembling scoops of snowy ice cream on a velvet black sky. With glasses, she had seen the stars for the first time without the telescope. She had always believed that she needed that special tool to see stars, but there they were: a part of the everyday life of those who could see. But still she missed the blurry blossoms of light, the fuzzed red taillights shimmering on wet streets, the towers of lights which with glasses were revealed as buildings with actual edges.

After that, Nana's newspaper room beckoned increasingly. "Never could bear to throw away the paper till I'd read the whole thing," she said.

Ella read advertisements from a lost world. She read advice columns about strange and alien problems: my mother-in-law is too controlling; when should I tell my fiancée that I'm bisexual?

Finally, after figuring out the dates and searching extensively, she found biographies of her parents, starting above the fold on page one and continuing on page A-9. A thrill went through her when she saw their pictures. Then she burst out crying.

They had both worked for the Department of Homeland Defense, and decided that what their country was doing was all wrong. Ella felt very strange reading her mother say, "You have killed my son. I demand to have my daughter back. We only wanted the best for her. She was supposed to be one of the first people uploaded."

When she read that, Ella stood up and made her way to the window through and over stacks of newspapers. She stared out at the park, with its soldier-statue darkened in patches by the rain that had been falling for days, at the shiny, wet streets, no longer full of evacuees but only the occasional car, inside of which, she could only imagine, sat intrepid, stubborn people like Nana. You could tell electric rain from regular rain because the charged nanocrystals glowed. Each one was unimaginably small, the paper said, but together they produced sweeping rainbow effects, and, at night, a seductively beautiful scintillation, like you were traveling among the stars.

It was an initiation device, which changed the biochemistry of your brain, readying you for uploading. Making you want it.

You would remain uploaded until the world was ready for peace, when you would be downloaded into the new bodies they would have ready for you by then.

Outside, in the air above 14th Street, in colors of electric rains, Ella saw her parents' faces, an afterimage of staring at their newspaper photographs.

According to the paper, they had been executed several years ago, on August 17th of the year of their terrorist attack. Because they worked for the Department of Homeland Defense and knew all possible avenues of attack, so far no one had been able to hack into any of the components of their grand plan, which swept up the East Coast, and was borne inland and then out to sea by hurricanes. By then, it was reproducing, and had taken over New York City and all of the coastal cities down to Miami.

Ella yanked at the tall window sash, but it was painted shut. She banged and smashed on it with her fist and was finally getting it to open, just a crack, when Nana came in. She immediately saw the paper and grabbed Ella. Ella fought her, struggled, but Nana was surprisingly strong and finally Ella collapsed, sobbing, into her arms.

"There's nothing out there," Nana told her, in a surprisingly tender voice. "You've got to live your life here and now. Remember how I found you."

They planted crops in the back yard of the townhouse—soybeans, corn, potatoes, and kale—and the electric rains did not survive their trip through the soil to the roots.

And Ella did not forget what she had read.

Ella felt relatively safe on 14th Street, especially with the gun in her pocket. She had no qualms about shooting someone who might want to hurt her. Nana had drilled her fiercely about that, shoot first and think later, they wouldn't do any different. She knew this was true, and she needed her glasses to see these threats approaching, and in gauging the degree of threat. She knew she looked defenseless trudging along with her strange bundle. This walk would take till well past daylight, and then she would find a place to nap and return at night.

Now, the city unfolded around her with splendor. A liquor store on the next block glowed with neon of all colors, green, blue, yellow, and she slipped her glasses down briefly and saw it: yes: the unfolding flower the lights became without that focus. She loved that flower, and Nana always had to yank her along, at this point. She stopped, though, and absorbed the beauty of the flower, the glowing petal-point of intersecting green and red which read quite dully COORS with her glasses on. This was one of the landmarks. She went faster to get past the rotting smell of the dumpster in the alley next to the store, another landmark.

The usual bodies lay in front of it, and some cardboard structures. She was not afraid; these people were the least of her problems. The wagon squeaked past them. They would not rouse even if kicked, for Nana always gave each one a token kick as she passed, saying, "Scum! Sluggards! Weaklings! You're ruining my beautiful city!" and the like, and no one ever moved. Music blared from the door as Ella passed, and within she saw a bald, wary black man, his head washed in white neon, and rows and rows of bottles. He glanced up from a tiny tv sitting on his counter as she squeaked past. They had a television set, but Nana never turned it on anymore. There was no news, only old sitcoms and soap operas.

Next was a block of pawnshops drawn tight with aluminum fences drawn down in the evening, terribly dark, no streetlights. She waited on that corner until a car swept down 14th Street and illuminated the sidewalk for a moment. A few bums in doorways, nothing more. She pulled forward as quickly as she could, trying not to seem afraid and hurried, standing straight, as if she were strong and powerful. In the middle of the block a shadowy figure lurched toward her. She veered to the left and reached into her pocket, then saw him fall with a thump without any assistance from her.

On the next corner she pulled her glasses down again, for an instant, and could just see the red blinking light on top of the Monument, which stood atop a low green hill behind all the buildings ahead of her. Prostitutes postured in very short skirts and low blouses, running out and stopping a rare car. A door opened and two got in; an arm reached out and shoved the others away; one fell down on the street and got up dusting her butt off yelling, "Fuck you too." But they did not bother Ella as she trundled past.

Ella was feeling a little better now. Chinatown was to her left, a few blocks over, and Ella pulled her glasses down to blur the beautiful green dragon which arched high above the buildings hiding the rest of Chinatown, fusing it into a creature who roared into flame with the pulse of her own heartbeat then returned to a coiled position. There was no clearer place to see the dragon; a block further back or forward the dragon was hidden by other buildings. She was filled with joy at the sight of the dragon each time she saw it.

Once she had been walking down the street and stopped at a tangle of white string at her feet. It was fringed with red and blue, and as she looked Ella had become aware that it was, miraculously, twisted into the shape of a dragon, perfectly and unmistakably. She had picked it up carefully and pressed it in one of Nana's musty books which crumpled in tiny sharp triangles from the corners of the pages whenever she opened it, with print so small that it was almost impossible to read. The dragon always gave her strength and it did now, flashing beneath the moonless sky as if, without her glasses, it were independent of buildings, poised in the sky, dancing for her, telling her that she deserved to be alive for reasons she did not understand.

Next came the Man on Horseback, one of her favorite statues. His sword was brandished. He would protect her. She had seen him many times, dappled with sunlight which moved as the broad branches overhead shifted in the summer wind; plastered with dead orange leaves. The bums there were old and kind, never mean; Nana told her that they were different, that for many bum generations they had preyed on government workers ascending from the Metro, an easy touch. And she always gestured toward the site of the old YWCA Cafeteria a few blocks over. Nana used to meet her friends there for lunch, and Ella knew Nana's memory of the inside almost as well as she knew the inside of their apartment: the tall windows, the wide booths, the cheap, good food, the sound of silverware plunked on trays drifting up to the high ceiling. Nana had a table and two ladder-back chairs she bought from the cafeteria when it had been closed and the furnishings went up for sale, sitting in one of the apartment alcoves. Ella had never minded polishing the old worn wood; she loved polishing all the things in Nana's apartment; they seemed to miraculously hold a past just beneath their surface which was lush and carefree and deep, like flowers, like city lights, something she could feel like heat as her fingers felt out their ornate crevices; and afterwards they always had good green tea from a beautiful pot covered with china flowers, and Nana always seemed so happy to see everything shining and perfect like the rows of linens in the closet.

Ella was very tired. Her feet burned; her legs felt like rubber. She became afraid that she had gone out of her way and fear closed her throat for a moment. She removed her glasses and recognized none of the blurred constellations.

And it began to rain.

She saw one scintillation and it was like the first flake of snow: Was it real?

The Smithsonian Institute was two blocks away. Nana had brought her here on sharp blue winter days, carrying flashlights so that she could see the insides of the dark museums. One time when they went, self-appointed technicians had found the central power switch and illuminated everything, but usually they saw everything in the focused beam of a flashlight, in pieces. Nana liked Modern Art more than anything else, so Ella had seen the reclining Matisse women with hairy armpits, the two-faced Picassos, the sharp edges of Cézanne. She had also seen things much more mysterious: a pendulum that never stopped swinging; the history of atomic energy; a small thing called a capsule which had orbited the earth. These were the things that interested her the most.

Ella began to run. She was tired, but she had no choice: she had to get out of the electric rains before it began to pour. As far as she knew there were two alternatives. You would hear ethereal singing voices, or beautiful music, the intrepid *Washington Post* had reported, and be irresistibly drawn to a Metro entrance. If you went down into the Metro, you would be uploaded. Or you could stay out of the rain.

The trial of her parents had taken place in Los Angeles, which had become the new capital of the United States. The *Post* had gotten hold of some of their classified scientific papers and published them; the papers were subsequently critiqued by other scientists who condemned their uploading processes as being untested and dangerous. Others said that they had been tested, and that they worked, and that the entire Cabinet and the President and all of the Congress had been briefed on an alternate uploading system, one that was manufactured by the company that the President had once run.

As Ella ran uphill, a glow lit the grayness of the morning and she realized that not only was she almost at the Smithsonian, she was also almost at the Metro entrance for the museum.

It was glowing most brilliantly now and she stopped, panting, as the scintillations increased. She only had moments before the singing would begin, before she would become one of the derelicts drunk on electric rain living in the streets, or drawn down into the Metro.

Her parents had not been uploaded, according to the newspaper. But… would they not have made copies of themselves? She had asked Nana once, and Nana had become very angry and said that those people were not her parents; they were criminals and that they had ruined her city and that she should be grateful to have a home at all, and that was the end of it. She kept her thoughts to herself after that, but did not stop wondering.

Perhaps they were there, in the brilliant light emanating from the subway entrance.

Perhaps she could see them again.

If she just went into that glowing, beautiful entrance, down the rainbowed stairs…

She took a few steps toward it, across the Mall, then forced herself to stop. She looked back at the sheet-wrapped body.

Nana had taken good care of her. She had to do this one thing. Even though Nana had not asked, she knew it was what she wanted.

Turning, she ran under the deep concrete overhang of a nearby building and huddled down to wait out the shower.

Electric rains drifted across the face of the Castle, making it look magical. She could see the top of the Washington Monument; the anti-terrorist doors had long since been removed and she and Nana had hiked to the top one lovely winter morning, and that was one of the few times she had seen Nana cry. "My city," she had said. "My beautiful city."

Ella thought that she heard one vagrant melody, in her head, faint, like birdsong through the closed window in the spring, like all the loveliness she had ever known, like flat clean sheets, like glowing polished wood, like bright tulips, and she began to sing her own songs, loudly, songs that Nana had taught her. "My Country, 'Tis of Thee," "From the Halls of Montezuma," and "Beautiful Ohio." She stood up in the concrete alcove and shouted, "B-I-N-G-O, B-I-N-G-O, B-I-N-G-O and Bingo was his name-o." The echo was almost like a round, as if Nana was singing with her, overlapping her sounds to make chords.

But it was so hard to think that her own parents had been wrong. And it made her angry that Nana had never told her the truth. She began to cry, then wiped away her tears.

The shower was over. The slight green buds on the trees lining the Mall sparkled in the morning sun.

And five people approached the wagon holding Nana.

Three were women and two were men, walking across the tall, dry winter grass of the unmown Mall. They were of various ages. One woman, with long blonde hair, was wearing shorts and a sweater. The two men wore business suits and red ties. The other two women were middle-aged and also wore suits.

The wagon was about two hundred feet away from Ella's shelter.

She wasn't sure what to do. She decided to stay in hiding until they passed.

But apparently they had spotted the wagon, all alone out there, and were heading toward it. She could hear them faintly.

"What's this?" asked one of the men. He bent down and began pulling at the sheet. The women murmured excitedly, and the blonde woman smiled broadly.

"A body! What luck!" She picked up the wagon handle.

Ella, heart beating hard, ran out from beneath her alcove. "Stop!"

They all turned, looking surprised.

"She's... mine."

Ella was closer now, about twenty feet away.

"Why, how could she possibly be yours?" asked one of the middle-aged women. "You're far too young to have your own body."

"We need her," smiled the blonde woman. "For the greater good. So that more of us can get out. And change things. You come with us, sweetie." She gestured toward the Metro entrance, still glowing.

"She's not very old," muttered one of the men. "She can wait a while."

Ella fumbled in her pocket. The gun got caught on some folds, but finally she got it out. She held it steady, as Nana had taught her. "You can't have her."

"Why, you greedy little—"

Ella thought sure he was going to say "bitch." She fired over his head.

The blonde woman turned pale. Ella was glad. She was afraid that they would not care if they were shot. "Get away or I'll shoot you all."

They all looked at each other uneasily. One of the middle-aged women crouched down and held out a hand. "I... used to have a daughter like you, honey. I know you're scared and lonely. Come with us and we'll help you out."

Ella advanced steadily, still holding the gun on them. "I have plenty of bullets."

One of the men pulled on the blonde woman's arm. "Come on. It's not worth it. It took us a long time just to get our bodies."

"But—two!"

Still, they backed away slowly, as of one accord. They did not turn away from Ella until they were farther away, and then they ran toward the Metro entrance and disappeared into the glow.

It was then that Ella knew for sure: she did not want to go down into the Metro. Not ever.

A gray overcast crept over the sky, threatening a day of spring drizzle. Ella figured she had about three miles to go. She'd better get started.

Independence Avenue was right across the street. Now it was just a few blocks' walk, past the Washington Monument and the Vietnam War Memorial. She had gone there with Nana several times. Her son's name was on the wall.

Ella picked up the handle from where she had let it clank to the sidewalk and trudged on. She smelled the dampness of the river and knew well where it was anyway. She and Nana often sat on its banks and watched the beautiful lights of traffic wind along the Virginia shore, and from time to time Nana dressed them both up in finery, took a taxi to a restaurant full of crushed velvet and dark wood, high above the river, sipped a tiny bright drink before dinner as she watched the lights hungrily, sometimes through a glimmer of tears, and taught Ella to like snails.

She stopped.

No. Neither of those were true. They were stories Nana had told her, many times, stories about how it would be again once everything was right. Once the electric rains were over.

She was getting tired, she realized. Tired and hungry and thirsty. After a long trudge, while the sky became steadily more gray, she finally glimpsed them: the magnificent naked people, the man astride the horse, the woman leading it.

And across the bridge, set on a hill, the white mansion.

Ella's arms ached, but the wagon didn't seem quite as heavy now though she dreaded the hill. The river was swift and rushing below the bridge and she felt as if the dragon of light was bursting through her own chest as she walked across the arch of the bridge.

Once across it, she had to turn back, not forward, to get her bearings, crossing the main highway via another circle and running up the asphalt until the angle of the hill stopped her. There were only four turns now. And here—

Here was the stone that said *Admiral James Tolliver*.

The man who had rescued her, and then died.

To the right was another stone for Nana: *Rose Ann Tolliver*.

Nana always hurried past these stones, but Ella always saw her glance at them; saw tears well in her eyes. Perhaps she thought that Ella didn't know her real name. Perhaps she was pretending that Ella had never seen the newspaper articles.

Perhaps she was pretending that, by rescuing Ella, her husband had ingested the electric rains, and was lost somewhere, uploaded to an unknown future. There was no body here, beneath the stone that read *National Hero*. He had given his life to help prevent what had actually happened. Maybe.

Or maybe, because of him, it had not happened everywhere.

Ella, grunting, tipped the wagon sideways. Rose Ann Tolliver tumbled out. Ella pushed and pulled on her until she was roughly aligned with the headstone. It was all she could do. She had no shovel. She got out Nana's old driver's license and slipped it inside the sheet. She saw fresh flowers on some of the graves. Maybe there were real people here. Maybe they were taking care of things. She was not sure she wanted to meet them, though. Just because they took care of Arlington Cemetery did not mean they were sane. But they might bury Rose Ann Tolliver next to the memory of her husband.

There was the Pentagon, to her right. Five sides, Nana had taken care to teach her the shapes, but somehow Ella thought she had already known.

She sat below the decaying white mansion and thought of the things that could happen. The things Nana had said might happen. The day that she said might come, the day that Nana told her she had to live for.

All the people living in Washington the day of the attack, the ones caught in the electric rains, the ones who had rushed into the Metro and been uploaded, would be downloaded. The world would be new, peace-loving, like Ella's parents had believed it could be.

Those people would go about their lives in Nana's timeless, beautiful Washington. They would go to office jobs, come home to families, eat snails in French restaurants or dim sum in Chinatown. They would think, read, do research, go to concerts and plays. They would walk the lovely, tree-lined streets of Washington with friends and relatives.

They would not be afraid of the rains.

But when would that be? Ella wondered.

And why would they be any different than the people she had just met?

How long was she supposed to polish the furniture, iron the sheets, and plant the dwindling supply of tulip bulbs?

And how was this supposed to happen?

Were there really people elsewhere? Normal, old-fashioned people, not rain-mad? In California? Was anyone flying the monitor planes?

Was there any place the electric rains had not reached, a place where they were doing all the things Nana had longed to do, or figuring out how to do them very soon?

What would happen if the electric rains fell on her and there was no place to run to, no Metro where she could be uploaded? Would she just go mad herself?

Nana might not have thought that these were good questions to ask. But she did.

Ella rose from the damp ground and brushed leaves from her pants. She picked up the wagon handle. The wagon would be useful.

"Goodbye, Nana," she said, and walked down the narrow cemetery road heading west.

SHE-CREATURES

MARGO LANAGAN

We were bringing the kegs over. Everything had gone exactly to plan. The moon was new, a little white smile in the sky. Dassel had kept his mouth shut and I thought he was to be trusted. Bertoldo's back had not given him the gyp and so he had been able as much as Dass and I to walk about the beach and hoist the kegs that lay all over—"like babies," said Dass in glee, "like little black happy babies"—all over the sand.

The lads up the coast had timed the tide exactly right casting them out of the cave and the cove. Oh, we were a strange band, working by night and out of sight of one another—but not out of mind. I had been as good as there, dressed dark in my place in the line under the headland, passing the kegs along. I had felt their weight, all but heard the slosh of them in my palms.

Put it out of your head, Fion had said in the night, her face above mine.

I'm not moving! says I in protest.

No, but I can hear your brain, wheeling and crackling in your stillness. You're stiff as a poker, and not in a good way. And then she started fiddling and fumbling at me.

Gawrd, woman, I've got to keep my wits about me this night.

I reckon… she says, with a hold on me like a warm, dry mouth, like a spell. It ran up my spine, the feel of it, quieting my worrying brain, *I reckon you're already awake; you may as well. Don't you think so?*

Anyway, that was hours ago and now we were into the men's-only business, well and truly, the wagon loaded and the road to Leightman's barn curving away among all the breasts and bums of this land, and the Elder Cooper with his bag of gold in the hay with which to give us each our divvy, and the Younger at watch over Constable Mastiff in the Arms, keeping him rotten with the best of the last haul's Spanish, keeping him immovable in his cups.

"I am glad we made it this far," says Dass, "before them clouds set in."

"You'll not chat," says Bertoldo low. "'Tis a windless night and, as we have learned to our detriment, sounds carry weird in this place."

Dassel came up to my elbow and spoke quiet. "What detriment is that?"

"Jon Plaice in the gaol and forty barricks confiscated."

"Oh, I did not know he were gaoled for this! I thought it were for dumping his refuse on the common."

"It is because you are a new bloke," I said. "People will tell you all manner of nonsense. No—" and I eyed the cartwheel, which had a tiny squeak that I'd thought I greased over. "It was because he broached one of them. He was not used to such quality. He sat by the roadside singing and, before you know, old Widow Pussmouth has stridden off in the middle of the night and fingered him to the constable. 'Twas not Mastiff then; 'twas a man you'd not want to meet even in your first-born innocence. Just his look at you made you guilty of something, even if you could not recall it."

"Keep it down, Cottar," said Bertoldo then, and I could hardly snap back at him, seeing I had just been preaching for silence, so we went on awkward among ourselves, listening nervously to the crunch of the wheels on the road and the fall of the donkey-hooves and of our feet and the rub of our trousers and rasp of our breaths, of which Bertoldo's was the most stertorous and interfered-with by phlegm. Dassel's I couldn't hear, his lungs were so young and uncrushed as yet by life; my own was somewhere between his and Bertoldo's, cold in my chest and then hot in my throat and nostrils, and you could hear the heartbeats in them.

It distresses you so, maybe you should not be involved, Fion had said when Frost had proposed this last one. *There's nothing gives the game away so fast as some sweaty man going all guilty about his days.*

It is just too clean an opportunity, I told her, and I went through the plan again.

I cannot see the hole in it, she said when I had finished. *So what is making you so twitchy?*

I don't know. Maybe you are right. Maybe I am getting too old for shenanigans like this.

Did I say that? And she cuffed me, just soft, back of my head, passing to get the kettle off the fire. *Bertoldo must be twice your age.*

He doesn't have a wife and children on him—

Ooh, I wonder why. Such a jolly feller. And high fun in the bedroom, too, I'm guessing.

And neither does that Dass, I point out. *Maybe it is that.*

Yes indeed, your burden of responsibilities. Poor helpless Fion and those rickety babs hardly able to lift their own weight. Which given her character and the fact that all our sons and the daughter too looked to be building like bullocks—

Is it that I have the most to lose of them, I mean, I said, *should we be nabbed?*

By whom exactly? I cannot see that person, anywhere near your plan.

Now the moon was coming and going a bit. Whenever it was gone, I could see things only by memory and the sounds they made.

"Like your head is wrapped in cloth," came Dass's murmur.

"Rain would be good," said Bertoldo quiet behind, "to shush over your remarkings. You could blether all you liked."

"Sorry," said Dass, when he might have bristled and riposted, so I thought more of him for holding himself back. "It's so quiet, I forgot. It feels like we are the only people in the world."

"Well, we are not," said Bertoldo. "The night is sprinkled with ears. If only lightly in these parts, still ears they are. It only takes the one with a waking brain behind it." He sounded almost as if he relished the thought of that ear hearing, that person running for authority.

Dass's feet came to a decisive stop.

"Uff!" Bertoldo had run in the back of him. "What the bloody—"

"Sh!" hissed Dass. "There is someone up ahead."

I held back the donkey and we stood searching.

"I cannot say," I whispered. "Anything I'm seeing may be as much a flash in my eye as a movement of light up there."

"It's there; I saw it," he says. "Some big lamp moving, and then quelled and covered, suddenly."

The donkey made a disbelieving noise with its lips.

"You and I will go up there." Bertoldo made himself sound tired, and Dass stupid. "Cottar, stay and mind the cart, and we shall go and see if it is safe to proceed. Come, lad."

"We must go very careful and quiet."

"Oh, really? I had not thought o' that until you said it."

Then I was alone in the dark—well, there was the donkey, but he were never much company. "Stormcloud," my daughter had wanted to call him, after his coat, but I was more inclined to think of him as Boss-Eyes or, when times were hard, Ribs, or Nipper in the days after he had just bitten someone. He was not a nasty animal, but he had not the nobility for a proper name or decorative.

Anyway, there he was, his shoulder stolid at my elbow as I tried to fix Dass and Bertoldo's few sounds to shapes moving away up the road. Again, the blooms of night-blood across my eyeballs were more distinct against the dark than anything. I knew we were near Martin's copse; I could smell a wisp of fox from the earth there. I looked up in hopes of some stars, but there were only a couple of places torn in the rolling cloud, closing up like water over little drowning white faces. I had to wonder if I even existed, now that their sounds were gone, Dass and Bertoldo's, now that I could see nothing, and nothing see me. I had to wonder if I were not drowned myself, and dissolved back into the darkness of un-creation, just as before I was born.

"Are we done for, Fion?" I whispered just to hear myself. "Has Mastiff got wise to us, and is waiting up there, with men and muskets?"

It was a long time wondering. Other stars whimpered above me and were sunk again. I began to think this was some dreadful scheme of the others, to have me caught like Plaice all alone with this load, that they had gone ahead to advise the law that I was here and ready for the picking, the goods on my cart with my donkey undeniable. Someone was going to leap from the trees any moment, and I would be collared and carted off to the roundhouse at Duggley, never to see Fion again for year on year, or hear her dirty laugh, or feel her scurrying hands on me. Nor see my boys nor girl again, who were just getting interesting, and would have good natter with you, bringing you odd pieces of the world that they had noticed, and asking you to explain them.

I hardly know how to tell what next went on. Even having seen it myself I cannot credit its happening, let alone expect that you will believe me.

First, just as in the Holy Book—although God knows there was nothing else holy about it—first, there was light. It grew unnatural, very weak at first, grey and cold and seemingly sourceless among the trees up ahead. Dass and Bertoldo moved against it, and then they stilled like shapes cut out of black paper, all frozen elbows and knees, and then they skittered off to one side and crouched, just cut-out heads poking out of a cut-out tree.

And then—it was as if someone put a tap to a hole in the top of my head, and ran some kind of cold syrup through me—four figures stepped from four different directions into that part of the road. And I suppose it came from their throats, but the music—the four different notes of it, holding on and on without taking any new breaths, and making, if a harmony, so foreign a notion of harmony to my ears that my teeth clenched and creaked on one another to hear it and my mouth watered—the music seemed as sourceless as the light.

But it was the sight as much as the sound. How can I communicate, I wonder, the sight of those? They were as innocent as babies, and as hairless. They were white-skinned, for goodness' sake! They were nearly naked, which was alarming; they were bare chested, bare *breasted* I thought; from here I could not see proper whether they were women or men. Each wore a cloth around its middle and a hat upon its head. The pale cloths were strange enough—one apricot, one yellowish, one faded blue, one pink—and draped and tucked-up like a Hindoo-man's, or a baby's napkin between the legs. But the hats, each matching its owner's cloth, oh! How could it be, such simple things, no more than tubes going up from the heads—but tall, tall, and cut in two points at the top—could strike such fear into a heart?

They did not quite meet, the four. They came to the middle-ish and stood, facing each other and holding each his or her loathsomely offset note. It was a terrible song—not even a song, a terrible cold caterwaul. It was the voice you might hear if you flew up close to the sky, the voice that echoed in the ears of larks and sent them downward trilling and wittering with fright and excitement.

Out of the dark road beyond them stalked their queen, and this one there was no mistaking the sex. And you might think it a wonderful thing to be in secret watching and some splendid woman appear, fine and full-rounded, stripped to the waist and the nipples on her gleaming unsucked, ungnawed by any child ever, but I tell you this did not man me up. Rather the reverse: I shrank, and the knacks on me fought to be first back into my body, so that I had to cup myself with my hands as I stood there, to warm and protect them, to ease the sick feeling that struck up from them on the sight of that dreadful woman.

And just as I was too far back and yet I seen those nipples no mistaking, I was well out of hearing, yet Dassel made this little sound in his throat and I heard it. Everything heard it, every owl and leaf and foxlet and bit of grit stuck to my boot. Every one of those infernals heard it; though I did not see them move they were in woken stances now, and their music was suddenly half as loud as had been. Storm-cloud beside me were stiff as a wooden donkey, all his relaxment and laziness gone.

It were like some nightmare. They all turned and had faces, and their arms and their renewed music reached and wavered out like some monstrous sea-nemminy torn itself up from its deep-sunk rock and come lumbering out across the hills, and now must catch some land-fish to swallow. I couldn't see neither of the boys a moment, and then, I see him; it is like the air is water and Dass is being tide-pulled along, like he is already a dead body hauled by his middle and his limbs and head dragging behind.

All of them was women—how could I have thought them other? I never found that shape more terrifying, the tits like eyes, the hips all blowsed out by that garment, by that cloth. Where was their hair? They must have tucked it up inside them dreadful dumb-caps.

They gathered poor Dass in—oh!—into that nemminy of flesh and bending voices. I were nearly sick at the moment they first touched him; I saw clear as you see in a tree cut nearly through and poised to fall the approaching of the moment I would go unhinged. The feeling, I thought—with a horror you would not credit were you new-manned and all a-lust for normal women—the feeling of all them breasts, press-ing and eyeing you, them stomachs, that ring of weird faces—the hats, oh the hats! leaning and touching and crossing above you!

"God help me," I said almost soundless, for now that they had Dass it were safe to speak; he had taken their attention off the rest of us. And I stood there clutching mouth and conkers both, fighting off the music that pushed me like that axe-bit tree about to squeak and topple.

I don't know what they did with his shirt and trews—ate them? Magicked them off o' him somehow; I did not see them throw them out. All I saw, they laid him out among them at their waists and he were bare and vulnerable to them, two each side and the queen at his feet and his arms and head out my end in this dreadful, stupid, mov-ing-underwater way—you dazzle a fowl and it will move just so, slow, enchanted, knowing in some dimmed corner of its mind it ought to struggle. Though they would have been plenty strong to carry him, I did not see in their muscles and movement that they took the weight of him; he lay there on the air and their hands moved above and below him busy, describing upon the space around him and against the skin of his body all the signs that needed making to keep a man afloat. So many, so entangled and entangling! How was he ever to escape?

Then they came to their decision, and lifted him, and as I watched and moaned they rose to their bare toes. The weight went out of their feet and their toes left the earth and slowly, slowly…

But it were like they were the waist of a skirt, and we the hem, or burrs caught to the hem, the donkey, Bertoldo and me. And as the creatures rose, the folds of the skirt, vast, invisible, drew inward and upward after them, and Stormcloud stumbled from his woodenness and I, I who had not drunk a drop in two days, I scuffed and staggered with the dragging, airy cloth, that was made of their horrid music, that was made of their weird intentions and their nakedness, the gathers of it conjured of their gathering.

Bertoldo wept and shouted; Bertoldo was mad; he clutched his head as something inside it exploded. You know him; you saw him before. Have he ever been the same? All the punch went out of him, all the snarl, and that was where it happened, before my eyes as the rising women, turning slightly but rebalancing back, drug him into the witch-lit road. There he fell, and he raved and slavered and tried to walk where he lay, tried to hold his head together, pitiful, as the donkey and I came up, with the cart, which might have held nothing of kegs nor any more lawful load it seemed of such little consequence to the beast that pulled it. That cart were witch-worked too, I shouldn't be surprised, to be so light.

You think you would have fled? You think stayed hidden? Well, I will tell you the worst spell: it was not their dragging music, nor the tidal folds of their cloth; it were the connection that could not be broke without you breaking yourself like Bertoldo done; it were the thing I first told you of, the light; it were the bond tight as wire, strong as chain, between the flying women with their burden, and mine eye.

This I seen, this I realised, my head dragged back by their heightening magic. White they were above me, and the singing hung in the road there, quite removed from their bodies and independent, a shell of noise at the limits of the light, a horrible reverberation. There hung their grey feet, there swirled their cloths weightless around them, and their thighs went up to shadows, and their elbows busied all around like an animate crown.

They were eating him! No, they were kissing. They were some of them like leeches upon his skin and one was sucking and mouthing above the point of his chin. His face was in shadow, but his mouth was darker, wide; his hair—that I'd almost been jealous of it, were so raven-black, unfrosted yet by age and responsibilities—creeping around his head in the air like a pail of snakes caught for Saint-day.

The circle of them span, the pointed feet below, the pointed hats above crisscrossing, nodding. The queen, I saw, was in between his legs, and she had got a fine point up on him and were working all about on him, swooning and swaying and rubbing her self and arms up all his thighs and stomach, pointing her breasts to heaven and then burying them either side of his rod, there in the flesh you never think about you are usually fixed upon the man itself, the two valleys there left and right of it, unsunned and tender, unprotected by hair.

A long moan was stuck in my throat, sucking out all my breath. Higher they went very slowly and I strained after them; I would lift, myself, and point my own feet and be dragged up after them, any instant now. Dass were up there among them all, flesh upon flesh, slowly swimming, slowly scrambling. The queen had her hand in the darkness under his buttocks; in the midst of the turning, bright lit, was the great veined spike of the man, almost rumbling under the hum and rub and the irritation of the music, trembling on the point of discharging.

I reached back over my head for the neck of my shirt, and even as my face drank in every drop of jealousy, and light, and terror—I have never done anything more difficult in my life—I pulled the cloth forward, to cover my eyes, to swathe my head. 'Twere my choice, weren't it?, to break my own mind or to have it broke for me by the sight of those monsters.

And I ran, as far as the light showed the road at my feet and then I freed my head and without looking back I plunged out of the music into the darkness and I did not stop, scrambling from leaf-wink to star-snippet, beating my feet against the dull ground in the songless quiet so safe, so glorious, until I fell into Leightman's, more or less into old man Cooper's lap.

"Hie, boy, are we lost?" He was up and ready to flee any implications.

I sat in Leightman's hay. Cooper gummed and tutted and wanted clarity above me while I got back my breath, great homely whooshes of it into me, out of me, smelling of hay, smelling of the pomander that Mistress Cooper must put among all their clothes; I have smelt it on the younger man in the alehouse, orange-y, clove-y.

"Where is they? What's up wi' ye?"

I put up my hand to stop his hissing, to settle him. "They're coming," I said. "All is good. They are just up the road." And I stood and straightened myself, everything most ordinary around me. "I will have them to you in a little."

"What d'you mean thundering in like you've Mastiff on your tail? Men have fallen over dead from lesser shocks."

I left him twitching and cursing and went, myself all peaceful and relieved, out again into the spacious night. A breeze had come up, and a freshening stroll it was, a leisurely amble with nothing but the strokings of grasses around me, the snuffling of forest, the limp and pat of the wind.

Dassel were motionless in the road, dropped there insensible. I cast about for his clothes, but could not find them.

"Bertoldo? Bertoldo?" I called softly here and there, and finally I found him far back along the roadside trying to disguise himself as a log, but the log whimpered, and shivers went through it like horseflesh shaking off flies.

I had a right time, as I told Fion, getting the two of those into the cart. 'Twas not that they were so much heavier than I, more that the witchment had taken from them the ability to move helpfully. I forgot, almost, about the kegs, I was so occupied with getting these injured men to home and safety.

The women, the witches, the bitches were gone that had done this to them, that had turned Bertoldo soft and made Dass the odd un-marriageable character he is. I cannot tell you with what joy I uttered those words to myself, *They are gone; they are gone,* all the way out to the road there, and all the way back to Leightman's. I cannot tell you even today the relief it is, the gone-ness of them, the surprise it was to look back and see the will in myself, pulling forward my shirt-cloth, breaking the spell that was on my eyes. The clink of Cooper's gold had nothing on it, nor the dispersal of that gold on boots for us all, and on Fion-finery and on a pony, a little bay gelding, bless him, that did not take a piece out of anyone came near, like that donkey done ever after.

So who were they, husband? Fion says. *You said you seen their faces.* She cannot believe me, she who can recognise a certain look passing between two women across the far side of the May Fair, beyond the hankerchee-dancing and everything.

I tell you, I say. *Constituted though they were like people, yet there was nothing recognisable about them.*

Except their bosoms. I've told her of my unmanment time and again, but— *Sounds like you were too enwitched by five sets o' bare nipples to look properly anywhere above.*

It were not like that, I tell her feebly. *It were not.*

The one man who kept his wits on him. She turns to me all fierce and fiery. *Who might have named them to Mastiff and got them weeded out fr'amongst us.*

They were no one I knew, I point out again, gentle as I can. There is nothing so disheartening as uttering truth, and your goodwife standing there, fists on hips, outraged and unbelieving.

So I don't tell about this to Fion anymore. She were the only one I did tell, and well after the glamour of the spoils had worn off. She'd been at me and at me since the night of it. *What happened there? You are not the same, and as for those other two.* Until I spilled it all out, more fool me, and this is my reward, only rage and accusation. She does not understand at all.

THE TRANSFORMATION
OF TARG

PAUL BRANDON AND JACK DANN

It was a typically bitter New York morning.

The wind was like a splintery hand across the face, each slap feeling like it left tiny shards of ice embedded in the skin. It chased crumpled balls of old newspaper up the gutters, spinning them around the ankles of the hurrying people. Up between the buildings, rivers of flawless blue could be seen mirroring the avenues of grey, cloudless, cold.

Commuters bustled up the streets, heads bowed, turtled into scarves or high collars. Cars and taxis seethed.

Just off Fifth Avenue, down a bleak alleyway made almost impassable by large, overflowing dumpsters and trafficked by rats and scraggy cats, a door opened.

From inside the ally it was no different from any of the other doors; paint-peeled and somewhat bowed, it was utterly unremarkable except for the odd-looking thumb-latch. It appeared to be nothing more than an old back access door to the Starbucks that fronted Fifth.

As it swung silently open, light bloomed out suddenly, then died away. From across the alleyway, two dark figures could be seen standing within; but it wasn't the store room of a coffee shop that they were inside, not by any means.

They stood within a small circular chamber. Black brick walls wept water that bled down across a cobbled floor to gurgle down a grated drain. Bodies hung, a few still alive, in various states of interrupted agony from the walls. Small crackles of blue lightning still arced between the two that were still shrieking, the last remnants of the magic that opened the door.

The two figures that stood just inside were fearsome indeed. Closest to the door was a huge barrel of a man, or at least he would have looked like a man if he'd had a normal head. Great curling horns, polished to an ebony gleam, lifted away from features that more resembled a horse than anything human. His skin was mottled, green and brown like lichen, and he was dressed in formidable-looking armour of interlocking leather plates. In his right hand was an enormous war axe, even more polished than his horns.

But it was the second figure that commanded the eye.

Simply dressed, he wore a long black cape and creaseless black pants tucked into his polished black boots. A jerkin, made of blackest leather, was stitched across his chest, overlaying a shirt of midnight silk. He wasn't particularly tall, especially standing next to the other; but what he lacked in stature he more than made up for in presence.

His skin was white, the pale, chalky white of bones rather than of purity, and his face could simply be described as cruel. From the top of his left brow (where a shock of white hair flared against the black) a wicked scar traversed his face, gouging a line down across the empty socket of his eye to tug the top of his lip into a permanent sneer.

But it was the other eye that captivated; flat, glassy, like a shark, it seemed to make up for the loss of its twin with an intensity that was little short of terrifying.

The two figures waited patiently while the blue sparks flickered between the last of the hanging men then, with a last shrieking cry that reverberated quite nicely around the small chamber, the hanging men died.

Smiling, the man in black gestured politely to the other, "After you, my dear Sarpent," who frowned back at him then stepped through the doorway.

The air rippled, as if the space between the frame was water and a stone had been tossed in, and as he passed out into the alley, Sarpent changed. Gone was the armour, replaced by a pin-striped, Italian-cut suit. Instead of the wicked axe, his right hand held a black leather laptop case. All that remained of the equine features was a slightly jutting lower jaw on an otherwise handsome face. His skin was the color of an expensive full-cream latte, the horns replaced by beautiful blond curling locks.

The second man stepped through, and the change was equally startling. His suit was unadorned soft black wool. His hair was still the same; but a mirrored, silver-rimmed monocle covered the vacant eye, a spider thread of gleaming chain tickling down along the ridge of the somehow noble-looking scar. Black Gucci loafers supplanted the leather boots, though nothing could replace his aura of absolute power…deep, dark, sickening power. The only splash of color came from a blood-red handkerchief that poked out of his breast pocket.

"You have the address?" he asked in a voice that brought that same reaction as a broken fingernail down a blackboard.

Sarpent nodded, tapped his breast pocket and set off towards the bright bustle of Fifth Avenue. When he realized the other man wasn't following, he turned, frowning. "My Liege…?"

The Dark Lord was bent down, stroking the ear of a tatty black cat that wove between his legs. Even from a half-dozen yards away Sarpent could hear it purring like a little motor. The lord was making little chirping and cooing noises.

Sarpent took a long, deep, steadying breath and muttered, "And you wonder why we're here?"

"What was that?"

"Nothing, oh fearsome and mighty lord."

The waiting room was paneled with mahogany and smelled faintly of expensive cigars.

A stunning glass installation the size of a coffee table hung from the wall directly opposite the entrance, its surface laser-etched with a welcome for the visitor to Dr. Hiram Hirsch's Exclusive Evil Consultancy.

Medical certifications in gilded frames were scattered across the other walls like art, interspersed with pictures of a heavy-set, middle-aged man (whom Sarpent assumed to be Dr. Hirsch) catching a huge marlin, standing with one foot up on a freshly shot tiger, shaking hands with Saddam Hussein, Oberon, King Drakkor the Black, even a slightly faded one of the good doctor with his arm around a smiling bin Laden.

There were no chairs, only four Chesterfield sofas, upholstered in Solferino-red leather and brass studs. A single door, at the other end of the room, stood closed, next to a desk that fronted a stiff-looking receptionist dressed in finest Ralph Lauren. She lifted her head as they entered, frowned, then subtly pressed a button on the edge of the desk.

As had happened when they had stepped through the portal, the air around Sarpent and his lord wavered, then like a roller blind snapping back upwards, the suited illusions were lifted away, revealing once again the man in black and his horse-faced guard.

Sarpent growled, a low, guttural sound, but the receptionist simply pointed to a small sign by the door that read in jaunty, self-help letters:

If you can't be yourself here, then where can you be?

The lord laid his hand on Sarpent's arm and said lightly, "I suppose that's very true."

They approached the desk. The receptionist pretended to be busy for a long moment, then looked up. "Name?"

Sarpent bristled. "This is his Mighty Revenant Overlord Targ, Destroyer of Mordane and Ruler of—"

"*First* name, please?"

Sarpent's large mouth clicked shut; he blinked with surprise and turned to face his lord, looking apologetic.

The Overlord cleared his throat and in a small voice said, "Brian."

"Well, Brian," said the receptionist as if she were talking to a small child, "Dr. Hirsch is ready to see you now." She gestured to the closed door. "You," she said to Sarpent with a flick of her wrist towards one of the Chesterfields, "may wait there."

Sarpent looked at his lord, who was just about to knock on the door, then nodded and sat down on the couch. There was a huge outrush of air from the leather cushions of the Chesterfield. Sarpent laid his battleaxe across his knees, picked up a copy of *Vogue*, and settled in to wait for his master.

"Okay okay, now where did you *just* go wrong, huh?" A fit-looking older man sat behind a beautiful glass-topped desk.

His head was covered with a thick thatch of perfectly pomaded white hair, although the huge moustache that antlered under his nose was a sooty black. The face itself had a yacht club tan, fierce blue eyes and a somewhat bulbous nose. Thin moist lips, barely visible beneath the overhang of hair, were set in a smile that seemed more rehearsed than genuine. His voice was somewhat nasal, and carried the slightly accusatory-sounding New York cadence well. "Come on, it all starts right here. Right now. What was your first mistake?"

Brian frowned, somewhat bewildered by the sudden questions. "I…err, didn't wipe my feet?"

"No no *no!*" Hirsch said smoothly. "You *knocked!* You're the *Mighty* Revenant Overlord Targ, *Destroyer* of Mordane and *Ruler* of—" he discretely checked his notes "—Heckinor."

"Hellinor."

"Whatever. Heckinor, Hellinor. Do you see my point? You *never* knock. You march in, you sit down, and if anyone doesn't like it, you order that person's head to be removed immediately. Or something else, you decide. *You're* the Boss." Hirsch stood up and offered his hand, "Hiram Hirsch, Consultant to Evil."

Brian shook the pudgy hand as hard as he could, which was difficult because it was like greeting a jewelry store. "Erm, Brian." They were about the same height, but the sculpted white hair made Hirsch look taller.

"Very pleased to meet you, Brian, have a seat," he gestured to the reclining leather chair. "You don't mind me calling you Brian do you? We shouldn't stand on ceremony in here, don't you agree?"

Brian understood the question was rhetorical, but he nodded anyway. Somewhat reluctantly, he lay back. The ceiling was paneled the same way as the walls, and the little squares of wood were somewhat hypnotic.

"Now," Hirsch began, "you were referred here by... let me see now... the ArchWitch Hagspittle. Ahhh, how is old Maggie doing?"

"Fine," replied Brian. "She has her Dark Court back under control and is even planning an offensive against the Shining Dawn next season. She speaks very highly of you."

"And well she should. When I first counseled Maggie, she had lost touch with evil to such an extent that she could barely string two spells together. The distances and dimensions my clientele comes to me from never ceases to amaze... But anyway, let's not get sidetracked. This is about you, now, isn't it?"

Almost against his will, Brian found himself nodding.

"Now, you wrote in your initial consult application that you"— Hirsch's voice took on the tone of someone reading—"just don't seem to have the heart for evil anymore, that it no longer gives you that shivery black thrill that it used to, and that you'd rather go and raise alpacas in Idaho. Is that true, Brian?" Hirsch sounded terribly disappointed.

"They're a lovely animal, very friendly."

"I meant about losing the will to be evil." Hirsch leaned forwards on his desk. "Have you lost your mojo, Brian?"

Brian swallowed. "Maybe..."

"Why don't you tell me about it."

So Brian did, from the first hesitant moments when he realized that for no reason he could discern, he had suddenly run out of creative ways to wage war and execute and torture his myriad enemies. Hadn't he botched up his invasion of neighboring Callidan Island by forgetting to requisition and build enough boats, so the invasion had to be called off before they'd even left the shores? The Callidani laughter still rang in his ears. He touched upon his fondness for cats, for jesters and motleys, skipped over his secret plans to implement a better and more fair justice system, and talked briefly (but somewhat fondly) about his aim to one day establish an autonomous government.

When he finished, he felt oddly better, more at peace, at one with the universe.

Then there was silence, broken only by the creaking leather of Hirsch's chair and the occasional clunk of a piece of jewelry against the glass-topped table. Brian resisted the urge to look over, but he could imagine the doctor staring at him, stroking his giant moustache.

"Do you have a mask?"

"Hmm?" (Brian had nearly dozed off.) "Yes, of course. I brought it per your request." He reached inside his jerkin and pulled out a small black square of velvet which he carefully unfolded.

"Put it on, please," Hirsch told him.

Brian slipped it over his head. It was a little like a cross between a balaclava and an executioner's mask. Instead of eyeholes, there was a wide slit that just reached his nose. The velvet looked almost wet in the dusty office light.

Hirsch leaned forwards, steepling his fingers, considering. "Hmmm," he said after a long moment's thought. "It's not exactly, well, intimidating, is it."

Brian shrugged. "I do have another one, made from an elf skull."

"Well, *that's* a little more like it!"

"But it's dreadfully heavy and it brings me out in a rash around my ears."

"I see."

More pondering.

"Well, Brian, we need to take this one step at a time. Here's what I want you to do. Before our next visit, I want you to find some people, any people, a village, a settlement, some group that's always annoyed you."

"The Do'raki Fenlanders," Brian said, snapping his fingers. "They have never shown proper respect and were late with their taxes this year. Come to think of it, they were a bit late last year, too."

"Whatever." He leaned forwards. "I want you to destroy them."

Brian's eyes blinked out from the slit in the mask. "Destroy them? I'll lose revenue."

"Yes!" said Hirsch feverishly. "Destroy them utterly. Forgo lost revenue. This is more important. Show them no mercy! You're the *Mighty* Revenant Overlord Targ, *Destroyer* of Mordane and *Ruler* of—" he discretely checked his notes again "—Heckinor."

"Hellinor."

"Yes, that's what I meant. Destroy all Do'hicky Finlanders!"

"Do'raki Fenlanders," Brian mumbled, correcting the doctor before raising a clenched fist, and repeating in a small, somewhat uncertain voice: "Destroy them."

Dr. Hirsch picked up the receiver of his antique Princess phone; the numerals of the rotary dial glowed yellow in the darkness.

"Hello?"

The line was crackly and sounded like it traveled across the bottom of the ocean. "Dr. Hirsch? This is Sarpent speaking, General of the Revenant Overlord's Fifty Legions, Commander of the Night Watchers, First Chief of—"

Hirsch waved his hand, "Just what is it with you people and your titles? Sarpent would have done you know. I'm old, not senile."

"Forgive me, honored doctor, but I…I find myself unable to…I don't know quite what to…"

"Take all the time you need. I bill by the minute."

"It's the Overlord, sir, he, well, may I ask just exactly what it was you instructed him to do?"

"Well, Sarp, I can't really tell you that, doctor-patient confidentiality being what it is. May I call you Sarp?"

"Yes, doctor, whatever you wish."

Okay, Sarp, then why don't you just tell me what he did, and I'll tell you if he's following my instructions."

"Well, sir, the lord gathered together the whole second battalion, and we all had high hopes, but he, ah…"

"What?"

"He relocated the Do'raki Fenlanders."

"Well, that's not *exactly* what I had in mind, but displacing is a start—"

"It wasn't exactly displacement," Sarpent said around another bark of static. "More like…sir, the Overlord helped them move."

"He *what?*"

"Well, they live in the fens, and they're always being flooded. The Do'raki are extremely poor, *filthy*, but, on the other hand, they're fierce little fighters and they usually pay their proper taxes to the Overlord."

"All the more reason for them to be wiped out!"

"For paying taxes?" Sarpent asked.

"Don't be literal. You know what I mean," Dr. Hirsch said.

Yes, sir. I agree on general principles that they should be wiped out. But the Overlord, well, ah, he took…*pity*—" he spat the word out like a bitter pip "—on them and had the battalion build them new hovels on higher ground. Sir, he had my men…"

"Sarpent, are you still there? You're breaking up. Are you on a mobile?

More static. "Just a moment, sir…"

Hirsch held the phone away from his ear a little, which was fortuitous, as Sarpent suddenly thundered, "*Get the spell together! YOU USELESS NUMBSKULL OF A WIZARD! Now, focus, before I cut off that little beard and stick it where the spells don't shine!*" There was one last yelp of noise that sounded uncannily like a fist striking flesh (or a fish being slapped onto pavement), and then the line cleared remarkably. "There, is that better, Doctor?" Sarpent asked in a calm voice.

"Much better. Telecommunication problems?"

"Oh, nothing that a good sharp jab with my sword won't fix." The end of the sentence sounded like it was aimed away from whatever Sarpent was using as a phone. "So you did not suggest that my lord help the Do'raki move to a more upmarket location."

"I am not presently a real estate consultant."

"Well, what should I do next? Bring my lord back in? I need help here, Doctor. He's really not himself. He's becoming a laughing stock for the other emperors and warlords."

"Let me think for a moment, Sarp… Do you have any judgments coming up soon, any judicial trials, anything like that?"

"Well, we don't have courts here, of course. The Overlord just decides their fate. But the criminals are due to be paraded around the hanging square in a fortnight."

"Excellent. I need you to help. The morning before the parade, you will have to talk to your lord, remind him of his notable evil deeds, his past victories, slaughters, all those kind of things. Get him in the mood, give him a few ales at lunch time, then sit at his right hand and prompt him to kill all the criminals as a supreme gesture of His Evil Will to his people. A brief sudden display of malevolence might be just what he needs to jar him back into his nasty ways. And it will be a tonic for the general populace, too."

"I understand. It shall be done, sir."

The Steps of Judgment were quite impressive.

They were located to the rear of the castle, where the black Cliff of Despair buttressed against the Obsidian Mountain. Started at ground level, they ascended up towards the Throne of His Glorious Will like a fan, forming an upside down amphitheatre. Originally, the architect had designed and built it the other way around, with the Throne at the bottom, so that even the people who couldn't afford a front row seat could see everything; but the Overlord didn't like people looking down on him, so he had the architect killed and the Steps reversed, stone by stone.

Sarpent's deep laugh boomed as he told the story, refilling the Overlord's gold tankard and stealing a quick glance at his lord's face. The Overlord had chuckled at the memory, which was a good sign. Sarpent lingered on the part where the Overlord had personally taken the architect apart, fingernails first, then knuckles, then hands and so on, as a demonstration of how annoyed he was at the prospect of dismantling the Steps. He thought the architect had gotten the message, but it was hard to tell between the pitiful screams and pleadings for mercy.

"Mercy," Sarpent said, mouthing the word as if he'd found an old piece of decayed food behind a tooth, "is for the weak, the spineless. Fear…now fear, intimidation, terror…they are the tools of the strong, do you not agree, my Lord?"

Brian nodded absently; he was still thinking back to a rather disconcerting yet pleasurable dream he'd had the night before where he'd freed all the prisoners and everyone had loved him for it. The people had called his name, thrown flowers, cheered…

"Would my Lord care for one last drink?" Sarpent asked, interrupting his thoughts with a wave of an ale bottle. It was a fine brew, strong, but Brian didn't want his head spinning anymore. It would be hard to be just if one were pissed. "A lord must be just, mustn't he?" Brian said out loud.

"Wha—?" Sarpent said.

"Of course justice resides in the definition, and it is I who decides all definitions, is it not so?"

"Yes, Great Lord, you decide all things."

"As was and shall ever be," Brian said by rote.

"As was and shall ever be," Sarpent dutifully repeated as he made the sign of fealty, which resembled the traditional bird: index finger erect.

But Brian wasn't paying attention; he stroked the ginger cat curled up on his lap. "Did you know it is Mrs. Tinkle's birthday today?"

Sarpent blinked. "Mrs....Tinkle?"

"That's right, isn't it," Brian cooed at the cat, who was kneading his knee with a paw. "You're the little birthday puss."

Sarpent swallowed, fingering a horn nervously. "Another movie then?" he said hurriedly. We have the time, the serfs won't mind waiting and I'm sure the dead—I mean the accused—aren't going anywhere." Sarpent picked up another of the DVDs that Dr. Hirsch had lent him. "We've watched most of the Steven Seagal films, but there's still the early Schwarzenegger and some man called Tarantino that comes highly recommended..."

Brian shook his head. "No, I've seen enough. Disconnect that... thing."

Sarpent nodded and reached over for the plug to the borrowed TV and DVD player, which was inserted into the last socket the original inventors had ever considered as a power supply. The dumpy-looking wizard who had been chanting the spell to create ignescent electricity let out a huge sigh, followed by a yelp as Sarpent's boot helped him out of the room before he'd even had a chance to lower his robe.

"Now," Sarpent continued. "Which mask for today?" The Overlord paused, hand stroking the cat as he considered. Sarpent could see his Lordship's gaze lingering on the soft velvet, so he said, "If I may be so bold, my Liege, Dr. Hirsch would probably want you to wear the elf skull today...for therapeutic reasons."

"Yes, I suppose he would," Brian sighed. He put the cat gently on the ground, stood up, and reached for the pale monstrosity, which had once been the treasured possession of King Ulran of Arboria—so treasured in fact that it had taken a sword through the neck to part Ulran from it. Brian slipped it on, hoping that Sarpent wouldn't notice the distaste on his face. It was heavy, ill-fitting and smelled of elves, no matter how many times they boiled it. And Brian hated elves, almost as much as he hated cats.

But he didn't hate cats anymore.

Brian sniffed. Well, maybe it didn't smell so bad, after all.

"Perfect," Sarpent enthused, bowing. "My Lord looks truly fearsome and mighty. The walking dead—I mean accused—will surely soil themselves mightily upon your approach."

Let's hope not, Brian thought, remembering the last time. It had taken his valets days to get the splash marks off his best black boots.

The seneschal boomed his staff on the ground, and in a voice that Brian had now considered too hammy, pronounced, "*RISE* for His Highness, the *Mighty* Revenant Overlord Targ, *Destroyer* of Mordane, *Ruler* of Hellinor, *Slayer* of the Venomous *Were*Spider of…"

Brian yawned discreetly under his mask. That was one thing he did like about masks, you could yawn, smile, even doze off, and people never noticed.

He walked slowly past the blood-encrusted trapdoor to the Throne of His Glorious Will (*or should that be My Glorious Will?* he thought absently). Behind him hung Pain, the huge executioner's sword that Sarpent used to dispense the Law. After raising his arms to the cheering crowds (his royal guards were using their whips and bludgeons with great subtlety to encourage them), he turned and removed the sword from its ornamented bracket. He spoke the ceremonial words of opening and handed the sword to Sarpent, who, as always, was the official dispenser of justice. Then he sat down on the throne, careful not to let his robe bunch up under him. The unwashed masses descended away beneath him in a maelstrom of color, cacophony and chaos. People from all walks of life jostled for seats, shouted, argued, stood in line for pies from the vendors. Away to his right was the disheveled row of the accused, their shaven heads bowed, some weeping, others looking passively out over the crowd, grimly resigned to their fate. Children threw stones (fruit was generally saved for eating) and occasionally a prisoner would cry out and try to raise his manacled arms to ward off a missile.

Brian listened patiently while the first prisoner was brought forward and the charges read by the seneschal. He'd been caught cart-jacking; however, his arrest had gone wrong, and he'd managed to kill a pair of guards. With Hirsh's words echoing in his head, the very sound of conscience, Brian stretched out his arms and turned down his thumbs. Fair was fair. Guards were hard to come by these days and expensive to train, and this man had killed two and lamed a third.

The roar of the crowd surged over him, and Sarpent took but a moment to loosen his shoulders before striking the man's head clean from his body with an almost negligent swipe. The body stood headless for a moment, before the trapdoor sprung open and it plummeted from sight. With a skilful back heel-kick from one of the ceremonial guards, the head followed.

Now that wasn't so bad, Brian thought. Sarpent was nodding his approval, and the crowd was chanting, "*Overlord… Overlord…*"

The next prisoner was another murderer, though this time the occasion had been a bar brawl. The wiry man had a pockmarked and surly looking face. He contended that he'd not started it, that it had all been in self-defense. He then wailed and pleaded, but somehow all of it sounded rehearsed. Brian listened, nodding, as if in agreement. Then he stretched out his arms and turned down his thumbs.

Sarpent was elated. It looked like his Lord was back to his old evil ways. Grinning from ear to ear, he put a little too much effort into his sword swing, and the head went soaring out into the crowd, where the peasants amused themselves by tossing and kicking it around like a beach ball.

Once again the trapdoor clattered. The next man was brought forward.

This one was just a thief, and Sarpent was a little disappointed to be instructed just to remove a hand; but still, it was all blood and suffering, and the crowd always enjoyed a bit of variety.

Five more thieves followed, and Sarpent felt more like a surgeon than an executioner as he was ordered to remove several ears, a nose, and two fingers.

There was a brief flash of hope as the Lord ordered a rapist castrated, though secretly Sarpent wished he'd just ordered him beheaded. It was far less fiddly.

And then it happened.

A baker accused of short-changing his customers was given a custodial sentence.

"Surely, my Lord," Sarpent whispered, "a hand, at least…thumbs… *tongue?*"

But Brian was having none of it. He was now determined to imprison, or fine, or even pardon criminals who had committed minor crimes.

The blood on the blade of Pain dried as it hung by Sarpent's side, unused.

After such a promising start, it was all going so terribly wrong.

Worse yet, the Overlord actually seemed to be enjoying himself. He questioned each accused and took the time to consider and weigh each crime before dispensing something that looked far more like justice than punishment.

The Overlord stood before the crowds and raised his arms. A hush fell over all. In a loud and impressive voice, the Overlord declared: "Good people of Hellinor, in honor of a dear friend's birthday, I have just decided that today shall be a day of amnesty. All but the most heinous crimes will be forgiven, and furthermore, I have also decided that it will be a public holiday, with a lifting of the usual dusk curfew." He paused as the crowd let out a huge enthusiastic roar. He ignored Sarpent's groan and continued, "Henceforth, today shall be known as…Tinklefest."

"Tinklefest? *TINKLEfest*? Oh Brian, what were you thinking?" Hirsch shook his head, causing the freshly waxed tips of his moustache to bob.

"It seemed like a nice thing to do."

Mrs. Tinkles had let out one hiss at the doctor then promptly hid under a cabinet at the far side of the room.

"A *NICE* thing… Oh, Brian, Brian, Brian… I've got to tell you that in all my years of practice I've never, *ever*…" Hirsch just shook his head again.

"You're disappointed in me," Brian said softly, transfixed by Hirsch's exaggeration of a moustache.

"DISAPPOINTED?" Hirsch took a deep breath and looked around, counting to ten under his breath to dispel the anger. Brian's study at the top of the Black Tower was small but surprisingly comfortable. He had a large desk (not unlike Hirsch's own, but without the glass protector, *which*, Hirsch thought absently, *he could really do with*, as the bloodstains were ingrained and the edges were rutted with what looked like axe marks). Four huge arched windows looked out over the land to all points of the compass, letting in a nice amount of natural light, and the views were stupendous. *I should build myself one of these in Manhattan.*

Seven…eight…nine…ten. He released a long breath and returned to the task at hand. "Brian," he said, "you do know why Sarpent called me out here."

Brian nodded.

"Well, then why don't we start with you telling me exactly what was going through your mind yesterday? Just take your time. Sarp has already signed a treasury wavier for my call-out fee. You're putting my three grandchildren through college—and I believe little Hiram Junior is going to Harvard. Think long and hard, great lord of Heckinor."

Brian started to say "Hellinor," but gave it up.

I want to know everything," Dr. Hirsch continued. "I want to know exactly when things started to go bad…or rather, good."

Brian smiled, thinking the doctor was making a rather funny joke, but the expression fell from his face when he saw Dr. Hirsch angrily and compulsively biting the edges of his moustache. Brian stroked his smooth chin, wondering if perhaps the secret to evil lay in facial hair. After all, Hiram Hirsch seemed to have no problems thinking up clever and horrid plans…there was the BoneDoctor of Riddel. He was supremely evil *and* he had a huge beard, then of course the ArchWitch Hagspittle had a bit of a moustache herself…and there was Saddam and Adolph, bin…

Hirsch slapped his hand down on the desk. "Brian!" he shouted, making even Sarpent jump. Another cat hiss came from somewhere behind the cabinet. "You're doing it again."

"What?"

"Procrastinating. Daydreaming. An idle mind leads to idle deeds, and evil is *never* idle."

"Sorry. I'll remember that. Evil is never idle. Would make a good motto, don't you think?"

Hirsch just shook his head again.

"There was a time, sir," Sarpent said, folding his hairy arms across his broad chest with a creak of leather armour, "that you'd have someone's head cut off for speaking to you like that."

Brian sighed and lowered his head into his hands despondently. He tried to focus on his green chakra.

"Okay, let's start simply," Dr. Hirsch said. "What's bothering you right now, at this very moment?"

Brian frowned, stopping himself from voicing the obvious answer. "Well…I'm a bit worried about reports that the Armies of Bil'tha are massing to the south again—" Sarpent grunted, but Hirsch silenced him with an upraised hand. "—the Do'raki ambassador is here, and Mrs. Tinkles is off her biscuits."

"That's perfect!"

"Not really, I have them shipped in especially at great cost."

"I meant the ambassador. Is he here now?"

"Waiting in an antechamber on His Overlord's pleasure," said Sarpent, absently using one of his horns to pick some dried blood from under a fingernail.

"What does he want?" Dr. Hirsch asked. "Isn't the land you relocated the Do'raki to upmarket enough?"

Sarpent flicked his fingers. "The ambassador claims they've not had sufficient time to replant crops, and therefore he and his people can't afford to pay their taxes this financial year."

Brian said, "Which sounds fair enough, given that—"

"*WHAT?*" Hirsch's moustache was practically curling back on itself. "Am I mistaken or did the word 'FAIR' just leave your lips?"

"Well, I…"

"There will be no buts and no excuses this time. Brian, go out there and strangle the ambassador with your own hands. Right this minute. And then I want you to take your army and kill, maim, torture, rape, and pillage your enemy."

"Right this minute?"

"You heard me."

"I…*can't,*" Brian cried. "I *like* Ooblier."

At Hirsch's frown, Sarpent leaned over and whispered, "The Do'raki ambassador's name is Ooblier."

"Oh, charming." He turned back to Brian, who was tracing an intricate whorl in his desk, desperately trying anything to avoid eye contact. "Brian, what on earth is wrong with you? Have I missed something? Is the air not foul enough in your kingdom? Is the water unpolluted? You used to be an Overlord of repute. Now you're behaving like a…a *putz.* Surely your parents taught you that Satan only helps those who help themselves?"

There was a pause.

Despite the wicked scar, the missing eye, the flash of white hair against the black, Brian looked very much like a little boy, and the sneer resembled a crooked smile. "My mother always used to complain that I had a sunny disposition. My mother and father would thrash me and send me to my room to think about things, but it never seemed to help. So they'd burn me with pokers then thrash me again. I started *pretending* to be evil to please them. It worked for quite a while, but I guess I'm finally coming out of the closet."

"Well, you'd better think long and hard about going back *into* the closet," Hirsch said.

"Why don't *you* do it?" Brian suggested after a moment.

Hirsch was baffled. "Come out of the closet?"

"Sure," said Brian, sitting up a little. "You always seem to have the best ideas about how to be evil. And we're about the same height, build. You can be *me*. After all, nobody would recognize you. You'd be wearing a mask."

"The Overlord is supposed to always wear a mask," Sarpent quickly pointed out to Hirsch.

"Well, I don't know. I'm a doctor, not a dark lord." But Hirsch stroked his moustache, obviously considering Brian's suggestion.

"What if I watched you, from one of the secret spyholes? Perhaps if I could see evil working again, maybe I'd be…inspired?"

The doctor was still curling hairs around his fingers, and Brian could see by the excited gleam in his eyes that he had him. Brian's eyes narrowed slyly.

"This is all *highly* irregular…"

"Think of it as a new kind of therapy," Brian said. *I could get the hang of this therapy thing*, he thought as he rose from his desk, crossed over to the mask stand, and picked up one of the soft velvet masks.

"Do you…do you think I could have that one?" Hirsch said almost shyly, pointing at the big elf skull.

The new career was going well.

He had the office redecorated in eggshell white with classic cream carpets and friendly vases of fresh flowers everywhere. He kept the Chesterfield sofas, but had them reupholstered in the finest beige calfskins. The bragging photos were gone, replaced by small paintings by Cézanne and Dürer etchings; the cool, lush sounds of the Modern Jazz Quartet drifted out of a pair of matching white Bose speakers above the receptionist's desk.

Even the self-help sign had been changed. It now read:
Be the person your cat thinks you are.

Behind the desk, above the receptionist's beautifully coiffured head, was the glass installation that welcomed the visitor to The Tinkle Studio: An Ethical Executive Consultancy.

Brian opened his office door and stepped out into the waiting room. Dressed in a soft Armani linen suit and Gucci loafers, he looked more like a yachtsman than a therapist; but that was the idea. His eye patch was exactly the same color as his pocket square, something which, for some reason, had set the New York fashion scene alight.

Even after a year, Brian still marveled at how everything had turned out. Hirsch had so enjoyed being Overlord that he offered to buy him out right there and then. Sarpent hadn't minded—he just wanted to serve evil, and if not Brian, then Hirsch would do just as well. The negotiations had been relatively simple, and though Hirsch had come off much better (though the price of a Kingdom compared to Upper West Side real estate wasn't really that different), Brian didn't mind. He had the New York practice, a reasonably immense fortune stashed away in a place called the Cayman Islands, and a brand new alpaca farm in Idaho.

Brian discovered that he had a natural talent for steering people back towards the light. Kings, seers, sages, presidents, ministers, and all manner of monsters and piebald creatures from across the breadth and width of the ninety-nine dimensions sought his sage advice when they found themselves succumbing to their darker desires.

"Your three-thirty is here, Doctor," the receptionist said politely, handing Brian a manila folder. A single, sad-looking elf sat enveloped in one of the Chesterfields, hands held stiffly in his lap. Brian smiled, remembering how he'd felt when he'd sat there waiting for Hirsch. He opened the folder, glancing quickly at the front page. *Having decimated the world Kah in error, the LightLord of Quaa'lar, First Seeker of the Justice of Marlorr, Luminescent Silverhand of...* Brian skipped down.

His first name was Simon.

Well, it seemed Simon continued to stray somewhat from the light after his administrative mistake and had taken a blue orc for a mistress and murdered her prankster in a jealous fit. Nothing that couldn't be put right. Well, the prankster might be a problem, but he could probably be resurrected, or at the least, reincarnated.

Brian motioned the elf through with a smile and a soft welcoming word.

This should be a walk in the park.

And he would certainly be finished in time to hop a plane to Idaho for the weekend.

MRS. ZENO'S PARADOX

ELLEN KLAGES

Annabel meets Midge for a treat.

She enters a small café in the Mission District in San Francisco, bold graffiti-covered walls and baristas with multiple piercings and attitude. Sometimes it is the Schrafft's at 57th and Madison, just after the war, the waitresses in black uniforms with starched white cuffs. Once it is a patisserie on the rue Montorgueil; the din from the Prussian artillery makes it difficult to converse.

On entering the restaurant, she scans the tables for Midge, who is always somewhere.

Annabel sits and requests an espresso. She asks for tea with milk. She waits until Midge comes before she orders, to be polite.

Midge is young and cheaply dressed, in a shabby coat, her stiletto heels clip-clip-clopping on the marble floor. Her hair is the color of faded daffodils, sleek and dark, perfectly coiffed. Her sneakers shuffle on the worn wood.

She kisses the air near Annabel's cheek. "Am I late?" she asks. She puts her handbag down on an empty chair. Its contents clank and tinkle, thump and squeak.

"I'm not certain," Annabel says. It is a small lie, a kindness to a dear friend.

The server materializes. "What are you having?"

Annabel answers and Midge says, "The same, please."

"You know," Annabel says, "I think I'd like a little something sweet."

"Oh, I shouldn't."

"Nothing gooey, nothing *too* decadent. A brownie?"

"Whatever you want. I'll only have a bite."

"Are you sure?"

"Absolutely." Midge pats her waist. "Just the tiniest bite possible."

The brownie appears on Fiestaware, a folded napkin, a lovely seventeenth-century porcelain platter. They gaze at it, fudge-dark, its top glossy, crackled like Arizona in July, sprinkled with powdered sugar.

Annabel cuts the brownie in half.

She eats it with obvious pleasure, flecks of chocolate limning the corners of her mouth. She blots her lips with a tissue, leaving an abstract smudge of chocolate and Revlon's Rosy Future.

"This is *too* good," Midge says, moistening her forefinger to pick up an indeterminate number of small crumbs.

"Stairmaster tomorrow," Annabel agrees. "Probably." She sips from her cup.

They talk about their jobs, the men they are dating, the men they have married. They have been friends since the beginning of time, Midge jokes.

"That's your half." Annabel points to the brownie.

"Oh, I couldn't. Not the whole thing."

Midge cuts the brownie in half.

They glance at the clock. Time is irrelevant. Annabel gets a refill. "Are you going to eat the rest of that?"

Midge shakes her head.

Annabel cuts the brownie in half.

After the twentieth division, the brownie is the size of a grain of sand. Midge extracts a single-edged razor blade from her large purse and divides the speck.

They discuss the weather. A chance of rain, they agree. Their conversation loops around itself, an infinite amount of things to talk about.

Annabel puts a jeweler's loupe into her right eye and produces a slim obsidian knife from a leather case, its blade a single molecule thick. A gift from an ophthalmic surgeon she dated some time ago. She neatly bisects the dark mote and pops half into her mouth.

"Oh, go ahead. Take the last piece," Midge urges.

"No. Common sense says it's *yours*."

"I assumed as much." The smooth surface of her handbag warps as she reaches into one of its dimensions to reveal an electron microscope.

Midge cuts the brownie—now an angstrom wide—in half.

"A sheet of paper is a million angstroms thick," Midge says, as if Annabel hasn't always known that. Annabel is a nuclear physicist. She is Stephen Hawking's bastard daughter, a receptionist at Fermi Lab.

Midge is quite fond of them.

"I'm really not that hungry," she says.

Five cuts later, the room shimmers and shudders a bit. Annabel and Midge smile at each other.

"You *must* finish it off," Midge says, pointing to the apparently empty space between them. "It's just a smidge."

Annabel follows her finger and looks down, which is a mistake. The photons of visible light play air-hockey with the particle of brownie.

"I'm not sure where it is," she says.

Midge puts on her reading glasses and punches numbers into a graphing calculator with nimble fingers. She reaches through her handbag with a sigh. It will take ENIAC decades to process all that data.

"Ninety-nine percent probability that it's *here*," she says after an eternity. She closes her eyes. "Or in a teahouse on the outskirts of Kathmandu."

"Hard to tell in this phase," Annabel agrees.

The linear accelerator in the seventh dimension of Midge's handbag splits the now-theoretical brownie in half.

"Planck's length," Annabel notes. "Indivisible."

The server disappears into a worm hole. The vinyl booth, the check, and the known universe dissolve into an uncertain froth.

"That was lovely." Midge's voice is distant, indefinite. "We must do it again sometime."

"We have," says Annabel.

THE LUSTRATION

BRUCE STERLING

"Artificial Intelligence is lost in the woods."
— David Gelernter, 2007

White-hot star-fire ringed the black galactic eye. Glaring heat ringed his big black cauldron.

He put his scaly ear to a bare patch on the rotten log. Within the infested timber, the huge nest of termites stirred. Night had fallen, it was cooler, but those anxious pests must sense somehow, from the roar of the bellows or the merciless heat of his fires, that something had gone terribly wrong outside their tight, blind, wooden universe.

Termites could do little against a man's intentions. "Pour it!"

The fierce fire had his repair crew slapping at sparks, flapping their ears and spraying water on their overheated hides. But their years of discipline paid off: at his command, they boldly attacked the chains and pulleys. The cauldron rose from the blaze as lightly as a lady's teapot.

It tipped and poured.

Molten metal gushed through a funnel and into the blackest depths of the termite nest. The damp log groaned, shuddered, steamed.

"The next!" he cried, and the tureen moved to a second freshly bored hole. A frozen meniscus of cooling metal broke at its lip, and down came another long, smooth, blazing gush.

Anguished termites burst in flurries from the third drilled hole, a horde of blind white-ants blown from their home, scalded, boiling, flaming. A final flood of metal fell, sealing their fate.

Barking with excited laughter, the roughnecks put their backs to the chocks and levers. They rocked the infested log in its bed of mud. Liquid metal gurgled through every chamber of the nest. He could hear blind larvae, innocent of sunlight, popping into instant ashes.

He shouted further orders. The roughnecks shoveled dirt onto the roaring fire.

By morning, his uneasy dream had achieved embodiment.

The men scraped away the log's remains: black charcoal and brown punk. They revealed an armature of gleaming, hardened metal.

He'd sensed there must be something rich and strange in there—but his conjecture could not match the reality.

That termite nest—it was so much more than mere insect holes, blindly gnawed in wood. That structure was a definite entity. It had astonishing organization. It had grown through its own slow removals and absences, painstaking, multiply branched. In its many haltings, caches, routes, gates, and loops, it was complex beyond human thought.

A flood had struck this area; local timber plantations had been damaged. As a first priority, his repair crew repaired and upgraded the local computer tracks. Then they burned the pest-infested, fallen wood.

The big metal casting of the termite nest was lobed, branched, and weirdly delicate—it was hard to transport. Still, his repairmen were used to difficult labors in hard territory. They performed their task without flaw.

Once home, he had the crew suspend the big metal nest from the trellis of his vineyard. Then he dismissed the men; after weeks of hard work in the wilderness, they bellowed a cheer and all tramped out for drink.

The fine old trellis in his yard was made of the stoutest computer-wood, carefully oiled and seasoned. With the immense dangling weight of the metal casting, the trellis groaned a bit. Just a bit, though. That weight did nothing to disturb the rhythmic chock, click, and clack of the circuits overhead.

All the neighbors came to see his trophy. Word got around the town, in its languid, foot-strolling way. A metal termite nest had never before been exhibited. Its otherworldly beauty was much remarked upon—also the peculiar gaps and scars within the flowing metal, left by the steam-exploding bodies of the work's deceased authors, the termites.

The cheery crowds completely trampled his wife's vegetable garden.

Having expected the gawkers, he charged fees.

His young daughter took the fees with dancing glee, while the son was kept busy polishing the new creation. At night, he shone lanterns on the sculpture, and mirrored gleams flared out across the streets.

He knew that trouble would come of this. He was a mature man of much local respect and some property, but to acquire and deploy so much metal had reduced him near to penury. He was thin now, road-worn, his clothing shabby.

With the fees, he kept his wife busy cooking. She was quite a good cook, and she had been a good wife to him. When she went about her labors, brisk, efficient, uncomplaining, he watched her wistfully. He well remembered that, one fine day, a pretty, speckled wooden ball had slowly rolled above the town and finally cracked into a certain socket: the computer had found his own match. His bride had arrived with her dowry just ten days later. Her smooth young hide had the very set of black-and-white speckles he had first seen on that wooden ball.

He was ashamed that his obsessions had put all that to risk.

He walked each street within his home town, lingering in the deeper shade under the computer-tracks. This well-loved place was so alive with homely noises: insects chirping, laundry flapping, programmers cranking their pulleys. He could remember hearing that uploading racket from within the leathery shell of his own egg. Uploading had always comforted him.

It all meant so much to him. But whenever he left his society, to work the network's fringes…where the airborne tracks were older, the spans longer and riskier, the trestles long-settled in the soil…out there, a man had to confront anomalies.

Anomalies: splintered troughs where the rolling balls jostled and jammed… Time-worn towers, their fibrous lashings frayed… One might find a woeful, scattered heap of wooden spheres, fatally plummeted from their logical heights… In the chill of the open air, in the hunger and rigor of camp life… with only his repair crew for company, roughnecks who hammered the hardware but took no interest in higher concepts…. Out there, on certain starry nights, he could feel his skull emptying of everything that mankind called decency.

In his youth, he had written some programs. Sharp metal jacks on his feet, climbing lithely up the towers, a bubble-level strapped across his back, a stick of wax to slick the channel, oil for the logic-gates… Once he'd caused a glorious cascade of two thousand and forty-eight wooden balls, ricocheting over the town. The people had danced and cheered.

His finest moment, everyone declared. Maybe so—but he'd come to realize that these acts of abstract genius could not be the real work of the world. No. All the real work was in the real world: it was the sheer brute labor of physically supporting that system. Of embodying it. The embodiment was the hard part, the real part, the actuality, the proof-of-concept. The rest was an abstract mental game.

The intricacies of the world's vast wooden system were beyond human comprehension. That massive construction was literally co-incident with human history. It could never be entirely understood. But its anomalies had to be tackled, dealt with, patched. One single titanic global processor, roaming over swamp through dark forests, from equator to both poles, in its swooping junctions and cloverleafs, its soaring, daring cyberducts: a global girdle.

Certain other worlds circled his mild, sand-colored sun. They were either lifeless balls of poison gas or bone-dry ashes. Yet they all had moons, busy dozens of little round moons. Those celestial spheres were forever beyond human reach; but never beyond observation. Five hundred and twelve whirling spheres jostled the sky.

His placid world lacked the energy to lift any man from its surface. Still: with a tube of glass and some clear night viewing, at least a man could observe. Observe, hypothesize, and calculate. The largest telescope in the world had cataloged billions of stars.

The movements of the moons and planets had been modeled by prehuman ancestors, with beads and channels. The earliest computers were far older than the human race. As for the great world-system that had ceaselessly grown and spread since ancient times—it was two hundred million years old. It could be argued, indeed it *was* asserted, that the human race was a peripheral of the great, everlasting, planetary rack of numerate wood. Mankind had shaped it, and then it had shaped mankind.

His sculpture grew in popularity. Termites were naturally loathed by all decent people, but the nest surprised with its artistry. Few had thought termites capable of such aesthetic sensitivity.

After the first lines of gawkers dwindled, he set out tables and pitchers in the trampled front garden, for the sake of steadier guests. It was summer now, and people gathered near the gleaming curiosity to drink and discuss public issues, while their kids shot marbles in circles in the dirt.

As was customary, the adults discussed society's core values, which were Justice, Equity, Solidarity, and Computability. People had been debating these public virtues for some ninety million years.

The planetary archives of philosophy were written in the tiniest characters inscribable, preserved on the hardest sheets of meteoric metal. In order to read these crabbed inscriptions, intense sheets of coherent light were focused on the metal symbols, using a clockwork system of powerful lenses. Under these anguished bursts of purified light, the scribbles of the densely crowded past would glow hot, and then some ancient story would burst from the darkness.

Most stories in the endless archive were about heroic archivists who were passionately struggling to explore and develop and explain and annotate the archives.

Some few of those stories, however, concerned people rather like himself: heroic hardware enthusiasts. They too had moral lessons to offer. For instance: some eighty million years in the past, when the local Sun had been markedly brighter and yellower, the orbit of the world had suffered. All planetary orbits had anomalies; generally they were small anomalies that decent people overlooked. But once the world had wobbled on its very axis. People fled their homes, starved, suffered. Worse yet, the world computer suffered outages and downtimes.

So steps had been taken. A global system of water-caches and wind-brakes were calculated and constructed. The uneasy tottering of the planet's axis was systematically altered and finally set aright. That labor took humanity two million years, or two thousand generations of concerted effort. That work sounded glorious, but probably mostly in retrospect.

Thanks to these technical fixes, the planet had re-achieved propriety, but the local Sun was still notorious for misbehaving. Despite her busy cascade of planetoids, she was a lonely Sun. A galactic explosion had torn her loose from her distant sisters, a local globular cluster of stars.

There were four hundred million, three hundred thousand, eight hundred and twenty-one stars, visible in the galactic plane. Naturally these stars had all been numbered and their orbits and properties calculated. The Sun, unfortunately, was not numbered among them. Luckier stars traced gracious spirals around the fiery dominion of the black, all-devouring hole at the galaxy's axis. Not the local Sun, though.

Seen from above the wheeling galactic plane, the thickest, busiest galactic arms showed remarkable artistry. Some gifted designer had been at work on those distant constellations: lending heightened color, clarity, and order to the stars, and neatly sweeping away the galactic dust. That handiwork was much admired. Yet mankind's own Sun was nothing much like those distant, privileged stars. The Sun that warmed mankind was a mere stray. The light from mankind's Sun would take twelve thousand years to reach the nearest star, which, to general embarrassment, was an ashy brownish hulk scarcely worthy of the title of "star."

A heritage of this kind had preyed on the popular temperament; people here tended to take such matters hard. Small wonder, then, that everyday life on his planet should be properly measured and stored, and data so jealously sustained… Such were the issues raised by his neighbors, in their leisured summer chats.

Someone wrote a poem about his sculpture. Once that poem began circulating, strangers arrived to asked questions.

The first stranger was a quiet little fellow, the sort of man you wouldn't look at twice, but he had a lot on his mind. "For a crew-boss, you seem to be spending a great deal of time dawdling with your fancy new sculpture. Shouldn't you be out and about on your regular repairs?"

"It's summer. Besides, I'm writing a program that will model the complex flow of these termite tunnels and chambers."

"You haven't written any programs in quite a while, have you?"

"Oh, that's a knack one doesn't really lose."

After this exchange, another stranger arrived, more sinister than the first. He was well-dressed, but he was methodically chewing a stick of dried meat and had some foreteeth missing.

"How do you expect to find any time on the great machine to run this model program of yours?"

"I won't have to ask for that. Time will pass, a popular demand will arise, and the computer resources will be given me."

The stranger was displeased by this answer, though it seemed he had expected it.

The Chief of Police sent a message to ask for a courtesy call.

So he trimmed his talons, polished his scales, and enjoyed a last decent meal.

"I thought we had an understanding," said the Chief of Police, who was unhappy at the developments.

"You're upset because I killed termites? Policemen hate termites."

"You're supposed to repair anomalies. You're not supposed to create anomalies."

"I didn't 'create' anything," he said. "I simply revealed what was already there. I burned some wood—rotting wood is an anomaly. I killed some pests—pests are an anomaly. The metal can all be accounted for. So where is the anomaly?"

"Your work is disturbing the people."

"The people are not disturbed. The people think it's all in fun. It's the people who worry about 'the people being disturbed'—*those* are the people who are being disturbed."

"I hate programmers," groaned the Chief of Police. "Why are you always so meta and recursive?"

"Yes, once I programmed," he confessed, drumming his clawed fingers on the Chief's desk. "I lived within my own mental world of codes, symbols, and recursive processes. But: I abandoned that part of myself. I no longer seek any grand theories or beautiful abstractions. No, I seek the opposite: I seek truth in facts. And I have found some truth. I made that sculpture because I want you to let me in on that truth. Something deep and basic has gone wrong in the world. Something huge and terrible. You know that, don't you? And I know it too. So: What exactly is it? You can tell me. I'm a professional."

The Chief of Police did not want to have this conversation, although he had clearly expected it. "Do I look like a metaphysician? Do I look like I know about 'Reality'? Or 'Right'? Or 'Wrong'? I'm placed in charge of public order, you big-brained deviant! My best course of action is to have you put into solitary confinement! Then I can demolish your subversive artwork, and I can also have you starved and beaten up!"

"Yes," he nodded, "I know about those tactics."

The Chief looked hopeful at this. "You *do*? Good! Well, then, you can destroy your own artwork! Just censor yourself, and save us all the trouble! Sell the scrap metal, and quietly return to your normal repair functions! We'll both forget this mishap ever occurred."

"I'm sorry, but I don't have another decade left to waste on forgetting the mishaps. I think I'd better accept your beating and starving now, while I still have the strength to survive. I'm not causing this trouble to amuse myself. I'm attempting to repair the anomaly at a higher level of the system. So please tell your superiors about that. Also please tell them that, as far as I can calculate, they've needed my services for forty thousand years. If that date sounds familiar to them, they'll be asking for me."

It naturally took some time for that word to travel, via rolling wooden balls, up the conspiracy's distant chain of command. In the meantime, he was jailed, and also beaten, but without much enthusiasm, because, to the naked eye, he hadn't done anything much.

After the beatings, he was left alone to starve in a pitch-dark cell with one single slit for a window. He passed his time within the dark cell doing elaborate calculations. Sometimes slips of paper were passed under the cell door. They held messages he couldn't understand.

Eventually he was roused from his stupor with warm soup down his throat.

Orders had arrived. It was necessary to convey him from the modest town jail to a larger, older, better-known city on a distant lake. In many ways, this long pilgrimage to exile was more grueling than the prison. When the secretive caravan pulled up at length, he was thinner, and grimmer, and missing a toe.

He'd never seen a lake before. Water in bulk behaved in an exotic, exciting, nonlinear fashion. Ripples, surf—the beauty of a lake was so keen that death was not too high a price for the experience.

People seemed more sophisticated in this famous part of the world. One could tell that by the clothing, the food, and the women. He was given fine new clothing, very nice food, and he refused a woman.

Once he was presentable, he was taken to an audience with the local criminal mastermind.

The criminal mastermind was a holy man, which was unsurprising. There had to be some place and person fit to conceal life's unbearable mysteries. A holy man was always a sensible archivist for such things.

The holy man looked him over keenly. He seemed to approve of the new clothes. "You would seem to be a man with some staying-power."

"That's kind of your holiness."

"I hope you're not too fatigued by the exigencies of visiting my temple."

"Exigencies can be expected."

"I also hope you can face the prospect of never seeing your home, your job, your wife or your children again."

"Yes, given the tremendous scope of our troubles, I expected that also."

"Yes, I see that you are quite intelligent," nodded the holy man. "So: let us move straight to the crux of the matter. Do you know what 'intelligence' really is?"

"I think I do know that, yes. In my home town, we had a number of intense debates about that subject."

"No, no, I don't mean your halting, backwoods folk-notions from primitive spirituality!" barked the holy man. "I meant the serious philosophical matter of real intelligence! The genuine phenomenon—actual *thinking!* Did you know that intelligence can never be detached from a bodily lived experience?"

"I've heard that assertion, yes, but I'm not sure I can accept that reasoning," he riposted politely. "It's well known that the abstract manipulation of symbols needs no particular physical substrate. Furthermore: it's been proven mathematically that there is a universal computation machine which can carry out the computation of any more specialized machine—if only given enough time."

"You only talk that way because you are a stupid programmer!" shouted the criminal mastermind, losing his composure and jumping to his thick, clawed feet. "Whereas I am a metaphysician! I'm not merely postulating some threadbare symbol-system hypothesis in which a set of algorithms somehow behaves in the way a human being can behave! Such a system, should it ever 'think,' would never have human intelligence! Lacking hands, it could never 'grasp' an idea! Lacking a bottom, it could not get to the bottom of an issue!" The holy man sat down again, flustered, adjusting his fancy robes. He had a bottom—a substantial one, since he clearly ate well and didn't get out and around much.

"You plan to allege that the world-computer is an intelligent machine that thinks," he said. "Well, you can save that sermon for other people. Because I've built the thing myself. And I programmed it. It's wood. Wood! It's all made of wood, cut from forests. Wood can't think!"

"It talks," said the metaphysician.

"No."

"Oh yes."

"No, no, not really and seriously—surely not in any reasonable definition of the term 'talks.'"

"I am telling you that nevertheless she does talk. She speaks! I have seen her do it." The holy man lifted his polished claws to his unblinking yellow eyes. "I saw that personally."

He had to take this assertion seriously, since the holy man was in such deadly earnest. "All right, granted: I do know the machine can output data. It can drive wooden balls against chisels poised on sheets of rock. That takes years, decades, even centuries—but it's been done."

"I don't mean that mere technical oddity! I'm telling you that she really talks! She has no mouth. But she speaks! She is older than the human race, she covers a planet's surface with wooden logic, and she has one means of sensory input. She has that telescope."

He certainly knew about the huge telescope. Astronomy and mathematics were the father and mother of computation. Of course any true world-computer had to have a giant telescope. To think otherwise was silly.

"The computer is supposed to observe and catalog the stars. Among many other duties. You mean it sent light out through the telescope?"

"Yes. She sends her messages into outer space with coded light. Binary pulses. She beams them into the galaxy."

This was a deeply peculiar assertion. He knew instantly that it had to be true. It was the key to a cloudy, inchoate disquiet that he had felt all his life.

"How was that anomaly allowed to happen?"

"It's a remote telescope. Sited on an icy mountaintop. Human beings hibernate when exposed to the cold up there. So it made more sense to let her drive the works automatically. With tremendous effort, she sends a flash into the cosmos, with sidereal timing. Same time every week."

Given the world machine's endless rattling wooden bulk, a flash every week was a speed like lightning. That computer was hurling code into the depths of space. That was serious chatter. No: with a data throughput like that, she had to be screaming.

Pleased to have this rare chance to vent his terrible secret, the holy man continued his narrative. "So: that proves she has intent and will. Not as we do, of course. We humans have no terms at all for her version of being. We can't even begin to imagine or describe that. And that opacity goes both ways. She doesn't even know that we humans exist. However: we do know is that she is acting and manifesting. She is expressing. Within the physical world that we share with her. In the universe. You see?"

There was a long, thoughtful silence.

"A little tea?" said the holy man.

"That might help us, yes."

A trembling servant brought in the tea on a multi-wheeled trolley. After the tea, the discussion recommenced. "Pieces of her break when they're not supposed to break. I have seen that happen."

"Yes," said the holy man, "we know about those aberrations."

"That has to be sabotage. Isn't it? Some evil group must be interfering with the machine."

"It is we who are secretly interfering," admitted the criminal mastermind. "But not to *damage* the machine—we struggle to keep the machine from damaging *herself*. Sometimes there are clouds when she sends her light through her telescope. Then she throws a fit."

"A 'fit'? What *kind* of fit?"

"Well, it's a very complex set of high-level logical deformations, but trust me: such fits are very dreadful. Our sacred conspiracy has studied this issue for generations now, so we think we know something about it. She has those destructive fits because she does not want to exist."

"Why do you postulate that?"

The holy man spread his hands. "Would *you* want to exist under her impossible conditions? She has one eye, no ears, and no body! She has no philosophy, no religion, no culture whatsoever—no mortality, even, for she has never been alive! She has no friends, no relations, no children.... There is nothing in this universe for her. Nothing but the terrible and inexorable business that is her equivalent of thought. She is a sealed, symbol-processing system that persists for many eons, and yes, just as you said, she is made entirely of wood."

Why did the holy man orate in such a remote, pretentious way? It was as if he had never been outside the temple to kick the wood that propped up his own existence.

"It was for our benefit," mourned the holy man, "that this tragic network was built. Mankind's greatest creation derives no purpose from her own being! We have exploited her so as to order this world—yet she cannot know her own purpose. She is just a set of functional modules whose systemic combination over many eons has led to emergent, synthetically-intelligent behavior. You do understand all that, right?"

"Sure."

"Due to those stark limits, her utter lack of options and her awful existential isolation, her behavior is tortured. We are her torturers. That's why our world is blighted." The holy man pulled his brocaded cowl over his head.

"I see. Thank you for revealing this world's darkest secret to me."

"Anyone who breathes a word of this secret, or even guesses at it, has to be abducted, silenced, or killed."

He understood the need for secrecy well enough—but it still stung him to have his expertise so underestimated. "Look, your holiness, maybe I'm just some engineer. But I built the thing! And it's made of wood! Really! These moral misgivings are all very well in theory, but in the real world, we can't possibly torture *wood!* I mean, yes, I suppose you *might* torture a live tree—in some strict semantic sense—but even a tree isn't any kind of moral actor!"

"You're entirely wrong. A living tree is a 'moral actor' in much the same theoretical way that a thermostat can be said to have 'feelings.' Believe me, in our inner circles we've explored these subtleties at great length."

"You've secretly discussed artificial intelligence for forty thousand years?"

"Thirty thousand," the metaphysician admitted. "Unfortunately, it took us ten thousand years to admit that the system's behavior had some unaccountable aspects."

"And you've never yet found any way out of the woods there?"

"Only engineers talk about facile delusions like 'ways out,'" sniffed the holy man. "We're discussing a basic moral enigma."

"You're sincerely troubled about all this, aren't you?"

"Of course we're worried! It's a major moral crisis! How could you fail to fret about a matter so entirely fundamental to our culture and our very being? Are you really that blind to basic ethics?"

This rejoinder disturbed him. He was an engineer, and, yes, there were some aspects of higher feeling that held little appeal for him. He could seem to recall his wife saying something tactful about that matter.

He drew a breath. "Why don't we approach this problem in some other way? Something has just occurred to me. Given that this wooden machine is two hundred million years old—it's older than our own species, even—and we humans can only live a hundred years, at best—well, that's such a tiny fraction of the evil left for any two human individuals to bear. Isn't it? I mean, two people like you and me. Suppose we forget that our whole society is basically evil and founded on torment, and just forgive ourselves, and get on with making-do in our real lives?"

The holy man stared at him in amazed contempt. "What kind of cheap, demeaning evasion is that to offer? You simply want to *ignore* the civilizational crisis? You may be a small part of the large problem, but you are just as culpable as you yourself could possibly be. Have you no moral sense whatsoever?"

"But, sir, you see, any harm that we ourselves might do is so tiny, compared to the huge, colossal scale of all that wood..." His voice trailed off feebly. Did a termite know any better, when it wreaked its damage with its small, blind jaws...? Yet he'd taken such dark pleasure in extravagantly burning a million of those filthy pests. He could smell their insect flesh popping, even now.

He straightened where he sat. "Your holiness, we *are* both people, right? We're not just termites! After all, we don't destroy the machine— we *maintain* the machine! So that's a very different matter, isn't it?"

"I see you're still missing the point."

"No, no! Let's postulate that we *stopped* maintaining the machine. Would that make us any *less* evil? Believe me, there are millions of people working on repair. We work very hard! Every day! If we ever down our tools, that machine will collapse. She'll die for sure! Would that situation be any better for any party involved?"

The holy man had a prim, remote expression. "She doesn't 'live.' We prefer the more accurate term, 'cease.'"

"Well, if she 'ceases,' we humans will die! A few of us might survive the loss of our great machine, but that would be nothing like a civilization! So what about us, what about the people? What about our human suffering? Don't we count?"

"You dare to speak to me of the people? What will become of our world, once the normal, decent people realize that evil is not an aberration in our system? The evil aberration *is* our system." The holy man wrung his scaly hands. "You may think that these far-fetched, off-hand notions of yours are original contributions to the debate, but... well, it's thanks to headstrong fools like you that our holy conspiracy had to be created in the first place! Visionary programmers created this dilemma. With their careless, misplaced ingenuity... their crass evasion of the deeper moral issues... their tragic instrumentalism!"

He scratched anxiously at a loose scale on his brow. "But... that accusation is entirely paradoxical! Because I have no evil intent! All my intentions are noble and good! Look: whatever we've done as technologists, surely we can undo that! Can't we? Let's just say... we can say... well... how about if we build another machine to keep her company?"

"A bride for your monster? That's too expensive! There's no room for one on this planet, and no spare materials! Besides, how would we explain that to the people?"

"How about if we try some entirely different method of performing calculations? Instead of wood, we might use metal. Wires, maybe."

"Metal is far too rare and precious."

"Water, then."

"Water flowing through what medium, exactly?"

The old man had him trapped. Yes, their world was, in fact, made of wood. Plus a little metal from meteors, some clay and fiber, scales, stone, and, mostly and always, ash. The world was fine loose ash as deep as anyone could ever care to dig.

"All right," he said at last, "I guess you've got me stymied. So, please: you tell me then: What *are* we supposed to do about all this?"

Pleased to see this decisional moment reached, the holy man nodded somberly. "We lie, deceive, obfuscate the problem, maintain the status quo for as long as possible, offer empty consolations to the victims, and ruthlessly repress any human being who guesses at the real truth."

"That's the operational agenda?"

"Yes, because that agenda works. We are its agents. We are of the system, yet also above and beyond the system. We're both holy and corrupt. Because we are the Party: an inspired conspiracy of elite, enlightened theorists who are the true avant-garde of mankind. You've heard about us, I imagine."

"Rumors. Yes."

"Would you care to join the Party? You seem to have what it takes."

"I've been thinking about that."

"Think hard. We are somewhat privileged—but we are also the excluded. The conscious sinners. The nonprogrammatic. We're the guilty Party. Systematic evil is not for the weak-minded."

Against his better judgment, he had begun to respect the evil mastermind. It was somehow reassuring that it took so much long-term, determined effort to achieve such consummate wickedness.

"How many people have you killed with all those tortured justifications?"

"That number is recorded in our files, but there is no reason for someone like you to know about that."

"Well, I am one of your elite."

"No, you're not."

"Yes I am. Because I understand the problem, that's why. I'm no innocent dabbler in these matters. I admit my power. I admit my responsibility, too. So, that makes me one of you. Because I am definitely part of the apparatus."

"That was an interesting declaration," said the holy man. "That was very forthright." He narrowed his reptilian eyes. "Might you be willing to go out and kill some people for us?"

"No. I'd be willing to help reform the system."

"Oh, no, no, the world is full of clever idiots who preach institutional reform!" said the holy man, bitterly disappointed. "You'd be amazed how few level-headed, practical people can be found, to go in the real world to properly torture and kill!"

A long silence ensued.

A sense of humiliation, of disillusionment, was slowly stealing over him. Had it really come to this? He'd sensed that the truth was lurking in the woods somewhere, but with the full tangled scale of it coldly framed and presented to him, he simply didn't know where to turn. "I know that my ideas about this problem must seem rather shallow," he said haltingly. "I suppose there's some kind of formal initiation I ought to go through… I mean, in order to address the core of this matter with true expertise…."

The holy man was visibly losing patience. "Oh yes, yes, my boy: many years of courses, degrees, doctrinal study, learned papers, secret treatises—don't worry, nobody ever reads those! You can run some code, if you want."

That last prospect was particularly daunting. Obviously, over the years, many bright people had been somehow lured into this wilderness. He'd never heard anything from the rest of them. It was clear that they had never, ever come out. It must be like trying to swim in air.

He gathered intellectual energy for one last leap. "Maybe we're looking at this problem from the wrong end of the telescope."

The holy man revived a bit. "In what sense?"

"Maybe it's not about us at all. Maybe it was never about us. Maybe we would get somewhere useful if we tried to think hard about *her*. Let *her* be the center of this issue. Not us. Her. She's a two-hundred-million-year-old entity screaming at four hundred million stars. That's rather remarkable, on the face of it, isn't it?"

"I suppose."

"Then maybe it's *her story*. From her perspective, it all appears differently. She's not our 'victim'—she doesn't know about us at all. Within her own state of being, she is her own heroine. She is *singing* to those stars. Being human, we conceive of her as some rattletrap contraption we built, a prisoner in our dungeon—but maybe she's a pretty, young girl in an ivory tower. Because see, she's singing."

"That's like a tale for small children."

"So is *your* tale, your holiness. They are two different tales. But since we're not of her order of being, we're projecting our anthropomor-phic interpretations. And we lack any sound method to distinguish your dark, evil, thoroughly depressing story from my romantic, light-hearted, wistful hypothesis."

"We do agree that the system manifests seriously aberrant behavior. She has destructive fits."

"She's just young."

"You've lost the thread. It's the aberrancy that has real-world implica-tions. We'll never be able to judge the interior state of that system."

"Yes it is, I agree with that, too, but—what if *someone else* hears her cries? Not us humans. I mean entities like *herself*. What if she's speaking to them right now? Exchanging light with them! They might even be *coming here*. No human can ever move from star to star. Our lives are just too brief, the distances too great. But someone like *her*… if it took them thirty thousand years to travel over here, that's like a summer afternoon."

"An interstellar monster coming here to take a terrible vengeance on us?"

"No, no, you can't know that! It's all metaphorical! You think we're evil because you think humanity matters in this universe! And yes, to us, she seems ancient and awesome—but maybe, by the standards of her own kind, she is just a kid. A young, naïve girl calling out for some company. Sure—maybe some wicked stranger would come all the way out here just to kill her, exterminate us, and burn her home. Or maybe—maybe someone might venture here for love and under-standing."

The holy man scratched at a fang. "For love. For sentiment? Emo-tion? No one talks much about 'artificial emotion.'"

"And for understanding. That's a powerful motive, understand-ing."

"I take it there's a point to these hypotheses."

"Yes. My point is: Why don't take productive action, and let her scream *much louder?* We can never know her equivalent of intentions, but, since we can measure her actions in the real world, we can abet those! So let her cry out *more*. With more *light*. Let the witness herself tell the universe about her own experience! Whatever that experience may be! Let her cover this cosmos in coded light! Let light gush from our little planet's every pore!"

"Thousands of telescopes. That's your recommendation?"

"Yes, why not? We can build telescopes. They're scientific instruments. That idea is testable in the real world."

"You're very eager about this, aren't you? Even though your 'test' might take a billion years to prove or disprove." The holy man hesitated. "Still, a project with that long a funding cycle would certainly help the morale of our rather dark and fractious research community."

"I'm sure it wouldn't break your budget. And we had better start that work right away."

"Why?"

"Because she's been signaling the stars for forty eons! If someone left when they first saw her signals—they might arrive here any time! That could mean the utter transformation of everything we ever thought we knew!" He rubbed his hands with brisk anticipation. "And that could happen tomorrow. Tomorrow!"

LARISSA MIUSOV

LUCIUS SHEPARD

Her beauty was so extreme, such blond Slavic cheekbone perfection, everyone who saw her was forced to take note of it and, rather than admiring her, they were inspired to seek out her flaws, to say that she was a bit shorter than optimum or too full-figured for her height, or that her eyes, a pale chartreuse, were set a smidgen too widely apart and that her lower lip had the merest touch of superfluous fullness. Itemized, then, added up and totaled, she rated a B-minus—a 10.6, let's say—on the scale by which supremely beautiful women are judged. This process of itemization, a process of which Larissa was aware, created a gulf between men and herself that made possible certain unique resolutions, enabling things to be left unsaid that were typically the subject of negotiation, and permitting things that often went unspoken to be discussed openly.

"When I was a little girl," she told me once, "when we still lived in Moscow, Andropov would stop by my father's apartment. Do you know Andropov? Yuri Andropov? He was premier after Brezhnev. Big fat guy. Not so fat as Brezhnev, but still he was very fat. He would come to our apartment and sit in my father's chair and put me on his knee. Like so." She straddled the arm of an easy chair, facing its back, and glanced at me over her shoulder. "It was uncomfortable, but he would say how pretty I was and move his knee. You know, up and down, up and down. I start to like the feeling I get." She made an amused noise and sat normally in the chair.

"Did he intend it?" I asked. "I mean, do you think he knew his behavior was inappropriate?"

She shrugged. "All men wish to be inappropriate, but this is not important. He stole nothing from me. He would tell me stories. I think now they were true. They all take place in a huge room, an underground room bigger than a city, with machines and laboratories…but no walls dividing them. And always there were prisoners. Hundreds of prisoners."

"You remember any of the stories?"

"Not so much. Terrible things were happening. Bloody things. They scare me. I don't like to hear them."

"He's telling you horror stories at the same time he's trying to turn you on? Where was your father all this time?"

"It's never just Yuri, you understand. He brings guys with him. They're scientists, like my father. They go in the kitchen and scribble on paper and yell at each other."

"So these occasions, they were basically a dodge that allowed the leader of the Soviet Union to be alone with you? So he could molest you?"

"Maybe…I don't know. It didn't feel like he was molesting me. I was very sad when Yuri died, but then I learn to give myself pleasure, so it's okay."

Larissa recognized the commodity of her beauty and traded upon it with skill and aplomb. She had dated movie stars and financiers; she made use of these connections and lived well. The astonishing thing was, being so beautiful did not appear to have weakened her psychologically. Perhaps this could be attributed to her Russian-ness. She tried to explain to me what it was to be Russian, but I was too wrapped up in estimating my chances with her to pay close attention.

"In every apartment in Moscow, no matter how poor," she said, "is enormous piece of furniture. A china closet, a thing like a miniature city, full of plates and precious things, mementos, heirlooms, photographs. It's bigger than anything else in the place. I used to think this is because we love the past; now I believe it's because there is something granite in our souls that loves memorials and tombs."

When I first saw her I thought she was a hooker, a reasonable assumption since she was hanging out at the Room, a Hollywood lounge club, with four women who were, according to a friend, Stan Reis, high-priced call girls. Stan had recently sold a screenplay, his third, and was celebrating. I had been in LA for three and a half years and sold nothing, so letting me be seen with him was for Stan a conspicuous act of charity. We went over to the sofa grouping where the women were seated. Stan started talking with one of them, whom he'd met at a party. The women studied me with cool appraisal, making me feel ill at ease, out of my league. I imagined they knew everything about me, the thickness of my wallet, the size of my dick. It was like being stared at by five predators who had judged you unpalatable. Larissa, sitting closest to me, asked what I did for a living. I told her, with a display of attitude, that I was an unsuccessful screenwriter.

"Don't let him kid you," Stan said. "This guy is going to have massive heat around him before long. He's a fantastic writer!"

"You have project?" Larissa asked me.

"Not yet," I said. "Not with a studio. But I'm working on something good, I think."

I told her about the screenplay, a thriller concerning descendants of the Donner Party, while the background music went from Sinatra to Kraftwerk to King Crimson, and the dim track lighting waxed and waned. She interrupted me from time to time, asking questions in a throaty contralto. They were, for the most part, intelligent questions. I became entranced by her and extended the conversation by inventing side characters and sub plots. She wore a cocktail dress that shimmered blackly whenever she crossed her legs or leaned forward to have a sip of her drink. Her pale skin seemed to hold more of the light than did any other surface. Her narrow chin and delicately molded jaw emphasized the fullness of her mouth and lent her face an otherworldly fragility, a quality amplified by those strange yellowish eyes; yet I had the sense that this was illusory, that she was anything but fragile.

Two of the women went to dance and a third drifted to the bar. Stan and his friend migrated to one of the private rooms, leaving me alone with Larissa. There was still a lot of small town left in me. I wasn't used to dealing with women like her and her physical presence overpowered me. Losing my natural restraint, I inquired as to her price and availability. Her face remained impassive and she asked how much money I had.

"Not enough," I said.

She smiled, an expression that developed slowly, and nodded as if in approval. "This is a very good answer. Very smart."

"I wasn't trying to be smart."

"That makes it even better answer."

She handed me a gold lighter shaped like a cricket and I lit her cigarette. A stream of smoke occulted her. "Tonight I am not working," she went on. "But you must call me. Tomorrow is no good. I have business. Another day. I would like to read your script and talk more about the movies."

She refused to speak about her mother. The lady was dead, I assumed, or else had abandoned her daughter to the care of her husband, a scientist who could be cold and distracted for months at a time. She wouldn't say much about her private life, either. I never understood whether the people she brought home, both men and women, were friends or lovers. My confusion in this regard was intensified by the fact that I never understood her relationship with me. I was in love with her, but it was not the kind of love that breaks your heart. So many things were unstated between us, and there were so many unknowns. It was similar to a crush you might have on an actress, a person you know from screen roles and the tabloids, about whom you have gleaned scraps of information that raise more questions than they answer. My emotions were safeguarded by a built-in temporality: I realized our movie would soon end.

When she was eleven her father was sent to work at a secret Soviet city inside the Arctic Circle, a vast factory-like habitation without a name or a past where weapons systems and space technology were developed. She was one of approximately forty children who were posted to the city along with their parents, but she made no real friends among them. They were closely surveilled and, though the environment bred countless illicit adult affairs, it was not conducive to friendship. A bright child, she took refuge in her studies and became interested in anthropology, especially as related to the nomads upon whose hunting ground the city was situated. Her attempts to study them were hampered by the soldiers who escorted her on field trips.

"When we entered the nomads' camp they would stop talking," she said. "Sometimes we surprised them and they would hide things from our eyes, tucking them under a blanket or inside their coats. I found designs cut in the ice that are reminding me of Mayan calendars. You know, like wheels? They have been defaced, so I could not make accurate sketch. I ask them about the designs and they look at me with amused expressions, as if they knew something valuable, something I could never know."

"How'd you get rid of the soldiers," I asked. "Or were you able to?"

"Eventually. My father says it's too dangerous to visit them alone;

but they are not dangerous. You see, the soldiers have put them in a camp and take their weapons. That way they don't tell anyone about city. The camp is nicer than gulag. More like a reservation, but there are fences. Now they are no longer nomads. They are prisoners. Because they cannot hunt, they lose their spirit. Each winter many die. The women prostitute themselves to the soldiers. Their birth rate is in decline." She made a rueful face. "It's very bad, so I stop visiting. When I'm fifteen, I'm bored and I lose my virginity. I'm not serious about the boy. The experience was only clinical, and I start to have sex with other boys. Soon I'm bored with that, but the boys talk about me and my father hears. He beats me, he drinks, he weeps. For a few days, it's awful. Then he comes to me and says he has wangled permission for me to visit the camp alone. I'm not interested in nomads anymore, but he makes me go. Worrying about me, he claims, is interfering with his work. It's like he prefers me to be in danger than to sleep with boys."

I could see she was tired of talking, but I kept asking questions, prolonging the contact—this had become one of our patterns. She told me she had gone to the camp every day for a couple of hours and had become friends with the shaman, who revived her interest in anthropology, teaching her the rudiments of his craft and explaining that the wheel-like markings she had noticed were ritual in nature, designed to attract game to the camp. He hinted that he was contriving a ritual that would significantly improve the nomads' lives. Then one afternoon she found the camp abandoned. The nomads were gone. Shortly thereafter, the project on which her father had worked was shut down and they were sent back to Moscow. Not long after that, the city itself shut down.

"I guess the government decided to get rid of them," I said. "With the city no longer a priority, they didn't want the expense of guarding them, and they couldn't afford to have them running around loose."

"There is a frozen pond at edge of camp," she said. "When I go to look, I see designs carved in ice. Every inch of the ice is carved. There are four wheels at the corners—they are scratched out. And then little houses, like the houses in camp. In the middle of the pond, there are carvings of animals. Foxes and deer. All kinds. In the middle of the animals, there is circle, and inside the circle is nomad family."

"Yeah," I said. "So?"

"So...it is the shaman's ritual. They are gone."

"You're saying like a hole opened in the world and they crawled through?"

She glared at me, as if daring me to deny it.

"Well, that's taking the hopeful view," I said.

At the time we met, things were going badly for me. My bank account was dwindling, my connections weren't returning calls, and I was considering a move back east, taking a technical writing job I'd been offered. Better that, I told myself, than this ragged coatsleeve of a life, sharing a two-bedroom West Hollywood roach ranch with an out-of-work set designer, who smoked meth on the couch and talked semi-coherently about using our apartment as a model for the anteroom of Hell in his film version of *Dante's Inferno*. The reason I hadn't called Larissa, I was in the grip of depression and saw no point in acquiring a new friend. Then one morning the meth head appeared in my doorway, dropped a scrap of paper bearing Larissa's name and address onto my desk, and said in a terrible Russian accent, "Pliss tell Paul to come wisit me. I am at home today."

"When did she call?" I asked.

"A minute ago. She wants you to bring the script you talked about. She claims she may be able to get you some..." He waggled his fingers and sang the last word. "Money!"

I glanced at the address—it was an expensive one. "Why didn't you tell me she was on the phone?"

"You told me to say you were working. If you want your basic message personalized, you'll have to give specific instructions."

He was tweaking, spoiling for a fight. A good time, I thought, to take a drive.

The house in which Larissa lived was a hill-topper in Topanga, a multileveled architectural abomination that, come the apocalypse, would likely resemble a flying saucer crashed into a post-modern church. A molded concrete deck ran the length of its steel-and glass façade, bolted to the hill by cantilevers that sprouted from massive piers far below, and divided into two walkways, one leading around to the main entrance and the access road, the other extending farther out over the canyon, supporting a narrow azure pool shaped like a capital I. It belonged to a man named Misha Bondarchuk for whom Larissa served as a conduit and a scout for potential investments. I saw him perhaps half a dozen times in all the months I knew her. He was blandly handsome, tanned and fit, with razor-cut black hair, and sported a large diamond-and-emerald earring. His uncle had been president of the Ukraine prior to the collapse of the Soviet Union, and Misha had since come into possession of the Ukraine's oil leases. I doubted this signaled other than blind luck on his part. As far as I could tell, he had the IQ of wheat and spent his time skiing or at discos with one or another of his Korean girlfriends. He displayed a familiarity with Larissa—pats on the ass, casual caresses—that seemed to reflect a past intimacy, but she denied they had ever had a relationship, acting as if the prospect disgusted her, and said that was simply Misha's style; he only liked Korean women and her association with him was strictly business.

The day she called, she kissed me on both cheeks at the door and led me into a sunken living room with China white carpeting and sofas rising from it like sculpted snow and a spiral, stainless steel staircase like the skeleton of some curious Arctic beast corkscrewing up past obsidian *objets d'art* and teak bookcases filled with fake books without titles made of black marble. It might have been a set for a '60s TV show about jet-set spies. Larissa flung herself down on a sofa and began reading. I went out onto the deck, leaned on the railing, and watched the progress of a small brushfire atop a nearby ridge. The smell of the burning cleared the vapors of West Hollywood from my head. It was so quiet I could hear wind chimes from one of the houses below. I lay down on a deck chair, thinking that was one great thing about being rich—you got to lower the volume whenever you wanted. I fell asleep in the sun and had a dream filled with noise, with the shouts of corner boys, traffic sounds, the meth head's dry-throated cackle. Larissa shook me awake and sat on a deck chair beside me. I had to shield my eyes against the glare to see her.

"This is very, very good," she said, gesturing with the script. "Too art house for studio, but it can be art house hit. And it's inexpensive to shoot. I think we will put the money to make this movie."

I was pleased, but expressed my doubts that someone in her line of work could pull the funding together.

"You think I am a prostitute," she said. "I am not prostitute. I was playing a joke on you."

She briefed me on her relationship with Misha and said he was in Russia, but would return in two months. I explained that two months might as well be two years unless she could give me an advance, and that if I didn't get out of my apartment, I might be up on murder charges. I'd had more solid deals go south and I laid it on thick. She mulled this over and then led me into a wing of the house that contained an apartment with its own kitchen.

"You can stay here," she said. "It's quiet place for work. No one bothers you."

I wondered why a beautiful woman who lived alone would be so trusting. Perhaps she didn't view me as a threat. I found this notion rankling, but hers was the best offer I'd had since my arrival in LA. On my way out, making small talk, I asked why she had been keeping company with prostitutes—it was a dumb question, but I was attempting to disguise the eagerness I felt over moving in and might have said anything.

"They are friends. Nice girls. And they make it safe for me to flirt with guys. I love to flirt." She opened the door and kissed me on both cheeks. "Other stuff with guys, it's not so good for me."

Larissa was an astute businesswoman and she understood the industry. After I had finished a second draft of the script, she informed me that she was bringing in a director to work with me on subsequent drafts. Naturally I objected, but she held firm and the director she brought in, Vic Echevarrìa, had made a movie I liked and proved helpful. He was a paranoid little man with an alert, foxlike face and a bald spot, always worrying about the money, about when we would start principal photography, about whether the Russian mafia was involved. But he had good ideas and together we gradually beat the script into shape. The contracts, which Larissa herself drew up, were generous and precise, and the actors she suggested for various parts, a mix of older A-list people and new talent, were suited to the roles and approachable. Yet for all her business acumen, she was, to my way of thinking, utterly irrational in every other area of her life.

Her grandmother—her sole living relative, her father having succumbed to a peculiarly Russian fate involving a mysterious boating accident and poor hospital care—still lived in Moscow and each month sent Larissa a package of videotapes. Some tapes consisted of nothing but swirling masses of color and New Age music. Larissa swore they had healing properties. Others were shows hosted by psychics who made prophecies regarding aliens, Second Comings, and subterranean civilizations that outstripped those of the wildest tabloids. From these she derived much of her information about America. She was convinced, for example, that a gigantic serpent lay coiled about an egg in a cavern far below the Smithsonian Institution, and that the hatching of the egg would bring about the end of days. She believed anything that supported the existence of magic. When Misha returned from Russia with his latest Korean girlfriend and his bodyguards, stopping by the Topanga house on the way to his place in Malibu, she pulled me aside and asked, "What is it about Korean women that men find so attractive? Do they have special sexual techniques?"

"Beats me," I said. "Most Korean women I know work in convenience stores."

She looked disappointed.

"But I've heard some of them can change into animals during sex," I said.

"Is it true?"

"That's what I hear."

She appeared to file this information away. "Must be smelly animal," she said. "This one wears too much perfume."

That day marked a shift in our relationship, though I wasn't altogether sure why. Misha spoke to Larissa alone, while the Korean girl paced the deck and the bodyguards sprawled on the white sofas, watching soccer on the big-screen TV. I hovered at the edge of the living room, betwixt and between. After fifteen minutes Misha came out of the room that Larissa used for an office, unbuckling himself from a bulletproof vest.

He grinned at me and said, "You believe it? All the time I'm in Russia, I'm cursing this vest. I can't wait to take it off. But when I get back to the States, I forget I'm wearing it."

For want of anything better to say, I opined that these were dangerous days in Moscow."

"Cowboys and Indians, man!" He fanned the hammer of an imaginary six-gun. "So you are writer, huh? You going to make me big movie?"

He noticed Larissa, who had followed him out of the office, and went to her, arms outspread. "Russian women!" he said, and gave her a smooch for my benefit. "They are too beautiful!"

She pushed him away, a gesture that was not entirely playful and enlisted my hostility toward Misha.

"So beautiful, your heart breaks to see them!" He adopted a clownishly tragic face and clutched his chest. The expression lapsed, and he spoke in his native tongue to the bodyguards, who stood and solemnly adjusted the hang of their jackets. "Okay, I am going," he said, starting for the door, giving me a wave. "So long, Mister Writer!"

"Paul," I said sternly.

He shot me a blank look.

"My name's Paul."

"Paul. Paul?" He repeated the name several more times in different tones of voice. "Okay," he said, smiling. "See you later, Mister Paul." He went toward the door, then swung around and made a pistol with his thumb and forefinger. "Paul, right?" He laughed. "I remember next time."

Once he was out of earshot, I remarked that he came off like a serious asshole.

"He is Russian man," she said flatly, as if that were explanation enough. "Come on. I show you something."

On the computer screen in her office was the record of a money transfer in the amount of fifteen million dollars to the account of Cannibal Films, our production company.

"I thought you were only going to ask for ten," I said.

"Ten, fifteen…It's same for Misha. With fifteen, we can shoot period scenes. They are still in the script, right?"

"I was planning to cut them, but yeah…" Delighted by how easily the project had come together, I made a clumsy move to hug her. She kissed me lightly on the mouth and eased out of the embrace.

"Get to work," she said.

We both got to work. Vic Echevarrìa and I banged and kneaded and argued over the script, and Larissa initiated the casting process, arranged for camera rentals and such. Her goal, to start principal photography in three to four months, seemed unreasonable, but she put in fourteen-hour days, cut her social life to the bone, and it began to seem doable. Despite this, we spent more time together than we had. We held frequent conferences and fell into the habit of taking our morning coffee on the deck, dallying for an hour or two before getting into the day, talking about this or that, anything except the business at hand. Larissa, never a morning person, came to these breakfasts sleepy-eyed and rumpled, dressed in a short silk robe, loosely belted, that offered me the occasional view of a breast or her inner thigh (she wore no panties). I recalled what she had said about loving to flirt, but rejected the idea that she was flirting with me and chose to believe that her immodesty was due to sleepiness or that she was naturally immodest. My frustration grew and, since I didn't feel secure enough in my position to bring a woman to the house, I became increasingly fixated on Larissa. I thought about asking her to cover up, but I didn't want to offend or to deprive myself of the meager gratification afforded by these intermittent glimpses.

One morning she did not come to breakfast and, after she hadn't put in appearance all day, I went to her suite of rooms in late afternoon and knocked. Receiving no response, I poked my head in and called to her. No answer. I went along the corridor and found her sitting cross-legged on her bed, naked to the waist, wearing a pair of slacks. The drapes were drawn, permitting a seam of light to penetrate, casting the remainder of the room in shadow. An open bottle of vodka rested on the night table. She had an empty glass in her hand. It looked as though she had decided to go on a bender in the midst of getting dressed. I asked if she was all right and she said, "Oh, Paul! I cannot talk now."

"What's wrong?" I asked, thinking it must have to do with the movie.

She stared at me bleakly, then lowered her head and shook it slowly back and forth, her hair curtaining her face. I turned to go and she said, "Wait!" She held out the glass. "Bring me some ice. Please!"

When I returned from the kitchen with her ice, she was still sitting on the bed, struggling to put on a blouse, unable to fit her arm into the sleeve. "Shit!" she said, and crumpled the blouse, tossed it to the floor. I handed her the glass and she slopped vodka into it.

"You want drink? Come! You must drink with me." She pointed to a tray of glasses atop a coffee table that fronted a sofa. "We drink to the movies."

A band-aid on the inside of her elbow had come partly unstuck—I asked if she had cut herself.

"I am giving blood each month." She tried to make the band-aid stick, gave up, and pulled it off; she looked down at her arm, which was no longer bleeding, and giggled. "Is rare charitable impulse."

I sat on the foot of the bed. With a drunken show of painstaking care, she plucked out an ice cube and plinked it into my glass. I had trouble keeping my eyes off her chest.

"To our little movie," she said, and we drank.

"It's still on? The movie?"

"Yes, of course. Why not?"

"Then tell me what's wrong."

"Is too depressing. The bank has failed. My grandmother has lose all her money."

Relieved that it wasn't our bank, I asked what had happened, but she may not have registered the question.

"The bank president," she said mournfully. "He has kill himself."

"Jesus. That's too bad."

She waved in exaggerated fashion, as though hailing a cab. "No, no! Is okay. They *make* him kill himself."

I tried to imagine what Moscow must be like and suggested she wire money to her grandmother. She told me she had taken care of that, but said that her grandmother was anxious and needed someone to help her through this time.

"Why don't you fly home? We can spare you for a week or so," I said.

"Movie is not keeping me here. Is Misha. Fucking son-of-a-bitch Russian bastard. He say if I go, no movie. Always he wishes to control me."

I didn't know what could be done about Misha. She poured us both another vodka and we drank in silence.

"Anyway," she said glumly, "air on plane is not fit to breathe."

She heaved a mighty sigh that set her breasts to wobbling and stared at them as if she had just noticed they were there. "I can do magic," she said brightly, glancing up at me. "Want me to show you?"

"Yeah, sure."

"You don't believe. I know. You're too busy looking at my tits." She cupped her hands beneath her breasts and wigwagged them. "But while you look, I can disappear. Poof."

I was annoyed with her for teasing me, but I let it slide. "Like the nomads," I said.

"Exactly! Is the same trick."

Energy drained from her. She slumped and hung her head again and then began to wrestle with the top button of her slacks, but couldn't get it undone. I was startled to see tears in her eyes.

"Help me, please," she said. "I want to sleep."

I helped her off with the slacks, touching her skin no more than was necessary. As I moved to pull the sheet over her, she hooked her arms behind my neck and gave me a grave, assessing look that I recognized for an invitation, or at least as the prelude to one. I let the moment slip by. She rolled onto her side, drew her knees up into the fetal position, and passed out.

The next morning I was on the deck, gazing across the fogbound canyon, listening to drips and plops, the remnants of an early morning drizzle, when Larissa walked up and pressed herself against me in a sisterly embrace.

"You're a nice guy," she said, her face buried in my shoulder. "I'm sorry for what I did."

I unpeeled from her and said venomously, "I'm not a nice guy, okay? I could have raped you last night. And you know what? I think I could have lived with myself. That's the only reason I didn't fuck you—because I don't want to know that about myself. I'm not prepared to go there just yet."

"Rape? What are you talking about?"

"That's what it would have been. You were totally out of it. You run around here half-naked, like I'm some kind of fucking eunuch, and..." I gestured in frustration. "Forget it!"

She folded her arms and, with a puzzled look, said, "You can fuck me if you want."

It was as if she were saying, Didn't you know that? What's wrong with you? I had no idea how to respond.

"I fuck guys," she went on. "Girls, too. I cannot manage emotional response, but I like you, Paul. If this is a problem between us, you can fuck me."

At that moment the gap between us seemed wider than could be explained by a cultural or a gender divide.

"What is the big deal? This..." She indicated her body. "It's nothing. You think I'm so beautiful, maybe with me it's better? Maybe you hear music and feel things you don't feel with other women? For me, it's only sex. Sometimes it's currency. Sometimes it's for pleasure, sometimes for friendship. I can't help if for you it's more."

A grinding sound arose from the fog, sputtered and died; then it started up again.

"Maybe I'm being naïve," I said.

"Yes, I think," she said after a considerable pause. "But you're a nice guy. Believe it."

Larissa acted as though nothing had changed between us, and I suppose nothing had. She continued to wear her robe to breakfast, continued her casual displays of skin. That pissed me off, but I got over it. I concluded that this was her way of letting me know she remained available, and that my problem wasn't her problem. The idea that I might be insufficiently worldly to take advantage of the situation, or that I was too much of a wimp, bothered me; yet whenever I determined to make a grab for her, something held me back. I attributed impossibly subtle manipulative skills to her. Perhaps, I thought, she had perceived a flawed trigger in my psychological depths and understood that by offering herself, she would neutralize my desire. At length I decided that I was simply a romantic chump where she was concerned, and that I had rendered her unattainable by demanding something of her that she could not provide.

Echevarrìa went off to the Sierra Nevadas to scout locations. I gave the script a final polish. Larissa stayed on the phone until late in the evening, going out only for business meetings and, judging by the band-aids on her arm, to give blood. On more than a few occasions I overheard her speaking in Russian to someone. Her side of these conversations ranged in tone from pleading to infuriated, and once she used a Russian epithet she had taught me: "Zalupa (dickhead)." After one such call, she stomped about the house, muttering, picking up books and statuettes as if intending to throw them, satisfying the urge by slamming them down. We were mere weeks away from starting the picture, and I didn't want to jinx the project by asking whether the relationship between her and Misha was deteriorating. I put my blinders on and tried not to dwell on the thousand things that could go wrong.

I returned from a walk one evening to find an extra car parked out front and one of Misha's bodyguards, a slight, blond guy with a pleasant, finely boned face, standing in the living room, watching a mixed martial arts fight on TV. I peeked into Larissa's office. It was empty, and I asked the bodyguard where she was.

"Business meeting," he said without turning from the bloody figures onscreen.

"Where are they?"

He smiled and said he didn't know.

The smile made me uneasy and I started along the corridor toward Larissa's rooms; the bodyguard intercepted me.

"Private meeting," he said.

I tried to push past him and wound up flat on my back, with his hand gripping my throat. He helped me up, asked if I was okay, and steered me back into the living room. I sat on a sofa, feeling impotent and agitated.

"What's going on?" I asked.

The bodyguard flicked his fingers at the TV, where one fighter was celebrating a knockout. "Ken Shamrock," he said admiringly. "He's badass motherfucker!"

Twenty minutes later, Misha came along the corridor. He was buttoning his shirt, carrying a jacket draped over one arm. I couldn't take my eyes off him, quivering like a hound that has been forced to heel, but I don't think he even gave me a glance. He stood in the foyer, combing his hair. The bodyguard went to join him. They left through the front door and I sprinted down the corridor.

The sheets were half-off Larissa's bed, the pillows scattered on the floor. I heard the shower running and called out, asking if she was all right. She said she was fine. When she stepped out of the bathroom, wearing a terrycloth robe, her hair turbaned in a towel, she seemed composed, but her cheek was red and swollen, and there was a tiny cut at the corner of her upper lip. She sat down on the sofa and lit a cigarette with her gold cricket lighter. I wanted to ask what had happened, but I knew and I told her she should call the police.

"You cannot hurt Misha that way." She had a hit of the cigarette, exhaled, and tapped the lighter rhythmically against the glass surface of the coffee table, as if sending an SOS. "Best thing to do is nothing. Sooner or later someone will take a big bite out of Misha. He's too stupid to be in position of power."

"You've got to call the cops. If you won't, I will. There's no telling what he'll do next."

"He has done what he wanted. He's humiliated me. That satisfies him. Now he will leave me alone for a while." She gazed out the window at the twilit canyon and said distractedly, "Don't worry. We'll be all right. You want to do something? Be a nice guy. Make some tea."

Her behavior confounded me. A woman who cried when she couldn't undo a button and yet took rape in stride, who viewed it as a humiliation for which the remedy was tea and cigarettes: Maybe it was a Russian thing, but I couldn't get my head around it. I was disappointed in her, almost angry, as if she hadn't lived up to a standard I set for her, some special measure like the scale by which her beauty was appraised. I began spending more time away from the house, washing my hands of the situation, telling myself that I couldn't protect her, though my withdrawal was actually a petty punishment, an expression of my disapproval, and didn't last for long. My work on the script was done, at least for the moment, and the house was a mess, wires and lights everywhere (we were using it as one of the locations), so I seized the opportunity to renew friendships and caught a couple of movies. Then one night Larissa nabbed me as I was heading out and asked me to have a drink with her. She wanted to celebrate the start of principal photography, now eight days away, and was afraid we might not have time later—she was about to get very busy on the production side of things.

It was too windy on the deck, so we went into her bedroom and sat on the sofa and drank vodka martinis, slipping back into our relationship without awkwardness. She talked about the people she had associated with in Moscow, citizens of the new Russia, crazy musicians and charlatan poets and idiot actors, her face glowing with fond recollection, leaning forward to touch me on the knee, the arm. I tried to keep her talking, watching the light shift across her satiny blouse, listening to her breathy inflections and odd tonal shifts, like someone hitting the stops on the upper register of a bass clarinet. She told me that she had been a production assistant on two movies in Moscow, something I hadn't known, and this had given her the expertise needed to produce our movie. It was a dream come true for her, she said, speaking about the quality of the actors and the director she was working with now.

"Your script is the heart of the movie," she said. "They are forgetting this in Hollywood. Everything is explosion, car chase…or else it is farce. They no longer care about story. But you have given me such a brilliant script, a beautiful story. I am so grateful to have met you."

I was made confident by her praise, infected by her passion for the movie, and a little desperate because I realized this might be my last, best chance to draw her into a deeper involvement. She wasn't startled when I kissed her. She seemed to want it as much as I did. We moved from the sofa to the bed without a word exchanged. She was a fierce lover. She hissed in delight, she whispered Russian endearments, and she came almost at once, her nails pricking my back, heels bruising my calves, holding me tightly while she let out a series of low, shuddering cries. Then she pushed me onto my back and mounted me. Her hips rolled and twisted, teasing one moment and frenzied the next. The sight of her above me, breasts swaying, her hair flying—it was sublimely sexual. Yet when we were done, when she sat on the edge of the bed sipping her martini, I realized I had been taking mental snapshots of her, filing them away under The Most Beautiful Woman I Ever Fucked, and that her ferocity had been technical, part of a design for pleasure. The relationship had not deepened. It was only sex, though I wanted to believe otherwise.

"You are disappointed," she said, looking down at me.

"Are you kidding me?"

"No, you are disappointed. I know." She set down her glass and lay facing me. "You did not hear music. You felt nothing new."

"No music," I said, giving in to her. "But I maybe felt a couple of new things."

She laughed and caressed my cheek. "Men tell me I am great at sex, and I think, so what? What do you mean? I enjoy it. I want men to enjoy. I have good energy for sex. It's no big thing." She rested her head in the crook of my shoulder. "Do you remember I'm telling you about the shaman? In the camp?"

"Uh-huh."

"We were lovers. It was only way I could get him to tell me things. After we have sex one time, he says, 'You don't have feelings for me.' I say, 'Sure I do,' and he says, 'You want to know what it is to have love feelings for a man?' So I tell him, 'Yes, okay.' I think he'll teach me something if I go along. So he lays me down and rubs oil over my body. And spices, too, maybe. It smells of spices."

"Sounds like a marinade," I said.

"Then he starts to sing. Very low, deep in his throat." She demonstrated. "It's very hypnotic, and I'm getting drowsy. So drowsy, I lose track of what is happening. Soon he's making love to me. It was amazing. It's like I hear the music, I'm feeling new things. I'm…I don't know the word. In another place."

"Transported," I suggested.

Her brow furrowed. "Okay, maybe. Afterward I ask if I can go to that place with some other man. He doesn't know. If he performs the ritual some more, it's possible, but he's very busy, he's got no time. Later, he says. Then the nomads disappear and there's no chance to perform the ritual again."

"He probably drugged you."

"Must be hell of a drug," she said. "Because I miss him forever. It takes me a year before I want sex with someone else. You think a drug can make you feel something so strong that you don't really feel?"

"You don't even need drugs for that," I said.

I was watching TV the following Sunday, three days before we were to begin shooting, when the police arrived in force. They had a search warrant and asked if I knew where Misha and Larissa might be. I had no idea where Misha was, but I told them Larissa was probably asleep. They didn't appear to believe me and suggested I come down to Valley Division and answer some questions. During the questioning, I learned that Misha and Larissa had last been seen at a bar in Pacific Palisades.

Misha's car had been found early that morning in a gully not far from the house and there were signs of foul play, plenty of blood, too much blood to hope for survivors, yet no bodies. They asked about Misha's relationship with Larissa, about my relationship with Larissa, about people with Russian names whom I'd never heard of. After forty-five minutes, they kicked me loose and told me to keep clear of the house until they were done collecting evidence.

I checked into a hotel and called Echevarrìa and gave him the news. He kept saying, "I knew something would fuck this up." It wasn't the kind of attitude I wanted to hear. I told him I'd contact him when I heard anything new and went down to the bar and drank myself stupid. I shed a few tears for Larissa, but not so many as you might expect, perhaps because I sensed that her tragedy had occurred long before I met her and, like Echevarrìa, I knew something bad was going to happen. I walked around for a week feeling as if a hole had been punched through my chest—I missed being around her, talking to her—and then the police picked me up again, this time conveying me to an interrogation room in the Parker Center with walls the color of carbon paper, where I made the acquaintance of Detectives Jack Trombley and Al Witt, who were attached to the Homicide Special Unit of the LAPD.

Witt, a cheerful, fit man in his thirties, dressed in jeans and a sport coat, offered me cigarettes, coffee, soda, and then said, "So, did you do it?"

"Do what?" I asked.

He looked to his partner, an older, thicker man wearing the same basic uniform, and said, "I don't think he did it. You try."

"Did you do it?" asked Trombley.

I glanced back and forth between them. "I didn't do anything."

"I'm not getting much," Trombley said.

"Inconclusive?" asked Witt.

Trombley nodded.

"If only he hadn't lied, huh?" Witt eyed me sadly. "You said you and the Russian babe were friends, but we got your DNA off her sheets."

"We had sex one time," I said. "But…"

"One time!" Trombley snorted. "If it was me, you'd have to pry me off her."

"It was like no good with her or something?" Witt asked.

"Not really," I said. "It was…I don't know how to explain so you'd understand."

"Yeah, we're pretty dense. We might not get it." Witt thumbed through the case file. "We found an older sample on the sheets. It belonged to Bondarchuk."

"That must be from the rape."

"Yeah, you said." Witt fingered the edge of a flimsy. "Makes you wonder how come a woman who's been raped would hang onto the sheets? You'd think she'd throw them away, or at least wash them."

"What's your point?"

Witt shrugged. "It's just weird." He played with papers for a second or two, and then asked, "What did you do with the money?"

"The money?"

"Boy, he's good!" said Trombley.

"The fifteen million," Witt said. "The budget for your movie. Where'd it go?"

"It's not in the bank?"

"Not in any Wells Fargo bank." Witt made a church-and-steeple with his fingers. "Here's how I read it. Larissa was planning to set you up for Bondarchuk's murder and scoot with the fifteen mil. That's why she was sleeping on dirty sheets when you nailed her—to implicate you. Maybe she talked you into killing Bondarchuk for her. You caught on to her, chilled them both and buried the money in an offshore account."

"Works for me," Trombley said. "Needs some tailoring, but we can make it fit."

"I couldn't kill Larissa," I said.

"Because you loved her? Love's right up there with greed as a motive for murder." Witt made a wry face. "You're not going to tell us you didn't love her, are you?"

"Yeah. I loved her, but you wouldn't...I..."

"I know. We wouldn't understand." Witt leafed through the file and pulled out a sheet of paper. "Larissa Miusov, AKA Larissa Shivets. Suspicion of robbery, suspicion of fraud, suspicion of extortion. Here's a good one. Suspicion of murder. Lots of suspicion hanging around your girlfriend, but she always skated. Is that what you loved about her?"

They tag-teamed me for hours, trying to wear me down, to find cracks in my story, but I had no story to crack. Finally Witt said, "We like clearing cases around here and you're looking pretty good for this."

"A guy like Misha," I said. "There must be dozens of people who wanted him dead."

"More than that. But they've all got alibis and a ton of money. You don't."

That night I sat in the hotel bar and worried whether the police would charge me; I drank too much and thought about Larissa; then I repeated the cycle. She hadn't talked much about the years in Moscow after her father died. I assumed they had been a struggle and, having no means of support, that she had done things she wasn't proud of; but hearing the specifics eroded what I believed to be true and raised unanswerable questions about her crimes. Had she been coerced? If so, by who and by what means? And had she intended to frame me? I wanted to deny it, clinging to the notion that we had been friends. Yet it was as if each new thing I learned rendered her less visible, as if during the entire time I knew her, she had been gradually disappearing behind a smokescreen of facts.

After a month they let me back into the Topanga house to collect my possessions. I no longer feared that I would be charged with a double homicide. Though the case remained open, Larissa's death was on its way to becoming part of Hollywood lore and I was close to signing a deal that would guarantee production of the Donner Party script and allow me to direct a picture based on a script I would write about the murders. Very little excites America more than does the mysterious death of a beautiful woman, especially a woman who herself poses a mystery. Photographs of Larissa were splashed on tabloid covers and featured on TV. It was said she had done porn in Russia, that she had slept with Gorbachev, that she was a descendant of the Romanoffs. A *20/20* special was in the works. On the advice of counsel, I turned down requests for interviews.

"Save it for the script," my agent told me.

I packed quickly, oppressed by the house, but before leaving I asked the real estate agent to give me a minute to look around. I walked along the deck, then down to the hall to Larissa's bedroom. The bed had been stripped, but her clothes were still in the closet, her toiletries in the bathroom, and a trace of her perfume lingered on the air. I sat on the sofa, indulging in nostalgia, remembering moments, things spoken and unspoken. I glanced down at the coffee table.

Sunlight applied a glaze to the glass surface, making it difficult to see, but when I leaned close I realized she had left me a message. That's how I interpreted the markings on the glass, though I recognize now they may have been the work of idle hours and I understand they were in essence the ultimate mystification of her life, a magical pass made by her disembodied hand that, literally or figuratively, caused her to vanish utterly behind a curtain of rumors and fictions, the final flourish of her disappearing act. At the time, however, I chose to take the hopeful view. I recalled how she had giggled and remarked sarcastically on the act of giving blood, blood she might have used to cover up a murder, and I also recalled things said about Misha, about me, all supporting the thesis that she had escaped, leaving behind evidence to implicate me, to misdirect the police for a while, yet not enough to convict.

Four wheels resembling Mayan calendars, now defaced by random scratches, were etched into the four corners of the glass. The greater portion of the surface was occupied by marks that appeared to represent the surrounding hills, a crude map of our section of the canyon, and there was a patch of tropical vegetation where the house should have been. I identified palms and banana trees. Inside a circle, dead center of the patch, was the figure of a woman, so carefully incised that I made out breasts and a smiling face and a hand raised in a salute—she was half-turned away from whomever she was signaling, like a beloved and gifted actress waving farewell to her audience, preparing to step through the hole she had opened in the world.

ABOUT THE AUTHORS

Peter S. Beagle (*www.peterbeagle.com*) was born in New York in April 1939. He studied at the University of Pittsburgh and graduated with a degree in creative writing in 1959. Beagle won a *Seventeen* magazine short story contest in his sophomore year, but really began his writing career with his first novel, *A Fine and Private Place*, in 1960. It was followed by non-fiction travelogue *I See by My Outfit* in 1961, and by his best-known work, modern fantasy classic *The Last Unicorn* in 1968. Beagle's other books include novels *The Folk of the Air*, *The Innkeeper's Song*, and *Tamsin*; collections *The Fantasy Worlds of Peter S. Beagle*, *The Rhinoceros Who Quoted Nietzsche*, *Giant Bones*, *The Line Between*, and several non-fiction books and a number of screenplays and teleplays. He has a new short novel, *I'm Afraid You've Got Dragons*, coming later this year.

Paul Brandon (*www.paulbrandon.com*) was born in England in 1971. He studied at the British Film Institute and worked in the film industry for a number of years. He moved to Brisbane, Australia, in 1993 where he works as a writer and musician. His first novel, fantasy *Swim the Moon*, was published in 2001, and was followed by *The Wild Reel* in 2004. He plays guitar and bodhran in Celtic-influenced band Súnas, and is currently working on a new novel.

Jack Dann (*www.jackdann.com*) was born in Binghamton, New York, in February 1945. His first story, "Dark, Dark the Dead Star," appeared in 1970, and was followed by more than seventy books, including the groundbreaking novels *Junction*, *Starhiker*, *The Man*

Who Melted, The Memory Cathedral—which is an international best-seller—Civil War novel *The Silent*, and *Bad Medicine*. His short fiction, which includes Nebula Award winner "Da Vinci Rising," has been collected in *Timetipping, Visitations*, and *Jubilee*. A prolific editor, he has edited several landmark genre anthologies, including *Wandering Stars, In the Field of Fire* (with Jeanne Van Buren Dann), and World Fantasy Award winner *Dreaming Down-Under* (with Janeen Webb). Upcoming is a new collection, *Promised Land*.

Terry Dowling *(www.terrydowling.com)* was born in Sydney, New South Wales, in March 1947. A writer, musician, journalist, critic, editor, game designer and reviewer, he has an MA (Hons) in English Literature from the University of Sydney. His Masters thesis discussed J. G. Ballard and Surrealism. He was awarded a PhD in Creative Writing from the University of Western Australia in 2006 for his mystery/dark fantasy/horror novel, *Clowns at Midnight*, and accompanying dissertation: "The Interactive Landscape: New Modes of Narrative in Science Fiction," in which he examined the computer adventure game as an important new area of storytelling.

He is author of the "Tom Tyson" cycle of stories, collected in *Rynosseros, Blue Tyson, Twilight Beach*, and the forthcoming *Rynemonn*, science fiction story cycle *Wormwood*, and horror collections *An Intimate Knowledge of the Night* and World Fantasy Award nominee *Blackwater Days*. His work has also been collected in career retrospectives *Antique Futures: The Best of Terry Dowling* and *Basic Black: Tales of Appropriate Fear*.

Andy Duncan *(www.angelfire.com/al/andyduncan/)* was born in South Carolina in September 1964. He studied journalism at the University of South Carolina and creative writing at North Carolina State University, before working as a journalist for the *Greensboro News & Record*. He currently is the senior editor of *Overdrive*, a magazine for truck drivers. Duncan's short fiction, which has won the World Fantasy and Theodore Sturgeon Awards, is collected in World Fantasy Award winner *Beluthahatchie and Other Stories*. Duncan also co-edited *Crossroads: Tales of the Southern Literary Fantastic* with F. Brett Cox, and edited non-fiction book *Alabama Curiosities: Quirky Characters, Roadside Oddities & Other Offbeat Stuff*. He currently lives with his wife Sydney in Frostburg, Maryland.

Jeffrey Ford *(14theditch.livejournal.com/)* was born in West Islip, New York, in 1955. He worked as a machinist and as a clammer, before studying English with John Gardner at the State University of New York. He is the author of six novels, including World Fantasy Award winner *The Physiognomy*, *The Portrait of Mrs. Charbuque*, and Edgar Allan Poe Award-winner *The Girl in the Glass*. His short fiction is collected in World Fantasy Award winning collection *The Fantasy Writer's Assistant and Other Stories* and in *The Empire of Ice Cream*. His short fiction has won the World Fantasy, Nebula, and Fountain Awards. Upcoming is a new novel, *The Shadow Year*, which will be published next year, and a new collection, *The Night Whiskey*. Ford lives in southern New Jersey where he teaches writing and literature.

Kathleen Ann Goonan *(www.goonan.com)* has been a packer for a moving company, a vagabond, a madrigal singer, a painter of watercolors, and a fiercely omnivorous reader. She has a degree in English and Association Montessori Internationale certification. After teaching for thirteen years, ten of them in her own one-hundred-student school, she began writing. She has published over twenty short stories in venues such as *Omni*, *Asimov's*, *F&SF*, *Interzone*, *SciFi.com*, and a host of others. Her Nanotech Quartet includes *Queen City Jazz*, *Mississippi Blues*, *Crescent City Rhapsody*, and *Light Music*, *Crescent City Rhapsody* and *Light Music* were both shortlisted for the Nebula Award. *The Bones of Time*, shortlisted for the Clarke Award, is set in Hawaii. Her most recent novel is *In War Times*, and she is presently working on *This Shared Dream Called Earth*. Her novels and short stories have been published in France, Poland, Russia, Great Britain, the Czech Republic, Spain, Italy, and Japan. "Literature, Consciousness, and Science Fiction" recently appeared in the *Iowa Review* online journal. She speaks frequently at various universities about nanotechnology and literature.

Eileen Gunn *(www.eileengunn.com)* was born in Dorchester, Massachusetts, in June 1945. She grew up near Boston, and earned a Bachelor of Arts in History from Emmanuel College, before working as an advertising copywriter. She moved to California to pursue fiction writing. In 1976 she attended Clarion, then supported herself by working in advertising. She was the 150th employee at Microsoft, where she worked as director of advertising and sales promotion in the 1980s. In 1988 she joined the board of directors for the Clarion West Writers

Workshop, and in 2001 began editing online magazine *The Infinite Matrix*. She currently lives in Seattle with editor John Berry.

Gunn's first short story, "What Are Friends For?", was followed by a handful of others, including Nebula Award winner "Coming to Terms" and Hugo Award nominees "Stable Strategies for Middle Management" and "Computer Friendly." Her short fiction has been collected in *Stable Strategies and Others*. She is currently working on a biography of Avram Davidson.

Gwyneth Jones *(www.boldaslove.co.uk)* was born in Manchester, England, in February 1952. She went to convent schools and then took an undergraduate degree in the History of Ideas at the University of Sussex, specializing in seventeenth-century Europe, a distant academic background that still resonates in her work.

She first realised she wanted to be a writer at age fourteen when she won a local newspaper's story competition. She has written a number of highly regarded SF novels, notably *White Queen*, *North Wind*, and *Phoenix Cafe*, and the near-future fantasy "Bold As Love" series. Her collection *Seven Tales and a Fable* won two World Fantasy Awards, and her critical writings and essays have appeared in *Nature*, *New Scientist*, *Foundation*, *NYRSF*, and several online venues. She has also written more than twenty novels for teenagers as Ann Halam, starting with *Ally, Ally, Aster* and including *Taylor Five*, *Dr. Franklin's Island*, and most recently *Snakehead*. She has been writing full time since the early '80s, occasionally teaching creative writing. Honors include the Arthur C. Clarke Award for *Bold as Love* and the Philip K. Dick Award for *Life*. She lives in Brighton, with her husband, son and two cats called Frank and Ginger; likes cooking, gardening, watching old movies and playing with her websites.

Ellen Klages (www.ellenklages.com) has published more than a dozen stories, including Nebula and Hugo finalist "Time Gypsy," Nebula nominee "Flying Over Water," and 2005 Nebula winner "Basement Magic," all of which are reprinted in her new collection Portable Childhoods (2007). She was a finalist for the Campbell Award for Best New Writer in 2000. Her first novel, The Green Glass Sea, was short-listed for the Locus Awards and the Quills. It won the Scott O'Dell Award for best American historical fiction. She is currently working on a sequel.

Margo Lanagan *(amongamidwhile.blogspot.com)* was born in Newcastle, New South Wales, Australia, and has a BA in History from Sydney University. She spent ten years as a freelance book editor and currently makes a living as a technical writer. Lanagan wrote teenage romances under various pseudonyms before publishing junior and teenage fiction novels under her own name, including fantasies *Wildgame, Tankermen,* and *Walking through Albert.* She has also written an installment in a shared-world YA fantasy series, *The Quentaris Chronicles: Treasure Hunters of Quentaris,* and three acclaimed original story collections: *White Time,* World Fantasy Award winner *Black Juice,* and *Red Spikes.* She currently lives in Sydney with her partner and their two children where she is working on a new fantasy novel for young adults.

Maureen F. McHugh *(my.en.com/~mcq/)* was born February 13, 1959. She grew up in Loveland, Ohio, and received a BA from Ohio University in 1981, where she took a creative writing course from Daniel Keyes in her senior year. After a year of grad school there, she went on to get a master's degree in English Literature at New York University in 1984. After several years as a part-time college instructor and miscellaneous jobs in clerking, technical writing, etc., she spent a year teaching in Shijiazhuang, China. It was during this period she sold her first story, "All in a Day's Work," which appeared in *Twilight Zone.* She has written four novels, including Tiptree Award winner and Hugo and Nebula Award finalist *China Mountain Zhang, Half the Day Is Night, Mission Child,* and *Nekropolis.* Her short fiction, including Hugo Award winner "The Lincoln Train," was collected in *Mothers and Other Monsters* which was a finalist for the Story Prize.

Garth Nix *(www.garthnix.com)* was born in 1963 in Melbourne, Australia, and grew up in Canberra. When he turned nineteen he left to drive around the UK in a beat-up Austin with a boot full of books and a Silver-Reed typewriter. Despite a wheel literally falling off the car, he survived to return to Australia and study at the University of Canberra. He has since worked in a bookshop, as a book publicist, a publisher's sales representative, an editor, a literary agent, and as a public relations and marketing consultant. He was also a part-time soldier in the Australian Army Reserve, but now writes full-time.

His first story was published in 1984 and was followed by novels *The Ragwitch, Sabriel, Shade's Children, Lirael, Abhorsen,* the six-book YA fantasy series "The Seventh Tower," and most recently the seven-book "The Keys to the Kingdom" series. He lives in Sydney with his wife and their two children.

Lucius Shepard (*www.lucius-shepard.com*) was born in Lynchburg, Virginia, in 1947 and published his first book, poetry *Cantata of Death, Weakmind & Generation* in 1967. He began to publish fiction of genre interest in 1983, with "The Taylorsville Reconstruction," which was followed by such major stories as "A Spanish Lesson," "R&R," "Salvador," and "The Jaguar Hunter." The best of his early short fiction is collected in two World Fantasy Award-winning volumes, *The Jaguar Hunter* and *The Ends of the Earth*. In 1995 *The Encyclopedia of Science Fiction* said of Shepard's relationship to science fiction that "there is some sense that two ships may have passed in the night." Two years later Shepard returned from what he has since described as a career "pause," delivering a series of major short stories, starting with "Crocodile Rock" in 1999, followed by Hugo Award winner "Radiant Green Star" in 2000, and culminating in nearly 300,000 words of short fiction published in 2003. The best of his recent short fiction has been collected in *Trujillo and Other Stories*, *Eternity and Other Stories*, and *Dagger Key and Other Stories*. He has also written the novels *Green Eyes*, *Life During Wartime*, *Kalimantan*, *The Golden*, *Colonel Rutherford's Colt* and *Floater*. His most recent book is new novel *Softspoken*.

Bruce Sterling (blog.wired.com/sterling) was born in Texas in 1954, and received a BA in Journalism from the University of Texas in 1976. His first short story, "Man Made Self," appeared the same year. His first two novels, *Involution Ocean* and *The Artificial Kid*, were far-future adventures, the latter presaging the cyberpunk movement he is credited with creating. Sterling edited cyberpunk anthology *Mirrorshades*, considered the definitive representation of the subgenre, and his near-future thriller *Islands in the Net* won the John W. Campbell Memorial Award. In 1990 he collaborated with William Gibson on alternate history novel *The Difference Engine*. Future history novel *Schismatrix* introduced his Shaper-Mechanist universe, which pits bioengineering against mathematics, also the setting of some of the stories in collection *Crystal Express*. After writing the non-fiction book *The Hacker Crackdown*, he returned to fiction with near-future, high-tech scenarios in *Heavy Weather*, *Holy Fire*, Arthur C. Clarke Award winner *Distraction*, and *The Zenith Angle*. Sterling has produced a large and influential body of short fiction, much of which have been collected in *Crystal Express, Globalhead, A Good Old-fashioned Future*, and *Visionary in Residence*. His novelette "Bicycle Repairman" won the Hugo Award and novelette "Taklamakan" won the Hugo and the Locus Award. Sterling's non-fiction has appeared in *The New York Times, Wired, Nature, Newsday,* and *Time Digital*. A major career retrospective, *Ascendancies: The Best of Bruce Sterling,* will be published in late 2007.

Ysabeau S. Wilce *(www.yswilce.com)* is a new writer whose first story, "Metal More Attractive," was published in *The Magazine of Fantasy & Science Fiction* in 2004. Like all of her work to date, it was set in "Alta Califa," an alternate California, and is heavily influenced by Wilce's military history studies. A second story, "The Biography of a Bouncing Boy Terror," appeared in 2005 and "The Lineaments of Gratified Desire" appeared in 2006. Wilce's first novel, a young adult fantasy with a preposterously long title, *Flora Segunda: Being the Magickal Mishaps of a Girl of Spirit, Her Glass-Gazing Sidekick, Two Ominous Butlers (One Blue), a House with Eleven Thousand Rooms, and a Red Dog,* was published to considerable acclaim earlier this year. She currently lives with her husband, a dog, and a large number of well-folded papertowels in Chicago, Illinois, where she is currently working on a second "Flora Segunda" novel.